15

W9-CNC-533

"Mary Mackey gives her readers yet another woman warrior, this one a fighter in the Civil War. We thrill to the story of Carrie Vinton as she travels from Brazil to Bloody Kansas to Missouri and courageously takes the side of freedom over slavery."

—Maxine Hong Kingston, author of *The Woman Warrior*

Praise for

THE NOTORIOUS MRS. WINSTON

"A deep look at the Civil War from the viewpoint of a feisty, independent female masquerading as a male . . . Strong, engaging historical fiction starring a wonderful protagonist."

—*Midwest Book Review*

"Using the Civil War as a backdrop for her story of a woman's struggle for freedom and independence, Mackey creates a strong feminist work of fiction that reads like true history. Her fascinating characters and actual events and battles of the war are drawn so clearly you'll feel you're in the midst of the war as well as inside the heroine's heart. This appealing, intelligent story will find a place on your bookshelf and in your heart."

—*Romantic Times*

Acclaim for Mary Mackey's previous novels

"A complex, colorful saga . . . Engrossing and realistic."

—*Publishers Weekly*

"Inventive and imaginative."   —*The New York Times*

"Deserves a place on the shelves next to the work of Jean Auel."

—*Booklist*

"Fascinating."

—Marion Zimmer Bradley, author of *The Mists of Avalon*

MAY 19 2011

Berkley Titles by Mary Mackey

THE NOTORIOUS MRS. WINSTON
THE WIDOW'S WAR

THE
WIDOW'S WAR

Mary Mackey

BERKLEY BOOKS, NEW YORK

MORSE INSTITUTE LIBRARY
14 E Central Street
Natick, MA 01760

THE BERKLEY PUBLISHING GROUP
Published by the Penguin Group
Penguin Group (USA) Inc.
375 Hudson Street, New York, New York 10014, USA
Penguin Group (Canada), 90 Eglinton Avenue East, Suite 700, Toronto, Ontario M4P 2Y3, Canada
(a division of Pearson Penguin Canada Inc.)
Penguin Books Ltd., 80 Strand, London WC2R 0RL, England
Penguin Group Ireland, 25 St. Stephen's Green, Dublin 2, Ireland
(a division of Penguin Books Ltd.)
Penguin Group (Australia), 250 Camberwell Road, Camberwell, Victoria 3124, Australia
(a division of Pearson Australia Group Pty. Ltd.)
Penguin Books India Pvt. Ltd., 11 Community Centre, Panchsheel Park, New Delhi—110 017,
India
Penguin Group (NZ), 67 Apollo Drive, Rosedale, North Shore 0632, New Zealand
(a division of Pearson New Zealand Ltd.)
Penguin Books (South Africa) (Pty.) Ltd., 24 Sturdee Avenue, Rosebank, Johannesburg 2196,
South Africa

Penguin Books Ltd., Registered Offices: 80 Strand, London WC2R 0RL, England

This book is an original publication of The Berkley Publishing Group.

This is a work of fiction. Names, characters, places, and incidents either are the product of the
author's imagination or are used fictitiously, and any resemblance to actual persons, living or dead,
business establishments, events, or locales is entirely coincidental. The publisher does not have any
control over and does not assume any responsibility for author or third-party websites or their
content.

Copyright © 2009 by Mary Mackey.
Cover illustration by Alan Ayers.
Cover design by Judith Lagerman.
Interior text design by Laura K. Corless.

All rights reserved.
No part of this book may be reproduced, scanned, or distributed in any printed or electronic form
without permission. Please do not participate in or encourage piracy of copyrighted materials in
violation of the author's rights. Purchase only authorized editions.
BERKLEY® is a registered trademark of Penguin Group (USA) Inc.
The "B" design is a trademark of Penguin Group (USA) Inc.

PRINTING HISTORY
Berkley trade paperback edition / September 2009

Library of Congress Cataloging-in-Publication Data

Mackey, Mary.
    The widow's war / Mary Mackey.—Berkley trade paperback ed.
        p.   cm.
    Includes bibliographical references and index.
    ISBN 978-0-425-22791-6 (alk. paper)
    1. Abolitionists—Fiction.   2. Women and war—Fiction.   3. African American soldiers—
Fiction.   4. Kansas—History—Civil War, 1861–1865—Fiction.   I. Title.
    PS3563.A3165W53   2009
    813'.54—dc22   2009021032

PRINTED IN THE UNITED STATES OF AMERICA

10 9 8 7 6 5 4 3 2 1

For John Edward Mackey

1920–2008

Historical Note

In 1854 fierce fighting broke out in Kansas as abolitionists and pro-slavers flocked to the territory to vote in an election to decide whether Kansas would enter the Union as a free or slave state. For the next seven years, until the official start of the Civil War in April of 1861, an undeclared civil war raged on the Great Plains as bands of Southern raiders massacred abolitionists and abolitionists retaliated. The violence in Kansas can be seen as a bloody rehearsal for the Civil War, a conflict that would rip the United States in half from 1861 to 1865 and end with the emancipation of over four million enslaved Americans of African descent.

Chronology

MAY 30, 1854   President Pierce signs the Kansas–Nebraska Act, a law that allows residents of the western territories to vote to decide whether or not those territories will join the Union as free states or slave states. Pro-slavers and free-soilers flock to Kansas.

AUGUST 1, 1854   Lawrence, Kansas, founded by New England abolitionists.

NOVEMBER 29, 1854   Election for first Kansas Territorial Delegate to Congress. Massive fraud as Missourians stream over the border to vote for pro-slavery candidate John W. Whitfield.

OCTOBER 7, 1855   Abolitionist John Brown arrives in Kansas.

MAY 21, 1856   Army of pro-slavers attacks Lawrence, sacks the town, and burns the Free State Hotel.

MAY 22, 1856   Massachusetts Senator Charles Sumner brutally beaten on floor of United States Senate by South Carolina Congressman Preston Brooks.

MAY 24, 1856   John Brown kills pro-slavery settlers at Pottawatomie Creek.

JUNE 2, 1856   Brown's men defeat pro-slavery militia at Battle of Black Jack (sometimes considered the first battle of the Civil War).

AUGUST 30, 1856   Pro-slavers attack Osawatomie and massacre Brown's supporters.

OCTOBER 16, 1859   Brown seizes United States arsenal at Harpers Ferry, Virginia, with intent of arming slaves of the South so they can free one another.

DECEMBER 1, 1859   Brown hanged for treason.

JANUARY 29, 1861   Kansas enters Union as a free state.

APRIL 12, 1861   Confederate batteries fire on Fort Sumter. American Civil War officially begins.

Carrie

The Kansas Territory, September 1856

Nine days ago, I shot my husband. Tomorrow, I am going to lead a band of escaped slaves into Missouri to free eight women, four men, and three children who were kidnapped by Henry Clark and his band of border ruffians. Actually, the escaped slaves are going to lead me. They were trained in the art of war by John Brown himself, and God help any slaver who gets in our way.

When I throw the divining shells and look into the future, I can see that this is only the first battle in a civil war that will soon engulf the entire nation. That war is racing east right now toward New York and Boston, Richmond and Savannah, cracking and roaring like a prairie fire, and there's not a thing any of us can do but prepare to stand and fight.

Henry Clark welcomes this war. For the past week he's been hunting me like game. He's plastered a poster with my description on it on the side of every jail in western Missouri:

WANTED: WHITE WOMAN, AGE 25. BROWN EYES, BLOND HAIR, 5'5" IN HEIGHT, APPROXIMATELY 120

LBS. SLAVE-STEALER, ABOLITIONIST, STATION MAS-
TER ON THE NOTORIOUS LAWRENCE LINE OF THE
SO-CALLED UNDERGROUND RAILROAD. GOES BY
NAMES "CAROLYN VINTON," "CARRIE VINTON,"
"CAROLYN SAYLOR," AND "MRS. DEACON PRES-
GROVE."

He got most of the details right, but that poster also contains additional information that reads as if it were composed by a madman, which leads me to believe Clark himself wrote it. "Armed and dangerous," I take as a compliment, but what am I to make of the charge that I am known to "consort with satanic spirits," or "kill men from afar by mysterious means"? Clark makes it sound as if I'm wanted for witchcraft. I wonder what he'd have written if he'd known I was coming after him with a cavalry unit of black soldiers?

To tell the truth, I'm surprised the word "adulteress" doesn't appear anywhere, because I'm not just riding into Missouri to free the men and women Henry Clark plans to sell back into bondage. I'm riding to a plantation called Beau Rivage to rescue my lover before Clark hangs him. His name is William Saylor, and I've loved him almost all my life. The first day I met him, I pulled a late-blooming orchid out of the mud and thrust it into his hands. "Have a Ca-lopogon pulchellus," I said. "You don't often see them in bloom this time of year." That was back in Mitchellville, Kentucky, so many years ago I can hardly count them. William was eleven and I was nine—just children both of us, but from the very first it was as if we had been born to spend our lives together.

William examined the orchid and then stared up at me with dark eyes that reminded me of the black waters of the upper Amazon—a tall, skinny, pale boy with thick, silky hair the color of caramel candy. "You speak Latin?" he said in an awed tone that I found very grati-fying. Even in those first few minutes of our acquaintance, I wanted to impress him. Neither of us had the slightest suspicion that we'd just fallen in love or that we'd stay in love forever.

Our lives have been full of so many missed opportunities that when I think about them, they drive me half mad. If I'd stayed in Mitchellville instead of going back to Brazil with my father, we would have married as soon as William got out of medical school, but instead I married the wrong man and spent almost an entire year grieving for William while he grieved for me. Each of us thought the other was dead, and by the time we found each other again, every penny of the great fortune my father had left me was gone, and the war in Kansas had begun. If William and I hadn't been deceived and lied to, I would never have lost him a second time to Henry Clark or seen my baby boy taken away by Clark's men, trussed up in a pillowcase like a dead rabbit.

Now it's up to me to undo the damage. I can't let innocent people be sold back into slavery because they hid us, fed us, and kept our whereabouts secret, so tomorrow we'll ride into enemy territory and rescue them. I'll get Teddy back and cut that rope off of William's neck before Clark lynches him. But I'd be lying if I told you I wasn't afraid. I have a Sharps rifle, plenty of ammunition, a brown gelding, and the bravest companions a woman could wish for, but still I wonder if I'll be alive this time next week.

My father always told me courage is the ability to do what you have to do no matter how frightened you are. Dear Papa, that was good advice, but I don't want to face the guns of the most vicious gang of raiders ever to make Kansas bleed. I'd rather go back to Rio before all this began and fix things so they don't turn out this way. But although you taught me the name of every orchid in the jungle, you never taught me how to fix the past, the terrible, beautiful past that is forever as unchangeable as death . . .

PART 1

Brazil

Chapter One

Rio de Janeiro, October 1853

Their child is conceived in a time of plague. Here is how Carrie remembers it: She and William in her bed in her father's house on the Ladeira da Glória with the shutters closed. Outside, panic in the streets as refugees flee the city, black flags in the port, ships in quarantine, the sound of church bells tolling ceaselessly. Inside, light slanting through the wooden slats of the shutters, the scent of freshly turned earth drifting in from the garden, William's eyes filled with despair, the tenderness and fierceness of his lovemaking, his hair thick and soft as brown silk.

Speaking his name, she pulls him closer and tells herself they will be together for the rest of their lives. That is the moment she first realizes he is burning with fever. And when she sits up, sweating and shaking, she understands that she is burning, too . . .

Chapter Two

She wakes several days later in an unfamiliar place where she can see nothing but a net of white lines and a brilliance so intense it makes her scream. Footsteps hurry toward her, shadowy white shapes loom up through the netting, and she's examined by terrifying figures in black robes with huge white wings sprouting from their heads. *I'm dead*, she thinks, *and these are either angels come to take me to heaven or devils come to take me to hell.*

She struggles to lift her head and the pain is so intense, she screams again. Every bone in her body feels as if it's been broken. Dear God, if she's dead, why is she in so much pain?

"*Senhorita,*" a female voice asks in Portuguese. "Who are you?"

She tries to reply, but she can't form words, and she has forgotten her name. Heat rises from her feet to her head in a long, shuddering coil. This must be hell then. The devils are tormenting her for her sins, feeding her to the flames, turning her slowly over hot coals. Again she tries to speak, but the sweet smut of fever fills her mouth, choking her.

"*Senhorita*, your name. We need to know your name."

Suddenly she remembers: the plague, her father's death, the hellish two weeks of tending the dying, and then . . . A pain sharper than broken bones fills her chest. Where is William? He was so sick, so terribly sick. She remembers sponging him down with alcohol in a desperate attempt to break his fever, begging him to drink a little water, kissing him and crying over him. What happened to him? Where is he?

She tries to ask one of the things that is hovering over her, but she has gone mute, and no matter how hard she struggles, she can't utter a single word. For a while she fights to speak, because she must know—even if she is dead and in hell—if William survived the smallpox epidemic. But the effort is too much and the pain too overwhelming. The net of light begins to dim, and a vast incoherent roaring fills her ears. She makes one last attempt to speak William's name and then falls into blackness as if into a deep well.

When she wakes again, the pain is still there but beaten back to a more bearable level. This time she understands that the net of white lines is not an infernal trap but merely a loosely woven cotton bandage someone has tied over her eyes. She lies still for a long time, too exhausted to move. All around her she can hear women's voices. They're speaking Portuguese, which must mean she's still in Brazil, perhaps still in Rio. Although they speak mostly in whispers, she understands a word here and there. She has been hearing Portuguese since she was six and her father and mother took her from her grandparents' house and plunged her into the wild, beautiful tropics. For a moment she's comforted by the sound of this melodious language, which she speaks as if she'd been born beneath the slopes of Corcovado. Then again, she remembers.

"*Senhoras!*" she cries. The conversations stop abruptly and footsteps approach. Through the bandage, she sees a large woman dressed in a black robe. The woman is wearing a starched white headdress that flutters like the wings of a bird. Not a devil or an angel but simply a nun in a wimple.

"So you're awake at last," the nun says.

Carrie manages to nod.

"What is your name, my child?"

"Carolyn Vinton." Carrie's tongue has finally been unlocked and the words slide out easily.

"You have been very ill, Dona Carolyn. We did not think you would live. You were given the *últimos ritos*."

"The last rites? But I am not . . ."

"Not Catholic. We knew that. But in times of plague, rules can be broken. Father Gilberto baptized you and then anointed you with holy oil and prayed over you. And you see, it worked. Many died, but thanks to the grace of God, you survived. And now you are a good Catholic girl, and if you relapse and die, you'll go straight to heaven."

Carrie struggles to find the nun's words comforting, but the idea that she might fall back into fever and die is terrifying. She wants to tell the nun that the priest didn't need to baptize her. She'd been baptized at the age of three when Grandfather Hampton dunked her in a freezing cold creek in mid-March over her mother's strenuous objections. Mama had yelled that Carrie would get pneumonia and die like her baby brothers, which had been a real possibility. There'd been no reason for that cold spring baptism except for Grandfather's own, famous bullheadedness . . .

She realizes with a start that her mind has wandered back to early childhood. Her memory seems to be returning in pieces. She looks up and finds the nun still standing over her, waiting patiently. There are things Carrie wants to ask her, but first she needs to put her own thoughts in order.

She's been ill, the sister said. Sometimes people wake from tropical diseases with their minds permanently scrambled, or worse yet, they return from the edge of death like little children, unable to read or write or remember their own pasts. Will her brain work normally once she recovers? Will she ever be herself again? Maybe if she could see . . .

"Could you please take this bandage off my eyes?" she asks. There's a brief silence while the nun considers her request. Carrie's mouth goes dry with fear. Something's terribly wrong.

"Do you think you can stand the light, Dona Carolyn? The last time we removed the bandage, you began screaming and begged us to put it back on."

"Am I going blind?"

The nun laughs softly. "No, quite the contrary. All your senses seem to have been sharpened to the point of agony. When the cat came into the room a few nights ago, you knew it was there, not because you could see it—that was impossible—but because you smelled it. You asked for us to put it up next to you, and we did. You slept with it for an hour or so, and then, as cats do, it wandered off, perhaps to hunt mice, which is why we allow it to live here." The nun bends over in a sudden black-and-white blur and plucks the bandage from Carrie's eyes. "There," she says, "how's that? No screaming? Ah, good."

Carrie blinks and finds herself staring up into a pock-marked face with coarse features. The nun has dark eyebrows, a large nose, and small, watery eyes. She's well into middle age and not at all pretty, but her smile is kind, and Carrie is grateful for it. She turns her head and discovers that her neck still aches, but the pain is minor compared to what it was before.

She is in a large room. The whitewashed walls are adorned with wooden crucifixes. Tall windows let in pink-tinted light—either sunrise or sunset; she's in no state to determine which. To her left, a row of cots covered with mosquito netting stretches toward an arched doorway through which she can see a courtyard, a bougain-villea vine in full bloom, and a fountain made of those blue-and-white Portuguese tiles that go by the name of *azulejos*. She notices that only a few of the cots are occupied. Most are not only empty but missing sheets and mattresses.

"Where am I, Sister?"

"You lie in the hospital of the Irmandade da Santa Casa de Miser-icórdia. We found you unconscious on the street and brought you here in a cart along with a dozen others, all of whom had the pox."

At the word *pox* another shiver moves through Carrie's body. She can feel horrible, inchoate shapes lurking at the back of her mind like caged animals impatient to be let out, but she doesn't know what they are. Memories? Nightmares? She knows her own name and her distant memories are clear, but she seems to have no recent past. Whatever's waiting for her has something to do with the word *pox*. Instinctively, she reaches up and touches her cheek, feels the warmth of her flesh, the curved plain of her forehead, the bridge of her nose. When she moves her hand up to her head, she discovers they've cut her hair.

She remembers it had been waist-length, blond; that it curled in impossible tangles. She remembers fighting it with a hairbrush every morning and winding it into a crown of braids. Most of all, she remembers being pretty, not beautiful perhaps, but pretty: dark brown eyes with flecks of amber in them, an oval face, a complexion that tanned in the tropical sun rather than burned, leaving a line of freckles across her nose. She remembers not minding that her skin darkened even though ladies were supposed to be as pale as milk.

Shutting her eyes again, she conjures up herself in an imaginary mirror: small, round breasts; long legs. Too tall by a good three inches for current fashions, but slender and high-waisted with curved hips, delicate, long-fingered hands, and lips so red that someone, whose name she cannot remember, once accused her angrily of using paint. She lists her flaws: a crooked toe on her right foot that never healed properly after she broke it, an overbite, a turned up Irish nose—

Her hand returns to her cheek and freezes. She lies still fighting a terrible suspicion. Slowly she lowers her hand and opens her eyes. She has a question she wants to ask, but she isn't sure she wants to hear the answer.

"I've had the pox, haven't I? Tell me the truth, Sister: Am I horribly scarred?"

"No, not at all, Dona Carolyn. There isn't a mark on you. You never caught the pox. You had some disease that we have no name for. Your fever was so great, we were sure you were going to die. You had a rash all over your body that we first assumed was the pox, but you never developed the blisters. Even so, your pain was beyond description. You suffered greatly. We prayed for you as we prayed for all who came to us during those terrible weeks, but in your case, by the grace of God, our prayers were answered."

The nun looks down the row of mostly empty beds. "I don't think you need to be afraid of catching the pox now. The plague has burned itself out. Some of the sick have recovered and gone home, but many died. Most of those empty beds were theirs. We've burned the sheets and mattresses and buried their bodies in our garden because there was no room left in our cemetery. We would have burned their bodies, too, but the poor souls could not go to God if we did that. For more than a week, they died nearly as fast as they came in. On the worst day we buried fourteen, two of whom were sisters in our order who nursed the sick until they fell down beside them and had to be nursed in turn. I don't know why I was spared."

She turns back to Carrie who is staring at her with a look of great agitation. "What is it? Are you feeling ill again? Is the fever back?"

"No, but your words have made me remember something."

"Remember what, my child?"

"That my father died. I buried him in a garden, our garden. Some-one . . . someone I love . . . William . . . yes, William helped me dig his grave." William's name suddenly comes back to her, releasing a torrent of memories so painful she begins to weep. She knows now why she hasn't been able to remember the recent past. It's unbearable.

"Where is he, Sister? Did he live or die? Tell me now, please. I can't bear not knowing." Sick with fear, she waits for the nun to answer.

"Did who live or die, my child?" There is a hint of weariness in the nun's voice as if a display of grief were out of place in this room full of ghosts and empty beds.

"William," Carrie says. "William Saylor. He'd come back to Rio, and we were going to be married, but as soon as his ship sailed into the bay, he saw the black flags. He's a doctor, so he knew at once what they meant. Once he realized there was plague in the city, he became desperate to get to me, but the captain forbade anyone to go ashore and announced that he was going to set sail for São Paulo as soon as the tide turned because only a madman would enter Rio in the middle of an epidemic. William said all he could think of was the danger I was in, so he waited until dark, lowered himself down the side of the ship, swam to the docks, and came to me as quickly as he could. He found me at home tending my father. William tried to help me save Papa, but all his medical knowledge proved useless. Papa suffered so, dear God . . ."

Carrie begins crying again.

"*Lentamente*," the nun says softly. "Calm down, go more slowly, and try to stop crying. You say this William Saylor who came to you when your father was dying was your fiancé?"

Carrie attempts to control her tears and only succeeds in sending herself into a choking fit. The nun jerks her upright and whacks her smartly on the back with the palm of her hand. "Breathe!" she commands.

Carrie takes a long, shuddering breath and finds her voice. "I've loved William since I was nine years old. We were to be married. He intended to come back to Rio sooner, but his—"

The nun interrupts her. "'Veelhum'" is an English name, is it not?"

"No, American. William and I were both born in the United States less than a hundred miles from each other. I was born in Bloomington, Indiana; he was born in Mitchellville, Kentucky." The nun stares at her blankly, and Carrie realizes she has switched into English.

"William and I are both Americans," she repeats in Portuguese. "Do you know where he is? Did he come here with me? When I fell ill, he was already running a high fever, and I'm afraid he may have caught the pox—although perhaps he only had what I've had, and like me he's recovered. Still, I'm afraid he came down with the pox. We spent two weeks nursing the sick together . . . "

"For which God will reward you," the nun says. She pauses and fixes her eyes on Carrie in a way that Carrie can't interpret. It's not an unfriendly look, but there's something speculative about it. "I'm sorry to say that there's been no one named William Saylor here, or at least no man who lived long enough to tell us that was his name. If you like, I can check the book that holds our records of births and deaths, but I've read it so many times over the past month that I know it by heart, and I can tell you without looking that you won't find your fiancé listed there."

"Of course his name won't be on your death list! William can't be dead. God wouldn't be that cruel."

"God works in mysterious ways, my child. It's not for us to question Him."

Under other circumstances, Carrie might have argued this point with her since her own grandfather had spent his entire life questioning God at every opportunity, but she's too busy struggling to sit up. "Where are my shoes and clothes? Please bring them to me, Sister. I need to go out and search for William. He may be lying sick and untended. He may need food, water . . ."

The nun puts her hand on Carrie's chest and pushes her back down. "What you need, Dona Carolyn, is to lie still and rest. You're in no condition to go out on the streets, and if you insist on trying, you may not live long enough to marry anyone. Rio is still in turmoil. The Emperor and his court have moved to the Summer Palace in Petrópolis. Anyone else rich enough to leave the city fled at the first sign of the plague and only a few have returned. Thieves and looters have taken over the streets. Be sensible. Think of your own safety. If you leave the protection of the *Irmandade*, you may be ravished and murdered if you don't relapse and fall down dead first."

"Please let me get up," Carrie pleads. "Please, Sister. I don't care what happens to me. I have to find William. If I die looking for him, then I die. If he's alive and sick with the pox, I want to take care of him, and if he's dead, I don't want to live."

"Calm yourself, Dona Carolyn. This is your illness speaking. Your life is precious. God gives each of us only one. The passion with which you speak of this man is not appropriate for a *senhorita*. It's hardly appropriate for a married woman. I think this Veelhum Saylor has been more than your fiancé, that you were with him for many days unchaperoned, and that you and he did more than simply tend the sick together."

"I could never be ashamed of anything I've done with William!"

"My dear child, I am not asking you to be ashamed. I am asking you if you are carrying his child."

Carrie is struck speechless. The thought has not occurred to her. She remembers lying in William's arms, the look in his eyes that told her better than words could that he loved her, a joy so intense she felt as if she might shatter under the force of it. And then she remembers how afraid they were, how people were dying all around them, how they only had each other for comfort.

"It's possible," she admits. "William and I . . ." She looks at the nun and thinks that there's no use trying to explain this to her.

A smile curls at the corner of the nun's mouth. "Do you think that because I've never been with a man, I don't know what love is? For twelve years I directed our shelter for fallen women. No doubt you don't think of yourself as 'fallen'. The girls never do until the babies come. I always encourage them to trust in the love of Christ. True, they've sinned, but I believe of all mortal sins, the sin of love is the most easily forgiven. After all, Veelhum was your fiancé. You were about to marry him."

"William and I searched everywhere for someone to marry us, but the epidemic kept getting worse, and in the churches they were having funerals, not weddings. The day before William fell ill, they even closed the . . ." A frightening thought suddenly occurs to her. "Sister, I've been very sick. If I'm carrying William's child, will it be normal?"

The nun seizes both of Carrie's hands and holds them in hers. "There is no way to tell. You must trust in God, my child."

"God can wait." Carrie jerks her hands back. "I have to find William."

"I am sorry, Dona Carolyn, but I can't let you leave."

Carrie says nothing. She's not afraid of going out on the streets of Rio. She just spent two weeks on them in the middle of an epidemic, not to mention that she's the granddaughter of Decimus Hampton, the most stubborn man who ever lived.

"We have guards at the gate," the nun says. "If you try to leave, they'll catch you and bring you back to me, and I'll have to tie you to your bed. You were tied when you were sick so you wouldn't fall out and harm yourself or claw at your face, and the cords are still in place. So lie still, Dona Carolyn, and rest until your strength returns. Later I'll bring you some hot broth."

The nun drops the mosquito net, turns, and walks out of the room, through the door, and into the courtyard, disappearing behind the orange blossoms of the bougainvillea vine. As soon as she is gone, Carrie again tries to sit up, but she's so exhausted she can hardly push her body off the mattress. When at last she manages to swing her legs over the edge, she's wracked by nausea and dizziness. For a few seconds she clings to the cot, trying to steady herself, but the sensation, which is a great deal like seasickness only worse, doesn't pass. At last she gives up and falls back.

Perhaps she passes out or perhaps she simply falls asleep, because the next time she opens her eyes, it's dark and raining furiously. An oil lamp sways above her, casting strangely shaped shadows on the walls. On the ceiling, in an ever-shifting circle of lamplight, a gecko is hunting mosquitoes. For a long time she lies awake watching the gecko, listening to the rain drum against the roof tiles, and praying William is somewhere warm and dry.

Chapter Three

Early November 1853

Mae Seja sits in the shade fanning herself with a palm frond. Her name, roughly translated from the Portuguese, means "Mother of Possibilities." Thin to the point of gauntness, she is so old hardly a hair remains on her head, but her eyes are small, bright, dark, and deeply intelligent. On her back, she bears scars from the lashes an overseer gave her many years ago when she was a slave in the cane fields. Now at eighty-three, she is the most respected woman in the *quilombo*, a spiritual leader who speaks with the *orixás*, those gods her people brought with them from Africa and have hidden from their Brazilian masters for hundreds of years.

Everyone in the *quilombo* believes Mae Seja is a visionary who can see into the future and the past and beyond both into the realms of the dead, which is why Carrie has come to consult her today. They have just drunk bowls of coconut milk and eaten slices of mango to celebrate Carrie's arrival. Now they are resting against the roots of a tree as tall as the mast of a ship. Its roots are bleached whitish gray, spread out like wings, curved, and large enough to serve as backrests. Through the leaves of this giant, which is only one of thousands that grow in the jungles surrounding Rio, sunlight filters down in small golden pools, and far overhead a flock of parrots takes flight, screeching like window hinges in need of oil.

"Mae Seja," Carrie says, "I have a favor to ask. I need to find a man who calls himself William Saylor."

She waits patiently for Mae Seja to speak. She has come to her in desperation after searching in vain for William. Brazilians are famous for keeping accurate records. Since the sixteenth century they have recorded the name of everyone who enters or leaves the country, not to mention every coil of rope and sack of coffee. Brazil has over two thousand miles of coastline, so some people have undoubtedly slipped past, most notably the thousands of slaves who are still being smuggled in from Africa to work on the coffee plantations even though importing slaves into Brazil has been illegal for nearly three years.

William would not have been one of those overlooked by the authorities, yet his name is not on the custom lists. This in itself is not surprising since when he arrived, he swam to shore, but his name is nowhere else to be found either. For a while Carrie kept expecting him to show up at her father's house, but there's been no sign of him. She has examined lists of the dead and ill and the passenger lists of every ship that left Rio for another port within the past two months. She's talked to anyone who might have seen William and even looked at lists of prisoners, although she can't imagine him committing a crime. On the off chance that he might have gone home, she recently wrote a letter to him in care of his mother, but it takes two months for letters to reach the States from Brazil and another two to receive a reply, and she doesn't think she can wait four months.

The nun at the Casa de Misericórdia was right. She has missed her menses, and thanks to an unfamiliar feeling in her body that she can't quite put into words, she strongly suspects she is carrying William's child.

MORSE INSTITUTE LIBRARY
14 E. Central Street
Natick, MA 01760

Mae Seja still hasn't responded. Finally she reaches out and helps herself to the last slice of mango. "Is the man you're looking for dead or alive?" she asks.

"I don't know, Mae. That's what I need to determine. I thought perhaps you could perform a ceremony to help me find out."

Sitting back against the tree, Mae Seja closes her eyes, and begins fanning herself again. "To summon the *orixás*, we'll need drummers. The hunters will have to stop hunting, and the women will have to quit hoeing their manioc patches. The children are going to have to stop gathering wood and help their parents get ready. The elders will be there, so we'll need to make sure they're comfortable. The babies and the sick will also be there. Curing the sick will simply be an extra benefit."

Carrie nods. In other words, Mae Seja is willing to perform the ceremony, but it's going to be expensive. "I'll be happy to pay, Mae. I've recently come into a great deal of money."

That, if anything, is an understatement. She has inherited a fortune so large she can hardly comprehend it. Her father made a substantial amount in his own right, plus he was always a soft touch for inventors. After Carrie got out of the hospital, she returned to their house on the Ladeira da Glória and began the sad task of sorting through his papers. She knew he had designated her his sole heir, but since his investments had a habit of failing, she didn't expect her inheritance to amount to much. To her surprise—among patents for steam-powered earthquake neutralizers and worthless promissory notes from inventors who planned to produce umbrellas guaranteed not to turn inside out—she discovered something of value. Two years ago, her father had bought shares in a silver mine and a telegraph company that was in the process of taking over all the lines west of Buffalo, New York. When she took these stock certificates to the bank, she was astonished to discover that they had appreciated astronomically. She was now one of the wealthiest women in Rio.

Even if she hadn't been rich, she wouldn't have begrudged Mae Seja whatever she cared to charge. The *quilombo* is a community of escaped slaves, half a dozen desperately poor white Brazilians, and a few Indians who have not died of European diseases or been killed or worked to death—one of perhaps eight thousand such communities in Brazil. Hidden in a steep jungle valley east of Rio, it has not only been a refuge for slaves fleeing from the coffee plantations where the life expectancy of a worker is less than seven years; it has also been a refuge for Carrie and her family. Carrie first came to this nameless place with her father and mother when she was eight, after her father decided to hunt orchids near a city where his wife and child could live in comfort and safety.

The day they arrived, Mae Seja was there to welcome them. She said she had seen them coming in a dream. For many years, the people of the *quilombo* helped Carrie's father find rare orchids in the Atlantic jungle, establishing his reputation. He in turn protected them from the *capitães do mato*, those armed bands of professional killers who hunted down escaped slaves. The route to the *quilombo* has always been a secret, involving three days of rugged travel through almost impenetrable terrain, but there is so much hunger for slaves that the *capitães* would have found it sooner or later. So Carrie's father did what was usually done in Brazil under such circumstances: He bribed the right people. Technically, of course, he bribed no one. He merely rented the land, which was of almost no value whatsoever, but in reality he paid a yearly protection fee to the growers who armed the *capitães*.

Thanks to this so-called "rent," the *quilombo* was left in peace, and Carrie had the unusual experience of growing up in two worlds: One in Rio where she wore white lace dresses, moved in the society of ex-patriots and wealthy Brazilians, and went to school with the children of British diplomats, and another where she ran barefoot in the forest with the children of the *quilombo*, learned the Afro-Brazilian-Indian names of plants, tormented sloths by tossing mango pits at them, gathered firewood, tracked animals, gambled away her allowance with wooden counters, took shots at birds with makeshift blowguns, cooked whole monkeys in iron kettles, and did a hundred other things that were endlessly fascinating and often dangerous—all the time dressed in a knee-length cotton shift or, on some occasions, in nothing at all.

She hasn't visited the *quilombo* much in recent years. When she turned twelve, her father decided she was too old to run wild in the jungle. But the *quilombo* and Mae Seja have always had a place in her heart, and she intends to go on paying the rent for this land just as her father did.

Mae Seja still has her eyes closed. Carrie wonders if she's fallen asleep. "I'll be glad to pay for the ceremony," she repeats.

Mae Seja opens her eyes and puts down her fan. "No, your father was a generous man. He bought the freedom of several people here. Zé's wife, Ynaie's uncle . . ."

"Papa hated slavery. After Mama died, he set me to copying his correspondence. He often wrote about how happy it made him to buy slaves from their masters and give them their liberty. He always said no one had a right to own anyone else."

"He was a good man. We all mourn his passing. We can't take money from his daughter for finding out if someone she loves is dead or alive." Mae Seja doesn't have to ask Carrie if she loves William. A woman who can see into the past and future is not likely to miss the signs of love on a young woman's face.

Carrie kneels, takes the hem of Mae Seja's shift in her hands, and kisses it. "Thank you, Mae," she says.

Mae Seja laughs. "No need to be so formal, Carrizihna. Help me up, and we'll go tell the men to pass the skins of their drums over the fires to tighten them. Tonight, the *Axé* will flow through me, the Ancestors will guide me, and my voice will become the voice of

William Saylor; but I must warn you of two things: First, you must sit with your back to me as I speak and never look around no matter how tempted you are. Second, I will not be able to tell you if he's dead or alive. Only he can tell you such things. Also, you will not be able to question him."

She must see disappointment in Carrie's face for she adds, "If he tells you nothing you don't already know, he may not be dead. If, on the other hand, he tells you of his death, he may still be living. Sometimes what you hear during the ceremony is not what a spirit is saying but your own fears and memories. I will search for your William in the realms of the dead, but often the dead are hidden from the living. In any case, I will do my best to bring him to you."

The ceremony begins a little after midnight in a clearing about a hundred yards from the *quilombo*. The moon has set, the stars are hazed by the moist breath of the jungle, and the only light comes from the candles on the altar. Approaching Carrie, Mae Seja's oldest son offers her a gourd filled with a black liquid. "Drink," he commands.

Accepting the gourd, Carrie drinks deeply of something so bitter she gags. Behind her, the candles on the altar flicker, casting shadows that rush over the vine-draped trees like swarms of butterflies.

For a long time everyone sits silently, waiting for the drink to take effect. Carrie feels nervous but not frightened. She trusts Mae Seja. Gradually, her throat grows dry, her ears feel as if they are being filled with cotton, her fingers begin to tingle, her legs grow cold, and a warm feeling spreads from her chest to her shoulders.

Suddenly, the jungle takes a step toward her. She starts, then forces herself to relax. The jungle takes another step and the vines on the trees become serpents. Impossible flowers blossom in the darkness. She sees pinwheels of light.

"*Á hora de começar*," she hears Mae Seja say. "Begin the drumming."

The drumming starts, the rhythms enter Carrie's chest, and her heart begins to beat in time to the drums. How long does this go on? She has no way of knowing, but at some point the men and women of the *quilombo* rise to their feet and begin the whirling dance of the *orixás*. They are dressed as gods, holding mirrors and wooden swords, their faces veiled by strings of beads. As they dance, they appear inhumanly beautiful, surrounded by auras of light.

Carrie finds these transformations disturbing. She tries to convince herself that the black drink is making her hallucinate, and this is why she's seeing these ordinary people—who she's known all her life—as gods, but no matter how hard she struggles to separate dream from reality, the dancers continue to change. Zé becomes a jaguar; Ynaie, a sinuous, green-scaled python. Even the children whirling in the shadows seem to change into toucans, parrots, red-winged tinamous, and chachalacas.

She's beginning to get frightened. She wants this to stop, but when she tries to stand, she finds she can't move. She opens her mouth to cry that she can't bear any more, but before she can speak, she hears William's voice. He seems to be sitting directly behind her. For a moment she's too shocked to put her thoughts in order.

Carrie, he says.

She starts to turn around, then remembers Mae Seja has forbidden her to. This is too cruel. How can she be so close to him and not speak or see his face or tell him that she's carrying their child.

All at once she feels something brush the back of her neck, light and quick as a kiss. The drummers find a different rhythm. The candles on the altar flare, and William speaks her name again.

She can bear this no longer. "William!" she cries, "Where are you? For God's sake, I must know! Are you dead or alive?"

At the sound of her voice, the drumming stops abruptly, and the dancers freeze in place. There is a sudden silence in the clearing. Carrie shudders and turns around. Mae Seja is gone, and the candles on the altar have been extinguished. She tries to see past the dark altar, but her eyes won't focus. Did she really hear William's voice just now or did she only imagine it?

There is no wind blowing, but when she looks back at the jungle, it's moving in a long, slow wave. *I'm drunk*, she thinks, *or in a trance or hypnotized. I can't tell what's real and what isn't, and I still don't know if William is dead or alive.*

What was in that drink they gave her? Papa would have known or at least he would have asked; but her lips are numb, she can't form words, and all she wants to do now is sleep.

Chapter Four

Late November 1853

In the parlor of her house on the Ladeira da Glória, Carrie sits at her writing desk trying to deal with the mound of correspondence that has piled up since she last had the energy to sort through it. She is wearing an old green cotton dress this morning because green was the color her father liked her in best. Papa would never have wanted her to put on mourning for him. He hadn't even dressed her in black when her mother died—an act that had scandalized Rio's entire English-speaking community.

"To wear black in the tropics is a mark of either insanity or idiocy," he'd said, but now she thinks he simply could not bear to be reminded of his own grief every time he looked at her.

In the garden beyond the open double doors, the fountain is playing over the ceramic rims of its bowls, each note of dripping water growing lower as it progresses. The air is filled with the scent of jasmine and the raucous cries of a band of monkeys who are once again harvesting the papayas before Carrie's gardener can get to them. In the past, she would have strolled out onto the patio to watch them feed. They are the tiny, amusing sort of monkeys who look like furry-faced squirrels. She spent her childhood longing to keep one as a pet but Papa would never let her.

"Not even a caged bird," he told her. "Wild things need to be wild."

"What about orchids?" she retorted once, when she was ten and in a combative mood and still determined to make him pay for leaving her in Kentucky after her mother died. There weren't many fathers who would have tolerated that kind of backtalk from a ten-year-old, but Papa merely laughed.

"A good point, but orchids don't have mothers and fathers, and monkeys do." And then being an honest man, he added: "So to speak."

Carrie cannot help thinking about her father this morning because every time she looks toward the garden she can see the spot where she buried him. There is a newly planted tree where his grave was, its trunk covered with the vivid purples of *Sophronitella violacea*, the delicate whites of *Brassavola reginae*, and an incomparable bunch of *Crytopodium parviflorum,* bursting forth in cream and burnt umber. She has had his body re-interred in the English cemetery after a proper funeral and used some of her newfound wealth to buy him a marble headstone carved with stone orchids, but these living orchids are his real memorial, and she can sense his presence in them even though he now lies next to her mother and the little sister and brothers who died before they ever really lived.

She turns away from the sight of the garden and picks up another black-edged condolence card. *Brazil is too full of death,* she thinks. *The tropics are merciless. They have killed everyone I love except perhaps—*

She stops herself from bringing this thought to its logical conclusion, grabs the letter opener, and slits the end of the envelope. The question of William's whereabouts is keeping her from properly mourning her father. There may be worse things than being perpetually suspended between hope and fear, but at the moment the only one she can think of is knowing for certain William is dead.

She's changed since the morning she woke up in the Casa de Misericórdia to find herself lying next to a row of empty beds. For the first time since she was a homesick child of six, she wants to leave Brazil. She has no ties in Rio. She has already bought the land the *quilombo* stands on, deeded it to the community, and set up a fund to pay the former owners ongoing bribes. Most of the girls she went to school with are married women, and she no longer feels particularly close to any of them. She is not attached to this house. If she wanted to, she could put it in the hands of an agent, pack her bags, and buy herself passage on the next ship bound for an American port. But where would she go when she got there? Her grandparents are no longer alive, and the idea of living in Mitchellville with Aunt Josephine sets her teeth on edge.

Fire ants in a box, she thinks, *that's what Aunt Jo and I would be if we lived together. We'd be fighting from morning to night. Not to mention that she owns her cook, her maid, and the old man who drives her carriage, none of whom she is about to free. Kentucky is a slave state and I've already lived too long among slavers. I don't have any friends or relatives in the north. I suppose I could go to Massachusetts and join the abolitionist movement, but a few months after I arrive—*

A few months after she arrives, her baby will be born. She no longer doubts she is carrying William's child. You do not miss your menses, have your breasts swell up like bladders, and feel as if you can't keep down dry toast in the morning if you are not going to have a baby. Most of her former schoolmates are so ignorant they won't know they're with child until their mothers tell them, but thanks to her parents, she has known the basic facts since she was seven, although—and this makes her smile—neither Mama nor Papa ever mentioned that the process of getting in a family way was pleasurable.

Again, she thinks of William. By day she can convince herself he survived the epidemic, but at night she wakes up gripped by panic.

She forces the thought out of her mind and turns back to her correspondence. The card in front of her is from a Mrs. Alice Montjoy, wife of a British coffee merchant. She studies Mrs. Montjoy's flowery protestations of sympathy with growing annoyance. She cannot recall meeting the woman and is fairly certain Mrs. Montjoy never knew her "dear, departed father."

The bank has not been discreet. News of Carrie's wealth has spread through the city faster than tidings of the California gold strike. She's surprised it hasn't made the front page of *The Rio Sentinel.*

Picking up her pen, she writes Mrs. Montjoy a brief, polite note, blots it with sand, and puts it aside. When she looks back at the pile of correspondence, she is seized by a desire to slam her writing desk shut and go out for a walk along the beach. Every mother of every eligible bachelor in Rio has sent her a card expressing sympathy on the occasion of her father's death. She stares at the pile, thinking that it is quite an assemblage of fine, convent-trained handwriting. What would those same eager mamas think if they knew the heiress they were pursuing was with child? The British and American mamas would cut her dead, but the Brazilian mamas might continue the hunt. Brazilians are more forgiving about such things, and the money would be a great compensation. Perhaps she should just marry some Brazilian from a good family and give her baby a father.

The thought chokes her. Dropping her head on the pile of envelopes, she begins to cry. *I feel a hundred years old,* she thinks. *Older than Mae Seja; old and ugly and exhausted and terribly sad. I know I'll never love anyone as much as I love William, and I don't want to raise our child with anyone but him.*

None of this was supposed to happen. She was supposed to be looking forward to her wedding day. Her dress is still hanging in the wardrobe in the spare bedroom. She needs to tell the maid to get rid of it. She can't bear to think of it hanging there. If William shows up, she'll buy another.

The crying sends her into a flurry of hiccups that jar her back to the job at hand. Wiping her eyes on her sleeve, she retrieves a kerchief from her pocket, blows her nose, and soldiers on with the task of replying to the condolence cards. She is crying too often these days, and she suspects it has something to do with being with child. Not, she thinks grimly, that she doesn't have good reason to cry, but it isn't like her to fall apart like this.

Around two, she stops working and retires to the dining room to eat a bowl of soup, some stewed chicken, and a plate of sliced fruit. Then she goes back to the parlor. She's just getting to the bottom of the pile of condolences when the maid comes in bearing a visiting card.

"A gentleman is here to see you, *Senhorita*."

"Please tell him I'm not at home." She has no desire to trade banalities with yet another man in hunt of a fortune. Besides there is only one card on the tray, which means her visitor has not followed the usual practice of coming with his mother or some other female relatives. Recently a male caller leaped at her under the mistaken impression that smothering her with unwanted kisses was the path to her heart. He had left humiliated and gasping for breath after she thumped him in the chest with the book of romantic poetry he had brought her. Word must have gotten out, because until this afternoon she has not had any more unchaperoned suitors. Still, the incident has made her wonder if it's been a mistake not to wear black.

"The gentleman is an American, *Senhorita*. He says he will only trouble you for a few moments, but that he brings you important news."

"News? Did he say what kind of news?"

"No, *Senhorita*."

"Please show him in."

In the time that elapses before the stranger enters the parlor, Carrie allows herself to hope. Perhaps he's bringing a message from William explaining his absence. She examines the calling card and discovers her visitor is Deacon Presgrove and that he's in the import/export business.

The parlor door opens and a man enters: tall, broad-shouldered, impossibly familiar. Springing to her feet with a muffled cry of joy, Carrie takes a few steps toward him, then suddenly checks herself. This is not William, only a man who looks something like him. He has the same long, straight nose and high cheekbones, but his hair and moustache are black, not brown; he is a good five years older than William, and there are other things about him—the way he stands, the way he holds himself, the shape of his chin . . . Sick with disappointment, she sits down.

Mr. Presgrove places his hat on a side table and puts a medium-sized package wrapped in brown paper next to it. She notices he is wearing mourning. At the sight of the black band on his arm, she experiences dread so great it is all she can do to keep herself from ordering him to leave immediately. She doesn't care what kind of news he has come to deliver. She doesn't want to hear it.

I mustn't jump to conclusions. This has nothing to do with William. One of Mr. Presgrove's relatives has died, so naturally he's in mourning. In a moment he'll state his business, and I'll find that it has something to do with orchids, or it will be a plea for me to contribute to a charity, or he'll have just arrived in Rio bearing a letter from Aunt Jo complaining that I never write to her . . .

She notices that his eyes are green and catlike. Later she will recall a subtle sense of being stalked, but at the time, the sensation passes so quickly she hardly registers it.

How could I have ever mistaken him for William? William has brown eyes. Yet for a few seconds, seeing this man was like seeing a ghost. She banishes the thought from her mind and forces herself to think of nothing at all. For a few seconds, she succeeds. Then Mr. Presgrove speaks.

"Miz Carolyn Vinton?" he says in a soft, unmistakably Southern accent.

"Yes," Carrie replies, rising to her feet. "I am Miss Vinton. What can I do for you, Mr. Presgrove?"

He looks at her, and for an instant something close to pity flickers in the depths of his eyes. "I am William Saylor's stepbrother."

Chapter Five

The news Carrie has dreaded for so many weeks has arrived on her doorstep: William is dead. As Mr. Presgrove gives her the details, she presses her fingernails into the palms of her hands so hard that she later discovers she has cut herself. Every atom of her being fights against accepting this final verdict. *Stop!* she wants to cry. *Stop!* But Mr. Presgrove goes on speaking.

She registers, as if at a great distance, the sound of his voice explaining that he came down from Salvador near the end of the epidemic and forced his way past the quarantine to search for William. *"And for you and your father as well, Miz Vinton."*

He found William somewhere—she does not recognize the name of the place—desperately ill and incoherent with fever, but he discovered no sign of her or her father. Somehow—and it does not occur to her until much later how unusual this is, what force of will it demonstrates—he managed to get the captain of the boat he arrived in to take William on board so William could be transported to São Paulo where he had a better chance of getting medical attention.

"This was made easier," Mr. Presgrove says, "by the fact that my stepbrother did not appear to have the smallpox . . ."

Carrie forces herself to listen as deep inside her, grief boils up in long, slow waves. "I need to sit down," she says.

Perhaps under the impression that she is going to faint, Mr. Presgrove moves swiftly toward her and offers her his arm.

"Allow me, Miz Vinton."

Carrie permits him to help her into a chair. Fainting would be a luxury. Being conscious is far worse.

"Perhaps I should not go on."

"No, please continue." She wants to tell him that she feels as if a boa constrictor is coiled around her chest crushing the air out of her lungs, but that seems a strange thing to say. No doubt he would look at her blankly. William would have understood.

Mr. Presgrove sits down across from her and clears his throat. "I hope you will not mind me saying, Miz Vinton, that I feel as if I know you. My stepbrother spoke of you constantly, calling out your name as his fever rose, and then, during that precious day when he regained his senses and we thought the worst was over— "

"He had a day free of fever?" Carrie finds it comforting to imagine William did not suffer too much at the end.

"Yes, a bit more than a day, actually. During that time, he told me a great deal about you, Miz Vinton. He was terribly worried about you, because you had fallen sick and wandered off, and in his own sickness he had not been able to find you. He asked me over and over again if you were alive, and I always told him that, yes, you were, although of course at the time I had no way of knowing I was speaking the truth." Mr. Presgrove pauses and looks at Carrie so kindly she nearly breaks down. "He said often that he loved you."

"Loved me." Carrie clutches at the words. "Loved me," she repeats.

"Yes. His affection for you was so strong that he thought more of you than of himself. When he realized he was going to die, he made me promise to take care of you and his mother. His mother's marriage to my father was recent, you see, and I think in his delirium he had forgotten she had a new husband. I am not sure he even recognized me, but he thought constantly of your welfare." Mr. Presgrove clears his throat again. "Miz Vinton, he died with your name on his lips."

Carrie doesn't believe this. She's seen people die and their last words are rarely memorable. But even though it's a lie, it's a kind one, and it comforts her almost as much as if it were true.

"A few hours later he passed away. He was buried at sea wrapped in the flag of his country. There was no minister on board, but the captain read the funeral service. I . . " He pauses again. "I hope you will not think I overstepped any boundaries, Miz Vinton, but I cut off a lock of his hair before he was sewn into the banner that was to be his shroud. I thought to preserve it as a keepsake because I had grown very fond of my stepbrother in the short time we were acquainted, but now I realize he would want me to give it to you." He pulls out a small twist of paper and hands it to Carrie. "You might have it worked into a mourning broach."

Carrie unfolds the paper. Inside is a lock of silky, chestnut-colored hair—all that is left of the man whose body she knew as well as her own.

"Thank you," she manages to say.

"Did he never mention me?" Mr. Presgrove asks.

Carrie closes the paper, puts it on her writing desk, and stares at it for a moment, unable to speak. "Yes," she says at last. "Yes, he did. He told me he came home to find his father dead and his mother remarried, and that his mother had a stepson who was, by coincidence, already in Brazil. He said you met in Salvador and shared a meal together, and that you had expressed a wish to come to Rio for our wedding. I admit I had forgotten all this until you arrived, and even then when your card was brought to me, I did not recognize your name. In the middle of an epidemic—well, I am sure you understand: confusion, no time to talk about . . . you can imagine . . ." How is she summoning up the strength to speak so calmly?

She closes her eyes. William gone. Blotted out as if he never existed. Where is he? In heaven? Trapped in darkness? Here in this room, a ghost listening? Nowhere at all? Where are the dead? Where do they go? Can Mae Seja really speak to them? Is there a country of the dead just like this one only separated from it by a veil? She wants to believe that somewhere, in some form, William still exists.

"Miz Vinton," Mr. Presgrove says, "are you feeling faint? Should I ring for your maid?"

Carrie opens her eyes. The afternoon light streaming in from the garden seems as blinding as it did when she first woke up in the Casa de Misericórdia. *I am seeing the sun*, she thinks, *a terra-cotta tiled floor, flowers in a green vase. I am alive and William—*

"I'm fine," she says to Mr. Presgrove who is staring at her with alarm. "Please go on."

"I do not have much more to say, I'm afraid. My stepbrother died so quickly. Before he lapsed back into delirium, he asked me to give you something. I hesitate to do so, knowing how painful receiving it will be for you, Miz Vinton, but I feel I must honor his wish." Mr. Presgrove rises to his feet, retrieves his package from the side table, and sits down again. Pulling out a pocket knife, he cuts the string. He hands the package to Carrie. "This was to have been your wedding present from him."

Carrie accepts the package, folds back the brown wrapping paper, and finds another layer of white tissue paper stamped with tiny golden flowers.

"Chinese paper," Mr. Presgrove says. "Fine, isn't it? William said he bought it from a merchant in Panama."

Thrusting her hand into the tissue paper, Carrie pulls out a silk shawl so beautiful it makes her gasp. Thin and light as sea foam, the cream-colored silk is a mass of flowers of every description. There must be hundreds of them, none bigger than the tip of her little finger. Unfurling the shawl, she holds it up to the light and the flowers glow, each surrounded by a tiny halo.

"It is . . ." Words fail her. She draws the shawl to her face and smells it, hoping William's scent still lingers, but all the silk gives off is an odor of incense—not gardenia or musk or anything else familiar. Perhaps this is the scent of a flower that grows only in China. Disappointed, she removes her face from the shawl and finds Mr. Presgrove still looking at her anxiously.

"Thank you," she says. "This means a great deal to me. I shall treasure it."

"I wish I could have done more, Miz Vinton. I wish I could have brought you William alive and well. I did everything in my power to save the dear boy. I should probably not call him that, but he was five years younger than I am, you see, and during the time I was taking care of him, I came to think of him as the younger brother I never had." He rises to his feet. "Now, with your permission, I'll take my leave. I imagine you want to be alone."

Carrie finds herself reluctant to part with him. He's the last connection she's ever likely to have to William, and there's something he should know, something she hadn't intended to tell him until the moment he called William "the younger brother I never had."

Folding the shawl, she puts it on her writing desk next to the piece of paper that contains William's hair. "Mr. Presgrove, are you returning to the States any time soon?"

"Yes. I plan to leave in a few weeks after I have finished my business in Salvador. Frankly, I'll be glad to go home. There is too much death in the tropics."

She is surprised to hear him utter the same thought she had been entertaining only a few hours earlier. "Could you carry a message to your stepmother for me?"

"It would be my pleasure. Would you like me to wait while you write it?"

"I do not need to write it, Mr. Presgrove. It's a very short message, and I doubt you'll forget it. Please tell her—" She pauses, trying to gauge what his reaction will be, then decides it doesn't matter because she will probably never see him again. "Please tell Mrs. Presgrove she's going to be a grandmother."

Mr. Presgrove looks at her in bewilderment. Suddenly he smiles. There's not a hint of censure in his face. "A grandmother! You are carrying William's child? Miz Vinton, this is the best news I have heard in . . . My stepmother will be overjoyed. Her health is frail, and I have been dreading the moment when I must face her and tell her of her son's death. Now I can bring her good news as well as bad. I think your announcement may well save her life. You are an angel, Miz Vinton."

"I am not . . ." Carrie says, but he waves away her protest.

"An angel, I say. Do not deny it." He looks as if he is about to weep with happiness. Carrie is moved by his reaction. For the first time since he arrived, she likes him. It's not his fault that he was forced to bring her the news of William's death.

"What a gift you are giving us," he continues. "I love children, Miz Vinton. I have always adored them. I have none of my own, you see, not being married, so to be told that I am about to become an uncle . . . well, I can't tell you what great joy this brings me. Thank you."

"You don't condemn me then?"

"Condemn you? How could I? Children are a gift from God, Miz Vinton. Now that we are to be related, I must call you 'Carolyn' and you must call me 'Deacon.' Would you mind that? I am sorry. I am being too familiar and probably not making sense. But a child! How wonderful! When is the happy event to take place?"

Again Carrie is touched. Overwhelming joy over the birth of a baby isn't a trait you often find in a man who isn't the father. She examines Mr. Presgrove's face and sees signs of tenderness and sympathy she missed earlier. *He's a good man*, she thinks. *A decent man.*

Later she will realize that she should have looked at his face more closely, but now in this parlor with her grief newly minted, she only sees a stranger with William's warm heart who looks something like William.

"I will have my baby in June," she says. *My baby.* The first time she has ever uttered those words aloud. *William's baby, too*, she thinks. Suddenly she experiences a passionate hunger to be held and comforted, and an ache so deep all she wants to do is run from it. Unable to meet Mr. Presgrove's eyes, she looks toward the garden and sees a hummingbird stabbing its beak into a purple and white-petaled flower. *Passiflora edulis*: *maracujá* in Portuguese; passionflower in English. The unspoken words fall on her tongue like dust. She chokes on her grief, turns the choking into a cough, masters her emotions, and turns back to Mr. Presgrove.

"June?" he says. "But Carolyn—Miz Vinton—you can't possibly stay here. You must come back to the States immediately and let my stepmother take care of you. You cannot go through the dangers that attend childbirth alone."

Again he echoes a thought that Carrie has been having. When she wakes at night in a panic, she not only worries about William; she worries about giving birth to their baby in the tropics. Her two brothers and only sister died as infants here. She is probably alive only because her mother returned to Indiana to give birth to her. She was six—well past the age of greatest danger—before her parents took her to Brazil where even in large cities like Rio the lives of babies are so short that sometimes their parents don't name them until they prove they can thrive. She can imagine nothing worse than bearing William's child only to have it die or dying herself and leaving their child an orphan. Her own mother succumbed to childbed fever not two miles from where she now sits.

Time is running out. She must choose between Brazil and the States while she can still travel. For a few more seconds she wavers. Then she comes to a decision. She cannot do less for her child than her mother did for her. She's been waiting to find out what happened to William. Now that she knows he's dead, what is there left for her here in Rio where every street reminds her of him? Since she came back to this house, she hasn't even been able to sleep in her own bed because they once made love in it. That bed is empty now, made up with fresh sheets, neat as a coffin. It would be better to leave it behind. She needs to start over. This is no place for her and no place for her baby.

She looks up and sees Mr. Presgrove waiting for her to speak. "I plan to return to the States," she says. "But—" She breaks off in mid-sentence. She intends to tell him she doesn't want to impose on William's mother, but the truth is, she'd like to have her baby's grandmother with her when she gives birth.

Mr. Presgrove looks relieved. "I'm glad to hear you are leaving," he says. "The fevers alone, Miz Vinton, not to mention the bad water, filth, heat, venomous snakes . . . well, Brazil is no place for a woman who is with child. If I had a wife, I'd ship her back home as soon as she told me the good news. Have you booked your passage yet?"

"Not yet."

"Then let me do it for you. My family has a sugar exporting business in Salvador. We are doing quite well, and I can easily book you passage to New York on a clean, sturdy vessel." He smiles kindly.

Under normal circumstances, Carrie would have smiled back,

but grief is bubbling up in her again, threatening to overflow, and she can hardly trust herself to speak. She wants him to go away now and leave her alone to mourn William, but if she's going to accept the hospitality of the Presgroves, there are arrangements to be made.

She is so busy trying not to break down that she pays no attention to Mr. Presgrove's description of the family business in Salvador. Not until much later does she play back this conversation and realize how strange it is that the Presgroves are making money in sugar when everyone in Brazil knows the sugar market has collapsed. *Coffee*, she thinks. *He should have said 'coffee', but what did it matter. I wasn't listening for warning signs, not then.*

"You must let me escort you," he continues. "There's no use protesting that you can easily find a suitable female companion to travel with you. She is welcome, of course, but I insist on coming, too. You should not make such a voyage without a man to look after you."

She is about to tell him she can look after herself, but he continues speaking with an enthusiasm that defies interruption.

"No, no, Miz Vinton, I beg you. Do not refuse. I will conduct you directly to my stepmother. At present she and my father are living in Washington. He's a senator, Senator Bennett Presgrove of Kentucky. Perhaps you have heard of him? He's been in the papers quite a bit lately."

Carrie shakes her head. She hasn't read an American newspaper in weeks. All she knows is that Franklin Pierce has been elected President and that the issue of slavery is becoming more and more divisive, but beyond that she has been out of touch ever since the epidemic began. She has never heard of Senator Bennett Presgrove.

"No matter, the point is, he and my stepmother have rented a very comfortable house in Washington, so you will not have to make the long trip to their plantation in Kentucky. As you know, the voyage from Brazil to the States takes two months—sometimes more. By the time you reach Washington . . ." He stops. "Well, you take my meaning, Miz Vinton."

"By then," Carrie says, "I will almost be ready for what is called 'my confinement.' In other words, my condition will start to become quite obvious, and no amount of raising crinolines or taking out seams will be able to disguise it." She knows she's being overly blunt, but she doesn't care. Her life is going to have to go on, and she intends to live as she has always has, straightforwardly without cloaking everything in cloying euphemisms.

"I need to warn you that I'm not a woman who puts much stock in conventions. When I was a child, my aunt despaired of turning me into a lady. I have no intention of shutting myself away for months in a dark house with the blinds drawn. It's unhealthy and boring and completely unnecessary. Being with child is not an illness, and despite the fact that I'm unmarried—" Although she fights to control her voice, it trembles at the mention of marriage. She stops and takes a breath.

"Despite that, I am not ashamed. I intend to go out in public as long as I feel up to it, and if that makes you want to reconsider your offer, you had better tell me now."

Mr. Presgrove doesn't seem to be the least disconcerted. "Of course," he says. "Whatever you wish. But you will allow me to escort you back to the States, won't you? And you will let my stepmother have the joy of being present when her first grandchild comes into the world?"

Carrie's desire to resist collapses. She wants to go home to have her child, and Mr. Presgrove is offering her a chance to do so in comfort and safety. She's surprised that she still thinks of the States as "home," but she does. All at once, she's overcome with nostalgia. She wants to experience winter again, watch apple trees bud out in the spring. How long has it been since she has seen a robin or eaten maple syrup on her pancakes?

"I'll travel to Washington with you," she says. "Thank you, Mr. Presgrove. It's a very kind offer, but are you sure William's mother will welcome me?"

"She will welcome you with open arms." He pauses. "And you must let me pay your expenses. Again I insist. After all, William's dying wish was that I take care of you and," he looks around the room, "I imagine you are experiencing financial difficulties. I hope you do not take offense at me saying this, but your father, famous though he was, could not have been a wealthy man."

Carrie studies him warily. She does not like the turn the conversation has just taken. He seems sincere, but is it possible he doesn't know she's wealthy? She glances at the pile of condolence cards on her writing desk. If so, he must be the only unmarried man in Rio who doesn't view her as a potential source of income.

"Surely you have heard that I recently inherited a great fortune."

"Yes, Miz Vinton. I heard that on the day I learned you were still alive. The news has spread to Salvador. Brazil is a large country, but Americans are few and when something happens to one, the rest know about it so swiftly it's enough to make one believe in thought transference. So, yes, I did hear you had come into money, but when I saw you—pardon me for remarking on this—in a dress that is becoming but obviously worn, living in a home that is simple to the point of starkness, I decided those rumors were untrue. To be frank, I hoped they were untrue."

"They are," she says. "What would you say if I told you that I am nearly destitute? That this house is rented? That I have less than fifty dollars American to my name?"

He does not flinch. "I would say that it is fortunate indeed that I came here today, and I would ask you to have the goodness to accept any monetary aid my family or I can offer you. I know my father and stepmother would feel the same. I am sorry to hear you have been experiencing financial difficulties, but you must put any anxiety about money behind you. You shall never want for anything, nor shall the child."

His face turns red; he seems to struggle for words. "Miz Vinton, I said just now that I hoped the rumors of your wealth were untrue, because I have something to ask you, and if you were rich, you might be inclined to think I had ulterior motives. I want to say, right at the outset, that I am thinking only of your welfare and the welfare of your child. I am a simple, plainspoken man. I know this is the worst possible time to ask you this question. You are grieving for William, as am I. I've never done this before and I don't know how to find the right words, but I wonder if . . . that is, if you would consider doing me the honor of becoming . . . my wife."

"No," she says sharply. "Of course not." So he is a fortune hunter after all. She is disappointed. She had thought better of him.

Mr. Presgrove looks agitated, as well he should. "I was afraid that would be your answer, Miz Vinton. That would be my own answer if I were in your position. I have heard you have been deluged with suitors who, despite your many obvious virtues, court you only for your money, but I am not one of these. Would you please hear me out before you give me your final answer? What I am about to say has grave implications for your child."

Carrie wants to order him to leave, but when a man says he is about to say something that has "grave implications for your child," what choice do you have but to listen? "Go on," she says.

He clears his throat. "Thank you. You are every bit as kind as William said you were." He clears his throat again. "I would hope that if you accepted my proposal you would in time come to feel affection for me, but however you choose to regard me, I will respect your feelings, and I will never attempt to compel your affections or ask you to do anything you do not want to do.

"If you wish, our marriage could simply be a legal arrangement for the benefit of my late stepbrother's son or," he adds quickly "daughter. Frankly, that would not be my preference, for, if you will excuse me for saying so, you are a very attractive woman, but for a daughter it is particularly important to have a legitimate father. You have not been back to the States for a long time, and perhaps you do not realize the stain an out-of-wedlock birth puts on an innocent child there. I don't care that you and William never married, nor will my father and stepmother care. No matter what you decide, we will embrace your child as our own, but society will not be so kind.

"America is still Puritan. Saving your presence, I must use the word *bastard* here, Miz Vinton. I can think of no kinder word, and that is what people will call your baby. I do not want that to happen when you and I can so easily prevent it. If we marry, no one will dare question the paternity of your child."

"Mr. Presgrove, please, stop. I can't possibly consider your offer. We have just met."

"Yes, Miz Vinton, we have, and that is why I now want to tell you something to prove my sincerity. I said that my father was Senator Bennett Presgrove. The name meant nothing to you, but it means a great deal in the States. Few men are more determined to extend slavery into the western territories, and few men make more ardent speeches in support of slaveholding.

"I will not attempt to deceive you by pretending that my father himself does not own slaves. When he argues for the extension of slavery, he speaks out of self-interest. He is one of the largest slaveholders in the state of Kentucky. I realize that in confessing this fact I run the risk of permanently alienating you, but I want you to know everything about me without reservation.

"Miz Vinton, please do not judge me on the basis of my father's reputation. I may be his son, but I do not share his views on slavery.

In fact, I find them abhorrent. William told me you were an abolitionist. So am I. My father and I have quarreled bitterly over slavery. I believe he may write me out of his will because of it, but whether he does or not is a matter of indifference to me.

"I'm an honest businessman, Miz Vinton. I'm not wealthy, but thanks to my late mother, I'm prosperous, and I can easily take care of you and the baby. You say you have no money, but even if you did, I would not need it, and I would insist that you agree to draw up a will leaving it all to the child.

"I know I am not a great catch, but I'm good-natured, and I love children, and, if you will excuse me for saying so, I'm told that I'm not bad looking. You deserve a better man than I will ever be, but time is of the essence. I am here and unmarried, and I would love this child as my own without ever attempting to replace his father. When the boy is old enough, we can tell him the truth. You can name him William Saylor Presgrove, and when he is of age, he can drop the 'Presgrove.' If you give birth to a girl, she will be my delight and treasure, and I will see that she marries well. Male or female, the child will not only inherit whatever money you may have; he or she will inherit my entire estate as well."

Carrie is impressed. Surely no man who was merely interested in her money would confess to being the son of a slaveholding father. Still, what he is proposing is impossible.

"This is a generous offer," she says, "a kind offer, very possibly a well-meant offer, but, Mr. Presgrove, I cannot accept it. My answer is still no. I cannot marry you. I will go back home dressed in mourning and tell people I am William's widow."

"Miz Vinton, that may work for a while, but although Brazil is on the other side of the globe, ships sail from the States to Rio more frequently than you might imagine. In the end people will find out. Sooner or later, they always do. I know my proposal has been unromantic, but do not think the less of me for that. I realize I can never take William's place in your heart. I would never try. But what I would try to do is make you happy."

Pulling out his card case, he removes a card, picks up Carrie's pen, dips it in the inkwell, and writes something on the reverse side. "Here are names of some people who know me. And here is where I am staying. I have friends and business acquaintances in Rio. You can ask them about my financial status and my character. They will confirm what I have told you. Please at least think over my offer, Miz Vinton. If you discover something about me that makes you adverse to becoming my wife, then I will never mention the subject again. But if after verifying my story, you change your mind, I would be honored to be your husband."

"I do not wish to be rude," Carrie says, "but I would appreciate it if you would leave now."

Mr. Presgrove rises to his feet, politely bids her good day, gives her a courtly Southern bow, and leaves. Two hours later a messenger arrives bearing a huge bouquet. There are so many flowers, Carrie cannot find enough vases to hold them. With them is a note, which reads:

My dear Miss Vinton,
Whatever you decide, I remain your loyal friend.
D.L.P.

Chapter Six

After pillaging the flower market of its most spectacular blossoms and ordering them sent to Carrie, Deacon hails a cab and spends the remainder of the afternoon making calls. Traveling to the docks, he speaks to two business acquaintances. Then he pays a short visit to the banker who handles his commercial transactions and asks for a favor. His banker is delighted and promises to do as Deacon has requested.

"You may rely on me, *Senhor* Presgrove," he says, shaking Deacon's hand with so much enthusiasm that a bystander might have thought Deacon had just been elected to political office.

After leaving the bank, Deacon dismisses the cab and strolls through the city. His pace is leisurely. From time to time, he pauses to admire something: a cage of green and red toucans being offered up for sale, piles of orange cashew fruits, clay pipes imported from Holland. Around four, he stops in a café for a small cup of coffee so strong and thickly sugared he can almost stand his spoon up in it. Legless beggars clack along the street in small wooden carts painted with the faces of saints, vendors hawk an unidentifiable purple fruit that looks like grapeshot, barefoot female slaves in ruffled skirts and turbans pass by balancing trays of sweets and baskets of laundry on their heads.

Tossing a few coins to the waiter, Deacon gets up and begins to walk again. When he reaches a section of smart shops, women dressed in the latest Paris fashions sweep by him like flocks of exotic parrots.

As he crosses the Largo do Praço, he sees a toothless old man in a battered straw hat clutching a lamppost with one hand and a bottle of rum with the other. *Rum is sugar and sugar is selling for next to nothing*, Deacon thinks. This is a thought that should worry a man in the sugar exporting business, but Deacon's mood remains sunny.

Pausing in front of the Igreja de Nossa Senhora de Candelária, he looks around for a cab. The church, which as usual is adorned with scaffolding, is still not complete. Deacon has long thought it should be renamed "Our Lady of Perpetual Construction," but he has not found anyone he can share this witticism with. Brazilians are touchy about foreigners making jokes about religion.

A cab appears. Deacon hails it and gets in. Half an hour later he is sitting in the parlor of the home of the military attaché to the American Diplomatic Mission, drinking sherry and having a lively conversation with the attaché's wife, a small, redheaded woman from Tennessee named Nettie.

"My stars!" Nettie cries. "You are the most amazin' man, Deacon Presgrove. How do you do it?"

"Necessity, my dear," Deacon says. "Pure, unadulterated necessity."

Nettie laughs and refills his glass, which, Deacon is sorry to note, is hardly larger than a thimble.

"You simply must take part in one of our amateur theatricals before you leave Rio. You are too talented to let yourself go to waste.

Christ Church is putting on a passion play at Easter, and you would be perfect for the role of Judas."

Deacon smiles and toasts her with the miniature sherry glass. "I will take that as a compliment, Mrs. Wiggins. Alas, I will be long gone before Easter, out on the high seas, tossed by the elements."

"Why, you selfish old thing, you. You simply cannot leave without sharin' your talents. You were such a favorite back in Washington City. I still remember the night I saw you do Shakespeare at the National Theater. I never saw a more handsome Romeo. I can't for the life of me recall the name you acted under?"

"Donald Lane. But my acting days are long behind me, Nettie. I had a brief career on the boards, again out of necessity. A single season only. Hardly a soul except you remembers and, darlin', I'd appreciate it if you didn't remind them."

"My lips are sealed," Nettie says. She takes a sip of sherry and laughs. "At least until you sail. Now don't go givin' me that dark look, Deacon. I'm only teasin'. Honey, you are lookin' at me like Othello looked at poor Desdemona just before he wrung her neck."

Chapter Seven

In later years when Carrie thinks back to the weeks when Deacon courted her, what she remembers most is how considerate he was. The day after he proposes marriage for the first time, he returns to her house and asks to see her. Instead of telling the maid to send him away, she admits him to her parlor to thank him for sending her the flowers.

That at least is the ostensible reason. The truth is, she's lonely. Deacon Presgrove is the only person in Rio she can talk to about William and the only person who knows she's carrying William's child. She decides in advance that if he renews his proposal, she will ask him to leave at once, but he never mentions the subject. Instead he is sympathetic and considerate, and they have a long conversation that leaves Carrie feeling as if she has found a friend.

Three days later, he comes back again, and again the day after that. Gradually she begins to expect him to call in the late afternoon and to look forward to his presence in her parlor. Deacon is charming, amusing, friendly; he distracts her from her grief, encourages her to imagine how much better her life will be once she leaves Brazil, and reassures her that she will not be lonely in the States.

Sometimes they talk about her baby: whether it will be a boy or a girl, whether or not it will look more like her or more like William, what name she should give it.

On other occasions, they discuss less personal things. Deacon is well-educated, well-read, and intelligent. He can talk about art, literature, and politics without being pompous or boring, and although he knows almost nothing about botany or even, to Carrie's surprise, how sugar is grown, he knows an amazing amount about the theater. His stories of the plays he has seen in Washington and New York help her remember there is another world beyond Brazil. Sometimes he acts out the best bits for her, calling up the lines from his apparently inexhaustible memory.

He is always most eloquent when he speaks against slavery. His commitment to the abolishment of the trade is not only absolute, it is passionate. Once, while speaking of the horrors of the slave ships that ply the Middle Passage, he breaks into tears, and Carrie finds herself comforting him.

The most amazing thing she discovers about Deacon is that she can say anything to him. One afternoon she confesses that she thinks he looks like William. Yes, he says, he and William also noticed the resemblance. In Salvador they were taken for brothers, which, Deacon says, flattered him, since he knew he was not nearly as handsome as William.

Carrie agrees and tells him so, and he laughs. "You're an honest woman," he said. "I like that, Carrie." By now, they are calling each other by their first names, which seems reasonable since Deacon is, after all, a relative of sorts. And if he ever feels jealous when Carrie talks about William, he never shows it.

Carrie is never sure exactly how it happens, but gradually she comes to believe marrying him might not be a bad idea. Sometimes after he leaves, she feels agitated and filled with desire. Deacon may not be as good-looking as William, but he is a handsome man with a way of sitting and talking and moving that reminds her of a caged tiger. There is a passion in him that is hard for him to conceal and hard for her to overlook, and often when they are talking about ordinary things, she senses it and responds. Sometimes she even feels as if he has reached out and stroked her when all he has really done is pass her a plate of tea cakes or made a remark about the weather.

She finds this confusing and does not know what, if anything, she should do about it. Is she responding to Deacon because he looks like William or is she attracted to him in his own right? Should she tell him or does he already know? Is she feeling lust, loneliness, or something more real? In the end, she gives up trying to decide. Her emotions are so tangled during this period, she cannot sort out one kind of longing from another.

She may not be sure how she feels about Deacon, but she has no doubt how he feels toward her. Those green eyes of his stare at her in a way that is hard to ignore, and although he is polite, discreet, and gentlemanly almost to a fault, she would have to be blind not to see how much he desires her. As the days pass, this becomes increasingly important since she knows she could never consider marrying a man who was only interested in talking to her, and by now she is beginning to seriously consider his proposal. Then, too, she is flattered. How could she not be? When a man sits in your parlor speaking to you with the utmost respect and looking at you as if you are the most desirable woman he has ever met, you are not likely to feel he is making a mistake.

In December, he proposes again, and again she refuses him. She is only twenty-three and not inclined to spend the rest of her life as a nun, but even though he has become a good friend, she does not love him.

That night after he leaves, she goes upstairs and looks in the mirror and sees the lines grief is putting on her face. She still loves William, only William, but at that moment she knows that if she keeps on loving him and refuses all offers of marriage, she will end up a bitter, unhappy old woman. She will have the child, of course, but the child will grow up as all children do and leave her, and then what will she do with her life? Devote herself to good works? Take in stray cats? Become a pillar of the church? Bake cookies for the neighbors' children?

She thinks of all the years that lay ahead of her, all the hours she will spend sleeping alone, all the nights she will wake up longing for an embrace; the solitary meals she will eat; the poverty of a life lived in the past instead of the present. Staring at her own reflection, she realizes she is on the verge of turning her love for William into a religion. *No matter how much I love him*, she thinks, *I can't go on worshipping his memory. William was a man of flesh and blood, not an idol, and he would not have wanted me to stop living just because he did.*

As if he senses she is thinking of accepting his proposal, Deacon becomes more intimate. He does not try to kiss her, but the look of desire in his eyes becomes more intense, and gradually he begins to confide in her. One afternoon when she is talking about how hard it has been to lose both William and her father in such a brief space of time, she notices he is not responding as usual. Instead he sits silently, looking at her with intense sadness.

She stops talking and lets the silence gather. At last, he sighs and says: "I also lost two people I loved within a few weeks of each other: my mother and a young lady I was very fond of. My mother had shown me nothing but kindness, and I loved her dearly."

"And the young lady?"

"A friend of my sister's. I loved her and thought to marry her someday, but it was not to be." He gives Carrie a sad smile. "She looked nothing like you, but she was pretty in her own way: small and full-figured with dark hair and a little mole right there." He reaches out as if to touch Carrie's upper lip, coming so close that she can feel the heat of his finger, then draws back and lets his hand fall into his lap.

"How did you lose her?" Carrie asks. The question feels awkward, but Deacon does not seem to mind.

"Consumption."

"And do you still love her?"

"No. I will always treasure her memory, of course. She was a sweet, gentle girl, but my heart is elsewhere now."

Later Carrie plays back this conversation and sees what she should have seen at the time: how unlikely it was that a young woman dying of consumption would be "full-figured." But on that Saturday afternoon, all she feels is sympathy for Deacon and a sense of comradeship in loss.

Two days after he tells her about his late fiancée, Deacon proposes again, and again she refuses him. This time, she does not go upstairs afterwards and look in the mirror because she knows what she will see. Instead, she goes to her writing desk, takes out the piece of paper that contains William's hair, drops it into a saucer, strikes a match, and sets it on fire. As the paper burns, she says a final goodbye to him.

"Dearest William," she whispers, "I will never stop loving you, but somehow I must find the strength to go on without you. If you can hear me, my love, give me that strength."

As the paper turns to ashes and the flames die down, she feels a sense of release. She won't forget William, but she vows that from this moment on she will never again allow herself to be frozen in the past.

The next day she begins to check Deacon's references. Everyone speaks well of him: his banker, his business associates, even Mrs.

Wiggins, the wife of the military attaché to the American Diplomatic Mission, who knew Deacon in Washington.

"A wonderful man," Mrs. Wiggins says. "I'd trust him with my life, Miss Vinton." Her eyes wander to Carrie's midsection, which is hidden under layers of petticoats. "Such a warm day," she observes with a bright smile, "and yet you dress so stylishly."

Five days later, Deacon makes a fourth proposal of marriage. This time Carrie tells him the truth: That she esteems him, feels friendly affection for him, and finds him attractive, but does not love him and is not sure she ever will. If he's content with this, she's willing to become his wife; if not they should stop seeing one another.

Deacon does not hesitate. Seizing her hands, he covers them with kisses. "Carrie, dearest Carrie," he says, "I can imagine no happiness greater than becoming your husband. I love you more than words can express, beyond everything I value, beyond all riches, beyond life and health and beauty and honor itself, so much so that I can hardly breathe or speak."

Carrie is touched by his words. When he leans forward to kiss her, she is even moved to tears. For a few seconds she feels the warm pressure of his lips on hers, then she feels dampness on his cheek and realizes he is crying, too. It's a touching scene, one she remembers for the rest of her life, but there is more to it than she suspects.

Months later, she discovers Deacon cobbled together a few of Goneril's lines from *King Lear*, twisted them to serve his purpose, and presented them to her that afternoon as if they were sweets on a tray, and she wonders how long he spent selecting them, and if he ever saw the irony of using the speech of a liar as he reeled her in ever so sweetly inch by inch.

Safado! she writes in her journal on the day she understands what a fool she's been. It is a fine Portuguese word for which there is no English equivalent. *Con man, Don Juan, liar, libertine, gigolo, philanderer, womanizer, rake, cad*: all fall short.

PART 2

Betrayals

Carrie

The Kansas Territory, September 1856

*T*he night is passing swiftly and dawn is almost upon us. Already the east is tinged with red and choked with huge thunderheads that are turning purple and gold. The violence of the sunrise makes me think of blood and slaughter. I am not a violent person by nature, but I will fight Henry Clark and his band of border ruffians with every ounce of strength, cunning, and courage God gives me.

I have no military training. I am only leading the men into Missouri because I know the way to Beau Rivage. My father taught me to track anything that doesn't fly, and even though my skills were honed in the jungles of Brazil, I can easily see the signs of men passing over the prairie. The long grasses bend and break, campfires leave indelible traces, horses rub themselves against trees more gently than buffalo, and there are fewer trees to inspect. As for foot and hoofprints: in the Amazon it rains constantly, but here the land can go for days without being thoroughly soaked. When rain does come, the result is a muddy gumbo that catches prints and dries like unfired pottery, so reading a trail isn't much harder than reading a book of nursery rhymes.

It takes skill for a band of men on horseback to leave no trace, and Henry Clark and his band of border ruffians not only know nothing about hiding their tracks, they have no interest in doing so. After they massacred my friends and took those I love best captive, they rode toward the Missouri border drunk on arrogance and cheap whiskey. I tracked them to Beau Rivage like an invisible ghost and killed three before they reached the river.

Yet although I spread terror through their ranks, there were too many for one woman to defeat, so I had to return to Kansas for reinforcements. Clark's Raiders are afraid of me now, but they still have their hostages. My greatest worry is that they will kill me, take the prisoners to a slave market, and sell them South. If they do, Ni has sworn to follow them to hell and back if necessary.

Ni is a better scout than I will ever be. His slave name was Toby, but after he escaped from his master, he went to live with the Kaw Indians, whose name, he tells me means People of the South Wind. The Kaw treated him well, and before they were driven off their lands onto the reservation, they sent him on a vision quest. Now he calls himself Ni, which means water in Kaw.

Like me, he has a special reason for risking his life: His wife, Jane, and his two little daughters are Clark's prisoners. I say "wife" even though slaves are not legally permitted to marry. Jane is more Ni's wife than I was ever Deacon's even though I was fool enough to marry Deacon in church in a white dress, surrounded by flowers and witnesses.

The courage of Ni and his companions humbles me. Even if I am captured, the slavers probably will not hang me, although the penalty for helping slaves escape is death. It would cause too great a scandal to execute a white woman, particularly the daughter-in-law of Senator Bennett Presgrove. So provided no one can prove I killed three of Clark's men, I have a chance to survive. But the men who ride with me can expect nothing but execution or re-enslavement. At best they will be sold back into bondage, and they have all sworn to die rather than become slaves again.

They are fifteen in number, all ages, some nearly as white as their masters, some dark as Africans. Two, Andrew and Charles, are actually African-born "saltwater slaves," smuggled into South Carolina twelve years ago, although the United States government has outlawed the importation of slaves since 1808.

John Brown secretly trained them to ride and shoot, and he trained them well. They were going to be the cavalry of his secret army, and he planned to have them lead the slave insurrection that he believes will ignite a second American Revolution. If they make it back from Beau Rivage alive, they may indeed help end slavery in the United States, but in the next few days their aim and mine is to end it on a much smaller scale.

The oldest of my companions is forty-two; the youngest not more than fifteen. The fifteen-year-old's name is Spartacus, by which you may deduce he was not named by his master. My friend Elizabeth Newberry named all three of her sons after the leaders of great slave rebellions: Prosser, Toussaint, and Spartacus. Nine days ago, Clark killed Prosser and Toussaint, so although I have pleaded with Spartacus not to ride with us, arguing that he is not old enough, he tells me defiantly that he is not too young to die if it means evening up the score.

Spartacus and the others are armed with Beecher's Bibles, those fine rifled muskets that New England minister Henry Beecher supplies to anti-slavery immigrants heading to Kansas. I doubt Reverend Beecher ever imagined his guns would fall into the hands of a guerilla band composed of escaped slaves, but having met him personally, I believe he would approve. None of us have uniforms, because the federal government has not yet recognized it is involved in a war with the slaveholding South. We wear what we can. I have put on one of my lover's old flannel shirts and a pair of his trousers, Ni

wears buckskin leggings, the others wear the clothes they were wear-
ing when they escaped from their masters or clothes that have been
given to them since. One is dressed in an old jacket of John Brown's,
out at the elbows but still serviceable.

Before we set out, I want to list the men by name because if any
fall in the coming battle, I am determined to build a memorial to
them in Lawrence, just as we have built memorials to honor the sol-
diers who fell in the Revolutionary War, the War of 1812, and the
Mexican War.

They are: Abel, Andrew, Bilander, Caesar, Cush, Charles, Ebenezer,
Ishmael, Jack, Jordan, Marcellus, Ni, Peet, Samuel, and Spartacus.
Only Spartacus has a last name because, unlike the others, he was
born free. The rest have no desire to adopt the names of their former
masters, although several are considering taking the name "Brown"
in honor of the man who trained them in the art of warfare.

I suspect that we are all afraid of what may happen once we cross
into Missouri—I know I am—but we don't discuss our fears. We
have food, shoes, horses, and guns. We have a righteous cause and the
will to succeed. We have each other.

Chapter Eight

Rio de Janeiro, March 1854

As *The Frances Scott* sails out of Guanabara Bay, Carrie stands at the stern and inhales for the last time the familiar, earthy scent of wet jungles, perfumed flowers, and wood smoke. She sees the jagged heights of the coastal mountains, their slopes covered with coffee plantations, and the city, which has taken the drunken heaving of the shoreline and marshaled it into a bank of low white houses, factories, warehouses, and church spires. By the docks, hundreds of tall-masted ships rock in unison as slow swells move under them and speed on to crash against beaches the color of unrefined sugar.

Carrie watches until she can no longer make out the faces of the friends who came down to the docks to see her off. Then she turns and walks toward the bow of the ship. For the first time in many days she finds herself alone. Deacon is down in their cabin tending to the luggage, her fellow passengers are nowhere in sight, and the crew is too busy to pay attention to her.

She stands in the bow until the ship has sailed out of the bay into the open sea. When she walks back to the stern for one more look at

Rio, all she can see is a low, dark smear on the horizon. She is just preparing to go below and join Deacon when something moves inside her. Clapping her hand over her belly, she feels a light tapping sensation like the soft beating of butterfly wings. For a moment she stands there puzzled. Then, suddenly, she understands.

"Hello, my darling," she whispers to her unborn child, and all at once, she feels a rush of joy and grief so tangled together that she doesn't know whether to laugh or cry.

Chapter Nine

The sun sinks into a bank of clouds, night descends on the ocean, and everywhere Carrie looks, water and sky meet in seamless blackness. Propping the porthole open so the sea breezes can enter the cabin, she goes back to the table and sits down. To her left, a small glass inkwell dances on brass gimbals. To her right lies a pile of blank paper weighted down by an opalescent, spiraled shell.

Picking up the shell, she examines it. It's as intricate as the cross section of seed pod. Where did it come from? Not from Brazil. Perhaps it washed up on a beach on the other side of the world. If she holds it to her ear, will she hear the ocean roar? She puts the shell to her ear and is rewarded with a pulsing sound, but the sound of the real ocean is much louder.

Putting the shell aside, she picks up the flowered shawl William intended as a wedding present and throws it around her shoulders. The touch of the silk against her skin makes her sad. Perhaps she should put the shawl away, yet every time she wears it, she feels as if William is holding her. Will she remember him less often and be happier if she gives up the only gift he left her besides their baby? Running the hem of the shawl between her fingers, she decides the price of happiness is too high.

There are three pens in the penholder. The nib of the first one she selects is so badly splayed it must have been used to tighten screws, but the next is brand-new. Taking a sheet of paper from the top of the pile, she dips the tip of the pen into the inkwell, and begins to write the first of eight letters:

March 17, 1854
Dearest Mama,

I am writing to you because I need someone to confide in, and there is no one on this ship I can trust not to judge me. I lack the talent so many women have of working by indirection. I have always been too plainspoken for my own good. You and Papa always taught me to say what was on my mind and damn the consequences, but as I grow older I find this is a trait more suitable for a man than a woman.

I am also writing to you because I was told to. There, you see: I am being blunt again, but I know you will not mind. You always were a woman of strong opinions. When you and Papa argued it was as equals, face-to-face with no words minced and nothing hidden between you.

Before I left Rio, I went to a fortune-teller who threw those polished cowry shells the slaves call buzios, the ones they believe the gods use to send messages to human beings. I think the fortune-tellers read the messages by counting how many shells land right side up and how many fall upside down, but I'm not entirely sure. In any event, I know getting my fortune told was not a logical thing to do. The woman I went to claimed to be a priestess, but she was not nearly as skilled or wise as Mae Seja, and you never believed Mae Seja could see any farther than the end of her own nose. Still, I longed to know if my baby would be born well and healthy, and if it would be a boy or a girl.

At first the fortune-teller refused to tell me what she saw. Instead she looked frightened, which alarmed me. When I ordered her to reveal what the buzios were saying, she told me I would give birth to a girl "more angelic, strange, and beautiful" than any child I had ever seen. I objected to the word strange and demanded to know what she meant, but she refused to say another word beyond repeating "If you want to know anything else, Senhora, ask your mother."

I called her a fake, told her my mother had been dead for fifteen years, paid her, and ordered her to go away since it was clear she did not know any more about the future than I did. But since then, I have had a change of heart. Recently, I realized I have never stopped talking to you although you have been dead since I was a child. I dream of you often, and although you can no longer reply, this one-sided conversation, which never stops, comforts me.

Do the dead know what happens to the living? Were you present at my wedding? Did you slip into the church unseen and watch me marry a man I do not love for the sake of my unborn child?

Yesterday, I left Rio to return to the States, and yesterday I felt my child move in my womb for the first time. Will she really be "angelic, strange, and beautiful?" Can you see her, or was the fortune-teller only pretending to read a message in the shells? Perhaps my baby is a boy. If so, I hope he will look like William. If the souls of unborn children and the souls of the dead are in the same place, please speak to my little boy and tell him that his mother already loves him.

As you may have deduced by now, I am not entirely happy in my marriage. No surprise there; I didn't expect to be. But I think if I were a person more capable of forgetting the past, I would at least be content as Deacon's wife. The problem, as you may have guessed, is William. I still love him. What am I to do with this love? Transfer it to my baby? I doubt that will work. I can love my child without ceasing to love its father. Transfer it to Deacon? I don't think that is possible.

You see, Mama, I misspoke a moment ago. I am not simply in love with William; I am obsessed with him. I think of him from the time I wake up until the moment I fall asleep, and at night he fills my dreams. I think if I described these dreams to you, you would not condemn me, but I am not sure how to put them into words. They are very physical. William and I do not simply talk to each other. We do a great deal more. I believe most women would be horrified to have such dreams. Those pious girls I went to school with would hurry to confession, but here, too, I am different from other women. I welcome passion. I long for William's embraces. Each morning I am sorry to wake up and discover they are not real.

Yet oddly enough, although I can write to you, I cannot write to him. I have no idea why, but when I sit down to put pen to paper, I circle the blank page like a moth circling a candle flame and produce nothing but blots and tears.

I am not sure how I will post this letter. Perhaps I will drop it in the sea or burn it, but in any event, I will keep writing. The baby inside me grows larger every day, and I am frightened. I am not used to experiencing fear. I have always been confident that I could take care of myself no matter what happened. But so much can take place between now and the time we reach the States, and the only other women on board are the Misses Turner, two spinster sisters who presumably know nothing about childbirth, and Mrs. Wiggins, wife of the military attaché to the American Diplomatic Mission in Rio.

Nettie, as she has urged me to call her, is very pretty and well turned out in the latest fashions, all of which seem to be designed to make a woman look like a church bell. As we sail north toward the equator, it will grow hotter with each passing day, but I am willing to bet she will never abandon her lace gloves, long sleeves, and multiple petticoats. Nor will she take off her much-beribboned bonnet, a sturdy piece of millinery which would keep her head at a tropical temperature even if she were visiting Antarctica.

To give you an idea of her devotion to the latest styles, she has confided that she is going back to the States to have her seamstress run up a series of ball dresses for her. Why a woman would undertake a four-month round-trip voyage for a few silk and taffeta dresses that could just as easily be made in Rio is a mystery I am not capable of comprehending.

In other words, although Nettie is friendly, she is as impractical as those travelers who used to come up the Amazon with bathtubs, bottles of scent, and pianos. I like her, but I do not believe I can rely on her in a crisis. However, she is a good conversationalist and bright enough if you can steer her away from the topic of crepe de chine. She knew Deacon when he moved in Washington society and has nothing but good things to say about him. Also, she is perpetually cheerful. At the moment, I hold my tongue, keep my thoughts about William to myself, and drink in Nettie's good nature like a woman dying of thirst in a lifeboat. I am grateful for her friendship, but I would give the next two months of her for ten minutes with you.

Love,
Carrie

March 21, 1854
Dearest Mama,

Mrs. Wiggins and the Misses Turner have taken to their cabins with mal de mer. I remain well: "healthy as a well-fed brood mare," as Grandfather liked to say. The nausea of the early weeks has passed and my skin glows. Of course, my belly resembles a melon and my *ankles don't bear examination, but on the whole I would say I am prettier than I have ever been, for all the good it does me.*

I know I should be happy to be in such good health, but I am too preoccupied to enjoy my strolls on deck or the cafezinho *the cook prepares for me each morning. Something has happened. I want to tell you about it, but it is considerably more serious than dreams of illicit passion, and I find myself reluctant to commit it to writing.*

I don't know why I hesitate. When I was a child I could talk to you about anything. Even though you have been gone for many years, I remember you so perfectly that if I close my eyes I can imagine you are here with me.

Remember how you used to let me sit next to you at night and comb out your hair before you went to bed? You had the most beautiful hair: light brown and soft as a baby's. It fell all the way to your waist. I knew at the time that you were proud of it, but now I realize how much Papa must have loved it. You were quite simply the most beautiful woman I have ever known and the kindest. I am told it is common for mothers and daughters to disagree and grow cold toward one another as the daughter enters womanhood and the mother moves into old age, but that never happened to us. Perhaps one of the few blessings of losing you when I was so young is that I can never remember anything flowing between us but love.

You always did what was best for me, Mama, even when it was not best for you. For six years you lived with Grandfather and Grandmother Hampton, enduring Grandmother's complaining and Grandfather's endless sermons so I could grow up safe and healthy in America, so I know you understand why I married Deacon. Like you, I am leaving a place I love for the sake of my unborn baby; but unlike me, you were married to a man you adored. You were certainly married to a man you knew; but, Mama, I am beginning to think I do not know Deacon as well as I thought I did when I ac-

cepted his proposal of marriage, or perhaps it is myself I do not know.

When Deacon proposed, he claimed he loved me, and I was convinced he did; but—and I find this peculiar—since the day after we wed, I cannot feel his love, particularly when he and I are in bed together. I can tell he desires me—he leaves me in no doubt about that—but I cannot feel what I always felt when I was with William: security, a deep trust that he will never hurt me, a sense that his arms are a refuge against the troubles of the world. Mama, I am confused and for once I hardly know how to continue. Still, let me try.

I told Deacon when I accepted his proposal that, although I liked him and found him attractive, I did not love him in return, but despite this, our wedding night was more than I hoped for. Deacon was kind, considerate, attentive, and remarkably skilled as a lover. He did not once make me feel that he was disappointed that I had not come to him a virgin. Before we began, he assured me that, if I did not want marital relations with him so soon, he would not press them on me; but I was having none of that and told him so. I had not married him to live in celibacy for the rest of my life, so with some misgivings and an ache in my heart for that other wedding night that should have taken place but never did, I invited him to come into bed with me.

I was awkward at first, preoccupied with my pregnancy and worried we might do something that would hurt the baby, but he was patient, and we consummated our marriage with mutual pleasure and, I thought at the time, mutual affection. During the act—and this is crucial—I did not think of William. I believed I had put the past behind me. But of course, as you already know, that has not proven to be the case.

The very next day, things began to change between Deacon and me. At first, I hardly noticed, but gradually it has become clear that *something is gravely wrong. A few nights ago, shortly after I had settled down to sleep, he came into my bunk, took me in his arms, and kissed me. To my shame, I responded eagerly to his kisses. I will tell you more about why I felt shame in a moment. For now, let me simply say that this was the first time I had been really passionate with him, and yet at the same time I could not shake the feeling he was making love to me merely to entertain himself. Perhaps this was untrue; perhaps I imagined it, but the worst part was that even as I doubted him, I said nothing.*

Mama, I have discovered a strange thing: even when my heart does not respond, my body does. During the day, I find myself longing for the sexual act, and I think Deacon knows this. I tell myself that he is my husband and that naturally I should welcome his embraces since they present the possibility of having more children, but I have a terrible confession to make: I welcome them for another reason, and this is the source of my shame.

When Deacon makes love to me, I close my eyes and imagine he is William. I fear this is adultery, but I cannot stop doing it. So you see, the lack of real intimacy between us is very likely my fault, not his.

Deacon does not suspect that every time he touches me, I pretend he is another man, and I think that if you were here, you would advise me not to tell him.

I will post this letter by burning it. Deacon must never see it. He may love me as much as he said he did when he proposed to me or he may not, but in any case he must never suspect that I betray him nightly.

I will write again soon.

Love,
Carrie

March 23, 1854
Dearest Mama,

I have struggled with my passions and lost. I still think of William when my husband takes me in his arms, but I have gone beyond shame. Deacon's caresses have become my way of forgetting my grief over William's death—only I do not forget. I get drunk on passion and dreams and drift away to happier times that I do not dare mention to anyone but you.

I am using Deacon, and I think he is using me. I suspect neither of us really loves the other. What kind of marriage is this? I hardly know who I am. I feel as if I am sleepwalking through my life, living in a trance as the baby grows larger in my womb. When Nettie Wiggins speaks to me, sometimes I do not hear her, and when Miss Turner or her sister ask me a question, often I do not reply. All the while, for no reason I can name, I have a terrible, irrational presentiment that a disaster I am powerless to stop is rushing toward me. I hear such fears are common on long sea voyages, but I suspect the source of my own anxiety is guilt. I am deceiving my husband with a dead man. There, I have said it as bluntly as possible. William is dead. I repeat this truth to myself a dozen times a day but I still can't make myself believe it.

The fortune-teller I consulted in Rio gave me her bag of buzios. This morning when Deacon was taking a walk on deck, I threw them and tried to see into the future, but if prophecy exists I have no talent for it. I saw exactly what I expected to see: sixteen polished cowry shells, ten turned right side up, six turned upside down. Still, you can deduce from this how unsettled I am becoming.

I am told that on our journey north we may expect to sight the vast sweep of muddy water that surges out to sea from the mouth of the Amazon. When we do, our ship is scheduled to turn west and put into port at Belém for three days to take on supplies. As we approach that city, I am overcome with memories. Do you recall the year you, Papa, and I lived far up the Amazon on a smaller river called the Rio Branco? I remember Papa sent his orchids down to Belém by dugout canoe and our mail—what little we got—came up to us the same way.

If you were still living there, I would go ashore and find someone to take this letter to you. But the jungle grows so fast that by now every trace of our camp has long been obliterated, so instead I will burn this letter as I have burned all the others and imagine you have received it.

Love,
Carrie

April 5, 1854
Dear Mama,

The catastrophe I feared has arrived, but not in the form I expected. I am so overcome with grief and weak from loss of blood that I can hardly hold my pen. Since the captain has been good enough to loan me his log book, I will copy out the entry and let it speak for itself.

Sunday, April 2, 1854: Delivered prematurely of passenger Mrs. Deacon Presgrove, a female child who lived less than a quarter of an hour.

Monday, April 3, 1854: Child of Mr. and Mrs. Presgrove buried at sea. Painting of stern boats continues.

I think that last sentence hurts more than all the rest. "Painting of stern boats continues." Did ever a sweet babe have less of an epi-

taph? I feel as if no one but me knows she lived and breathed and was part of this world.

I am being unfair. The captain has been very kind as has Deacon and everyone else. Both the Miss Turners tended me with great skill and compassion, and Mrs. Wiggins did her best to help although there was nothing she or anyone else could do to save my baby.

I will write more when I am stronger.

Your grieving daughter,
Carrie

April 8, 1854
Dearest Mama,

I named her Willa. She never opened her eyes, but I like to imagine they would have been dark like William's and that her hair would have been like his, too—thick and brown and silky. She was indeed the "angelic, strange, and beautiful" girl the fortune-teller promised me, so white and transparent that she seemed to come from another world. She could not have weighed more than a pound and a half, but everything about her was perfectly formed: her ears, her lips—even her tiny fingers had nails.

Before we buried her, I wrapped her in the shawl William meant to give me for a wedding present. In her arms I put one of the orchids I brought from Brazil. It is only a root and even though it cannot live in salt water, I like to imagine it blooming in Willa's arms far beneath the sea, a great purple blossom signifying her mother's love.

The ocean will never again look the same to me. When this voyage is over, I want to move inland.

Love,
Carrie

April 9, 1854
Dearest Mama,

Although I wrote to you only yesterday, I take up my pen again this evening to say how good Deacon has been to me and how kindly he has comforted me. When I told him I wanted to use some of the money I inherited from Papa to establish a memorial for Willa, he not only made no objection, he encouraged me to think of what would be best.

I said I had two things in mind. First, I want to fund the construction of a glass house in Washington at the new United States Botanical Garden to shelter the rare orchids I am bringing from Brazil. I would like it to be called the "Willa Saylor House." Although this will virtually be a public admission that Deacon is not Willa's father, he made no objection and, indeed, encouraged me.

Second, I told him, I want to do something to help the struggle against slavery. Deacon thought for a while and then said that it was likely Congress would soon pass a bill giving the people in the Kansas Territory the right to vote on whether or not they want the state to enter the Union free or as a slave state. I knew about the Kansas problem of course, but I had no idea that a plebiscite act was so near to being approved. I had been under the impression that the representatives of the free states would never tolerate such a betrayal of the Missouri Compromise.

"It may have already passed," Deacon told me. "If it has, President Pierce will certainly sign it, for although he comes from New Hampshire, he is nothing more than a doughface and a drunkard to boot." By doughface Deacon explained, he meant a Northerner with Southern sympathies.

Once a date for the plebiscite is set, he warned, slavers and free-soilers will be rushing to the Kansas Territory to vote in the election since there is no residency requirement. How, he asked, would I feel about using some of my inheritance to sponsor a group of abolitionist emigrants?

He could not have chosen a subject closer to my heart. I told him I could think of no more fitting memorial for Willa. Taking my hands, he kissed them and proclaimed I was "a saint," and that suffering people presently held in bondage would someday bless my name. I thought this was excessive and told him so, but he said he would not take his words back, that I was a saint, and he would not hear me deny it.

If he could have seen into my heart, he might not have been so quick with praise. Mama, do you know what I thought when Willa died? "Now I am married forever to a man I do not love and for no reason."

I am ashamed of myself. Deacon has been good to me. He has never made me do anything I did not want to do, and I believe now that all my suspicions about him were born of my inability to forget William. I have decided that from now on, I will do my best to love my husband in return without questioning his motives.

If ever a letter needed to be burned, it is this one. I will thrust it into the candle flame and send it to you before Deacon comes back to the cabin.

Your loving daughter,
Carrie

April 29, 1854
Dearest Mama,

Last night, for the first time since I lost Willa, Deacon and I had marital relations. I did not resist him even though this time neither my heart nor my body responded. I do not think—at least I hope—he did not suspect this.

I hope that in time this numbness will pass, and I will be able to enjoy Deacon's caresses and, more important, give him my heart.

Love,
Carrie

May 1, 1854
Dearest Mama,

Last night I managed to make love to Deacon without thinking of William. To be honest, I did not feel the kind of passion I felt when I took guilty pleasure in my dreams of past lovemaking, but when we were finished, I felt sincere affection for my husband. What Deacon felt, I cannot say, since I have vowed never again to attempt to read his mind. From now on, I will take him at his word when he says he loves me, and I will trust him.

Mama, I do not think I will write to you again. Before Willa died, I sensed your presence, but now I feel that I am alone here with nothing but the creaking of the ship and the sound of the waves to keep me company. It makes me sad to go on writing to you when you can never respond. I must look to the future, not the past.

I will always carry you in my heart.

Love,
Carrie

Chapter Ten

The United States, May 1854

The journey from Baltimore to Washington has already taken two hours longer than scheduled, and Carrie is impatient for it to end. When she was a child, she loved trains, but now the continual rocking reminds her of *The Frances Scott*, and *The Frances Scott* reminds her of Willa.

Sitting back, she closes her eyes, and surrenders herself to grief. *My life is a train to nowhere*, she thinks. That's so grim a thought, it's almost ridiculous. She forces herself to count her blessings: health, youth, wealth, a handsome, considerate husband. As she lists the good things in her life, the pain gradually recedes. After a while, she opens her eyes again, looks out the window, and notices they are approaching a muddy river crowded with barges and ships. She sees white sails, an eddy of currents, a long bridge, and then gets her first glimpse of Washington itself.

But wait. Something's wrong. Pulling out her handkerchief, she rubs the coal dust off the windowpane and stares in disbelief. This can't possibly be the capital of a great nation. Where are the parks, the monuments, the throngs of well-dressed people? Nettie Wiggins swore Washington was the Rio of the United States, but this appears to be no more than an overgrown town.

She leans forward to take a closer look. *Small*, she thinks, *sleepy. Where is everyone?* Most of the streets appear to be paved, but the ground looks swampy. Pulling down the window, she takes a deep breath and inhales something that tastes like warm molasses laced with mud and dust. How can you have dust and mud at the same time? Yet here the two are: the stagnant wet odor of undrained swamps, and dust—clouds of it—swirling down the avenues.

She coughs, claps her handkerchief over her nose, and feels a fine layer of federal grit joining the soot on her face. As soon as she arrives at Deacon's father's house, she'll have to take a bath.

The train rolls on, spewing out cinders as it pants into the city. What is this odd-looking, truncated column? Could it possibly be the Washington Monument? Nettie said that someday it would rise over five hundred feet into the air, a gleaming obelisk of marble and granite that would be the envy of the world, but this is nothing more than a stumpy tower of blocks, several of which bear Temperance Society mottos.

WE WILL NOT BUY, SELL, OR USE MALT LIQUORS.

George Washington would not have appreciated that sentiment. As Carrie recalls, the first thing he did after stepping down from the presidency was build a distillery at Mount Vernon.

Wadding up her kerchief, she stuffs it back into her sleeve as the train moves past the National Mall, which is supposed to rival the gardens at Versailles when finished but which at present is swampy and unkempt. Only this morning, Deacon told her that parts of the Mall had been sold off for private development. What's left reeks.

Near the canal, the stench becomes overwhelming. Shoddily

built houses, some no more than shacks, crowd up against tanning yards filled with rotting animal remains, blacksmiths' sheds, sawmills, and a few dilapidated stores selling chicken feed and wilted vegetables.

The squalor passes by, made worse by coal dust, wood smoke, horse dung, and trash. Carrie has to admit that her first view of the capitol building is impressive, although its small, aging dome is obviously timber-framed and out of proportion to the rest of the structure. Since she cannot see the White House, she hopes there's more to Washington than first meets the eye, but the prospects are not encouraging. Deacon has not mentioned malaria, but she would be willing to bet it lurks here somewhere along with typhoid and perhaps cholera. So much for leaving Brazil for a healthier climate.

Suddenly she spies an elegant three-story red-brick house surrounded by a wrought-iron fence that encloses a flower garden ringed by blossoming spirea bushes and showy purple and pink hydrangeas. Pulling out her handkerchief again, she rubs the last of the grime off the window, and inspects the house more closely.

"Who lives there?" she asks Deacon, who has finally come back from the club car and is sitting beside her puffing away contentedly on his cigar.

"Elegant ladies." He flicks an inch or so of ash onto the floor and laughs. "So you like it do you?"

"Very much. Or rather, I like the house but not its location." Giving him a smile, she goes back to looking out the window.

The train has lurched to a temporary stop in front of the house. She can now see ladies moving in and out, all dressed in clothing more brightly colored and flamboyant than anything she has seen since she left Rio. A plump, dark-haired girl in a green dress and a tall blonde in blue emerge from the gate and begin to stroll down the street arm in arm. All at once, the dark-haired girl puts the tip of her gloved hand to her lips and blows a kiss at the train window. A tiny mole on her upper lip quivers as she purses her lips. Carrie has a sense of having seen the girl with the mole before but that, of course, is impossible.

"Ah, ha!" Deacon exclaims. "What a pretty little miss!"

"Do you know her?"

"Know her? I should say not."

"Is she a whore?"

Deacon grins and makes a clicking sound with his tongue. "If you must say such words, Carolyn, say them in Portuguese or you will shock our fellow passengers into conniption fits."

"Is she?" Carrie repeats in a conspiratorial whisper.

"Yes." Deacon grins again and takes another pull on his cigar. "But it's a bit unfair to call her that. She's one of Mrs. Elizabeth Springer's girls. Mrs. Springer runs the most elegant brothel in Washington. It's a Congressional favorite. In fact, it's often said that Mrs. Springer's darlings are the unacknowledged legislators of the United States of America. Her girls frequently use their considerably well-displayed assets to get laws passed through Congress."

"Are they paid to do that?"

"Tsh, tsh. What do you think? Of course they are paid, and handsomely too."

"Paid by whom?"

"Railroads, telegraph companies, merchants who provision the military—in other words, anyone and everyone who hopes to feed at the national trough. Don't pity them. It's quite a profitable business. If that little brunette who blew us a kiss saves her pennies, she may make enough to start her own house of ill repute. Some of Mrs. Springer's girls retire and are rehabilitated as respectable members of society. Some even marry, although few find husbands in Congress. Their past is too much of a liability. Are you shocked?"

"No. It's the same in Brazil. I just didn't expect to find that kind of arrangement here in America."

Deacon claps his hand on her knee and gives her a friendly pat. "You have a lot to learn, my girl."

Five minutes later they roll into the Baltimore & Ohio Railroad's Italianate terminal at New Jersey Avenue and C Street. By now their train is over two and a half hours late, but Deacon's father is waiting for them on the platform.

Senator Presgrove is in his mid- to late fifties, tall and broad-shouldered like Deacon with the added bulk of several decades of good eating and soft living. He wears an elegant black suit and carries a heavy gold-headed walking stick. Like Deacon, he has high cheekbones and a long nose, but the senator's nose is red-tipped and slanted to one side as if it has been broken in an accident, or perhaps, Carrie thinks, a fight, and his eyes are a bloodshot blue with whites the color of yellowed linen. Beardless and square-chinned, he wears his gray hair to his shoulders in the senatorial fashion. He might have once been a handsome man, but in old age he is as spotted as a turkey egg with the jowls of a bulldog and a voice to match.

"Mah dear girl!" he roars upon catching sight of Carrie. "Welcome! welcome!" Striding toward her, he envelops her in an embrace redolent of cigar smoke and brandy. Crushed into the starched linen of his shirtfront, Carrie has the momentary sensation of being taken prisoner by a bear. No wonder the senator has been such a success in Congress. Even she, who disagrees with everything he stands for, is impressed. He is a natural force like a hurricane or an earthquake. Who could resist him?

Senator Presgrove releases her, stands back, and holds her at arm's length. "I have always wanted a daughter," he says in a Southern accent much stronger than Deacon's, "and at last I have one. Frankly, I never thought Deacon was going to settle down. The cards and ponies always called to him more than the ladies—"

A sharp cough from Deacon interrupts whatever the senator is about to say next.

"Daddy," Deacon says and stretches out his hand. Instead of taking it, Senator Presgrove envelops his son in his arms and lifts him off his feet.

"My boy! My wandering boy! Welcome home!"

"Daddy," Deacon pleads, "please put me down." Carrie is amused. She has never heard Deacon beg before. Senator Presgrove deposits his son on the platform and steps back.

"You have to shave off that moustache, son. It may do well enough in that godforsaken country you've been living in, but lip hairs aren't worn in Washington, at least not by respectable men. Great Gawd, what were you thinkin'? You look like a pirate. If your mama were still alive, I'd have to take you to a barber before I could bring you home."

Deacon turns bright red and bites his lower lip. He is obviously furious, but all he says is: "Yes, Daddy. I'll see to it."

"You do that, son." Having dispensed with Deacon's moustache, the senator turns back to Carrie. "I hear you are recently bereaved." For an instant Carrie thinks Deacon has broken his promise and told his father about Willa, but then the senator continues. "The loss of a parent is a grievous thing."

"Yes," Carrie agrees, "it is."

"Y'all aren't wearin' mourning?"

"No, sir." She wonders if she should be calling him "Father," but she cannot bring herself to give him that name yet. Perhaps in time.

The senator stares at her as if trying to pick something out of her brain with a sharp needle. "Does your choice to eschew black spring from religious convictions or lack of sentiment? Frankly, honey, I don't know which would be worse. Although you're as pretty a little thing as has ever entered this city of windbags and tobacco chewers, I'm not pleased by the thought that my only son has married a girl who belongs to some cant-ridden, abolitionist sect. And the very idea that a child doesn't love her father enough to mourn him, particularly when that father left the girl with a nice fat pile of Double Eagles, so to speak, well I— "

Another sharp cough from Deacon interrupts this line of conversation, which is fortunate because Carrie is starting to take a strong dislike to her father-in-law. Resisting an urge to tell him just how much she loved her own father and how poorly he stacks up in comparison, she forces herself to give him a polite reply.

"My father was opposed to the wearing of mourning," she says. "He would not have wanted me to dress in black on my honeymoon. Besides, he always said that only Englishmen, fools, and madmen wear dark clothes in tropical heat, and . . ." The desire to be polite passes. On less than three minutes' acquaintance he has just made a nasty crack about abolitionists and insulted her family.

"Now as far as I can tell, Senator, the difference between Washington and Rio isn't worth spit when it comes to heat. The day is sultry, sir. I see that you have on a black suit. You're certainly not an Englishman, so . . ."

"Carolyn!" Deacon cries.

Senator Presgrove gives Carrie a surprised look, then throws back his head and laughs so loudly heads turn. "Why aren't you the spunky one! Deacon, you are gonna have to keep this pretty little wife of yours on a short leash. In fact, I'm not sure you're man enough to handle her."

"I don't need to be handled," Carrie says. "I can handle myself."

"Please!" Deacon begs. Carrie suddenly remembers the pains Deacon has taken to get along with his father. Swallowing her anger, she turns the conversation to more neutral subjects—the voyage, the weather, the food on the train—and within a few minutes she is no longer the center of Senator Presgrove's attention. In fact, it would be fair to say Deacon and his father forget about her entirely; or at least if they don't, they appear to.

Senator Presgrove summons porters who carry their trunks and boxes to his carriage. As they roll north on Pennsylvania Avenue toward Georgetown, Carrie finally sees elegant shops and fashionably dressed women. She is just wondering if the haughty lady in brown silk is the wife of a senator when she becomes aware that Deacon and his father are discussing politics. Their conversation is not what she expects, and the more she hears of it, the more alarmed she becomes.

The Missouri Compromise, which has outlawed slavery north of thirty-six degrees latitude for more than thirty years, is apparently on the verge of being overturned. It seems that in January, Senator Presgrove's old friend and colleague Senator Stephen Douglas of Illinois introduced a bill that would allow settlers in the western territories to vote to decide whether or not they want to permit slavery. In other words, the plebiscite act Deacon warned her about is on the verge of becoming a law.

"The Senate went for it right away," Senator Presgrove says, "but the House has been draggin' its feet all spring, squabbling like a pack of coonhounds fightin' over a squirrel. Then, mirabile dictu!, last Monday the House finally voted. Result: thirty-five yeah, thirteen nay. A Joint Committee of Congress approved the whole kit and caboodle on Friday, and if Pierce can sober up enough to hold a pen, he'll probably sign it sometime this week."

Carrie is not surprised by the news, but she is astonished by Deacon's reaction to it. Deacon and his father are supposed to have argued bitterly over slavery. If territories above thirty-six degrees latitude are allowed to enter the Union as slave states, slave owners will soon be able to seize control of Congress. In no time at all, slavery could be legal from Canada to the Mexican border. Deacon should be outraged, but instead he's sitting there smiling and nodding as if this is the best news he's heard in months. How can he laugh, accept a cigar from his father, and talk to him in level tones while the whole future of the country is hanging on the pen stroke of a President who claimed in his inaugural address that the Constitution supported slavery?

Suddenly Deacon looks up and sees Carrie staring at him. Something in her face must convey her shock and dismay, because he abruptly shifts from politics to horses. To be fair, he warned her in advance that he would need to humor his father by pretending to agree with him, but this . . .

Carrie stares grimly out the window. She had no idea her husband had such a talent for acting. If this is what it is going to take to get along with her father-in-law, perhaps they should return to the station and board the next train to Boston.

Chapter Eleven

Senator Presgrove has rented an elegant house in Georgetown surrounded by a lawn so smooth it looks as if it has been clipped with embroidery scissors. It is a ship of a house with white pillars that look like masts, odd windows shaped like portholes, and a railed widow's walk that reminds Carrie of the deck of *The Frances Scott*. In back is a large garden in the French style, each tree and bush cut into a geometric form, each path a hedge-bordered grid that ends at a bit of marble sculpture or a fountain. If the jungle is nature with its hair let down, this is nature with its hair put up in a tight bun, and as Carrie gazes at the garden through the windows of the back parlor, she feels pity for the flowers, which must grow in straight lines or suffer execution at the hands of the senator's gardener.

She and Duncan have washed off the soot of the train, changed their clothes, and spent a mercifully short quarter of an hour talking to Bennett before he climbed back into his carriage and disappeared on official business. Now it's time for something that Carrie has been looking forward to for months. She thought it would occur sooner, thought the woman she longs to meet would be standing beside Deacon's father on the platform when their train rolled into the station, but the near-mother who won her heart long before she met Deacon is nowhere in sight because, as Deacon explains, she is ill.

"How ill?" Carrie asks as they step into the front hall and begin to wind their way up the great caracole of stairs that fills the center of the house.

"Very." There is something about the stark simplicity of the word that makes her not want to ask for details. Up they go, round and round, doubling back on themselves, always a little higher, until the parquet floor of the entry hall looks like a chessboard seen at a great distance. Here and there round windows appear, punched into the walls, letting in thick shafts of light.

Carrie looks at Deacon who is making his way up the steps just in front of her and thinks how strange it is that despite everything, William's mother has become her mother-in-law. For that is who lives on the top floor of this house like an angel gone into flight: Mrs. Bennett Presgrove, formerly Mrs. Patrick Saylor. Too ill to meet the train, too ill to come downstairs and greet Carrie and Deacon when they arrived, so ill that Carrie and Deacon are lifting their feet carefully from step to step as if she can be shattered by sounds.

Fourteen years have passed since Mrs. Presgrove and Carrie last met. Mrs. Presgrove has been widowed, lost her only son, seen her health destroyed, and according to Deacon, become an invalid who never leaves her room. Will she greet Carrie with the warmth and affection Carrie remembers so well, or will she blame Carrie for William's death?

The staircase turns and Carrie's mind turns with it, running back into the past. She remembers that years ago, when Matilda Presgrove was still Matilda Saylor, she was always laughing. During the eleven months Carrie spent living in Mitchellville with Grandfather Vinton and Aunt Jo, she visited the Saylor house almost daily, coming and going like a member of the family. Mrs. Saylor was always there, sitting by the fire in the winter or on the front porch in the summer, drinking lemonade, telling jokes, and fanning herself with a Chinese paper fan that looked like a multicolored lollipop. Carrie was fascinated by that fan—she had never seen one like it. She knew if she asked for it, Mrs. Saylor would give it to her, but she never got up the courage, and besides she knew Aunt Jo, who had very strong ideas about what was suitable for young girls, would never let her keep such a gaudy trifle.

Years later she realized Mrs. Saylor had probably pitied her for being motherless and living with a grandfather who was never at home and an aunt who had about as much of the milk of human kindness as a crow, but at the time Carrie never suspected William's mother was making a special effort to comfort her. Mrs. Saylor teased her, fed her sweets when she was not supposed to be eating them, and sometimes even took Carrie's side against William when the two squabbled. Carrie can still recall Mrs. Saylor hugging her and putting a bandage on her knee when she skinned it playing catch, and when she ran away from her grandfather's house, Mrs. Saylor was the only person in Mitchellville besides William who seemed to understand.

One of Carrie's most vivid memories of Mrs. Saylor is how pretty and exotic she was. She came from New Orleans and claimed to be three-quarters French. Born Mathilde Gabrielle Vallios—a name no one in town could attempt to say without sending her into a fit of giggles—she was under five feet tall, with delicate hands, tiny feet, a narrow waist, and a thin, fine-boned face. Her hair was black and it curled in ringlets, framing her forehead and emphasizing her large, dark eyes.

"Folks say Mama's quite a looker," William once volunteered, and even Carrie, who at nine was not much of a judge of the beauty of adult women, had to agree. Yet there was an aspect of Mrs. Saylor's beauty that would have been a warning sign if Carrie had been old enough to understand it: Her complexion was on the dark side, but her cheeks were always red.

Aunt Josephine and the other women in Mitchellville whispered disapprovingly that she painted, but they were mistaken. The truth was, Mrs. Saylor drank and used patient medicines to control the coughing that would sometimes wrack her body with such violence that she once cracked a rib. Carrie discovered this by sneaking a sip of Mrs. Saylor's lemonade and finding that it was laced with whiskey and something called Madame Bonville's Female Restorative.

The spiral staircase gives one final turn and coils out onto the third-floor landing. Deacon turns right, and Carrie follows him. The hall is long and narrow. At the far end, large windows look out over the back garden. As Carrie and Deacon walk down the hall, the sound of their footsteps is muffled by the carpet.

I wonder what made Mrs. Saylor cough like that, Carrie thinks. *I should have asked William.* She thinks of all the other things she never bothered to ask him, and a small pain, like a sliver of glass, passes through her.

There are three identical doors on each side of the hall. Deacon stops in front of the second door on the left and pauses as if listening. Carrie listens, too, and hears nothing.

"Knock," she whispers.

He knocks and enters without waiting for a reply. Carrie crosses the threshold after him. The drapes are drawn, and the room is as dark as the inside of a cave: a junglelike, slightly green-tinged sort of darkness that smells damp and unhealthy, as if the carpet needs to be taken out and aired and the mold washed off the walls with white vinegar. Directly in front of them, occupying most of one wall, is a large, elaborately carved bed piled with blankets and pillows tossed helter-skelter as if someone had begun to strip off the sheets and stopped halfway. Mrs. Presgrove should be in that bed, but it appears empty.

A large, red-faced woman stands by the night table with her arms folded across her bosom. She wears a dark blue dress made of coarsely woven cotton, and her hair is tied up in a white kerchief. Deacon approaches the bed and peers into the blankets as if trying to locate something. Straightening up, he turns to the nurse.

"How is Mrs. Presgrove doing this afternoon, Aideen?"

"Ah, the poor soul is not doing well, bless her," the nurse replies in a lilting Irish accent.

"Did she take her medicine?"

"No, sair, she did not. I tried to give it to her, but she refused it."

Deacon gives an exasperated sigh and turns back to the bed. "Mother Presgrove," he says.

There is a scuffling sound, and a small, withered figure rises up from the mound of blankets and props itself against the headboard. "What do you want?" a slurred, shaking voice inquires.

The woman who speaks looks so different from the woman Carrie remembers that Carrie has the sensation of having come into the wrong room. Matilda's beauty is a thing of the past. She cannot be more than forty-five, but she looks decades older. Her eyes are red-rimmed as if she has been crying. Her glossy black hair has turned into a dull, gray tangle that hangs around her face in stringy curls, and every inch of her skin is folded and wrinkled as if she has been dried in the sun. On the third finger of her left hand she wears a gaudy gold wedding ring, half an inch thick. Perhaps the ring fit her on the day she married Bennett Presgrove, but now the only thing that's keeping it from slipping off is a diamond-studded ring guard.

"What do you want?" Matilda repeats in that same strange, slurred voice. This was once a woman who spoke clearly and decisively, a woman who could sing loud enough to rattle church windows. Carrie notices a small clay pipe resting on the night table among the medicine bottles.

"Opium?" she whispers.

Deacon nods. "For the pain."

Matilda waves her hands in front of her face and makes a motion as if sewing cloth. "Who . . ."

Deacon raises his voice. "Mother Presgrove," he says clipping off the end of each word. "It's me, Deacon. I have returned from Brazil, and I have brought my wife to meet you. You know her, Mother Presgrove. She is—"

"Deacon, you say?"

"Yes, Mother Presgrove, Deacon, your stepson."

"I don't want Deacon. I want William." Matilda clutches at the hem of the sheet. "Where is he? Where is my son? Why isn't he here? Why hasn't he come to see me? Deacon, you evil boy, why do you tear up William's letters and refuse to give them to me?"

"Mother Presgrove," Carrie says gently, "William can't come visit you. William is—" Deacon lays a warning hand on Carrie's arm and shakes his head. Carrie begins again.

"Mother Presgrove, it's me, Carrie. Carrie Vinton. You remember. I was William's childhood friend, and now I'm Deacon's wife."

"Carrie?" Matilda's eyes light up for a moment. "Carrie, dear, you must not keep climbing trees. You've ripped your pinafore again. Come closer and I will mend it." She lifts her right hand and again makes a sewing motion.

"She knows me," Carrie whispers.

"In her way," Deacon agrees.

"And William? She doesn't know he . . . ?"

"She's been told. Father informed her of his death as soon as he got my letter. He says he's told her repeatedly, but she never remembers. She believes my stepbrother is still alive. She even imagines that he came back from Brazil and paid her a visit and told her—" Deacon pauses. "I am not sure I should tell you the rest, my dear. It will only cause you pain."

"Tell me. I can't imagine anything William's mother could say that could cause me more pain than I've already experienced."

"My stepmother is under the illusion that William came to her and told her that *you* were dead. She imagines that he grieved terribly for you and that she comforted him. I'm sorry, Carolyn; this must be very painful for you."

"Where is William?" Mrs. Presgrove repeats. Her voice cracks and tears roll down her cheeks. "Carrie, where has he gone? Why isn't he here?"

Deacon approaches the bed, puts his hands on his stepmother's shoulders, and gently pushes her back down onto the pillows. "Mother Presgrove, you must not agitate yourself." Curling in a ball with her knees to her chest, Matilda begins to cry.

"Poor thing," Carrie says.

"Her heart is not good. The doctors warn that these fits may kill her if we can't control them." He picks up a bottle from the night table, uncorks it, measures out a spoonful of brown liquid, and mixes it with water.

"Here, Mother Presgrove," he says. When Matilda refuses, he lifts her upright, opens her mouth, carefully pries her lips apart, and pours the medicine down her throat. Finished, he turns to the nurse. "See that Mrs. Presgrove gets another dose of medicine before supper."

"Yes, sair."

"If she refuses, call one of the male servants to help you administer it."

"Bless ye, sair, I can take care of Mrs. Presgrove my ownself. The poor soul is as weak as a newborn babby."

"Well then, you must be firm with her. We cannot allow her to refuse her medicine."

"Yes, sair."

A moan comes from the bed, soft as a breath of wind blowing

across the mouth of a bottle. Carrie starts toward the sound, but Deacon restrains her.

"You can't comfort her, Carolyn. God knows I wish you could, but you can't. She no longer knows where she is or what she's doing. She's living in a world of dreams."

"More like a world of nightmares," Carrie says. She removes his hand from her arm, approaches the bed, and looks down at Mrs. Presgrove who has burrowed back under the blankets. She feels heartsick. Matilda had been like a mother to her. If only she could rip those hideous curtains off the windows, let in light and air, throw away the opium pipe and the medicine bottles, take William's mother in her arms, and tell her . . . Tell her what? That William is dead? Perhaps it's a mercy she doesn't know.

"Come away," Deacon says. "You're upsetting yourself unnecessarily. There's nothing more we can do for her."

Blinded by tears, Carrie lets him take her by the hand and lead her out of the room. She remembers that moment for the rest of her life: the bedroom door swinging open, light from the hall flooding in, a clean white wall laced with the shadows of blowing leaves, a gold-framed painting, the cool, rough sensation of Deacon's hand in hers. Although she does not yet know it, this is the last time she will completely believe anything he tells her.

In the months that follow, she will think of herself as a blind woman, a woman unwittingly crossing a chasm on a thin sheet of ice, a woman trapped in a net, a woman hooked like a fish. She will search in vain for the perfect metaphor to describe how quickly things fall apart after that sickroom encounter: an explosion, a wildfire, a single glass jerked from the bottom of a pyramid of glasses, but no comparison she can come up with begins to describe the terrible rapidity of events.

The first hint that things are not as they seem comes in the form of a question, and Carrie is the one who asks it.

"How long has your stepmother been ill?" she says when she and Deacon are again alone together.

"For years, as far as I know."

"But surely . . ." Carrie stops herself from asking the question that is on her lips: *But surely your father would not have married a woman so sick unless . . .* She pauses, warns herself not to make hasty assumptions, and then decides the question is worth asking. If she is going to live in the same house with Senator Presgrove, she needs to know why he has chosen to marry an invalid who smokes opium and does not recognize her own stepson, or perhaps for that matter, the senator himself.

"Deacon—" Carrie pauses, searching for the right words to convey her suspicions. None spring to mind. Perhaps it's better to be blunt.

"Is your stepmother wealthy? William and I didn't talk much about his mother. We were too busy taking care of the sick and trying not to fall sick ourselves, but before he became ill, he told me that, like you, he and his father had quarreled over slavery, and that his father had cut him out of his will. I assume that means that when William's father died, your stepmother inherited all of his estate—"

Carrie stops speaking. Deacon's face has darkened. For a few more seconds she believes his expression conveys nothing more than the jealousy a newly married man might feel on hearing his wife mention her lover's name. Then he speaks.

"Carolyn, are you asking me if my father married my stepmother for her money?"

"No, of course not." Although, of course, that's exactly what she's asking.

"Why my father and Mrs. Saylor married is none of our business. I trust you appreciate that."

"Yes," Carrie says, but she doesn't say it meekly. Deacon has never spoken to her so sharply before, and she hopes he's not going to make a habit of it.

He gives her another look that she does not like in the least. "If you must know, it was a love match. Mrs. Saylor was not bedridden when they met. My father was besotted with her and she with him. In fact, I have never seen a couple so devoted to each other."

He smiles. As always, it's a charming smile, but Carrie does not return it because at that moment she knows beyond all doubt that he's lying.

The second indication that she is being deceived comes the following Tuesday in the form of cannon fire. The concussions are so loud, they rattle the chandeliers, make the windows tremble, and knock a small porcelain shepherdess off the parlor mantelpiece. As Carrie hurries toward the front door to see what is going on, gunshots ring out from the back of the house. Reversing direction, she runs toward the garden. There she finds Deacon and Bennett standing beside a fountain, shooting their pistols in the air, and whooping at the top of their lungs.

"What's happened!" she cries. "Are we at war?"

"He signed it!" Deacon yells.

In the distance, over the cannonades, Carrie can hear church bells simultaneously ringing and tolling in a wild cacophony of joy and grief. A series of smaller explosions fills the air, smoke trails from fireworks, and Roman candles crisscross the sky.

"Seventeen!" Senator Presgrove bellows as the cannons thunder.

"Eighteen!" Deacon cries.

"Nineteen!"

"Twenty!"

"Twenty-one!"

The salute being over, the cannons fall silent. Laughing and cheering, father and son embrace and slap each other on the back, and as they do so, Carrie realizes two things: first, President Pierce must have signed the Kansas-Nebraska Act; and, second, Deacon and his father are both happy about it.

That night at dinner Deacon makes no attempt to hide his joy at the prospect of Kansas entering the Union as a slave state. As Carrie sits at the far end of the table, feeling invisible, he and his father drink, smoke, and talk politics, and what she hears them say makes her feel as if a blindfold is being ripped off her eyes.

All day the telegraph wires have been speeding the news to other parts of the country and bringing back descriptions of how Americans are reacting to President Pierce's approval of the plebiscite. The evening papers are reporting that in Massachusetts people are wearing black armbands. In Indiana they are flying the American flag at half-mast. In Chicago banners have been strung over the streets, proclaiming: NO MORE SLAVE TERRITORY! NO MORE SLAVE STATES! NO MORE SLAVERY!!

Yet as effigies of President Pierce burn all over the North, the South is celebrating. In Charleston people have taken to the streets to express their approval. In Atlanta wealthy slave owners are rejoicing, balls are being planned, and women have sewn victory banners onto their parasols.

Senator Presgrove throws aside the newspapers and thumps his fist on the table so hard the water goblets dance. "By God, we're winning!"

"Yes, Daddy," Deacon agrees, "we are."

We. The word sticks in Carrie's throat. She gags on it, puts down her knife and fork and glares at Deacon, but he doesn't notice. Father and son go on congratulating themselves. By the time dinner is over, Carrie is convinced Deacon is not an abolitionist and never has been. In other words, he's been lying to her for months. He must have lied when he proposed, lied when he comforted her after Willa's death. This is a very disturbing thought, but when she confronts him, he denies everything.

"Carolyn, be reasonable. We're living in my father's house. What do you expect me to do? Tell him he's the devil incarnate?"

"Yes. You told me you and he disagreed bitterly over slavery, but I only see you rejoicing with him. Pierce has done evil work this day. The Kansas-Nebraska Act is an infamy. How can you even pretend to celebrate it!"

Deacon gives her an apologetic smile. "You're right. I shouldn't play along with the old man, but I did it for your sake."

"What does that mean?"

"It means, I want you to be able to live here in peace and quiet until I can find us a suitable home of our own. As I told you when I asked you to become my wife, my father is not simply pro-slaver; he believes in slavery the way a circuit-riding Methodist preacher believes in God. It's his religion. He knows I believe the institution should be abolished, but if I were to mention this openly, he would charge me like a bull elephant. He's a formidable orator when riled. When he was practicing law, he used to chaw up his opponents on a daily basis.

"You should go to the Capitol someday and sit in the Senate visitors' gallery and hear him, and then you'll see what I'm up against. He's half-bloodhound, half-cougar, and half-grizzly bear, and if you tell me that's one half too many, I'll tell you that's because Bennett Presgrove's got more meanness in him than Caligula and more stubbornness than a mule pulling a load of bricks uphill in a wagon with no wheels."

"In other words, you're afraid of him."

Deacon smiles. "Yes, ma'am, I surely am. And you would be,

too, if you knew him better. So let me humor him as long as we're living under his roof. What does it matter if I pretend to agree with him? You know what's in my heart."

"Yes," Carrie says, "I do." But she must not say it very convincingly, because Deacon seizes both her hands and presses them to his lips.

"I adore you," he says. "If you want to leave my father's house, I'll take you out of here tonight, but I have to warn you that Washington hotels aren't very comfortable."

He could not have said anything more calculated to make her feel guilty. She cannot reply that she adores him, too, and she certainly cannot say she loves him, although she is still trying to, so instead she says: "Humor your father if you feel you must, but don't act so enthusiastic about it."

"Thank you," he says. "You're an angel."

For a fleeting second just before he drops her hands, she sees a look of triumph cross his face. In the months that follow, she often asks herself what that look meant. Did he believe he had won the game? Did he think she would never again question him about his political beliefs? Did he really believe he could go on deceiving her?

Perhaps the truth was less complicated. Perhaps he simply did not care if she found out what a fool she'd been. After all, he had her in his power. She had married him of her own free will and come to a country with him where she had no friends and only one relation, who she couldn't stand and who couldn't stand her. Looked at from Deacon's perspective, those lies were a kind of courtesy. He need not have lied to her at all, but no doubt he thought a gentleman who had deceived a lady owed her a bit of fiction.

In retrospect she finds it astounding that he went to the trouble. His story holds up for exactly two hours, and then it falls apart.

Dropping her hands, Deacon gives her another smile warmer than the first, more winning, more handsome, a smile designed to melt marble and carve roads through the wilderness. "Get dressed, honey," he says. "We're going to a party."

"Not to celebrate Pierce's foul act. I don't care if your father has an apoplectic fit, I have no intention of watching pro-slavers rejoice."

"It's a reception at the French Embassy. The French completely abolished slavery six years ago. *Liberté, égalité, fraternité*, and all that." He smiles again, warmly, convincingly with so much truth in his eyes that she suddenly feels ashamed of herself for doubting him.

Reassured, she goes up to her room to change. She would rather retire with a good book and a glass of milk, but before they married, Deacon explained life in Washington was an endless string of social events and warned she would rarely have a night free.

My wifely duty, she thinks as she examines her dresses. As she sorts through them, fingering the skirts and examining the lace, she silently thanks Nettie Wiggins. On the voyage from Brazil, Nettie decided Carrie could not possibly arrive in Washington wearing what she called "those sweet, but impossibly unfashionable little frocks," so she willed Carrie most of her wardrobe, all of which Nettie intended to replace as soon as she landed.

Carrie and Nettie might be different in spirit, intellect, and complexion, but by a miracle of couture they are the same size. As a result, Carrie has morning dresses, tea dresses, ruffled ball gowns, flower-bedecked bonnets, a light summer evening cloak, dozens of shawls, and even a gilded lightning bolt designed to hold up her hair, which Nettie warned must be arranged casually *à la Grecque*.

"Please, sugar," Nettie insisted, "no braids or you will look like a servant. You must let your curls *emerge*." Nettie also told Carrie she should get Deacon to set up accounts for her with dressmakers, but Carrie figures she can set up her own accounts, and besides, she has no intention of wasting money on clothing—at least not at the rate Nettie says it is wasted in Washington.

Nettie's frocks are not to Carrie's taste. She prefers simplicity, a concept Nettie probably abandoned on the day her mother took her out of pinafores, but after considering all the possibilities, she selects a low-necked blue silk dress with short sleeves and a Bertha collar of sheer lace. The dress is so draped with artificial flowers that she feels as if she should water it before she puts it on, but she has to admit it's pretty, and she's always liked pretty things.

The ladies' maid, who like Mrs. Presgrove's nurse is Irish, helps Carrie slip the dress over her head and then arranges her hair. All of the servants in Senator Presgrove's house seem to have come with the place, and none of them appear to be slaves. As Carrie slips on her evening gloves—also a gift from Nettie—she thinks how fortunate this is. She might be able endure the senator's political views by gritting her teeth and holding her tongue, but if he had brought his slaves to Washington, she would have been sorely tempted to put something nasty in his coffee. The garden is filled with possibilities: foxglove, Devil's trumpet, lily-of-the-valley . . .

Throwing one of Nettie's shawls around her shoulders, she descends the spiral staircase, is admired by both Deacon and his father, and is loaded into the carriage like an over-sized bouquet. Twenty minutes later they arrive at the French Embassy, and half an hour after that, she gets up in the middle of a conversation and walks out. The French ambassador may represent a country that has freed its slaves, but as far as she can tell there's not a single American at this gathering who believes in abolition, and they are doing just what Deacon promised her they would not do: celebrating the signing of the Kansas-Nebraska Act.

"Washington is so terribly divided these days," a senator's wife says shortly before Carrie rises to her feet. Mrs. Greenleaf is a pretty, kind, well-meaning woman with a soft Southern accent, and Carrie takes an instant liking to her, but she does not like what Mrs. Greenleaf says.

"Oh, people still pay formal calls, and sometimes, when compelled, they attend the same public assemblies, but no one invites the wives of Northern and Southern senators to the same parties anymore. What a pleasure to meet you, Mrs. Presgrove. Your husband and father-in-law are such strong supporters of States' Rights. You must be terribly proud of them."

"No," Carrie says, "I'm not."

The senator's wife looks at her in confusion. "But how can you not be? Your husband and his father are among the staunchest allies of the South in Washington. I hear President Pierce himself consulted Senator Presgrove before he signed the act and that your husband was present at their meeting."

"Excuse me," Carrie says. "I feel unwell and must leave at once." Rising to her feet, she throws Nettie's shawl around her shoulders and walks out of the French Embassy, passing within a few feet of Deacon who is so involved in conversation he does not notice her exit.

The doorman hails her a cab, and she tells the driver to take her back to Georgetown. When she arrives, she finds the Presgrove house dark except for the lamp that hangs over the front door. Seizing the knocker, she rouses the servants and is conducted to her room where she sheds Nettie's fancy frock. For hours, she paces back and forth waiting for Deacon to return so she can confront him with his deception, but he does not put in an appearance. Finally, she gives up and goes to bed.

The gunshots and fireworks go on all night. She sleeps fitfully, turning her sheets into a damp, tangled pile. It is viciously hot and more than once she is awakened by the high-pitched whine of a mosquito. Around two in the morning, the Presgrove carriage returns bearing only the senator who, by the sound of it, is drunk.

"Oh, I come from Alabama!" he bellows, "with a banjo on my knee!" Carrie pulls a pillow over her head, muffling the rest of the lyrics.

That night she dreams of Brazil and the Amazon, of ships with tall masts going down in seas the color of buttermilk, of William making love to her on a warm beach, and a small girl floating away on the waves with a purple orchid clutched to her breast. Just before sunrise she wakes up alone in bed, wracked by nausea. Staggering to the chamber pot, she vomits. When she touches her breasts through the thin cotton of her nightgown, she finds they are heavy and sore. For the past few days, she's been aware of this, but she's been pushing it to the back of her mind and telling herself it doesn't matter.

Walking over to the dressing table, she unties the strings of her nightgown, pulls it off her shoulders, and inspects herself in the mirror. *No!* she thinks. *Not now!* But her menses are two weeks late, and once again all the other signs are present.

Sitting down on the edge of the bed, she tries to absorb the implications of being with child by Deacon. Only a few hours ago, she was seriously considering leaving him and returning to Brazil, but she can't possibly make the voyage if she is carrying a child. This baby has come at the wrong time. It ties her to a man who lied to her, a man who most likely never loved her, a man who must have married her for her money just the way his father married Matilda for hers. She has fallen into a nest of fortune hunters, and a baby will anchor her here. If she leaves Deacon after she gives birth, the law will give the child to him. And if she stays: What then?

She needs to know as soon as possible if what she fears is true. Is there any way to tell for sure if she is with child? Has her waist thickened? She doesn't think so. Her corset laces are no shorter. She rests the palm of her hand on her belly and remembers how Willa moved inside her, that sensation of butterfly wings and rising bubbles that will not happen for weeks yet—

Suddenly she feels a rush of happiness so intense it makes her gasp. This baby exists; it lives inside her. She doesn't know how she knows this, but she's sure of it. For a moment she allows joy to wash over her. This child will never replace Willa, but it is a gift, and no matter what sacrifices she has to make, she'll love it with all her heart and do what's best for it.

Grabbing one of Nettie's shawls, she throws it over her nightgown and walks downstairs and out into the garden. Overhead, the stars are intense and unfamiliar. She is used to seeing the Southern Cross and Carina, but what does it matter? The sky of the northern hemisphere is as beautiful as the sky of the south; the flowers in this garden smell as sweet as the flowers in Rio. She will teach her baby the names of new plants and new constellations. Maybe she can make a life with Deacon for the sake of their child. She's young. She has a whole life in front of her filled with possibilities. Somehow things will work out.

Chapter Twelve

The next morning on her way to breakfast, she encounters Senator Presgrove's valet coming out of the senator's bedroom with a tray of empty whiskey glasses.

"Did my husband come home last night?" she asks.

The valet balances the tray on the palm of his hand, and stares down at the carpet. "No, madam." He looks up, still not meeting her eyes. "Mr. Presgrove sent word that he was sleeping at his club."

His club? She didn't know Deacon belonged to a club. How many other things has he kept from her? Retreating to the garden with a book, she waits for him to reappear, but he doesn't come home that night or the night after. Senator Presgrove also disappears, so for the next three days she's alone except for the servants and William's mother. She visits Matilda several times, but always finds her sleeping. When she offers to help take care of her, Aideen begs her not to.

"Ma'am, the senator has ordered me to give the poor soul her medicine and see to her needs. If ye come in here and take over, Himself will fire me."

Not wishing to get Aideen fired, Carrie goes down to the kitchen to see if she can help run the household, but the servants have everything in hand. For an hour or so she sits at the kitchen table drinking coffee and watching the cook make vol-au-vent pastry shells. Then she gives up and goes back to the garden.

By the morning of the second day, she's bored beyond endurance. If she were in Rio, she could go down to the market and haggle with the vendors, take a walk on the beach, or call on friends, but she doesn't know anyone in Washington except Nettie Wiggins, who has temporarily decamped to New York to have her dresses made, and pro-slavers like Mrs. Greenleaf, who she's not inclined to visit.

She thinks of many things during those days she spends alone. Sometimes she imagines herself working things out with Deacon and discovering that, although he married her for her money, he cares for her. She doesn't think that's likely, but perhaps, even if he never felt affection for her, they can come to some kind of understanding. When he proposed, he told her he adored children. Was that the truth or another lie? Can a man be a bad husband and a good father? Can she raise a child with someone who believes in slavery?

Three nights in a row, she dreams of William. He always comes to her unexpectedly, bearing a handful of orchids or some strange, exotic object. One night he gives her a spiraled seashell carved with Brazilian and African symbols. In another dream he brings her an Amazonian tiger that licks her face and caresses her with great, soft paws.

In these dreams William caresses her, too: moves his hands across her shoulders and down her arms, outlines her hips and thighs with his fingers, draws heat across her face and eyes, and breathes into her mouth. They make long, slow love in her bed in Rio or in a boat that rocks each time they move. They laugh and cry and cover one another's mouths with their hands so no one will hear them.

She sees William, alive and well: his dark eyes, the tiny scar above his right eyebrow, the mole on his left shoulder, the white spot on the sole of his foot left by a nail he stepped on fifteen years and a whole lifetime ago. As she strokes his hair and measures the length of his body with hers, she feels happier than she's felt in months.

Dearest Carrie, he whispers. *Darling.*

Don't ever leave me again, she begs him. *Don't ever go away.* And in dream after dream, he promises not to.

In the past when she dreamed of him, she woke feeling guilty. Now she wakes feeling cherished. It's as if William has come back to comfort her. Each time she opens her eyes to find herself back in Senator Presgrove's house, she experiences a mixture of joy and longing and grief; but in the end, the joy outweighs the grief, and gradually she comes to understand that these dreams are a gift from Deacon, although not a gift he ever intended to give. By lying to her, Deacon has freed her from feeling guilty about loving William, and although she's not inclined to thank him, she's grateful, although what this means for her marriage in the long-term is something she's not yet ready to contemplate.

By day, she puts the dreams aside and starts to make plans. She needs to find a way to live the rest of her life, if not happily, at least with dignity. She would like to confront Deacon and have it out with him, but what good will that do when she can't believe anything he tells her? She's not sure exactly what steps to take, but she decides she'll begin by insisting he move into another room. Perhaps he'll object. Perhaps he won't care. In any case, she can no longer sleep in the same bed with him. After that, she'll wait and see what develops. It will be better for the child if they can at least appear to get along.

As for her plan to use some of her inheritance to sponsor a group of abolitionist settlers and endow a glasshouse in memory of Willa, there's no reason to sit around waiting for Deacon to come home so she can ask his permission to spend her own money. The time to act is now. The newspapers are reporting that a group of slave owners have met in Westport, Missouri, to plan a mass migration to Kansas. Armed, bent on driving out anyone who opposes them at gunpoint, and loudly declaring their right to take their "human property" into the territory, they are filing land claims at the rate of fifty a day. If something isn't done immediately, Kansas may enter the Union as a slave state.

Appropriating a pen, a bottle of ink, and a sheet of the senator's personal stationery from his study, she writes to Eli Thayer, Vice President of the newly organized Massachusetts Emigrant Aid Company, and offers to donate enough money to outfit thirty emigrant families. As she blots the letter, folds it, and seals it, she thinks how furious her father-in-law would be if he knew his letterhead sat above such a message.

Next she unpacks her sketch pad and draws up a plan for the glasshouse. She decides it will have two wings converging on a central domed atrium. There will be palms and other tropical trees, wild figs, lianas, and a small stone-rimmed pool filled with exotic fish. One wing will be filled with orchids. The other will feature brightly colored tropical flowers. Would it be possible to have parrots? They would be able to survive Washington winters, since the glasshouse will be heated by subterranean ovens, but would it be cruel to confine them to such a small place?

Yes, she decides, it would be. Reluctantly, she erases the parrots and replaces them with hummingbirds, then erases the hummingbirds and decides to have no birds at all. There's too much similarity between her own situation and theirs, and as far as birds are concerned, a cage will be a cage even if it's warm and filled with orchids.

On the evening of the third day, Senator Presgrove reappears and takes dinner with her. Picking up a silver carving set, he deftly removes a slice of chicken breast and has it sent down to her end of the table on a small china plate.

"Senator," she asks, "where is my husband?" Senator Presgrove lifts his eyebrows and goes back to carving.

"Sir, please tell me where my husband is. I need to talk to him. I've discovered he's deceived me about his opinions on slavery, and I have a right to know the truth."

The senator grins at her in a way that makes her acutely uncomfortable. "Honey," he says, "didn't your mama tell you that you could catch more flies with honey than vinegar?"

"Does that mean you won't tell me?"

"Yes, ma'am. My own dear mama didn't raise fools, and it's a foolish man who steps between husband and wife."

Carrie is furious, but she masters her temper. She needs to know how extensively Deacon has deceived her. If the senator won't tell her where Deacon is, perhaps he'll tell her other things. "Senator, it appears none of the servants in this house are slaves? Is that true?"

"That's correct. Would you care for a drumstick?"

"How many slaves do you own?"

"Honey, I own sixty-three slaves, which is pitiful by the standards of South Carolina or Georgia, but those sixty-three make me the fourth largest slave owner in the great Commonwealth of Kentucky, and I'm damn proud of it. You don't much like that do you?"

"No. I think it's abhorrent."

"Well then, in the interest of family harmony I think you and I should avoid speakin' of such topics at the dinner table. You know, Deacon told me you were a wide-eyed abolitionist. If you were a man, I suppose I'd have to call you out and shoot you, but political opinions don't count in a woman. You can't vote, honey. You can't even testify in a court of law now that you're married to my son." He finishes cutting off a drumstick and puts it on his own plate. Picking a bit of salt on the tip of his knife, he sprinkles it over his food in a way that is somehow menacing.

"What you can do is keep your mouth shut. I say that with the utmost respect. Take it as a friendly warning. Deacon needs a wife who will go to parties, bat her eyelashes, talk sweet, and charm the gentlemen."

He points the knife at her. "Now you got a long way to go before you're gonna be a Southern belle. In fact, it's my considered opinion that my son made a mistake when he married you, even if you are as rich as the Rani of Jhansi and were raised about as far south as a person can go without strikin' an iceberg." He repositions the knife, picks up the carving fork again, and inspects the platter. "Light meat or dark?"

That does it. The next morning, Carrie gets up, puts on one of Nettie's day dresses, eats a quick breakfast, and calls for the carriage. While she's waiting for it to roll up in front of the house, she opens her trunk and takes out a package wrapped in brown paper. For a few seconds she bends over it with her eyes closed, inhaling the clean, earthy scent of the jungle. She remembers a flock of toucans fighting over ripe brazil nuts and Papa far above her, perched on the limb of a Cecropia tree reaching out to gather a stem of white orchids.

Cutting the string, she opens the package, selects three orchid roots, and rewraps them in a clean linen hand towel. Half an hour later, she is standing in a somewhat dilapidated greenhouse speaking to Arthur Kroll, assistant to the director of the United States Botanic Garden. Placing the bundle of orchid roots on a potting table, she gets straight to the point.

"Mr. Kroll, I'm Mrs. Deacon Presgrove, and I wish to donate these plants to the garden as a memorial to my daughter, Willa Saylor, who died at sea."

Kroll examines the bundle from a distance and tugs at his cravat as if it were strangling him. "Mrs. Presgrove, that's most generous, but I am sorry to say we cannot accept donations from individuals. We're a scientific organization. We need to know when and where each plant was collected."

"Each plant I am donating bears a tag that contains all that information as well as the Latin name of the genus and species. If you open this package, you'll discover that I'm giving you a gift of rare orchids collected by my father, Canan Vinton."

Her father's name has an electrifying effect. Turning to the bundle, Mr. Kroll opens it, lifts out the orchid roots, and reads the tags. The roots look more like hanks of muddy rope than plants, but he immediately knows what he has.

"These are priceless! Collected by Canan Vinton himself—good heavens, Mrs. Presgrove, why didn't you say so at once! I would never have dreamed of refusing such a generous gift. I apologize if I sounded ungrateful, but we have so many ladies dropping by with daffodil bulbs and cuttings from their tea roses. These orchids are a treasure indeed! If we tried to buy them, they would cost the garden hundreds—perhaps thousands—of dollars each; but, as you know, no one can buy such orchids. The only other specimens I am aware of are presently being cultivated at Kew. They were also collected by your late father. The head gardener at Kew told us Mr. Vinton saved them from being destroyed when their portion of the jungle was logged for tropical hardwoods and . . ."

He suddenly realizes that while he has been rhapsodizing over the orchids, she has been standing. "May I offer you a chair, Mrs. Presgrove? Some coffee?"

Carrie smiles. It's been a long time since she has seen an orchid lover in ecstasy. "No, thank you, Mr. Kroll. I must leave in a few moments, but I'd like to return at a later date to meet with Mr. Howard, the director of the garden. I have something else to donate in memory of my late daughter."

"More orchids?"

"No. I wish to endow a glasshouse. I was thinking of something along the lines of the new Palm House at Kew."

Kroll looks stunned, which is not surprising. Carrie doubts many ladies drop by to donate a building.

"Mrs. Presgrove, that would be wonderful! Unfortunately, Mr. Howard is not here at present, but I know he will embrace the idea with enthusiasm. It is generous beyond— Well, ma'am, words fail me. The Presgrove House will be the first great glasshouse of the United States Botanic Garden."

"The Willa Saylor House," Carrie reminds him. She points out the window. "I would like to build it over there, Mr. Kroll, where it will catch the morning light. It will shine like a soap bubble. We'll have a domed atrium with marble benches where members of Congress can sit and discuss the affairs of the nation, and a small courtyard where ladies can take tea. I'll heat it with ovens in winter and fill it with tropical plants so that even in January the people of Washington will have a warm, green place to take shelter from the cold."

"Perhaps you would like to name the rare orchids in the glasshouse 'The Canan Vinton Collection' in memory of your father."

Agreeing that this is an excellent idea, Carrie thanks Mr. Kroll, shakes his hand, and promises to return later to discuss the details with the director and show him her sketches for the Willa Saylor House, but she's never able to fulfill that promise, because that afternoon when she goes to her trunk to get her stock certificates, she discovers they're missing.

"I imagine Deacon sold them about an hour after you two cleared U.S. Customs," Senator Presgrove tells her at dinner. "And I imagine he's got the proceeds tucked away somewhere you can't get your hands on them."

"He couldn't have done that! Those stocks were mine, not his! I inherited them from my father!"

"Maybe in Brazil they were yours, but if you'll look around, you'll see you're now living in the United States of America. I understand that where Portuguese law is the law of the land, a woman continues to own her own property after marriage, but under U.S. law, what's yours became Deacon's the second you said 'I do.'"

Carrie rises to her feet, grabs her water glass, and hurls it to the floor. "*Puxa saco!*" she cries. "First Deacon lies to me about being against slavery! Then he steals my money! Your son is a thief and a fortune hunter and so are you! What other lies have the two of you told me! Tell me, or I swear, I'll raise such a scandal, you'll be run out of Congress."

Senator Presgrove studies her thoughtfully. "You know," he says softly, "until now I didn't think you had it in you to cause real trouble, but I am in the process of changin' my mind. I'm gonna have to tell my son to quit tomcattin' around and keep a better eye on you."

He leans forward. "You want the whole truth, do you? Well then I suggest you ask Deacon the name of that 'club' of his. But you know . . ." His voice becomes a low, threatening purr. "You know, I wouldn't do that. No, ma'am, I wouldn't. Because you sure as hell aren't gonna like the answer. Now sit down and finish your dinner and try to impersonate a lady, or I'll order the servants to drag you upstairs and lock you in your room until that son of mine comes home. In other words, it's manners or incarceration. How does that sit?"

"You've already taken your wife's money, drugged her, and imprisoned her upstairs, but you'll find me harder to bully."

"Is that so?" The senator rises to his feet. "Listen and listen well: Deacon has your money and you can't do a damn thing about it. You want a penny from him? You'll have to beg for it. Now if you'll excuse me, I'll retreat to my study and smoke a cigar. In the future, I think I'll follow my son's example and dine out. Eating at the same table with you is a surefire recipe for dyspepsia.

"By the way, if you try to cause trouble, you're the one who's gonna get run out of town on a rail. Around here gentlemen can do whatever they like provided they don't do it in the middle of the street, but ladies who curse in foreign tongues and throw tumblers end up with no calling cards on their front hall tables. If you repeat the things you've said tonight, every lady in town is going to pity Deacon for having burdened himself with an insane wife.

"Against all odds, I myself already have garnered quite a reputation for being a merciful saint when it comes to women. There's more than one room in this house with a door that bolts from the outside. Think it over."

Putting the palms of her hands on the table, Carrie leans toward him. "I'm not afraid of you. I once chopped the head off of a nine-foot pit viper, and I know a snake when I see one."

The senator grins, exposing a row of yellow teeth. "My, my, you are a feisty one. I'm tremblin' in my boots. Now if you don't have any more Brazilian obscenities to hurl at me, I have work to do, and I reckon you need to get back to your knittin'."

Carrie retreats upstairs to her bedroom, slams the door, and locks it. Splashing cold water on her face, she forces herself to calm down. What a useless conversation! She's been insulted and threatened and condescended to and all for nothing. She still doesn't know where Deacon is.

For the better part of an hour, she paces back and forth trying to decide what to do next, but no coherent plan emerges. Around nine, she walks to the window, throws open the shutters, and looks toward Washington. In the distance, she hears the sound of a bottle breaking, the low whistle of the night train, the clatter of running footsteps.

For a long time she stands there trying to put her thoughts in order, and as she does so, a story gradually begins to unfold in her mind. It's Deacon's story of his sister's friend who died of consumption leaving him desolate, but it's not the same tragic story of grief and loss he told Carrie when he was courting her. Carrie breaks that story apart, lays out the pieces, and puts them back together into another story, one glued together with lies.

Obviously Deacon stole the dead girl's illness from his stepmother. The sister was a fabrication. Deacon has no sister. There are other bits and pieces stolen from other lives. She can't recognize all of them, but it's likely he stole the story of his quarrel with his father from the quarrel William had with his own father. Deacon's claim that he was nearly cut out of his father's will because of his support of abolition—that's William's story, too.

But back to the girl. She obviously never existed, which means Deacon must have made up everything about her from other sources. What were those sources? Was she a friend of the family? An acquaintance? Someone Deacon had only seen in passing and admired? What had he said about her? That she was "full-figured." Yes. That was it. Full-figured, with dark hair, and a mole on her upper lip.

Carrie walks over to the mirror and touches her upper lip. She remembers Deacon's finger drawing back just before it made contact, the heat of it, how at the time she had believed he respected her too much to touch her. *A mole right there. But who is she?*

Suddenly, she remembers the train: the clattering of the wheels, Deacon beside her, the smell of his cigar, and then the hiss of steam as they halted for a few moments beside an elegant red-brick house. A girl in a green dress puts the tip of her gloved hand to her lips and blows Deacon a kiss. *Know her?* Deacon protested. *I should say not!* But he did know her. He had even taken something from her.

Carrie turns away from the mirror. She knows now where she'll find her husband. She even knows the name of his club.

* * *

The red-brick house near the canal is ablaze with lights. Carrie can hear laughter and the tinkling of a piano.

"I am sorry, ma'am," the maid says. "I am afraid you have made a mistake. There ain't no Mr. Deacon Presgrove here."

Carrie smiles and leans forward. She has anticipated that she will not be admitted to Mrs. Springer's—no decent woman would be—so she's taken Nettie's most flamboyant dress, a yellow silk ball gown, and made it even more flamboyant by ripping out the panel of lace that covers the wearer's bosom. Burning a bit of cork in a candle, she's darkened her eyebrows and outlined her eyes. The red that glows on her lips and cheeks comes from the box of paints she uses to make botanical drawings.

Pulling off her gold earrings, she presses them into the maid's hand. "Please let me in," she says. "I won't be a moment." The maid inspects the earrings, lifts one to her lips, bites down on it, and nods.

"Go ahead then," she says, stepping aside.

Later, Carrie cannot recall much about the interior of Mrs. Springer's establishment except that it is tastefully decorated. There are no garish chandeliers or purple velvet drapes, only a well-appointed entryway with a brass umbrella stand, and beyond it a room that is like the parlor of any respectable home except that it features a gaming table covered in green felt. Five people sit around the table engrossed in cards. Carrie recognizes two as pro-slavery senators, two are complete strangers, and the one with his back to the door is her husband.

"Deacon," she says.

Deacon stiffens at the sound of her voice. Slowly he turns around. "Gentlemen," he says, rising to his feet. "Allow me to present my wife."

The men sitting around the table look startled. Throwing down their cards, the two senators beat a hasty retreat, no doubt hoping Carrie has not recognized them. Deacon ignores them. Walking into the front hall, he takes Carrie by the hand and leads her into the gaming room.

"Mr. Ipswitch, Dr. Vemeer, my wife, Mrs. Presgrove." The two remaining gamblers put their cards facedown on the table, rise to their feet, and give Carrie nervous bows.

"A pleasure, ma'am," they mutter. Behind the gaming table is a long sofa covered in yellow silk the exact shade of the dress Carrie is wearing. On it, sit three women dressed as elegantly as senator's wives. Two are blondes. The third is the dark-haired girl with the mole on her upper lip. Carrie notices she has twined artificial violets in her hair.

Deacon follows Carrie's gaze. "Lily," he says, "come here. I want you to meet my wife." He turns back to Carrie. "I suppose you are wondering who she is, yes? Well, since you've arrived unannounced, let me save you the trouble of asking: I own her."

"Own her? You mean she's your slave?" Carrie feels a sense of vertigo. She puts her hand on the gaming table to steady herself. "You're despicable."

"Am I?"

"Yes. How can you own another human being?"

"Slavery is legal in Washington, Carolyn. By law Lily is only three-fifths human, so perhaps I'm only three-fifths despicable." He shrugs. "In any event, the question is not how could I own her, but how I could have refused her. She was given to me by my father when I was—" He turns to the girl. "How old was I when the senator gave you to me, Lily?"

"Around twenty-eight," the girl says softly.

"That's right, I was twenty-eight and Lily was twelve when I became her master. Don't let her looks fool you. She's a mustee. You don't know what that is, do you? Well then, we must educate you. A mustee is one-eighth black. That's all it takes. One drop of black blood and a female can legally be bought and sold like a horse; only a fine, fifteen-year-old mustee like Lily brings in considerably more income than a racehorse. I rent her out, you see. Or at least I did until I married you. Now I have enough money to keep her to myself. Lily, thank Mrs. Presgrove."

"Thank you, Mrs. Presgrove," the girl says.

Carrie looks at Lily and feels such a mix of anger and despair she cannot speak. The girl, who is little more than a child, is obviously a Presgrove. The family features are evident in her face, her hands, the way she holds her head. Even her eyes are the same clear green as Deacon's.

She turns away and stares at the grease-smeared cards on the table, the poker chips stacked in toppling piles, the half-emptied glasses of whiskey, the cigar butts stubbed out in brass ashtrays. She came here this evening to let Deacon know she was carrying his child and give him an opportunity to tell her the truth so perhaps, for the sake of that child, they could go on being married. She expected him to lie, grow angry, even tell her to leave; but she never expected him to introduce her to his sister.

"For God's sake," she says, "set her free."

"Set her free? She's worth over two thousand dollars, and on a good night she brings in thirty more. Someday I may lose her at cards like a gentleman, but I'll be damned if I'll give her away just to make my wife feel virtuous. Go home, Carolyn, and stop meddling in things you don't understand."

Turning back to his remaining gambling companions, he picks up a deck of cards. "Gentlemen," he says, "I believe it's my turn to deal."

*   *   *

Carrie takes a cab back to Georgetown, lets herself in the back door of the house, walks upstairs to her bedroom, takes off the yellow silk dress, and scrubs the red paint and burned cork off her face. She still has no idea what to do, but one thing is certain: She cannot let her child grow up with Deacon Presgrove as a father.

She spends the rest of the night weighing her options. By the time the smell of coffee drifts up from the kitchen, she has come up with a plan for her life that does not include Deacon. To make it work, she will have to start by getting some ready cash. That part at least is easy. Deacon has a gold cigar case that he has left out on the dresser in plain sight. Perhaps he bought it or won it at poker. In any event, it's quite valuable. As soon as the shops open, she'll drive into Washington and pawn it. Then she'll buy a train ticket to Boston where she'll sell the rest of the orchids to Mordecai de Gelder. De Gelder was one of her father's best customers. He made a fortune supplying boots to the military during the Mexican War, and his enthusiasm for orchids knows no bounds. He even has a glasshouse attached to his mansion. If she offers him half a dozen rare orchids in one lot, he'll pay her perhaps as much as five thousand dollars.

Once she's settled in Boston, she'll look for some way to support herself and her child. Perhaps she'll be able to teach botany in a female seminary or work in the herbarium at Harvard. Herbariums don't usually hire women, but she is Canan Vinton's daughter, and perhaps that will be enough to convince them to bend the rules. In order to explain the fact that she's with child, she'll do what she should have done when she was carrying Willa: pose as a widow. She'll even wear black. And if Deacon comes after her and tries to take the child from her? Well, she'll deal with that if and when it happens.

Dashing cold water on her face, she puts on Nettie's soberest day dress, and goes down to breakfast hoping Senator Presgrove will keep his promise not to dine with her. He doesn't put in an appearance, and she eats in peace, fortifying herself with coffee, pancakes, and bacon, and then running upstairs to be sick. By the time she has finished and is rinsing out her mouth, any lingering doubts she has about being with child have disappeared.

Slipping the gold cigar case into her reticule, she goes back downstairs and calls for the carriage. It's just rolling up when a man appears with a message from the director of the Botanic Garden requesting she drop by his office at her earliest convenience.

"Please tell Mr. Howard that I cannot pay him a visit this morning. In fact—"

"Excuse me, ma'am," the messenger says, "but there's more, and since I get paid to deliver the whole message, I reckon I should give you the whole lot." He clears his throat.

"Mr. Howard also said to let you know this concerns a Mr. William . . . Bless me if I can remember his last name. A 'Mr. William' and a last name that has something to do with the ocean." He frowns. "Please don't tell Mr. Howard about me forgetting the man's last name. Say, are you all right? Because, ma'am, forgive me for remarkin' on it, but you're lookin' kinda pale."

Chapter Thirteen

Howard's office is tucked into a corner of a large brick building in a room so crammed with wooden specimen cabinets that Carrie has to press down her crinolines to make her way to his desk.

"Good morning, Mrs. Presgrove," he says, rising to his feet. Suntanned and lanky with a head of wiry brown hair, he gives off such an aura of good health and outdoor living that only when he reaches for a cane and takes a few steps toward her does she realize he's lame. "It's a pleasure to meet you. Do sit down."

Limping over to a straight-backed wooden chair, he sweeps up a pile of books and papers and deposits them on his desk. "I apologize for the mess. We have so few lady visitors, and I can't have anyone clean this room for fear something will be lost or damaged."

Carrie makes a gesture that indicates she's accustomed to such chaos. *For God's sake, stop talking about housecleaning and tell me about William!* she thinks.

"As the daughter of Canan Vinton," Howard continues with

maddeningly slow cordiality, "I am sure you know how fragile herbarium sheets are."

Resisting an urge to beg him to get to the point, Carrie yields to the necessity of preliminary small talk. "Yes," she says. "I used to remove the specimens my father had collected from the plant presses and sew them onto special sheets of paper he ordered from London. I spent many hours helping him preserve what he had gone to so much trouble to obtain, but of course, I was not always successful. We were often living in the jungle, and insects were a constant concern. What we could not dry, I sketched."

"Indeed?" He makes his way back to his desk, sits down, and props his cane against the nearest cabinet. "If you have no objection, I would like to ask you a question. The specimen sheets that come to us from collectors who work in the tropics often show insect damage, but your father's were an exception. How did he keep so many from being consumed?"

"Camphor."

His face falls. "We also use camphor. I was hoping your father had discovered a tropical plant that contained a superior insecticide. We have just experienced an alarming incursion of beetles due perhaps to the heavy rains, which . . ."

He pauses. "I'm sorry for running on like this. As everyone who knows me can attest, I am a monomaniac when it comes to preserving herbarium sheets, and frankly I am somewhat in awe of you, Mrs. Presgrove. Canan Vinton was one of my heroes, and it is not every day I get to meet one of his daughters."

"I am his only daughter."

His smile disappears. "Of course—his only living daughter. I learned of your sister's death from smallpox. What a grief her passing must have been to you and your father. Or did your father predecease her? I regret to say I cannot remember the exact sequence of

events. But still, such a young woman, a budding flower taken before it had fully blossomed—"

"Mr. Howard, I don't understand. Who are you talking about?"

"Your late sister, Mrs. Presgrove. I hope I do not add to your
grief by mentioning her, but I heard so much about her beauty and
intelligence and good nature that I have come to feel her loss as if I
had known her."

"Mr. Howard, my only sister died at birth. I have no other
sister."

Howard looks at her in confusion. "But you are Canan Vinton's
daughter, are you not? That is to say, you were born a Miss Vinton?"

"Indeed I was, Mr. Howard. I am the only Miss Vinton."

He blinks, opens his mouth, and closes it without speaking.

"Excuse me, sir, but you are staring at me as if I were a ghost.
Could you please tell me what is going on and what this line of questioning has to do with my late fiancé, William Saylor? I don't mean
to be rude, but I'm growing more confused by the minute."

"As am I." He clears his throat. "Mrs. Presgrove, I realize this is
an impertinent question, but could you please tell me your Christian
name?"

"Before I married Mr. Presgrove I was Carolyn Josephine
Vinton."

He sits back and looks at her with disbelief. "Impossible."

"Why 'impossible?' Do you doubt I am who I say I am?"

"No, Mrs. Presgrove. I'm sorry if I gave that impression, but this
is quite a shock. William Saylor and I are old friends. We went to
school together. When he came to visit me in April, he told me you
were dead. He showed me a Brazilian newspaper that contained
your obituary. He was a changed man, thin and pale from a recent
illness and quite undone. I have rarely seen a man so grief-
stricken."

"William came here in *April*?" Carrie rises to her feet, collides with the pile of books on Howard's desk, and sends them crashing to the floor. "Two months ago? My God! I thought he was dead!"

"Mrs. Presgrove, are you going to faint?"

"Faint? No, Mr. Howard, I . . . in April, you say? William's alive then? You're sure he's alive?"

"Yes, Mrs. Presgrove. As sure as I am sitting here."

"Where is he? I must see him at once. I believe I have—that is, I believe we both have—been the victims of a terrible misunderstanding."

"I fear you can't see him without making a long journey, Mrs. Presgrove. He's emigrated to Kansas."

"To Kansas?"

"Yes."

"Where in Kansas?"

"I'm afraid he didn't say exactly."

The room suddenly twists sideways and the specimen cabinets begin to move back and forth in a wavelike motion that is sickening. Carrie falls back into her chair. Her ears ring and black spots swim in front of her eyes.

"Mrs. Presgrove, are you sure you're not going to faint?" Howard's voice comes to her as from a great distance like the buzzing of an insect. She has an urge to laugh and cry and rage all at the same time. Gradually she comes to her senses. When she lifts her head, she finds Howard standing over her with a glass of water. She swallows and takes a gasp of camphor-scented air.

"Could you please open a window?"

He goes to the windows and throws them open. The smell of camphor is replaced by the steamy odor of the swamp Washington is built on. Carrie sits silently for a moment, trying to calm the beating of her heart. When at last she speaks, she manages to sound coherent. "I am sorry if I alarmed you, Mr. Howard. It appears we have both given each other a shock this morning."

"You were his fiancée?" Howard says, offering her the glass of water again. Carrie accepts it, takes a sip, and nods. The water tastes muddy, as if it had been dipped out of the river.

"And you and William each thought the other was dead?"

She nods again.

"Mrs. Presgrove, I am so sorry."

The sympathy in his voice nearly sends her into tears, but she manages to control her emotions. She has almost fainted on Howard's floor, and she does not want to break down completely in front of him even if he is an old friend of William's. She needs to gather her wits.

"Do you still have the newspaper William showed you? The one with my obituary in it?"

"No, Mrs. Presgrove. William took it with him. He said he was going to show it to his mother. He told me she was old and ill and was having trouble remembering things. He thought seeing the news of your death in print might help her understand what a grave blow losing you was, and why he had decided to leave instead of staying in Washington where he would be closer to her."

"Mr. Howard, I examined every mortality list in Rio when I was searching for William, and I never found my name on any of them. I can't understand this, because I always checked to see if my father's name was there, and it always was. Since at the time I also bore the last name 'Vinton,' I should have been listed just below him. Did William say how he came by my death notice?"

"He told me that a relative mailed it to him from Brazil."

"Do you recall the date on the newspaper, Mr. Howard?"

"I'm sorry. I'm afraid I have no idea of the exact date, but as I recall, the list of names was short because most of the dead had already been identified. I think it might have been published in late November or perhaps early December."

"Did William say which relative mailed the notice of my death to him?"

"I think he said his stepbrother sent it to him, to confirm—"

"To confirm what his stepbrother had already told him: that I was dead?"

"Yes."

Carrie stands and grips the back of the chair. For a moment she sways, her skirts brush against the cabinets, and she knocks a small paper label off one of the drawers. The label floats through the air and lands on Mr. Howard's desk upside down. She steadies herself, picks up the label, and hands it to Howard. She is almost too angry to speak. It's a different kind of anger than she has ever felt before.

Late November and early December—exactly when Deacon began courting her. Had he looked up her bank balance before he appeared in her parlor with that black band on his arm? Did he know his lie would kill any hope she had of being happy? Did he feel guilty when he saw how she was suffering, or did he light a cigar and congratulate himself on a job well done?

"Do you have—" Her voice breaks. She stops, takes a breath and begins again. "Do you have a map of the Kansas Territory that I might consult?"

"Certainly." Howard goes over to a cabinet, opens it, and takes out a leather map case. Moving everything off his desk, he removes the map from the case and spreads it out, anchoring the corners with books. It's a new map, published in New York only a few months ago by J. H. Colton & Co.: expensive, hand-colored, handsomely drawn; decorated with images of elk, bears, buffalo, wagon trains, and dancing Indians, so large that it covers the entire desk, yet no matter how hard Carrie studies it, it tells her nothing, because except for the border near Missouri, the territory has not yet been properly surveyed.

Kansas is simply a huge, rose-colored oblong that stretches over six hundred miles from the Missouri border to the crest of the Rocky Mountains. Within that oblong, the mapmakers have not indicated any towns unless you count Council Grove and Big Springs where the wagon trains assemble. Here and there, the names of forts appear, most established to keep the Indians in check and protect wagon trains traveling the Oregon and Santa Fe trails.

There is a huge area labeled *Catholic Missions* on a river the mapmakers have not bothered to name. Other rivers, and sometimes creeks, are marked in ways that makes Carrie wonder if anyone has really traveled along them: the Kaw, the Big Blue, the Arkansas, the Smoky Hill, the Cimarron, the unpronounceable Shawacaskah. Except for rivers, missions, and forts, the rest of the territory is a blank, which might as well bear the warning "Here Be Dragons."

She leans closer and sees there are more labels, equally unhelpful since they merely indicate where the various Indian tribes were settled when Kansas was still part of the Indian Territories: Potawatomie, Kickapoo, Iowa, Cherokee, Wyandot, and Kansas in the east; Arapaho and Cheyenne in the far west.

Some of these Indians emigrated to Kansas in the 1830s when all tribes east of the Mississippi underwent forced relocation. Now they and the others are being forced to moved again to make way for settlers. For a moment, Carrie contemplates the cruel irony of the Indians being pushed out to make way for abolitionist homesteaders who plan to make sure Kansas enters the Union as a free state. If she could do something about this, she would, but since she can't vote and has no influence on anyone who can, the chances of her being able to help are next to nonexistent, so she returns to the map and her own problem, namely: *Where in the 126,000 square miles of the Kansas Territory is William?*

Mr. Howard said he left in April before the territory was legally opened to settlement and just before, or possibly just after, the Massachusetts Emigrant Aid Company was formed. Logic dictates that since there were no established towns, he must have headed for one of the forts—probably Fort Leavenworth, where his services as a doctor would have been in demand. But there is another possibility, one that almost makes her despair when she allows herself to contemplate it.

In the summer of 1849, after quarreling with his father over slavery, William left Kentucky for the gold fields of California, joining a wagon train traveling west via the Oregon Trail. For eleven months he served as the train's doctor and, when all three guides came down with cholera, he became its leader.

That wagon train mostly carried families with no idea of the hardships that lay ahead of them and men so greedy for gold they forced the wagons to leave Salt Lake City in mid-April. It was a miracle any of them survived. In fact, if it hadn't been a mild winter, if William hadn't managed to save the life of one of the guides, and if they hadn't been rescued by another wagon train, they would have all died in the Sierra Nevada Mountains. William had come close to freezing to death when he tried to snowshoe out to get help, but of course he didn't die. Instead, he lived, came to Brazil, and made love to her in her father's house, and together they made Willa.

Still, if he joined one wagon train, might he not join another? She runs the tip of her finger across Kansas into the Rocky Mountains and over to Utah where the map ends in a burst of blue. Her search for him will almost surely fail if he has ridden off the map.

She straightens up to find Mr. Howard looking at her. "Mrs. Presgrove, he could be anywhere."

"I'll find him," she says stubbornly. She goes back to studying the map. "I understand the Massachusetts Emigrant Aid Company plans to found an abolitionist town somewhere in the territory. Do you have any idea where it's going to be located?"

Mr. Howard shakes his head. "No, I'm afraid the site hasn't been chosen yet."

"Did William say what he intended to do?"

"Not in so many words. He said he'd grown disillusioned with the practice of medicine. He told me he'd been reading about new techniques a Hungarian physician named Semmelweis had tried out in the Vienna General Hospital Obstetric Clinic—something simple that mostly involved hand washing, soap and water, chlorinated lime solutions, things of that nature. Semmelweis appeared to have had remarkable success in reducing patient mortality, but his colleagues treated him with contempt.

"William claimed this mistreatment of Semmelweis proved physicians, himself included, have no idea what they're doing. The thought that he had failed to save your life as well as the life of your father was a torment to him. I got the impression he was going to Kansas to start over again."

"Was he planning to farm?"

"Not that he mentioned."

Carrie runs her finger up the rivers and touches the crest of the western mountains. "He couldn't have been intending to prospect for gold."

"No, there's no gold in Kansas that I know of."

"I can't imagine him keeping a store or running a boarding house." Mr. Howard is silent. Carrie looks up and finds him staring at her as if he has something to say but isn't sure he should say it. "You know something you're not telling me, don't you?"

"Perhaps. I'm not sure. You see, I think—that is, I'm fairly sure he was planning to do something . . . dangerous."

"Dangerous?"

"Mrs. Presgrove, I wouldn't tell anyone else this, but I feel you should know that it's possible what he planned to do was illegal. When I asked him what he had in mind, he refused to tell me. I found that strange, since we'd always confided in one another. Still, I wouldn't have made much of it except he said—in a very joking way, mind you—that if certain people found out what he was up to they'd hang him."

"Hang him?"

"Those were his exact words."

"That's impossible. William would never commit a crime. He's the most honest man I've ever known."

"He is indeed. I'd trust him with my life. So you see, he must have been joking." Removing the books from the corners of the map, Howard allows it to roll up again. "Is there anything else I can do for you?"

"No, thank you. You've been very helpful." She pauses, then remembers she has bad news to deliver. "But I'm afraid I won't be able to endow the Willa Saylor glasshouse after all."

"I'm very sorry to hear that, Mrs. Presgrove."

"My husband," Carrie nearly chokes on the word, "has made it impossible for me to access my funds." Howard is giving her a look of pity. She'd like to tell him that revenge is more her style, but this has already been too intimate a conversation. "I'm sorry. It's something I'd like to do, something I will do if I ever get access to my money again. Meanwhile, I hope you'll take good care of the orchids I gave you. I brought them such a long way."

"Mrs. Presgrove, we will treasure them."

"Thank you."

Howard looks at her for a moment and then looks down at the map case. He slips in the map, picks up the leather top, and fits it on the end of the tube. "You're going to go to Kansas, aren't you?"

For an instant she's tempted to lie. But why? Whose reputation is she protecting? Deacon's? "Yes," she says, "not that it's any of your business."

Howard snaps the catch closed and looks up. She's surprised to see admiration in his eyes. "I apologize," he says. "My question was overly direct, but you see last fall I lost my wife. I miss her as I imagine William misses you. When you find him, please tell him I send my affectionate regards."

"How can you be so sure I'll find him?"

"I believe you'd find anyone you loved, Mrs. Presgrove. You're everything William said you were and more." He holds the map case out to her. "I'd be obliged if you'd accept this as a small token of thanks for the orchids you've given us. I think you'll find it useful."

As soon as she gets back to Georgetown, Carrie goes upstairs, walks into Matilda's room, and throws the drapes aside, letting in light and air.

"Mother Presgrove," she says, "wake up!"

The sick woman sits up, leans back against the headboard, and stares at Carrie blankly. "Who are you?"

"I'm Carrie Vinton. William's friend. You remember me, Mother Presgrove. I was here before."

Matilda runs her fingers through her hair and coughs. "I don't remember anything." Reaching out, she attempts to pick up the opium pipe, but her hand is nowhere near the night table. Carrie wants to snap the pipe in half and smash the medicine bottles so she can talk to the real Matilda, the one who has a mind and a memory.

"Matilda, Mrs. Presgrove, Mrs. Saylor—"

William's mother smiles at the name Saylor, and Carrie realizes she has made a lucky hit. "Mrs. Saylor, it's me. Carrie Vinton. William and I played together when we were children."

Matilda's face softens. She turns away from the opium pipe and reaches toward Carrie. "Carrie, dear, come closer and let me touch you. I want to make sure you're not a dream."

"I'm real." Carrie draws close to the bed. Matilda leans forward, reaches up, and runs her fingers over Carrie's face. She strokes Carrie's hair and twists one of Carrie's curls around her finger.

"Such pretty hair. So very pretty. Like spun gold. That's what William said. But you're dead, Carrie. That's too bad. I remember now that William said you and he were going to be married, but you died. He came to me and told me all about it and cried and I tried to comfort him, but . . . " She grows confused. "I couldn't." She lets go of Carrie's hair, coughs, and struggles for breath. "I always liked you, Carrie."

"I know," Carrie whispers. "I always liked you, too. I loved you, Mrs. Saylor." Scooping the sick woman up in her arms, she holds her close. Matilda is so light, Carrie can hardly feel the weight of her. "Mrs. Saylor, what's wrong with you?"

"They won't let me out in the garden." Damn Deacon and his father. No one ever loved flowers more than Matilda Saylor unless it was Carrie's own father and mother.

"No, Mrs. Saylor. I mean, do you know what sickness you have?"

"I don't know what it's called, but Deacon and Bennett say it is a very fashionable disease. Poor dead Carrie, I'll be dead soon, too, and then we can walk in the garden together. You always knew the names of the flowers. Do you see different flowers now or are the flowers of the dead the same as ours?"

"The same," Carrie whispers. "The same." She had meant to ask Matilda about William, but Matilda is so far out of reach there is no way to talk to her, and this conversation is heart-breaking.

For a few minutes longer, she holds Matilda. Then she gently puts her back down on the pillows. "Mrs. Saylor," she whispers, "I'm with child by Deacon. Deacon doesn't know, but I want you to know, because you are about to become a grandmother."

Matilda gives her a puzzled look. Does she understand? It's im-

possible to tell. Leaning down, Carrie kisses her on the forehead.
"Good-bye," she whispers.

A very handsome piece of work," the pawnshop owner says as he inspects Deacon's gold cigar case. "How much do you want for it, ma'am?"

"How much will you give me?" Carrie asks him.

He flips the cigar case upside down and squints at the proof mark on the bottom. "It's gold, alright, made right here in Washington." He turns the case back over, inserts his fingernail into the catch, and opens the lid. "Hmm," he says, "I think thirty dollars is the best I can do for you."

"So little?"

"You can take it around to other shops if you like, but I doubt you'll get a better offer. It's the inscription, you see. Lowers the price. No one likes to buy a cigar case inscribed to someone else."

"What inscription?"

The pawnshop owner looks at Carrie suspiciously. "Who did you say this cigar case belongs to?"

"My husband."

The pawnshop owner snaps the lid shut. "Never mind," he says. "Let's say thirty-five dollars? How does that sit?"

Carrie reaches out, takes the cigar case from him, and opens it. On the inside of the lid she finds an inscription, which reads: *From Nettie to Deacon with love.*

A n hour after discovering Nettie Wiggins's love note inscribed inside Deacon's cigar case, Carrie confronts him at Mrs. Springer's, pulls out her father's pistol, and aims it at his heart. "I'm leaving you," she tells him, "and if you try to follow me or threaten me or set the law on me or make any attempt to drag me back, I'll defend myself."

Clutching his glass of whiskey, Deacon backs up against the fireplace, opens his mouth, and begins to speak, but she doesn't hear him out. She's finished listening to his lies.

"Remember that I wasn't raised like other women. You may have my money, but you don't own my soul. Don't underestimate me, Deacon. I've shot plant specimens out of trees since I was nine. Remember: I never miss."

PART 3

The California Road

Chapter Fourteen

Missouri, September 1854

Carrie sits at the main table in the ladies' lounge of the *Magnolia Queen*, poring over her map of the Kansas Territory. Thanks to Mordecai de Gelder's insatiable appetite for orchids, she has five thousand dollars, and thanks to Professor Asa Gray of Harvard, she has a job. Once again the name Vinton has worked miracles. Professor Gray has overlooked the fact that she is a woman and has commissioned her to collect specimens of the plants of the Kansas Territory, which she is to dry and mount in the proper fashion and send to him as often as possible. He is also paying her to paint botanical portraits of each plant.

"Canan Vinton's daughter!" he said when she introduced herself. "You are a godsend! I am in the throes of assembling material for another volume of *Genera of the Plants of the United States*, and my collector in the Kansas Territory recently fell victim to smallpox. I trust you will not succumb to the same disease, Miss Vinton."

"If I were going to die of smallpox, I would already be dead," she told him, but she did not mention the plague in Rio or William, because there were questions Professor Gray was sure to ask that she did not wish to answer. Nor did she tell him she was married, pregnant, and leaving her husband to search for her lover.

Smoothing out the map, she weighs down each corner with the stones she collected the last time the steamer ran aground on a sandbar. Around her, sleeping women and children occupy the floor jammed so closely together that it's almost impossible to walk across the room without stepping on someone. Old women are snoring, babies are crying, and more than one New England matron is having dreams that have set her moaning and thrashing about. Add to this the thumping of the steam engine that powers the paddlewheel and the racket a party of drunken land speculators is making as they stand at the stern firing off their pistols for sport, and it's a wonder anyone can sleep at all; or perhaps not such a wonder, because by this point in the journey almost everyone aboard the *Magnolia Queen* is exhausted enough to sleep through anything short of a boiler explosion.

When it sought incorporation from the Massachusetts Legislature, the Emigrant Aid Company stated that the Kansas Territory was "accessible in five days continuous travel from Boston," but you could not prove it by the women and children in the ladies' lounge, most of whom have been traveling so long that clean sheets and hot food are already distant memories.

Carrie stares at the map and thinks about the real route to Kansas, the one ordinary people take that wanders west, north, south, west, and north for days by train and boat. When the *Magnolia Queen* finally reaches the Kansas Landing near Westport, most of the free-soilers on board are going to be loading their possessions into wagons and heading across forty miles of open prairie to the new abolitionist settlement of Lawrence. Should she go with them or stay on board and go up to Fort Leavenworth to see if William is there?

Lawrence is probably her best choice. It's the kind of place William would be attracted to. The first settlers pitched their tents beside the Kaw River only six weeks ago. They've already built a boardinghouse where emigrants can stay until they get settled. The next wave of settlers is not simply bringing ploughs, seed, and spades with them. They intend to build an entire New England village from scratch, so they're bringing gristmills, steam-powered sawmills, forges, chisels for shaping prairie limestone into building blocks, bells for their churches, Bibles, printing presses, even patent apple peelers, although it will be years before the orchards will bear enough apples for pies. And they're bringing guns, a great many guns, because the pro-slavers would like nothing better than to see Lawrence burned to the ground and every man, woman, and child driven out of the Kansas Territory or massacred.

She returns to the map, puts her finger over the blank spot where Lawrence is, and again considers her options. *Is William there?* She has asked everyone if they have seen him: land speculators, soldiers being posted to Fort Leavenworth, the clerks who sell train tickets, a mountain man in buckskins who has waist-length hair and a beard like a rat's nest, a Canadian trader, a Mexican cattle baron in silver-tooled chaps and a sombrero who told her he had ridden all the way from Matamoros to St. Louis, the captain of the *Magnolia Queen*, the women in the ladies' lounge, the men who are presently sleeping on the floor of the main salon.

So far her search has not yielded any clues to William's whereabouts. Most people have told her they have never heard of him, which makes sense since the majority are traveling to Kansas for the first time and thus not likely to know much about the Territory. But sometimes the answers she has received have been suspicious.

For example, some of the ladies on the *Magnolia Queen* are Missourians traveling to Westport with their personal slaves. So far none of these ladies will admit to having seen or heard of a tall, lanky man with dark eyes and chestnut-colored hair named William Saylor. Are they telling the truth? When Carrie speaks to them, they look at one another in ways that suggest they harbor secrets. Do those secrets concern William or do they merely dislike her because she's an abolitionist?

The New Englanders have been sympathetic, but here, too, something seems amiss. Only yesterday a minister's wife from Boston left a tin of oatmeal cookies in front of her stateroom door, but the minister himself will hardly speak to her, and whenever she mentions William's name, he changes the subject.

To avoid scandal she has told everyone William is her half-brother, so why are they being so reticent? Is it because they don't know anything, or do they pity her? Has William done what he told his friend Charles Howard he was going to do—something illegal and dangerous that he could be hanged for? That seems ridiculous, but if he hasn't, then why this conspiracy of silence? Maybe there is no conspiracy. Maybe she's just imagining people know more about William than they're willing to say.

For a moment she allows herself to picture how shocked they'll be when they see her kissing this "brother" of hers. That's what she will do when she finds him: kiss him senseless. And she will find him. It's simply a matter of persistence.

Rolling up the map, she blows out the candle, and puts her head down on the table. She should go back to her stateroom and sleep in a real bed, but if she tries to get out of the ladies' lounge, she will probably tread on someone's hand or foot, or worse yet, face, and she is too tired to deal with the yelling and confusion.

Closing her eyes, she forces herself to imagine sheep jumping over a fence. When that fails, she dismisses the sheep and begins to silently recite the Latin names of orchids. Gradually, the courage and stubbornness that have carried her through the day dissolve, and she finds herself thinking about the unthinkable.

If I can't find William, I will . . . what in God's name will I do?

For a long time she is neither asleep nor awake, but trapped between the two. Then she must doze off because she sees tall grasses swaying in the wind and hears a voice that she recognizes as her own.

If I can't find William, I'll buy land and settle in the Kansas Territory near Lawrence. I can get 160 acres for about $1.25 an acre. They say the soil is rich. I don't know anything about farming, but I know more about plants than most people. Surely, I can raise enough food on 160 acres to feed myself and my child . . .

She dreams of driving a wooden claim stake into the ground. As she does this, her anxiety dissolves, and she feels determined and self-sufficient, as if her life will turn out well no matter what happens. Then gradually the vision of the tall grasses fades. She opens her eyes and again feels loneliness and longing.

What will I do if I can't find William? How will I bear it? Reaching out in the darkness, she touches the rolled-up map, and begins to cry quietly so as not to awaken women who are on their way to join their husbands, and children whose fathers are waiting for them in Westport.

Chapter Fifteen

Limestone bluffs, gold and gray in the early morning light; wooded banks without a sign of human habitation; bottomlands filled with reeds that shine as they sway in the wind; mudflats, sandbars, unpredictable currents, the sound of the hull scraping something, the laboring of the engine. Smoke from the stacks drifting downriver like long gray scarves; more bluffs, more woods, more bottomlands, another steamer stuck fast in the mud.

Soldiers stand on the deck of the beached ship and wave to the *Magnolia Queen* as it steams by, and Carrie and her fellow passengers wave back. She thinks of the times she has gone up the Amazon, how different this river looks, how much broader the sky is, how much bluer; how the water is a clean green instead of a muddy brown. Below the hull, large fish flit like dark shadows over the white skeletons of sunken trees. Instead of tropical frogs, locusts sing in the underbrush; instead of parrots and macaws, hawks and eagles soar overhead.

Yet this trip up the Missouri to Westport is as hot as anything she ever experienced in the tropics. The wind has died down; not a leaf moves. The air is as wet and heavy as a boiled sheet. Gasping and fanning themselves, the other passengers seek shade, but it is even hotter inside than on deck, so Carrie holds her ground as the land speculators retreat to the main salon and order iced wine, and a plump, pretty woman from Worcester faints and has to be carried to the ladies' lounge, unlaced, and revived with smelling salts.

I should be fainting, too. Carrie thinks. *After all, I'm with child.* Fortunately, all the nausea of the first few weeks has disappeared, and after days of being fed nothing but salt pork and biscuits, her fantasies at the moment are equally divided between ice, William, and ripe mangos.

Suddenly the western sky turns black. Clouds boil up out of nowhere, and Carrie hears the rushing of wind. On shore, trees and bushes suddenly show the silver undersides of their leaves. Branches crack off and fly through the air. The wind hits the *Magnolia Queen*, and everything goes rocking. Wine bottles fly off tables, cargo slides across the deck; the sky opens up. Rain falls in torrents, blowing sideways, soaking everyone. In the Amazon, it would have been a warm rain, but here it is cold as ice. As lightning races across the sky in long jagged lines, the thunder is deafening.

Carrie hangs onto the rail, continues to stand her ground, and waits it out. Within seconds she is soaked to the skin and her skirts are plastered to her legs. Then as suddenly as it began, the rain stops, the sun comes out, and except for a wet deck, wet passengers, and soaked cargo, it's as if nothing has happened.

"That weren't so bad," the mountain man in buckskins says. He takes off his cap and beats the water off it. "You ever seen a twister?"

"No," Carrie says. "What's a twister?"

He smiles at her, exposing three missing teeth and two black ones. "Whirlwind." He makes a spiraling motion with his index finger. "Whoosh. And there goes a buffalo, miss. Up in the air to be dropped like a rock."

"I've never seen a buffalo."

He shakes his head in amazement and spits a mouthful of tobacco juice over the rail. "Welcome to the prairie, miss. You look like you got some grit, but most of them other dudes look like they're runnin' blind toward a cliff with a band of Sioux warriors shooting arrows into their butts." His face suddenly turns bright red. "Excuse me, miss. I been away from cities too long. I need to recollect to temper my language in front of ladies."

Reassuring him that she's not offended, Carrie excuses herself and goes back to her stateroom to change into dry clothing. *I may die in Kansas from fever, disease, weather, starvation, gunshot wounds, or—if I'm lucky—old age*, she thinks, *but apparently I'm not likely to die of boredom.*

Three hours later they reach Westport. The town sits on a high clay bluff above the Kansas Landing. Thanks to the rain, the mud is ankle-deep, so while the Southern ladies strap small metal rings onto the bottoms of their shoes, Carrie and the New Englanders pull on sturdy rubber boots and make their way to an oxcart, which takes them up to the city.

She stays at the Gilliss House, a hotel recently purchased by the Emigrant Aid Company. Above the front desk is a banner that proclaims: KANSAS MUST BE FREE! and another, smaller sign that warns that anyone who draws a gun on the premises will be "Summarily Evicted and Possibly Shot Dead."

"Vigilante groups," the desk clerk says, "that's what we fear, miss. We've had threats."

"What sort of threats?."

"This is Missouri, miss. Slavery is legal here. You walk out on the street around the time the saloons are filling up—which I wouldn't advise—and proclaim yourself an abolitionist, and well, I imagine a lady would still be safe, but a man might just up and disappear."

"Disappear?"

"Or worse," the desk clerk says cheerfully as he checks her into a room with a view of the river. "That will be one dollar and fifty cents, unless you are staying for a week, in which case we have a special rate of ten dollars, all meals included.

"By the way, if you do decide to step outside the hotel after you unpack your trunk, you will see notices offering a reward of two hundred dollars to anyone who will deliver Eli Thayer up to the pro-slavers. Reportedly, the original wording of the posters was 'deliver up Eli Thayer, founder of the Emigrant Aid Company, dead or alive,' but the moderates appear to have prevailed, for which we can all be thankful. Since Mr. Thayer remains in Massachusetts, he is in no great danger, but the existence of such posters is one of the reasons I keep a loaded shotgun behind the front desk."

"What time do the saloons start filling up?"

"Around six."

"Then they're filling up right now?"

"Yes, miss. Excuse me for asking, but you aren't thinking of going into any of them and preaching temperance, are you? We had a very unfortunate incident with an elderly lady a few weeks ago. She went into the Black Dog and tried to break some whiskey bottles with her umbrella and a drunken bushwhacker shot at her. Fortunately, he missed."

Reassuring the desk clerk that she will not attempt to save bushwhackers from the evils of alcohol, Carrie pays for one night and accepts the key to her room.

Chapter Sixteen

There are six saloons within a hundred and fifty yards of the Gilliss House. The nearest is the Black Dog. Hoping she'll have better luck than the elderly lady who preceded her, Carrie pushes aside the swinging doors and enters.

Her first impression is of a large, rectangular room so blued with cigar smoke she can hardly see across it. Men stand at an elaborately carved mahogany bar resting their feet on a brass rail and drinking beer from tin mugs and whiskey from small glasses. Behind the bar is a shelf of bottles and a large oil painting of a plump, naked woman that leaves nothing to the imagination. The woman is smiling and beckoning to a platter of ham sandwiches, some jars of pickled eggs, and a sign that says: FREE LUNCH.

As her eyes adjust to the darkness, Carrie sees other men sitting at the back of the saloon at small tables playing card games. Although some wear suits that would not attract notice in any eastern city, most are decked out in high boots, flannel shirts, and broad-brimmed hats. Many wear their hair long and their beards wild, and there is a fierce air about them, as if they would as soon fight as talk.

The fact that they are, to a man, armed increases this impression. Even on the upper Amazon, where civilization is only a distant rumor and the law is enforced by gun thugs, Carrie has never seen so many revolvers and knives in one place.

One of the men at the bar looks up and catches sight of her. "Boys!" he yells. "We got a visitor."

She is prepared for catcalls, taunts, and obscenities, but what she gets instead is a sudden, terrifying silence as every face in the saloon turns toward her.

"What do you want?" the bartender says.

"I'm looking for William Saylor."

"Get out, lady," he snarls. "*Now*!"

There's a kind of seething in the saloon, violent and nasty as a bag of snakes. A man at one of the back tables stands up and his companions pull him down again. Deciding she's not going to find out anything about William here, Carrie turns and leaves. Behind her, she distinctly hears someone say the words "abolitionist bitch."

Her experience at the Black Dog turns out to be a preview of what's in store for her. The Mule Skinner is a hastily thrown up tent where men sit on wooden packing crates. Before Carrie can enter, two saloon girls stop her.

"You don't want to go in there, miss," the youngest says. She cannot be much older than sixteen, and the hem of her pretty blue silk dress is stained with mud.

"There's twenty men in this town to every woman," her companion warns. "And they're all hungry."

"Have either of you seen or heard of a man named William Saylor? He's a little under six feet tall, lanky, very dark eyes, brown hair. He has a small scar just above his right eyebrow."

"Handsome, is he?"

"Very."

"Your sweetheart?"

"You might call him that."

"I wish I'd met him, but no such luck."

"Well maybe someone in the Mule Skinner will remember seeing him." Carrie starts for the tent, but the girls step in front of her.

"You can't go in there, miss."

"Why not?"

"Because, you got abolitionist written all over you, and that's a bushwhacker saloon if there ever was one. Me and Annie here know what places is dangerous and what ain't."

Carrie tries to persuade them to let her pass, but they just keep repeating that if she steps inside the Mule Skinner, she isn't going to come out in one piece.

Giving up, she moves on. The Mud Flat is a billiards parlor, the Holy Moses a dance hall, the River Rat an icehouse with a sign that promises cold beer. Instead of being greeted with silence, Carrie is taunted, propositioned, and pawed at. Since no decent woman ever walks into a saloon, men take her presence as an invitation. They offer her money, grab at her skirts, pull her into drunken embraces, and assail her with whiskey-flavored kisses.

Carrie wiggles out of their grip, raises her voice, asks if anyone has seen William. No one has, or if they have, they aren't talking.

The last saloon she enters is called the Bon Ton. Despite the French name, it's like all the rest: carved wooden bar, gilt-framed mirrors, floor slick with tobacco juice, advertisements on the walls for Bristol's Sarsaparilla and German beers. Perhaps the beer is flat or the whiskey is laced with tea, because the men here don't seem quite as drunk, and when Carrie walks up to the bar, none of them grab for her or offer to buy her a drink. They just stand there, drinking and staring at her.

"Good evening," she says to the bartender. "I'm looking for a man named William Saylor."

The bartender looks her up and down and grins. "Ain't we all," he says.

Carrie doesn't know what to make of this. "William's about six feet tall," she continues. "Dark eyes, brown hair, a small scar above—"

"Above his right eyebrow? Yep, that's the one." The bartender reaches behind the bar, brings out a rolled up piece of paper, and hands it to Carrie. When she unrolls it, she finds herself looking at a poster.

WANTED
DEAD OR ALIVE

WILLIAM SAYLOR
FOR ARMED ROBBERY

5'11" tall, black eyes, brown hair
1" scar above right eyebrow

$150 REWARD

Leaning forward, the bartender peers at the poster. "Could you describe him some more? There ain't no picture of him on this poster, and that's a tempting sum of money they're offering."

Carrie doesn't reply. She's staring at the poster and things are falling into place: William hasn't joined a wagon train and gone to California. He's living somewhere in the Kansas Territory. And where would he live? Why Lawrence, of course, because there's only one thing he'd steal at gunpoint, only one thing both Southern ladies and a New England minister would refuse to talk about, and Lawrence is the only place he could live and go on stealing it without falling into the hands of the law.

Handing the poster back to the bartender, she tells him that the description is all wrong. William Saylor has no scar above his right eyebrow. His hair is coal black, his eyes green, and he often uses an alias.

"What does he call himself?" the bartender asks.

"Deacon Presgrove," Carrie tells him. "You really should get a pencil and write this down."

Chapter Seventeen

She returns to the Gilliss House feeling more hopeful than she has since William first arrived in Brazil and asked her to marry him. That night at dinner, she meets more emigrants headed for Kansas. One is a missionary named Samuel Adair who has come from Michigan to see about resettling his family near Osawatomie Creek and founding a Congregational church there. Reverend Adair sits next to Carrie, and as they eat, he engages her in conversation.

"Are you headed to Lawrence?" he inquires after he introduces himself. "Almost everyone staying at this hotel seems to be."

"Yes," Carrie says. It's a relief to finally be able to tell someone where she's going.

Adair helps himself to the mashed potatoes and passes the bowl to Carrie. "Florella, my wife, is reluctant to live so far from her family, but we both believe we are called by God to enter into the spiritual struggle against slavery." He pauses, fork in hand. "My brother-in-law, John, is even more determined."

"He, too, supports the cause of abolition?" Carrie inquires politely.

Reverend Adair puts down his fork. "'Supports,' is putting it mildly. John believes he is the right hand of God sent to free the slaves and punish the masters for their sins." Adair lowers his voice. "He has consecrated himself to the destruction of slavery. He says most New England abolitionists are all talk and no action. He speaks of insurrection. When I remind him violence is unchristian, he quotes scripture at me: *Thou shalt break them with a rod of iron; thou shalt dash them in pieces like a potter's vessel!*"

"Psalm Two," Carrie says.

"You know your Bible."

"My mother taught me to read from it. When I was a child, it was the only book we had. The termites ate all the others."

Adair nods and goes back to his meal. If he wonders why termites ate their books, he doesn't ask. In fact, he stops speaking to her altogether even though she hasn't mentioned William. She finds this peculiar, but a few years later, when the name John Brown becomes a household word, she remembers this conversation and realizes Reverend Adair feared he had already said far too much about his brother-in-law.

The next morning, she meets another person who is destined to play an important role in her life. It's Sunday, and in honor of the Sabbath, the New Englanders hold a church service in the lobby of the hotel, presided over by Reverend Adair who takes as the text of his sermon Isaiah 58:6: "Loose the bands of wickedness, undo the heavy burdens, and . . . let the oppressed go free."

Except that it is given in a slave state in a hotel under siege, Reverend Adair's sermon is not particularly memorable, but what is memorable is a brief speech given by a free black woman named Elizabeth Newberry who stands up at the end of the service just before the benediction. Mrs. Newberry is tall and thin with graying hair, piercing eyes, a square, stubborn jaw, and a voice that could fill a cathedral.

"I was a slave in Maryland," she says, "and my mother was a slave before me, taken out of Africa and illegally smuggled into this country by slave traders who mocked the laws of the United States and cursed the federal government. When my master died, he freed me. As a condition of my freedom, I was forced to leave the state of Maryland immediately, thus abandoning my mother who had not been freed. When I told Mother I would give up my freedom in order to stay with her, she pleaded with me to leave, saying that no life was worse than that of a slave, and reminding me that a new master might sell me in which case she and I would never see each other again.

"In Michigan I met and married a good man and had three sons with him. My sons and I are now on our way to Kansas to do what we can to help ensure the territory enters the Union as a free state. We cannot vote in the plebiscite. That goes without saying. But we can help defend those who are able to vote. Yet because of the color of our skins, we cannot travel openly through Missouri without risking death or re-enslavement. Instead, we must pretend to be Mrs. Elijah Hulett's slaves.

"Mrs. Hulett, who sits quietly among us today, is a Quaker. I do not want you to think this good woman is actually a slave-owner, so I stand before you to thank her for providing my sons and me with her protection, and to urge you to do everything in your power to make sure that in future years when my grandchildren are grown, they will not be forced to choose between being murdered or traveling around their own country in disguise."

She gestures toward the back of the room. "Mrs. Hulett, will you please stand." There is a protest and some whispered urging. Finally an old woman rises to her feet. She looks frail, but when she speaks her voice is surprisingly strong.

"I am doing nothing except what my conscience dictates," she says. "All men and women are equal in the sight of God. I am sixty-three. My children tell me I should be putting up preserves and quilting, but I tell them I am going to Kansas to fight. Yes, fight. Do not delude yourselves that the slavers will let us settle peacefully. War it will be. I would call it a holy war but no war is holy, so instead I will simply say that if you are not ready to fight with me to bring Kansas into the Union free, than you should turn around and go back to New England."

No one turns around or goes back, or at least if they do they slink off quietly in the middle of the night. The next morning just before dawn, the emigrants board wagons headed for Lawrence. In preparation for what is likely to be a hot day, the women put on sunbonnets with flapping blinders that make it impossible for them to see anything not directly in front of them. Carrie, who intends to enjoy the scenery, wears a straw hat with a wide brim, which earns her stares of disapproval.

"'Tisn't very feminine," a lady whispers. "Would you like to borrow a sunbonnet, Miss Vinton?"

"No, thank you," Carrie says.

"Your hat looks like a Mexican sombrero," confides another. "I can't imagine why you wear it."

"I wear it to keep my nose from falling off," Carrie tells her, and reaching down she plucks a stem of blue sage and sticks it in the headband.

When she climbs into her wagon, she is pleased to discover she will be sharing it with Mrs. Newberry, Mrs. Newberry's sons and their wives, and several other members of the Newberry family, including three children under the age of seven.

"Biscuit, Miss Vinton?" Mrs. Newberry asks, opening a large carpetbag. "Or would you rather have cold ham?" Carrie looks into the bag and sees that Mrs. Newberry has brought enough food to outlast a siege.

"Both, thank you."

Mrs. Newberry pulls out a cold biscuit, tears it in half, slathers it with butter, and puts a slab of salt-cured ham between top and bottom. Carrie is just finishing the last crumb, when the teamster slaps the reigns against the backs of the oxen.

"Walk on!" he yells.

As the oxen begin to plod toward Lawrence, the wagon moves through a thin mist that rises off the river. For a little over half an hour, trees, bushes, and grass all look as if they have been draped in gauze. Then they put the river behind them and roll into sunshine so intense it makes Carrie wish the brim of her hat were even broader.

Since the city of Lawrence was founded beside the Kaw River less than two months ago, only about five hundred emigrants have settled there, but the road is as wide and well-worn as a turnpike. After a while, the teamster sits back, drapes the reigns around the whip holder, and explains why.

"Yer on the famous Santa Fe Trail," he tells Carrie and the others. "Where it meets up with the Oregon Trail, also known as the California Road, we'll be turnin' north toward Lawrence. 'Bout a million mules and oxen done stomped both trails hard as rock. Then you got your horses and your shoe leather packing them down even more. Number of pour souls walked all the way to California thinkin' they was gonna get rich. I don't hold with walkin'. Give me an ox team any day."

He points to the two beasts that draw their wagon. "The big one there goes by the name of Brock and the smaller by Whitehorn. As fer me, I'm what they call a *bullwhacker*, seeing as how it's my job to whack my team down this trail if they shows signs of lingerin'. But I hardly ever have to whip 'em. Brock and Whitehorn is fast fer oxen. I reckon we're gonna move at a good clip. Two and a half miles an hour or more unless it rains. Then all bets is off, and Betty bar the door!"

Carrie scans the sky for clouds, but it's blue and clear for as far as she can see. They are moving west across a rolling, open prairie of tall grasses broken by small creeks lined with oaks of all varieties, tall white-barked sycamores, willows that sway in the wind, red cedars, honey locusts whose dangling pods look like giant peas, ash, dogwood, hickories, black walnuts, pecans, and cottonwoods. This is the timber that will supply the materials for cabins and fences, and the Newberrys are relieved to see it.

"I feared Kansas might be flat as a plate and bare as a tabletop," Mrs. Newberry says. "But I see pies in those trees. Pecan, walnut, and—"

The wagon strikes a rut, gives a lurch, and she slides off the bench in slow-motion and tumbles to the floorboards. Prosser and Toussaint, her two oldest sons, grab her under the arms and put her back on the bench again. They are identical twins who must once have been hard to tell apart, but who now must rarely be mistaken for each other. Prosser sports a scalded place on his cheek that suggests someone once threw a pan of hot water at him, and Toussaint is missing an earlobe. Except for these differences, they are both handsome, tall, healthy men in their early twenties with dark skin and curly black hair: broad shouldered, good-natured, and not above teasing their mother who they clearly adore.

"You're gonna break yourself, Mama," Toussaint says.

"Gonna shatter like an old lantern shade," Prosser agrees.

Mrs. Newberry settles back on the bench, arranges her skirts, and looks at them the way she probably looked at them when they were four years old and pilfered cookies out of the cookie jar.

"Sons, you may be grown men with wives and children of your own, and I may be an old woman, but I can still tan your bottoms when you get too big for your britches."

"Sorry, Mama," Toussaint says.

"Sorry," says Prosser.

"Don't whip 'em," begs Spartacus, the youngest of the three, thirteen at most, with his mother's high cheekbones and a chin already showing signs of stubbornness.

"I'll spare 'em this time," Mrs. Newberry says. "You hear that, sons? Your baby brother has intervened for you." She turns to Carrie. "Spare the rod and spoil the child. What do you think?"

"I think they're too old to spank."

"Wouldn't do any good anyway. Like the time they told me they were going to go to California, strike gold, and become millionaires. You remember that, sons?"

"Yes, Mama," Prosser and Toussaint say in chorus. Prosser's wife, Eulie, laughs, and Toussaint's five-year-old daughter giggles and buries her head in her mother's apron.

"And what did I tell you?"

"You said we were damn fools, Mama."

"I said *damn*?"

"Yes, ma'am, you did."

"Toussaint Newberry, I got half a mind to wash your mouth out with soap."

"Your words, Mama, not mine."

"What did I say when you and your brother told me your fool plan?"

"You said we'd have to cross to Missouri if we wanted to join a wagon train, and that Missouri was a slave state, and sure as God is in Heaven, we'd be captured and sold South."

"And was I right?"

"No, ma'am. We didn't cross Missouri. We decided to take a boat instead, but it put in at Charleston, and we went ashore—"

"And got drunk," Spartacus supplies eagerly.

"And perhaps had a drink or two beyond what we should have,"

Prosser continues. "And while we were walking back to the docks, wham! Something hit me on the head and something hit Toussaint, and the next thing we knew, we were chopping cotton on the plantation of Mr. Horace Labrie for one pair of pants a year, and a peck of cornmeal, a pinch of salt, and three dried fish a week, and those fish stunk to high heaven."

"But you were free men!" Carrie says. "Surely you had your papers on you!"

"Oh, we had our papers on us all right," Prosser says, running his finger over the scald mark on his cheek. "But when we tried to show them to our kidnappers, they weren't impressed. In retrospect, I suspect they could not read. In any event, they didn't seem to have a firm grasp on the finer points of the laws governing free men of color."

"They were drunken barbarians," says Toussaint, "with the manners of hogs."

"Hogs or not, they had you," Mrs. Newberry says, "and if it weren't for me, you'd still be chopping that cotton and eating those nasty fish."

Carrie turns to her, amazed. "You helped them escape?"

Mrs. Newberry sighs. "Fools or not, they were my baby boys, so what choice did I have? Not all Southerners are in favor of slavery. Some are abolitionists, although they have to tread mighty softly. I contacted some Quaker friends in Charleston. They told me rumor had it that a planter named Labrie had just bought two black men who'd been kidnapped off a boat headed for the Panama crossing. Labrie wasn't satisfied with his purchase. He complained his new slaves were 'overeducated' and didn't know their place. He said they were so 'uppity' they quoted Shakespeare at the drop of a hat. When I heard that, I knew I'd found my boys.

"I arranged for a rescue. I would have gone myself if I could have, but given their particular situation, I was more likely to end up chopping cotton next to them than setting them free if I did. In short, someone else picked their locks—I'm not naming any names here—nailed them into crates, drove them down to the Charleston docks in the dead of night, and loaded them on a clipper headed for Boston."

"They escaped on the Underground Railroad?" Carrie whispers. Mrs. Newberry nods.

"Are you a conductor?"

"Yes." She moves closer to Carrie. Putting her lips to Carrie's ear, she says: "You might as well know it all, Miss Vinton, since it won't be a secret in this party much longer. My boys and I are headed to Osawatomie Creek to establish a station for slaves fleeing from Missouri. Reverend Adair and his wife will soon settle there, too. The Adairs and Newberrys worked together in Michigan running slaves over the border to Canada, and in Ohio before that we helped fugitives from Kentucky move farther north. I've been South five times, usually accompanied by Mrs. Hulett, who pretends to be my mistress."

"You're very brave."

"Brave, am I? Every time I go into a slave state, I'm scared witless. Helping slaves escape is a hanging offense for a white man. Can you imagine what they'd do to a black woman? Mrs. Hulett's sixty-three and white, but I don't doubt that they'd shoot her and throw her in some swamp if they discovered she was helping me."

She sits back and glares at Prosser and Toussaint. "You show me a man so brave he doesn't take account of human meanness, and I'll show you a fool. Am I right, boys?"

"Yes, Mama," they say.

Carrie wonders if she should ask Mrs. Newberry about William. Mrs. Newberry has just come from Michigan, which means she's unlikely to know anyone living in Lawrence, but she's an Underground Railroad conductor. She might have heard something. *If I do ask her,* Carrie thinks, *I need to wait until we're alone. Given that the slavers are offering a hundred-and-fifty-dollar reward for information about William, I'm probably going to have a lot of explaining to do before she'll trust me.*

At noon the wagons stop beside a creek. White linen tablecloths appear accompanied by elegant wicker picnic baskets. Some of the ladies carry chairs out of the wagons and arrange them in a circle. Jugs of lemonade and unfermented cider are passed around, and the liquids are poured into china teacups temporarily removed from the straw that protects them from breaking. A tall, nearsighted lady from Concord produces a small travel harp and plucks it as the men retreat to the shade of the wagons to smoke, the children play hide-and-seek, and the female emigrants wander arm in arm along the creek exclaiming over the clarity of the water and the size of the fish.

"Civilization has come to the prairies," Carrie says to Mrs. Newberry. She is biding her time. Making small talk. They are still not out of earshot of Prosser's and Toussaint's wives and children, and it appears they are not likely to be any time soon.

Mrs. Newberry contemplates the settlers for a moment and shrugs. "They remind me of a flock of chickens waiting for the axe. I just hope they can shoot straight."

"Don't underestimate them. Some are veterans of the Mexican War."

"From here they look more like preachers. They're wearing coats, ties, and stovepipe hats."

"You can fight in a stovepipe hat just as easily as in a plainsman's cap. Take Dr. Robinson for example, the man who picked out the site where Lawrence now stands. I've been told he also looks like a preacher, but he held off pro-slavers at gunpoint the very day Lawrence was founded. The newspapers say his motto is 'suffer and grow strong.'"

Mrs. Newberry laughs. "Grim, but fitting. Thank you, Miss Vinton. You've relieved me of considerable anxiety.

They chat for a while longer. Then Carrie goes back to the wagon and retrieves her sketchbook and a small spade. Grabbing an apple and a hunk of cheese from the lunch that has been spread out for the travelers beneath a large oak, she walks through the forest, up a limestone bank, over the lip of the wash, and out onto the prairie. Here the grasses tower over her, seven feet high or more, their stems purple and red with hints of green. She cannot see more than a few feet in front of her, and as the wind blows the grasses bend and brush against her arms and cheeks as lightly as the tips of birds' wings.

Making herself a nest of sorts, she sits down and watches a monarch butterfly drift from one purple thistle to another. Above her, a stand of sunflowers forms a golden ring. A meadowlark calls and is answered by another, and when she digs her fingers into the earth, she finds it so matted with roots it feels as if it's been woven into a carpet.

Pulling out her sketchbook, she stands up again and draws a stem of bluestem grass, known to botanists as *Andropogon gerardii*. Bluestem is not a rare plant. It grows from Massachusetts to Missouri, but here it grows more luxuriantly than she has ever seen it grow: nine feet tall, with three dense flower clusters at the top that look like a turkey's foot.

When she finishes sketching, she picks up the spade, kneels down, and starts to dig up the roots so she can send the entire specimen back to Professor Gray at Harvard. A quarter of an hour later, she is three feet down and still digging. Later she discovers that the roots of a single clump of Kansas bluestem can be more than fifteen feet long.

She digs for a while longer, and then gives up, chops off the roots, and stares at the result. How is she going to dry and press a plant this big? She will need a piece of mounting paper as long as a roll of wallpaper. And who would have wallpaper in the middle of the wilderness? Why the same people who have harps, crystal glasses, good china, and linen tablecloths.

Making her way back to the wagons, she buys a roll of wallpaper from Mrs. Arthur Crane of Cambridge, Massachusetts. The paper that was destined for the walls of Mrs. Crane's cabin is decorated with large pink roses, and as Carrie breaks the stem of the grass into a zigzag pattern and folds it into the paper so it will unfold like an accordion, she hopes Professor Gray will be amused. She decides she will press the plant by putting it between two boards and sitting on it.

Lunch over, the wagons move on across the prairie, through the grasses, which form a high wall on either side of the trail. Overhead, hawks circle. Once they come upon a buffalo standing in the middle of the road chewing its cud. When the teamsters yell at it and crack their whips, the great beast lumbers off slowly, leaving a space in the grass a buffalo-width wide. Carrie has not expected buffalo to be so big. This one looked powerful enough to tip over their wagon.

In the late afternoon, they pass two graves set side by side, marked with marble stones. Carrie is surprised to see tombstones in so remote a place, but the teamster driving their wagon tells her that some emigrants to California carry their own grave markers with them.

"Farther west, the trail is lined with graves," he says. "Children and women, mostly, but a good scattering of men, too. And such stuff as you wouldn't believe: barrels, ploughs, pianos, trunks full of fancy suits and ball dresses, clocks, carpets, perambulators, tin bathtubs, fiddles, whole sets of china, more books than a fellah could read in a lifetime. There ain't a thing known to man that ain't scattered along the gold routes. Folks just give up and give out. Cholera takes 'em, or the oxen die, or they just cain't stand it no more, so they lighten up the wagon, throw things out. They starve, too. Crazy thing to starve when there's buffalo to be had, but starve they do. And freeze and die of the heat. Not all as sets out for California gets there."

This is a sobering thought, and as the graves disappear into the tall grass, Carrie finds herself wondering how many of her fellow passengers will be alive six months from now.

"Winter," the teamster continues, "now that's the worst. Blizzards come howling down from the north and the frost gets so thick you could use it as window glass. Take a breath and the inside of yer nose freezes. Go out to the necessary, and you can't find your way back. Many a man's frozen to death less than a hundred yards from his own cabin. Last time I was in Lawrence, they was still livin' in tents. I don't mean teepees like the Indians live in. Teepees'll stand up to the wind. I mean little canvas tents not fit for hogs." He pauses. "Say miss, I ain't scaring you, am I?"

"No, I've seen worse," Carrie tells him, but secretly she wonders if she has.

Chapter Eighteen

As Carrie walks beside the wagon, the night smell of the prairie rises up around her, sweet and dry, perfumed with the scent of grass and flowers. To her right, the oxen plod along with a muffled clopping sound that reminds her of coconut shells being softly clapped together. On his perch, the teamster is asleep and snoring. In the grass, crickets hum and fireflies give off bursts of light. Everything else is lost in the silence of wilderness, sleep, or exhaustion.

At noon it was over one hundred degrees, so they are taking advantage of what relief night has brought to push on toward Lawrence. To amuse herself, Carrie is silently reciting the names of the wildflowers she has identified so far. *Clover, blue-eyed grass, mullein, milkweed, black-eyed Susan, oxalis, ironweed, asters of all kinds, lespedeza, goldenrod, poppy, sunflower, coreopsis coneflower...*

She comes to the end of the list and goes back to the beginning, turning the names into a chant that moves in time to her footsteps. Most of the plants are not in bloom this time of year, so she has had to identify them by their leaves. This has not been particularly difficult. They all grow in Indiana and Kentucky as well as in Kansas, so their names have come back to her like a foreign language she has not spoken since childhood.

Clover, blue-eyed grass, mullein, milkweed—

Waking up with a start, the teamster jerks on the reins to restrain the oxen who have suddenly taken it into their heads to gallop, or at least to do what an ox might consider a gallop, although it strikes Carrie as more of a disorganized lumbering.

"Whoa!" he yells. All the oxen in the train are now hurrying forward as if wolves are at their heels. Carrie runs to catch up and arrives just in time to see the teamster jerk the beasts back to a slow walk. Whitehorn snorts and Brock looks sideways at Carrie as if hoping she'll intervene.

"What's gotten into them?" she asks.

"Trout's," the teamster says as he slips his whip back in the whip holder. "I reckon they're hungry."

"The oxen eat trout?"

The teamster guffaws and spits a mouthful of tobacco juice between the traces. "No, miss. Oxen don't eat nothin' but hay and corn and such, but there's a place up ahead run by a Mr. Everett Trout. Trout has what some calls a travelers' hotel, although I'd call it more of a saloon. Not that Trout himself touches a drop of whiskey. The man's as sober as a Methodist preacher. Farms about a hundred acres of corn, has a store where he sells kegs of nails and salt and calico and such, buys skins and hides if they're in good condition. Everyone who travels the California Road has got to pass by Trout's Hotel. Why, it's a famous landmark."

"So if you were looking for someone who'd emigrated to the Kansas Territory, it's likely Mr. Trout might have heard of him?"

The teamster nods and spits another mouthful of tobacco juice between the traces. "I reckon that would be a good bet. Like I said, if you take the California Road, you purty much got to stop at Trout's. He's even hired hisself a Yankee widow lady to do the cooking. The woman makes biscuits so light you got to hold 'em down to butter 'em, but the oxen don't care none about cookin', Yankee or Southern. All they want is to git unyoked and shove their muzzles in a pile of hay. They ain't like horses. Your horse eats slow, but your ox is a gobbler and a glutton. These know we're gittin' close to Trout's place, so they've decided to run for it."

Sure enough, not more than fifteen minutes later they see a large, two-story wooden building. In this treeless land, it stands out like a lighthouse, but on the prairie things are much farther away than they seem, so it takes another quarter of an hour before they pull up in front. As the teamsters unhitch the oxen, Carrie and the others go inside where they are welcomed by Mr. Trout, a tall, lean man with a weathered face who wears a black hat with an unusually broad brim, a wool jacket, and elaborately tooled boots with pointed toes. In his belt he has thrust a large knife and two Colt revolvers. For a moment he stares at them without speaking. Apparently he decides they are no threat, because he takes his hands off his guns and says: "Welcome to Trout's folks. Make yourselves at home."

Gesturing in a way that indicates that there is luxury to be found at every turn, he sits down on a rush-bottomed chair, pulls out a small cigar and a match, strikes the match with his thumbnail, and commences to smoke. Carrie looks where he has pointed and sees she is standing in a single large room with loosely boarded walls. A long table runs down the center. Everything is dimly lit with tallow candles. Beneath her feet she can feel a soft planked floor that gives as she steps on it.

"Where do we sleep?" one of the men in Carrie's party asks.

Mr. Trout exhales a stream of smoke and thinks this over. "Everybody sleeps upstairs."

"Separate rooms?"

"No, sir, just one big one. Ladies and children got a curtain for decency."

"Do you have actual beds, Mr. Trout?"

"One or two."

To Carrie's surprise, none of the abolitionists complain about these accommodations. Retrieving blankets and pillows from the wagons, they climb a steep flight of stairs and settle in for the night: women on one side of the curtain, men on the other. There are two beds in the women's section. Mrs. Hulett gets one; Mrs. Crane the other. Everyone else sleeps on the floor. All in all, Carrie thinks, Mr. Trout's hotel is very much like a hotel in the Amazon minus the hammocks.

It is still punishingly hot. Unable to sleep, she goes back downstairs hoping to find Mr. Trout alone so she can draw him aside and ask him about William, but once again privacy is in short supply. As she steps out on the porch, she hears Mrs. Newberry and Mrs. Crane's voices. They, too, have come downstairs to get out of the heat.

"Mrs. Newberry and I were just about to walk out to look at the stars," Mrs. Crane says. "Do come with us, Miss Vinton." Linking her arm in Carrie's, Mrs. Crane draws her down the steps and they walk away from the hotel, following a trail that leads toward the creek. When they stop to look up, Carrie sees the Milky Way dividing the night sky in a wide, glittering band.

"I've never seen the stars so brilliant," Mrs. Crane says. "I can see my own shadow by the light of them."

"They're the glory of God," Mrs. Newberry says. They fall silent. After a while, Mrs. Newberry speaks again. "Trout saw us," she says. "And he didn't see us."

"I don't take your meaning," says Mrs. Crane.

"He saw the color of my skin and that of my sons and their wives and children, and he didn't say a word."

"What would he say, Mrs. Newberry?"

"Well, he could have said: 'Sleep outside with the stock,' or 'Get out of this hotel before I shoot you.' There are numerous possibilities, Mrs. Crane, but Mr. Trout pursued none of them." Mrs. Newberry looks up at the stars and then stares across the open prairie. "I think I'm going to like Kansas if the pro-slavers don't get hold of me."

They fall silent again. Everything is so still it seems to be encased in black glass. After a while, Mrs. Crane clears her throat. "I regret to move from the sublime to the mundane, but I need to pay a visit to the necessary. What if I encounter a bear?"

"I doubt you will be eaten by a bear in the necessary," Mrs. Newberry says, "but on the off chance one has decided to hibernate there, I will accompany you."

Mrs. Crane and Mrs. Newberry walk off, leaving Carrie alone to stare at the stars. She picks out Pegasus and Cassiopeia before she hears the sound of men's voices. Somewhere, not far off, a horse whinnies.

"Excuse me, miss."

Startled, she turns around and almost collides with Mr. Trout, who has come up silently behind her. "Hiram says you're lookin' fer someone. He thought it might be yer brother or maybe yer father or perhaps some fellah who done run off and left you."

"Hiram?"

"The teamster who drove yer wagon. Good man, but he has a hard time keepin' his tongue in his head. Given to imagin' things. A romantic, Hiram is. Reads them Penny Dreadfuls the way other men drink. If you ain't lookin' fer no one, just say the word, and I'll skedaddle."

"No, Mr. Trout. Please don't go. Hiram was right. I am looking for someone. His name's William Saylor. He's about six feet tall, black eyes, brown hair."

"You lookin' to claim the reward the bushwhackers are offerin' for him?"

"No, I need to find him for another reason."

"And what egzactly would that be?"

"You want a blunt answer or a ladylike one?"

Trout takes a cigar out of his shirt pocket, lights it, and inhales. "Try the blunt one out on me."

"I've run away from my husband."

"That don't surprise me none." Trout inhales again, and the tip of his cigar glows in the darkness. "Womenfolk are in short supply in these parts. There's many a wife who runs off from the old and finds the new. So is this fellah you're lookin' for the husband you done run from or the one yer runnin' to?"

"The one I'm running to."

"I don't mean to insult you. Yer a fine-lookin' woman, but what makes you think he wants you to find him?"

"We were engaged to be married."

"Do tell. But I take it you ain't now, you being a runaway wife and all. So let me ask you again, what makes you think this fellah wants you trackin' him down, particularly given there's a price on his head?"

"He does. I'm sure of it."

"How long's it been since you seen him?"

"Over a year."

"Lot can happen in a year. Man with a price on his head can just disappear. Get himself a new name, cross the border into Mexico, court himself a señorita, get married, and start a new life. But that hundred-and-fifty-dollar reward makes him worth lookin' for, don't it?"

Carrie starts to speak, but Trout holds up his hand. "Whoa, there. Before you start tellin' me how you wouldn't take money for turnin' him in if you wuz starvin', I got to know yer tellin' me the truth. Let's start with yer name."

"Carolyn Vinton. Or rather that was my name before I married.

It's Carolyn Vinton Presgrove now. Mr. Trout, if you know any-thing about William, please . . ."

"You an abolitionist or a slaver?"

"Abolitionist."

"Well that makes sense. Yer travelin' with a whole passel of 'em. What if I was to tell you that I was a dyed-in-the-wool slaver, would that change yer tune?"

"No."

"I'm likin' you better already. I ain't no slaver." Trout taps the ash off his cigar and stares at her. "But I still ain't sure about you, so let's jest suppose sumpthin. Let's suppose some fellah once came into my place, ordered hisself up one drink too many, and ended up tell-ing me a story about a girl he'd been engaged to who'd died tragi-cally in a furrin land. Now where do you reckon that poor girl might have passed away?"

"Rio de Janeiro."

"Nope."

"Brazil."

"Well, well. I'm not sayin' that's the right answer, but I'm not sayin' it's not neither. Now let's suppose this same fellah, in his cups and thus unreliable, claimed that besides bein' sweet and kind-hearted, his greatly mourned beloved weren't like other girls due to the fact that she could shoot a gun better than Kit Carson, Daniel Boone, and Davy Crockett combined. What would you say to that?"

"I'd say William greatly exaggerated my talents."

"So you can't shoot a gun?"

"I didn't say that. I'm a good shot."

"But how good? That's the question, ain't it? You got the name, but I still ain't sure you got the game." Trout drops his cigar, grinds it out with the toe of his boot, and lights himself another.

"I tell you what, you show me you can do some fancy sharp-shootin', and if I know anything about William Saylor—and I still ain't sayin' I do—I might tell it to you. If it were day, I could just toss a dollar in the air and you could try to plug it, or I could set you to shooting at a playing card. I once knew a feller who could drill out the eye of a one-eyed jack from ninety paces. But it bein' night, I reckon we're gonna have to do with snuffing candles. So if you'll jest excuse me a minute—"

"Wait," Carrie says. "You don't have to go get a candle. I can shoot at your cigar."

"Whoa, Nellie!" Trout jerks his cigar out of his mouth and backs away from her so fast he nearly trips. "I don't fancy an encounter with an armed woman. Last time I made that mistake, I had to spend most of a summer eating my grub off the mantelpiece. Of course, the circumstances was different. The lady in question was riled because I was not being properly forthcomin' on the subject of marriage and— are you armed, miss? Do you have a gun concealed about you some-wheres? One of them little ladylike derringers?"

"No. I was going to ask to borrow one of your revolvers. I wasn't proposing to shoot your cigar out of your mouth, Mr. Trout. I thought you might toss it up in the air and let me try to hit it."

Trout stares at her for a minute, then removes one of his revolvers from its holster and hands it to her grip first. "On the count of three," he says, putting his cigar back between his lips. He draws on it until the end glows. "One, two, three!"

Up goes the cigar into the air. Carrie aims, pulls the trigger, and blows it to pieces.

For a few seconds Trout stares at the place where the cigar met its fate. Then he grins and tips his hat. "Miz Carolyn Vinton," he says, "it's a pleasure to meet up with you. For the past month, William Saylor has been livin' in Lawrence. I reckon if you saw that wanted poster, you know what he's been doin'. Fact is, he's doin' it again tonight. We expected him to pass through here earlier with his 'freight,' but he appears to have been delayed. On the other hand, he could have already arrived. While you was busy blowin' my cigar to bits, I heard the sound of riders comin' down the California Road. Of course there's a big wagon train making up in Independence, so it might just be some fellahs headed over there to—"

Carrie doesn't wait for him to finish. Thrusting his revolver into his hand, she turns and begins to run back toward the hotel. When she comes out into the open, she sees that while she and Trout have been talking, four men on horseback have arrived and are now preparing to leave.

"Stop!" she yells. "Wait!"

The men rein in their horses and look toward her. She examines their faces eagerly, but they're all strangers.

"Beggin' your pardon, ma'am," one of them says. "Is there somethin' amiss?"

"No. I'm sorry. I thought you were someone else."

The one who appears to be their leader tips his hat. "Well then," he says, "we bid you good night."

Disappointed, she sits down on the front steps and watches the men ride off. Somewhere in the distance she hears an owl hoot.

"Excuse me, ma'am," a voice behind her says, "could you move over a bit? We need to pass by."

She realizes she is blocking the steps. Sliding sideways, she watches two pairs of boots tramp past her. As the men walk away, she stares at their backs. One is short and heavyset; the other tall and lanky. There is something familiar about the way the taller man walks. She stands up.

"William?" she says.

When he hears her voice, he turns around and sees a woman standing on the hotel steps wearing a white dress with a

muddy hem. The lantern above her is swaying and shadows are passing over her face like swift, gray birds. Her hair is wound around her
head in a braid, but small strands are escaping, shining in the lamplight like a halo. The woman looks so much like Carrie that for an
instant he manages to convince himself that it's really her standing
there. But of course it can't be.

Since she died, he's dreamed of her repeatedly, run toward her
and watched her dissolve, reached for her and seen his hand pass
through her body. He's even touched her hair, but when he buried
his face in it, it gave off no scent. That's how he knew for certain he
was dreaming. When the dead visit you in dreams, they never come
back whole.

Awake, he has seen her at least two dozen times in the faces of
women who looked almost nothing like her and heard her voice in
places where there was nothing to hear but wind. A few days before
he left for Kansas, he even followed a strange woman because she
was swinging her parasol the way Carrie always did when she was
feeling happy. He knew the woman wasn't Carrie; but from the
back, he was able to imagine she was. When the woman turned into
her own gate and two small children ran out to greet her, he felt
ashamed of himself.

Try to forget her, Charlie Howard had advised. Up at Fort Leavenworth, before he came down to settle in abolitionist Lawrence, the
advice had been cruder and more practical. *Buy yourself a whore,
Saylor. Or if you're too much a prig for that, go back east and court
yourself a wife.* But he doesn't want a wife or a whore. He wants
Carrie so much that sometimes he thinks he's not quite sane.

"William," the woman on the porch says again. He can't risk
responding to his name, not here, not under the circumstances. He
needs to turn around and walk away from her, but—

Suddenly, she's running down the steps, coming toward him with
her arms outstretched, repeating his name, and as the lantern light

catches her face, he sees— No. Impossible! Carrie's face, Carrie's eyes, Carrie's hair. Carrie taking him in her arms, Carrie pulling him to her and kissing him, Carrie solid and alive. The familiar scent of her skin and hair, a smudge of dirt on her cheek, her body warm against his.

"My God!" he cries, "you're real!" And all at once, she's laughing and crying and kissing him again and telling him that, yes, she's real, that she didn't die, and his head is spinning and his knees are buckling; and before he knows it, he's sitting on the hotel steps with his head between his knees the way they taught him to do in medical school; and when he lifts his head and opens his eyes, Carrie, who he loves more than anything in this life or the next, is still there: laughing and crying and very much alive.

Chapter Nineteen

The wind has risen and died, risen again and died again; and near Trout's Hotel, in the tall grass under a buffalo robe, Carrie and William are sleeping side by side.

The prairie that surrounds them seems peaceful, but the calm is deceptive. Kansas is about to explode into a violence that will shock the world. In Chicago and Albany, abolitionists are holding mass rallies urging free-soilers to arm themselves, go to Kansas, and vote in the plebiscite. In Missouri, a group that calls itself the Platte County Self-Defensive Association has recruited five hundred men to repel the coming army of "Yankee slave-stealers," and the slave owners who grow the hemp that binds up bales of Southern cotton are wearing hangmen's nooses in their lapels.

In Salt Creek, a man making a speech in favor of a free Kansas has been attacked and stabbed through the lung; while in Atchison, Senator David Atchison—after whom the town is named—has recently given a speech advising Missourians to hang "negro thieves and abolitionists without judge or jury." But in the bluestem grass near Trout's Hotel, the coming war is still only a smudge on the horizon.

Carrie stirs in her sleep and her eyes flutter. She's dreaming of Brazil. In her dream, the tall trees of the jungle are dancing around the mud huts of the *quilombo*, and Mae Seja is drinking the black drink, calling for the drummers to drum, and letting the *Axé* flow through her again.

As the drummers beat out the sacred rhythms and the men and women of the *quilombo* rise to their feet and begin the whirling dance of the *orixás*, Carrie dreams of Africa and Brazil mixed in one cauldron, of human beings transformed into gods. Zé becomes Changó, who calls down thunder. Ynaie becomes Yemaja, Great Mother and protector of children.

The humans-turned-gods surround Mae Seja and place their hands on her. At their touch, Mae Seja's spirit breaks away from her body and rises over the jungle like smoke. Down below, the humans-turned-gods clap their hands and send her from Brazil to the Great Plains of the United States.

Mae Seja hovers over Carrie. *You've found your man,* menina, she whispers. *Love him well.* Taking a small gourd out of her apron pocket, she pours seven drops of a powerful love potion on Carrie's lips and seven on William's. *You'll love each other forever. You'll never be parted.*

The rose-colored liquid smells of pineapple, mango, *cupuaçu*, *umbú,* papaya, açai, and oranges. Kissing Carrie and William, Mae Seja blesses them and sends her spirit back to Brazil. As she leaves, Carrie's dream ends, and a great silence envelops everything. Clouds stream out of the west, cushioning the sky. Voles, mice, and shrews return to their dens. Moths close their wings. Owls land in trees so silently not a leaf stirs. In the creek, the fish sleep motionless as stones.

An hour passes. At last a cock crows, and Carrie wakes to the sound. She has had a beautiful dream, which she cannot remember. She yawns and curls closer to William, feeling the warmth of his body. The prairie is so quiet, she can hear every breath he takes.

They have made love three times since they found each other: once with the hungry passion of long separation; once slowly; and finally, just before moonrise, tenderly, mouth to mouth and breast to breast in the waxing light. Each time she read his body with her fingertips, she found it leaner and more muscular than she remembered. His right arm is creased by a long scar that she suspects comes from a bullet wound. On his leg is the unmistakable V of a snakebite.

She has swept her hair over his chest and between his thighs and made love to him with the first real, uninhibited passion she's felt since they lay together in her bed on the Ladeira da Glória behind closed shutters as church bells tolled and people fled in panic from the plague. He has clasped her to him, and together they have traveled to a place where words weren't necessary. While they were making love, she forgot everything, but now, as she lies beside him listening to him breathe, she wonders if he's noticed that her waist is thicker, her belly fuller, her breasts rounder than they were in Rio. She has so many things to tell him, things she should have said before they lay down together; but the news she brings is bad, and there's so much of it. How do you tell the man you love that you're with child by his stepbrother? How do you bring the news of a lost daughter to someone who never knew he was a father?

William stirs, reaches toward her, and for a while they lie there quietly, holding each other. "My love," she says. She knows she needs to start telling him what's happened since they last met, but she can't bring herself to. Maybe it would be easier if she started with the present and worked backwards.

"Where were you going when I stopped you?" she asks.

William wraps a curl of her hair around his finger and plays with it. "Missouri," he says.

She sits up abruptly. The buffalo robe falls off her shoulders. Shivering, she draws it back up around her. "Missouri! Do you know that in Westport the slavers are offering a hundred-and-fifty-dollar reward for you, dead or alive?"

"I know."

"They say you're wanted for armed robbery. I can only think of one thing you'd steal—"

He puts his finger over her lips. "Don't say it, Carrie. Not even here. Prairie grass is a good place to hide if you want to eavesdrop."

"I'm afraid for you."

"I'm afraid for myself. I wasn't until a few hours ago. Without you, I couldn't feel much of anything. But now—" He sits up. "It's complicated. A lot of people depend on me. I'm not all that important, but I'm one link in a chain that can't be broken. I can't stop doing what I'm doing."

"I wouldn't want you to." She has something else to say, and to say it, she needs to see his eyes. "Come closer." He comes closer. Leaning forward, she puts her hands on his shoulders and looks into his face. "I need to tell you something. I should have told you last night, but I couldn't bear to. Things have happened that you need to know about."

"Bad things?"

"Very bad."

"Are you ill?"

"No, I'm married." He flinches and starts to speak, but she silences him with a gesture. "Please, let me go on before you say anything or I'll never be able to finish. I'm married to your stepbrother, Deacon Presgrove. I inherited a lot of money from Papa, but I don't have it any longer. Deacon was—is—a fortune hunter. He wrote my obituary and had it published so you'd have no reason to return to Brazil. He told me you were dead, but even so, I never would have married him except—"

The words stick in her throat. She swallows and tries again, but she can't even whisper them. It seems as if no time has passed since she watched the tiny bundle that contained Willa sink into the sea. She remembers the masts creaking in the wind, the waves pounding the hull, the wake spreading out behind *The Frances Scott* as she watched all trace of her daughter disappear. Tears burn behind her eyes, but she can't cry. Turning away, she looks off across the empty prairie.

"Come here," William says. He pulls her onto his lap and wraps the buffalo robe around her. "Let me hold you while you tell me the rest of it."

She nods, struggles to speak, and again fails. At last she puts her lips to his ear. "You and I had a child. A daughter."

He starts and draws her closer. "Dear God," he says.

"She was born too early, and she died. Her name was Willa. She was beautiful. Small and perfect. She looked like both of us. I wrapped her"—her voice breaks—"in that shawl you were going to give me as a wedding present and buried her at sea. I know you're going to blame yourself for not being with me, but it's not your fault. Deacon told you I was dead."

William makes a strange sound. She looks up and sees he's crying. "I'm going back East and shoot the son of a bitch," he says.

"No, you aren't. If you go to Washington, Bennett Presgrove will see you're arrested before you can get anywhere near Deacon. Shooting him isn't worth getting hung for. It won't bring back our child. If all this was anyone's fault, it was mine. I was a fool to marry him, but I did it of my own free will, and I have no one to blame but myself. Can you ever forgive me?"

"You weren't a fool. You were a woman with child left alone to fend for herself. As for forgiving you—hell and damnation, Carrie Vinton! There's nothing to forgive! Here, hold up your face and let me kiss you. I won't shoot Deacon, but only because you're asking me not to, and if you ever change your mind, let me know."

He kisses her, and they sit in silence as the sun rises, the tall grass takes on color, and the first shadows of morning appear, long, cool, and thin as straws. Somewhere in the direction of Mr. Trout's hotel another cock crows.

"They'll be hitching up the teams soon," Carrie says. Rising to their feet, they put on their clothes. William helps her with her laces, bends down and slips on her shoes, stands and kisses her again.

"I have to stay at Trout's for a few days. Stay with me. I'm meeting some men here, and I'm not sure when they'll arrive. When they show up, I'm going to ride into Missouri with them. I'll only be gone a day and a half at most, and then I'll come back and get you, and we can travel to Lawrence together. Don't worry about your things. You can send them on ahead, and they'll be there waiting for us when we arrive."

Carrie turns away from him and stares at the row of trees that borders the creek. She has more bad news to deliver. It's not as bad as the rest, in some ways you might even call it good, but why can't things ever be simple? Why can't she and William just pick up where they left off?

"What's wrong? Don't you want to stay with me?"

"More than anything, but before we make any plans, there's something else I have to tell you." She pauses, tries to find the right words, and decides there aren't any. "I'm carrying Deacon's child."

"I know."

She stares at him in astonishment. "You know? How?"

"I'd have to be a fool to hold you in my arms and not know."

"Deacon certainly managed to." An expression of pain crosses

his face, and she realizes he doesn't like the image she just con-
jured up.

"Did you tell him?"

"No, but if he finds out, he may come after me and try to take
the child away. I'm not going to let him do that. He's not fit to be
my child's father."

"Then let me be." William pulls her to him, and stands for a moment looking at her. Then he smiles. "Damn it, I've never been good
at this and I'm not improving with practice. I'm trying to find the
right words to ask you to marry me. Like I said that first time when
I proposed in Rio, I've loved you since I was eleven, and I'll never
love anyone else. Kansas is a hard place for women and children. I
can protect you and the baby. If Deacon comes to the Territory,
maybe I'll get a chance to shoot him with a clear conscience. Meanwhile, I'll start practicing medicine again. A doctor can always make
a decent living, even one who insists on scrubbing his patients with
soap and water. There'll always be food on our table and love in our
home, and we'll be happy, I promise."

"I can't—"

"Can't marry me? I know that. I don't mean legally. I mean in the
sight of God. What do we care about some piece of paper stuffed in
a musty Brazilian archive? We've been married for three years in the
only way that counts, so kneel down right here with me and tell
me again you'll be my wife. Say 'yes' just like you did in Rio. Promise me we'll stay together until death parts us. Will you do that?"

"What if I say no?"

"Well then, I guess I could take to drink, but I discovered a while
ago that I don't have the head for it. But you aren't going to say no
are you?"

"Are you absolutely sure? With the baby being—"

"Being mine," he says. "Being mine from the moment he's born as much as if he were my own blood. Girl or boy. Part of you, part of me. Forever. So will you marry me, Carrie Vinton?"

"Yes," Carrie says. She sinks to her knees, and William sinks down beside her. Pulling out his pocket knife, he cuts a blade of grass and twists it into a ring, and together, in love and in the sight of the gods, African, Brazilian, and Christian, they marry each other in a ceremony witnessed only by the tall grass and the sky.

Chapter Twenty

Missouri, September 1854

A sod hut dug into a hillside, front and side walls made of bricks laid in double rows. No windows; one door, barred from the outside. To the right of the hut, a comfortable-looking, two-story house, porch empty, windows dark, chimney producing only the thin smoke of a banked fire. To the left, a large field of dry corn that hisses every time the wind sweeps through the stalks.

This is definitely the Hawkins' place. Zachariah Amandson described it right down to the last detail as he sat in Trout's Hotel drinking lemonade, whispering to William, and looking up nervously every once in a while to make sure he wasn't being overheard.

Amandson is a free black who is able to pass for white. This allows him to travel through Missouri unchallenged. For over two years, he has had a small business that consists of mending pots and pans and gluing broken china back together. One of the most important links in the local Underground Railroad, he rides from farm to farm, noting which farmers own slaves and where those slaves are kept when their masters are asleep. When the conditions are right, he draws the slaves aside, speaks to them, tells them who he is, and offers to help them escape.

When people think of the Underground Railroad, they usually assume it's being run by Quakers, New England abolitionists, free-thinkers, and the like; but free blacks and former slaves are the heart and soul of the railroad. Some five hundred former slaves travel to the South each year to bring out those still in bondage. Without men like Amandson, William and his companions would be going in blind tonight.

Slinging the bag of drugged meat over his shoulder, William walks into the corn, grateful for the rustling that covers the sound of his footsteps. The wind is blowing away from him, which is fortunate because Amandson warned that Hawkins keeps four of the most vicious dogs in Missouri. They're part wolf, raised to attack and kill. The last slave who tried to escape from this place had his throat torn out.

Sure enough, the moment William steps out of the corn, the dogs charge toward him, barking like the hounds of hell. Tearing open the mouth of the bag, he throws them the meat, praying they'll stop to gobble it down. Then he turns and runs for the creek. Dashing into the water, he keeps on running. Hawkins's dogs aren't blood-hounds, they're probably going to be too busy with the meat to bother coming after him, and if they do, the water should wash away his scent, but there's always a chance they'll decide to hunt him down.

When he figures he's run far enough, he grabs an overhanging limb, pulls himself up into a tree, and sits there, gasping for breath. His heart is beating so fast he can feel it pounding against his ribs, his stomach is churning, and the inside of his mouth is dry. He's ridden into Missouri on four previous occasions and never felt so much as a prickle of fear. It's an odd sensation, like coming back to life, and it's all due to Carrie.

When he left Brazil, convinced she was dead, he changed. He'd always been a cautious man, but losing her brought out something wild in him that was both useful and extremely dangerous. For the better part of a year, he didn't care if he lived or died. He was willing to take risks other men were reluctant to take—risks perhaps no man with a wife and children to go home to would take. As a result, he's earned a reputation for bravery he doesn't deserve. It wasn't brave to be unable to feel fear. It was a kind of insanity brought on by grief. But now he has something to lose.

Gradually his breathing slows, and his heart begins to beat normally. Looking toward Hawkins's farm, he sees that someone has lighted a lamp in an upstairs bedroom of the main house. A few moments later, a man and a woman walk out onto the front porch. The woman wears a cotton nightgown and holds a lantern. The man, presumably Hawkins, wears long underwear and holds a shotgun.

Hawkins yells something, but William can't make out the words. Maybe he's demanding to know who's out there, maybe he's cursing the dogs for waking him. It's probably a little of both, because suddenly he lifts the shotgun and fires into the corn. Then he calls the dogs to him and gives each a hard kick.

The dogs grovel at his feet and follow him docilely to the sod hut where Hawkins checks the bar on the door to make sure it's still firmly in place. Again he yells. No doubt he's making sure the slaves are inside, but if they reply, their voices don't carry to where William is sitting.

After walking around the place and peering into every corner, Hawkins returns to the house, and he and his wife go back inside. The lantern light traces their progress up the stairs and into the bedroom. For a minute or two the light goes on shining before they blow it out.

After that, there's nothing to do but wait. Climbing down from the tree, William settles on a pile of dry leaves and tries to make himself comfortable. It's a chilly night with a hint of rain in the air. He wishes he knew exactly how long it will take for the opium to do its work, but you never can tell with animals. A veterinarian once told him about being called to a circus to extract a decayed tusk from an elephant. The vet said he had calculated how much opium it would take to sedate a man, and then multiplied by the weight of the elephant. The tusk came out successfully, but the elephant slept for three days. The circus owner had been so upset, he'd challenged the vet to a duel.

William sits for the better part of an hour listening intently. Finally, he rises to his feet and walks back toward the farm. He's out of meat and if Hawkins's dogs are still awake, he's going to be in serious trouble.

Stepping out of the corn, he freezes in place and waits for the barking to begin, but the only sound he hears is the dry stalks rattling behind him. Keeping to the shadows, he makes his way toward the sod hut. Just before he reaches it, he comes on one of the dogs stretched out full-length, fast asleep. It's a nasty-looking beast with a large head and powerful shoulders, but its pelt is a beautiful grayish white that looks silver in the starlight.

Giving the dog a wide berth, William walks up to the door of the hut and draws back the bar. When the door swings open, the slaves are waiting for him. They're taking nothing with them except some thin blankets and the clothes on their backs, most likely because they have nothing else to take.

"By the strength of hand, the Lord brought us out of Egypt," William whispers.

"Out from the house of bondage," one of the slaves replies.

Signals successfully exchanged, they shake hands all around, and William leads them away from Hawkins's farm toward the woods where horses and armed men are waiting to conduct them to Kansas and freedom.

Chapter Twenty-one

Wolf hen William slips in beside her, Carrie rolls toward him. Usually she's the one who has cold hands and feet, but tonight it's her turn to warm him. "Done?" she whispers.

"Yes. Are you all right?"

"Yes." The truth is, not a minute has passed since he rode off when she hasn't wondered if he'll come back alive. Last night, she dreamed the slavers had caught him and hung him, and she couldn't get to him in time to cut him down.

A strange honeymoon, she thinks. *Sleeping outside the hotel for privacy, William disappearing and then coming back as if he hasn't been gone, neither of us asking questions: no "Where have you been?" or "What have you done?"*

She closes her eyes and thinks of the limestone caves they explored when they were children. They'd been forbidden to go anywhere near them, but they'd crawled in anyway with nothing but the stub of a stolen candle to light them back to the entrance. She remembers the bullets they threw into a bonfire, the bear they tracked to its den, the fast current that pulled her under when they were swimming

in the river where they had no business swimming, and how William
had gone in after her and pulled her to safety and called her a fool;
and how afterwards they'd fought for hours over who was the big-
gest fool: her for nearly drowning herself or him for risking his life
to save her. *We're really no different than we've ever been*, she thinks,
and moving closer to him, she falls asleep.

A little before sunrise, she wakes to find the top of the buffalo
robe wet with dew. Giving William a quick kiss, she crawls out and
gets dressed. When she looks toward Trout's Hotel, she sees another
wagon train has arrived during the night. It must have come in late,
because the oxen are still in the corral, and no one is moving about.

William picks up the buffalo robe, gives it a shake, and folds it
over his arm. He is about to bend over to retrieve his guns, when
Carrie puts her hand on his arm. "Listen," she says. "What's that?"

They listen and hear the drumming of hoofbeats. Looking east,
they see a dark smudge on the horizon growing larger by the second.
The smudge divides into five, six—perhaps seven—men on horseback. The riders are whipping their horses, urging them forward
with all possible speed.

"Travelers?"

"Not at this time of day, not at a full gallop. Stay here. Hide in
the grass. Don't come out where they can see you." Throwing down
the buffalo robe, William scoops up his guns and runs toward the
hotel.

"Border ruffians!" he yells.

Carrie has never heard the term, but she instantly understands it
means pro-slavers come over the border from Missouri. Crouching
down, she parts the grass and sees William pounding on the door of
the hotel.

"Trout, wake up! Gentlemen, arm yourselves!"

A few moments later, the riders gallop up in a cloud of dust. One
leaps off his horse and points a pistol at William's head. The man

wears a flannel shirt, broad-brimmed felt hat, tall boots, a fringed buckskin jacket, and buckskin leggings with beadwork up the sides. He's blond with a red beard: Irish or maybe German.

"You slave-stealing, abolitionist sonofabitch!" he yells as he advances on William. "I should shoot you where you stand, but I ain't got time for it. Throw down your guns and surrender the fugitives."

"What fugitives?" William's pistols are pointed at the man's chest. Can one of them shoot the other before getting shot? Carrie scrambles around looking for something to use as a weapon, but all she comes up with is a rock. William should have left her one of his guns. What if they recognize him as the man described in the wanted poster?

"You know damn well what fugitives! We got warrants to repossess three males slaves that go by the names of Bilander, Cush, and Marcellus, all legal property of one Amos Hawkins, and you're concealing them in violation of the Fugitive Slave Act."

"What are their last names?"

"They ain't got no last names, damn it! They're slaves."

"Never heard of them."

"We know you got Hawkins's property," another rider says. "Hand 'em over, or there's gonna be one less abolitionist bastard voting come election time."

"Trout!" a third rider yells, "open your damn door right now or we'll break it down!"

The door of the hotel opens and the barrel of a shotgun emerges. Behind it stands Mr. Trout. "Go back to Missouri, boys," Trout says. "We ain't got no runaway slaves in here, and if you'll look up, you'll see why breakin' down my door is a mighty poor idea."

The raiders look up. At each of the six second-story windows stands a New England abolitionist with a gun. Most wear the long underwear they were sleeping in when awakened, but one has slipped into a suit coat and another has put on a top hat. In the light of day, it's clear Trout's is constructed to serve as a fortress. The windows are narrow with heavy shutters that can be slammed shut, and there must be a hatch somewhere because more armed men stand on the roof.

"Damn yer eyes!" yells the leader of the Missourians. "Y'all brought a whole army out from Massachusetts!"

"We reckon we got a right to defend ourselves," Trout says.

"You treasonous bastards are in violation of the laws of the United States of America!"

"And proud of it," William says. Carrie is afraid this remark is going to get him shot, but the man in the buckskin jacket merely spits a mouthful of tobacco juice on the ground and glares at him and then at Mr. Trout.

"Trout, we know you're harboring them fugitive slaves, but you got us outgunned. You damn well better keep a bucket of water handy, because someday soon we're gonna come back and burn you out." He gestures to the other raiders. "Come on, boys."

They ride off, but apparently they don't go far, because as the teamsters are hitching up the oxen and the emigrants are climbing into the wagons, another smudge appears on the horizon. This one is long and gray with dirty yellow borders, and it brings with it the smell of smoke.

"Prairie fire!" shriek the New England ladies. Gathering up their children, they start to head for the creek, but Mr. Trout stops them.

"No need, ladies. The fools got the wind wrong." And sure enough, the flames that were meant to burn Trout's Hotel sweep by without touching it. Still the fire is an alarming sight. The red, crackling inferno moves faster than a horse can gallop, driving animals out of the grass. Carrie sees soot-covered rabbits running for their lives, deer, a small herd of buffalo.

"Buffalo fur burns right slow," Mr. Trout remarks, "which is why they ain't runnin' full out." He is standing beside Carrie picking his teeth with an ivory toothpick. "This is a pissant fire as fires go. I cleared a firebreak around this place last spring. About all this blaze is gonna do is clear a bigger break, so those Missouri bastards—saving your presence, Miz Vinton—can't try this particular trick again for at least a year."

Marching down a gully, the fire finally puts itself out in the creek, leaving a black swath of burned-out prairie in its wake. *Such a waste*, Carrie thinks, but when she voices this sentiment to Mr. Trout, he grins.

"No use getting' upset about a prairie fire, unless it burns down your house or takes your crops. The Indians light 'em all the time to clear the brush. Makes hunting easier. Of course a big one, well that's another matter. You get in the way of a big fire racin' across the prairie, and you'll go deaf from the roar of it, if you don't choke yourself sick or burn to a crisp first."

"Thank you, Mr. Trout. I find the idea of burning to a crisp very encouraging."

Trout nods and says without a trace of irony: "Yer welcome, ma'am."

Again the wagons prepare to leave, but there is still another surprise in store, for when the fire has burned itself out completely, three figures emerge from the charred grass so covered with mud and soot that for a few seconds it's impossible to tell if they're male or female.

"You Bilander, Cush, and Marcellus?" Trout yells.

"Yes, sir," the tallest of the three yells back.

"Well come on in and wash up."

The last Carrie sees of the three fugitive slaves, they're being handed pans of water and soap by Mr. Trout's Yankee cook.

* * *

"Of course, I already know how they escaped," Carrie says, "not to mention why they chose to sleep out in the open last night instead of bedding down in the hotel where they might be trapped and retaken, but I'll hold my tongue and ask no questions." She is riding beside William on a mule, Trout not having had a horse to rent, and as a result they are moving slowly in the wake of the wagon train.

William flicks her a sideways glance and grins. "You ever hear the term 'jayhawk,' sweetheart?"

"No, I can't say that I have."

"Well, you should learn it because you just married one."

"What's a jayhawk?"

"A mythological bird that sneaks like a jay and pounces like a hawk."

"I take it that the jayhawk is the only bird that can ride a horse, shoot a gun, steal slaves out of Missouri, and vote in a territorial election?"

"The only."

The wind picks up, and the tall sunflowers that line the road begin to sway. The grass rustles as if an invisible army is marching along beside them. The dust from the wagons rises and is tinted by the light of the setting sun. Some of the dust goes into Carrie's mouth and eyes. Some turns as gold as the centers of the sunflowers; some as pale and red as blood.

Carrie laughs and kicks her mule forward toward Lawrence and whatever is coming next.

PART 4

The Siege of Lawrence

William

Lawrence, Kansas, November 1854

You are sleeping on a grass-stuffed pallet under a pile of buffalo robes: your mouth slightly open, your head turned to one side, your hair spread out on the pillow like a golden net. I want to walk over to you, bury my face in your hair, smell the sweetness of it, kiss you awake, and plead with you to take better care of yourself, but I can no more control you than I can control the wind that blows across Kansas tonight like the breath of an angry god.

It's a cold wind that smells of snow. Winter is arriving. I want to keep you warm and safe, but you will have none of it. You're the same wild girl I knew when I was a boy—just as stubborn, just as unpredictable.

You insisted on working side by side with me as we built our house. You lifted boards out of the wagon and nailed them to the studs, cut grass and tied it into bundles so we could thatch the roof, then climbed up on the roof and helped me with the thatching. When the walls were up, you mixed up a paste from flour and water and papered the inside with old copies of The Herald of Freedom *and* The

Kansas Free State, joking that this abolitionist wallpaper would not only keep out the wind but give us something to read on long winter nights.

Even after we bought a stove, you refused to sit in front of it knitting baby clothes. Instead, you cut up one of your dresses and sewed the curtains that hang at our windows, braided a rag rug for our floor, made a broom out of prairie grass, searched out herbs and traded them for buckets and books and butter molds. One day while I was out tending to a patient, you put up shelves for my medical texts. Then you began to study them.

You have a talent for healing. Already you've learned how to set dislocated shoulders, splint broken limbs, and pick buckshot out of human flesh. You are amazing, my love. You never stop working. I admire your energy, yet sometimes I'm afraid it's fueled by fear. You tell me you will not lose this baby as you lost Willa, that you carry the child high, that you are healthy and in love and that our love will protect you. I wish I believed this, but tonight when I look at you, I feel such a grasping in my throat that I can hardly breathe. I have seen too many women die in childbirth to believe anything short of divine grace can protect them, and I am not sure I believe in divine grace.

Do you? I can't tell. You go to church every Sunday and sing the hymns as loudly as anyone, but I think that you mostly do it to defy public opinion. You and I are a scandal. Only Mrs. Crane comes to visit you, and even men occasionally cross to the other side of the street when they see us coming.

Dearest Carrie, I'm afraid for you. Lawrence is an abolitionist town surrounded by slavers who would like to see it burned to the ground. Trouble is coming; it's simply a matter of time. I know that when the raiders attack, you'll insist on putting yourself at risk. I can't forbid you to do this. I can't nail up the windows and doors and imprison you. If I tried, you'd simply escape, and I'd never try.

I've known you too long to underestimate you. You'll always do what you want to do. You always have. But take care of yourself, I beg you. I lost you once. I couldn't bear to lose you again.

Chapter Twenty-two

Savannah, Georgia, November 1854

In early September, a violent hurricane had struck Savannah, wiping out bridges, killing slaves on the barrier islands, and endangering the city. On the day the storm made landfall, the sky became a green-black cauldron, the wind wailed like a demon, roofs blew off the warehouses that lined Factors Walk, and thousands of dollars' worth of cotton was pummeled into a sodden, unsalvageable mess. Now, in early November, the fall storms are over, the temperature is in the high seventies, and in Oglethorpe Square in the parlor of a private home where the Marquis de Lafayette once occupied an upstairs bedroom, Senator Bennett Presgrove is red-faced and sweating from an hour and a half of almost uninterrupted oration.

Bennett has been traveling through the South for nearly a month now on a speaking tour that has taken him to Nashville, Memphis, Richmond, Petersburg, Birmingham, Mobile, New Orleans, Charleston, and nearly every other Southern city with a population over fifteen thousand. He has even spoken in the newly founded town of Atlanta because his train stopped there unexpectedly.

The subject of Bennett's speech this afternoon is ostensibly

States' Rights, by which he means the right of the citizens of Georgia to resist the federal government by any means necessary, including joining with other slave states to form a new nation. But the meat of his topic—the real reason he is dripping with sweat, mopping his brow, and waxing eloquent—is Kansas. The first territorial election is about to occur—not the one that will decide if Kansas joins the Union free or slave, but an important election, nevertheless; one that will select Kansas's first delegate to Congress.

"Gentlemen," Bennett says, "we cannot let this election slip through our fingers! We must send John W. Whitfield to Washington." He pauses and looks intently at his audience. They are the usual mix of merchants, professional men, exporters, and slave owners from the rice and cotton plantations. Sixty some years ago Eli Whitney invented the cotton gin not more than twelve miles from where he now stands. Cotton has made Savannah one of the most important ports in the South. It is planted by slaves, cultivated by slaves, and harvested by slaves. Slaves gin it; slaves bale it; slaves carry it onto the ships that transport it to the mills of England and New England. A strong, healthy male slave between the ages of fourteen and thirty-three is currently selling for as much as $700 with some bringing as much as $1500.

For reasons he does not care to acknowledge openly, Bennett knows these prices right down to the penny. For the last ten years he and Deacon have been smuggling slaves into the United States from Africa and Brazil in defiance of federal law. Presgrove ships always carry legitimate cargo—sacks of refined sugar, bolts of cloth, casks of rum—but before they off-load these goods at U.S. ports, they stop at the Southern barrier islands and off-load their human cargo in the dead of night.

Slave smuggling is a very profitable business and not particularly dangerous. Thanks to the high death rate of native-born slave children, there is always a labor shortage on the larger plantations. When rich, powerful men are eager to buy your goods, you are not likely to find yourself charged with a crime. In fact, at this very moment some of Bennett's best customers are sitting right in front of him. He knows the exact worth of their slaves, which means he also knows exactly how much they stand to lose if the abolitionists triumph.

He lets the silence gather. The grandfather clock in the corner chimes the quarter hour. Outside a carriage rolls by.

"Do y'all know what the Yankees are up to?" he says. "Have y'all any idea what nefarious schemes they have concocted in the Sodoms and Gomorrahs of New York and Boston? Well, gentlemen, let me show you."

He reaches for a string, gives a dramatic tug, and unrolls a map that has been fastened to the parlor wall over the protests of the mistress of the house. It's the same map Carrie consulted, but it has been scribbled over, altered, and brought up to date by Bennett himself.

Seizing his gold-headed walking stick, he points to the great, rose-colored oblong of the Kansas Territory. "See here where the Indians are said to dwell? Well, cross them out, gentlemen. We've driven most of them off. They're either going, gone, penned in reservation, or dying. Smallpox and pneumonia have done our work for us. You won't find any wagon trains burning in Kansas these days, but what you will find is savages—Yankee savages—a whole army of them, gentlemen, a damnable army of New England abolitionists streaming into the territory like vultures coming down on a dead mule. Y'all know what they've done? Well, look here." Again he raps the map with his stick.

"Here's Kickapoo, Lecompton, Atchison, and Leavenworth— good southern, pro-slave towns mostly founded by boys from Missouri. But here's Osawatomie. An abolitionist rats' nest, gentlemen. A vermin-harboring, slave-stealing town that will vote to bring Kansas into the Union as a free state, and then vote to take away your God-given right to own slaves.

"And what's worse than Osawatomie? What's the carbuncle on the face of freedom that should be burned down and sown with salt? Lawrence. The name turns my stomach, gentlemen. I hate to even utter it. It's not a normal city. It's an abomination: an entire New England village brought out to the prairie piece by piece.

"I have a map of it, drawn up by men who sympathize with our cause. I reckon I don't have to explain why I posses such a map. The honorable gentlemen of Savannah have a long history of military service. Why right here, not more than a few blocks away, stands a cemetery filled with the graves of heroes of the first Revolutionary War."

He leans forward, smiles, and lowers his voice. "I say the *first* Revolutionary War because I believe there's going to be a second. Yes, a second. But more of that later in private over cigars and whiskey." Straightening up, he resumes speaking in a normal tone.

"As y'all know, when y'all are contemplatin' a siege, you got to know the lay of the land." Reaching up, he draws down another, smaller map.

"This is Lawrence, Kansas, gentlemen. As of the first of August of this year, it consisted of about fifteen tents and had a population of thirty or so abolitionist squatters. Now look at it. This is Lawrence as of three weeks ago. The Yankees have surveyed the prairie and are selling off land to emigrants who are leaving Massachusetts in packs to the sound of hymns and trumpets."

"They've brought out an entire sawmill in pieces and set it up on the bank of the Kaw River. Right this very minute, it's churning out milled lumber faster than shit goes through a goose. The Yankees brought printing presses with them and are already publishing two abolitionist newspapers. No, I misspoke. They came with the first editions of those inflammatory, traitorous rags already printed up and ready for distribution. They're making barrels and wagons, nails, and guns. Well, they don't have to make too many guns since the New England abolitionists are arming them to the teeth. I hear tell they even got mortars.

"You want to talk treason, gentlemen? You want to talk rebellion against the elected government? What do you suppose those Yankee squatters intend to use those mortars for? Hunting quail?" He raises his stick and begins to strike the map of Lawrence repeatedly.

"Lawrence, Kansas, population approximately seven hundred. Emigrant Aid Company Sawmill, Emigrant Aid Office, Land and Lumber Company, U.S. Post Office, Miller and Elliot's Printing Office, Offices of *The Herald of Freedom* and *The Kansas Free State*, Stern's Eating House, Pioneer House—a shelter for recent arrivals— Simpson's Meat Market, First Church. Schools, shelters made out of sod not fit to house pigs being replaced with fine homes you could bring your wife and daughters to, not that any of you would ever subject the ladies of your family to such company.

"And like Adam in the Garden, the Yankees are renamin' everything. Good old 'Hogback Ridge' has become 'Mount Oread.' The portion of the California Road that runs through the town is now 'Massachusetts Street.' Am I makin' my point, gentlemen? Do I have your attention?

"Lawrence, Kansas, has approximately two hundred free white males over the age of twenty-one. That's two hundred abolitionists qualified to vote. Lawrence is going to swing the territorial election if we don't stop it. And with your help we shall."

Lowering his stick, he leans forward and again becomes confidential. "We need money, and we need men. We'd rather have the men than the money because we intend to send an army of proslavers into Kansas to vote for Whitfield, but if you can't go yourselves, we'll take your donations and thank you for them. One patriotic Southern gentleman has already sold forty of his slaves and donated the proceeds to the cause. My own son—" He pauses and gestures to Deacon who is sitting at the back of the room. "Stand up, son." Deacon stands.

"My own son, Deacon, here had the good fortune to marry a lady of property. He has already spent a good portion of what she brought him to equip a boatload of pro-slavery emigrants who will leave from St. Louis this coming Monday. Let's give him a round of applause."

The men in the room clap, although not with as much enthusiasm as Bennett would like. Savannah cotton growers are a tight-fisted lot, and even though their very way of life may hang on this election, here in Georgia, Kansas seems very far away.

Deacon frowns as if he, too, has noticed the lukewarm quality of the applause. For a moment he seems ready to sit down, but then he does something brilliant. Waving aside the clapping, he smiles modestly.

"Ah cannot take credit for such a little thang," he says, in a Southern accent so strong Bennett realizes he is going to have to remind Deacon to continue speaking this way until they leave Savannah. "Mah only desire is to ensure the freedom of gentlemen like y'all to own their property in peace. For what other reason did your ancestors fight side by side with the Marquis de Lafayette to defend the beautiful city of Savannah against the tyranny of George the Third?"

Now it is Bennett's turn to frown. As Deacon would know, if he had paid the slightest attention to his history lessons, the Marquis de Lafayette never fought anywhere near Savannah. Worse yet, Lafayette was an abolitionist who freed his own slaves.

Bennett never knows how to reign the boy in when he launches into one of his theatrical soliloquies. He wants to tell Deacon that a French admiral named Valerie D'estaing was the one who teamed up against the British during the Battle of Savannah, but it's too late. Deacon has the bit in his teeth and is running with it.

"Freedom!" Deacon cries. "Yes, gentlemen, freedom from government interference. There's no more sacred word than *freedom* unless it be *honor*. How can y'all applaud me for doin' only what any of y'all would do in my position, for doin' what you're gonna do now." Whipping off his hat, he begins to walk through the room like a preacher taking up a collection.

To Bennett's amazement, this works. Maybe it's Deacon's Southern accent or his apparent sincerity or the modest way he puts his hat in front of men who cannot now decline to contribute without losing face. In any event, those tight Savannah fists open, and later when Bennett inspects the take, he discovers he has received substantial pledges as well as cash.

He has also received a short note from a young man named Henry Clark. Clark is not a gentleman, nor does he come from Savannah. Deacon picked him up on the docks last night and went drinking with him, and where Clark comes from or who his family is, is anyone's guess. Still his note is intriguing. It reads, in full:

I want to kil me some Yankees.

Murder is not on Bennett's Kansas agenda at present, but violent men have their uses. Bennett makes a mental note to keep Clark in mind if he needs a madman to do a job no sane man would do. He's fairly sure Clark is insane. The boy has eyes like glass marbles and a smile that would freeze a fire.

Money, pledges, and a willing assassin: Deacon has done well today. If they could just find out where in damnation his bitch of a wife has gone and get her back before Deacon becomes known as the "Cuckold of Kentucky," the boy might have a profitable political career in front of him.

Congressman Deacon Presgrove, Bennett thinks. *Yes, that has a nice ring to it. But not* Senator. *Deacon isn't stepping into my boots until I am dust in my coffin. Of course I may not continue to serve as a senator until my dyin' day. When the Southern states secede they'll be lookin' for a president to head up the new nation.*

Bennett examines himself in the beveled, gilt-framed mirror that runs half the length of the parlor wall. He decides that if he tidied up his hair a bit and turned himself sideways, he'd look damn fine on the face of a twenty-dollar bill.

Chapter Twenty-three

Kansas, November 1854

The night is moonless and cloudy. Up ahead, dozens of camp-fires surround Lawrence in a siege of flame. Every now and then the silhouette of a man passes in front of one of the fires casting a long, distorted shadow. Suddenly, there is a burst of light as if someone has tossed whiskey on the flames. The light runs through the grass, exposing every seedpod and stem. William ducks down, puts his face to the ground, and smells the cold odor of winter soil waiting for snow. "Elizabeth," he whispers.

Elizabeth's hand emerges from the grass and motions for him to be quiet. Falling silent, he lies there listening to the drunken singing and the crack of pistols. Elizabeth is leading this expedition, and he figures she knows what she's doing. She and the Adairs have established their Underground Railroad line and are running slaves to freedom from Osawatomie, which is closer to the Missouri border than Lawrence and—more important—not under constant siege; but tonight an emergency has brought her west along roads patrolled by gangs of bushwhackers.

It's November twenty-eighth, and Kansas is about to elect its first territorial delegate to Congress. Bennett Presgrove has raised his army, and Senator Atchison of Missouri has strapped on his Bowie knife and pistols and led the army across the border. The pro-slavers have surrounded Lawrence. Tomorrow morning at eight o'clock, they will ride into town to vote as permanent residents of Kansas even though most of them have been in the territory less than a week and will be returning to Missouri and other Southern states before the final votes are counted.

Go! Go! Go! Harriet Beecher Stowe!

the pro-slavers sing,

Go to hell and don't come back no more!

Although they're damning the author of *Uncle Tom's Cabin* to hell, this song is a considerable improvement on the one they were singing a few minutes ago.

Run, run Harriet Beecher,
The hounds'll track yah, and then they'll eat yuh.

Crawling back through the grass until she's even with William, Elizabeth points to a fire on the outermost ring of the encampment. They crawl silently toward it, moving a few feet at a time, then lying still until they're sure they haven't been spotted. The pro-slavers should have posted sentries, but the only man they see is sprawled facedown in a drunken stupor. Elizabeth gestures at him, and William nods. Good. It looks as if this is going to be easier than they anticipated.

When they reach the last stand of grass, they lie concealed for a long time, watching and waiting. Five men are sitting around the fire.

The closest two are white Missourians dressed in wool coats, wool caps, leather gloves, and the kind of canvas britches sold in Westport to emigrants heading west. Heavily bearded and bristling with Bowie knives, rifles, and pistols, they are sharing a jug of whiskey in sullen silence punctuated by an occasional oath.

The three remaining men are dark-skinned. One is perhaps forty years old with a creased face and graying hair. He wears wool trousers and a patched jacket. The other two, dressed in the coarse, light-weight clothing of slaves, are no more than twenty at most. They are not wearing jackets, gloves, or hats, and despite the chill of the evening, they have on open-toed shoes made of hemp.

Hemp is one of the main exports of Missouri, and the slaves are bound hand and foot with a rope woven of it. The loose end has been knotted into a hangman's noose and tomorrow, after the pro-slavers have voted and their votes have been tallied, they plan to hang the slaves to celebrate the victory of their candidate, J. W. Whit-field. The ostensible reason for the hanging is that the slaves were plotting to murder their master, but as far as William and Elizabeth are concerned, this is a human sacrifice waiting to take place.

Less than three hours ago, Elizabeth had appeared at William and Carrie's door, dripping wet and shaking with cold. She told them she was rowing a boat across the Kaw to avoid being seen by the pro-slavers when the boat had hit a snag and overturned. She asked for dry clothing, hot food, and a gun. William and Carrie supplied her with all that, and after she told them about the slaves who were about to be hanged, William supplied her with himself as well.

Before they left, they sat down at a table so new they could smell the freshly milled boards, joined hands, and prayed for success. Then Carrie took out her shells and cast them. Recently she had begun to believe she could read the patterns they made, although she wasn't sure how. Tonight the shells said: *Trouble, fraud, death, fire.* So far this evening, William has seen trouble and fire. Tomorrow at the polls there will certainly be fraud. That leaves death.

Lifting his head, he peers through the grass at the slaves and wonders whose death. Theirs? His? Elizabeth's? Carrie's? The problem with the shells is they have no sense of time. Today, tomorrow, and yesterday are all the same to them, which means Carrie can never tell whether an event is hours, days, or a whole lifetime in the future. It's a sure bet they'll all die someday, but William hopes it will be a good sixty years from now.

Elizabeth points toward the guards who are rapidly drinking themselves into oblivion. Her meaning is clear: If they don't spew out the whiskey, they should be unconscious soon. Until then, all she and William can do is wait.

An hour passes. It's cold and uncomfortable lying in the grass, but William has on a buffalo robe coat, and Elizabeth is wearing a sheepskin jacket and a wool cap pulled down over her ears. Once one of the guards steps out of the firelight to relieve himself, but fortunately he chooses the opposite side of the fire. The slaves are awake, but they aren't talking. They sit silently, staring into the flames, perhaps thinking about how their lives will end tomorrow. Maybe they'd be beaten if they spoke.

Finally, one of the Missourians goes over and checks the rope that bind their hands and feet. Satisfied that they can't wriggle free, he reaches into his pocket, takes out a cowbell, and ties it to the hangman's noose.

"Good night, boys," he says. He grins, the firelight catches his face. Ragged beard, eyes like gimlets. "Sweet dreams."

Returning to the opposite side of the fire, the bushwhacker rolls up in his blanket and goes to sleep. His companion sits beside him, drinking steadily. At last, he, too, lies down on the ground and begins to snore.

William and Elizabeth wait a quarter of an hour more to be sure the guards are asleep. It's now time to make their presence known to the slaves, but if they do this too suddenly, they're likely to startle them and set the cowbell ringing.

Sticking his knife between his teeth, William crawls through the grass, sneaks up behind the slaves, reaches out, and closes his hand around bell and clapper. Within seconds he has cut the bell off the noose and the clapper off the bell.

When Elizabeth is sure he's silenced it, she rises to her feet with her finger over her lips. One of the younger slaves starts and begins to speak, but before he can make a sound, the older man slaps his hand over the younger man's mouth. Keeping her finger over her lips, Elizabeth points silently to William and nods. As William stands, the men look alarmed, but they don't make a sound.

Drawing out her pistols, Elizabeth approaches the sleeping Missourians, and stands over them. If they wake, she may have to shoot them before they can yell for help. On any other night, the sound of gunshots would bring men from the neighboring campfires but this evening so many bushwhacker guns are being discharged it's unlikely anyone will pay attention to one more.

Working as fast as possible, William severs the rope that binds the slaves together. *Crawl*, he mouths.

The slaves immediately see the wisdom of this. Falling to their hands and knees, they crawl away from the campfire into the tall grass. Elizabeth and William crawl after them. As soon as they're outside the ring of light, they stand up and begin to run. When they finally stop running, Elizabeth takes the slaves aside and talks to them for a while. William has no idea what she says, but they seem to come to an understanding.

Half an hour later, they are all in Carrie and William's house clustered around the stove, eating cheese and biscuits and drinking hot tea laced with sugar. The slaves introduce themselves as Ebenezer, Sam, and Peet. Ebenezer, who is the oldest, has a burn on his arm. William doesn't have to ask him how he got it, but as he washes it off, puts salve on it, and binds it with gauze, he says: "That's a cruel mark."

Ebenezer shrugs. "It would have been crueler to be hanged. I'm a valet. I couldn't get a stain out of my master's coat this morning, so he took his cigar and gave me what he calls a 'souvenir of his disapproval.' I got a lot of these marks. Master does it when he gets drunk and then apologizes when he sobers up."

"Were you really planning to murder him?"

"Nah, we was just planning to run away," says Sam. "Problem was, I had a kitchen knife on me when they found us. I wasn't gonna slit his throat. I'm a cook. I could have poisoned him six ways to Sunday any time I had a mind to, but I didn't figure it was gonna do much good to tell a passel of Missouri slave owners that. They hang you just for thinkin' about it."

"So I suppose you're on your way to Canada now?"

Sam looks at Elizabeth. Elizabeth shakes her head, and William knows that he and Carrie will never hear whatever Sam was about to say. That's just as well. The less they know, the better. But Peet must not get the message for he says: "I have a mind to go join John Brown. He's better 'an Canada any day."

The name *John Brown* means nothing to William and Carrie. Like most Americans, they have not heard of Brown's plan to arm fugitive slaves and fight a guerilla war in the Allegheny Mountains.

"Do you plan to work for this Mr. Brown?" Carrie asks.

Elizabeth coughs pointedly, and Peet falls silent. Later William and Carrie will realize Peet told them something they had no business knowing, but at the moment all they can think about is how to send Elizabeth and the fugitives safely on their way before the Missourians discover they're missing and sound the alarm. There are no more boats to be had, the only way to get out of Lawrence is to cross the river, and Sam and Ebenezer can't swim.

They discuss the problem and decide that Elizabeth and the slaves will sleep in the root cellar tonight and hide out there tomorrow until the election is over. Once the stove goes out, the cellar will be warmer than the rest of the house, and although sleeping on a dirt floor may not be as comfortable as sleeping on one made of planks, it's a great deal safer.

William and Carrie provide them with blankets and a lantern. When they're safely hidden, William straps on his pistols, kisses Carrie good-bye, and goes out to patrol the streets of Lawrence. He hasn't been gone more than fifteen minutes when Elizabeth reemerges from the cellar. Brushing off her skirts, she looks around the room.

"We have to leave tonight," she announces.

"Why? You're safe and warm in the cellar."

"Fire. That's what those shells of yours predicted. Do we believe them? I don't know. But what they foretell worries me. They remind me of those knucklebones my mama used to throw when she had to decide something important. I'd say shells and bones don't so much speak to a person as help a person concentrate her mind, and at the moment I'm concentrated on one bothersome fact: If those bushwhackers burn the town, Ebenezer, Peet, Sam, and I will be trapped."

For an instant Carrie imagines Lawrence in flames. Then she casts off the fear, which after all is no worse than half a dozen others she has had to deal with tonight. If Lawrence burns, it burns. She and William can build another house. They can live in a tent for that matter. Or a sod lean-to. You can't burn sod.

"Fine," she says. "How do we get you out of here? You can't ride through an army of drunken bushwhackers, and at least two of you can't swim."

Elizabeth points to an object in the center of the room. "Give me that."

"How did you get so smart?"

"Practice. If I wasn't smart, I wouldn't be alive. Can I have it?"

"It's yours." Throwing her arms around Elizabeth, Carrie embraces her. Then she goes out to the woodshed to get a hammer.

T he next evening, after the polls close, William comes home from patrolling the streets to find Carrie sitting in front of the stove drinking tea and reading *A Treatise on the Blood, Inflammation and Gunshot Wounds*. Her hair is freshly washed, and she is wearing a clean dress and apron. At her feet lie four table legs.

"Where did the tabletop go?" he asks.

"We made it into a raft."

William sits down across from her, takes off his hat, and hangs it on the back of the chair. "Sweetheart, I don't know what you've been up to, but please don't tell me you've been out rafting on the Kaw in the middle of November."

"Oh, no, nothing like that. I only went in up to my ankles when I was giving the raft a push. I was more worried about Elizabeth and the slaves. I thought they might make the crossing safely, and then come out of the river wet and freeze to death; but Elizabeth told me she had mules and dry clothing waiting for them on the other side." Carrie puts her book down on the floor beside the table legs. "So who won the election?"

"J. W. Whitfield, I'm sorry to say."

"What a surprise. How many votes were cast?"

"Considerably more than there are eligible voters in Lawrence.

The pro-slavers showed up with premarked ballots and stuffed them in the boxes." He leans down and kisses her on the forehead and then kneels beside her and puts his arms around her. "Carrie—"

"You're going to ask me to take better care of myself, aren't you?"

"Yes."

"I promise I will."

"What?"

"Don't look so surprised."

"But you've always been—"

"Wild? Reckless? Pigheadedly stubborn?" She laughs. "That's what Elizabeth called me. Before she left, she sat me down and told me that I'd been a fool to work so hard building this house. She said you could have done it by yourself, and that I should have let you. She said what I was doing was understandable and that she'd seen it before in women who were carrying a child, but that I needed to recognize that the way I've been acting is a danger to me and my baby. She got me to confess that I feel that if I coddle myself, I'm admitting I may be in danger of losing this baby like I lost Willa.

"'You're not immortal,' she told me. 'No one is. But sometimes we feel that we have to act as if we are.' She said that if I go on pushing myself and not resting, I may regret it for the rest of my life, but if I take good care of myself, I'll give birth to a healthy baby."

"You actually listened to her?"

"Elizabeth can be terrifying when she's a mind to be. She's helped hundreds of babies come into the world. She told me some stories I don't want to repeat. Her lecture sobered me up considerably. Before she left, I promised her I'd stop splitting kindling and carrying water up from the river and do more sitting in front of the fire. Then we sat down together and threw the *buzios* to see if I was going to have a boy or a girl."

"So which will it be?"

"The *buzios* wouldn't say, so Elizabeth helped me pick out two names. Do you want to hear them?"

"Yes."

"Alice and Edward." She takes his hand and puts it against her belly. "Say 'hello.'"

"Hello, Alice or Edward," William says.

In the stove, the fire burns with a low hiss. Gradually the hiss of sleet joins in, slapping against roof and windows like loose gravel. That night William and Carrie sleep in each other's arms. When they wake the next morning, every blade of grass is coated with ice, and the prairie looks as if it has been strewn with diamonds.

Chapter Twenty-four

Three days after the election, the first great winter storm sweeps across the prairie. As the wind howls and the snow piles up, all emigration comes to a halt, and peace descends on the Kansas Territory. In St. Louis, the steamboats are locked in ice until spring. Blizzards block the California Road, and Mr. Trout, seeing no prospect of business for some months, sends his Yankee cook, Mrs. Witherspoon, off to Lawrence for the season. Retreating to a small room, he burrows down under a pile of buffalo robes and sleeps away the short days, only waking to feed the stock, shovel off the roof, and stoke the fire.

Despite the weather, Lawrence prospers. The Emigrant Aid Company Sawmill continues to spit out boards, and with them the New Englanders build schools, houses, and churches. The empty lots on Massachusetts Street fill up, and the town spreads well beyond the edges of the map Bennett Presgrove showed to the slave owners of Savannah.

Cold weather builds character, the citizens of Lawrence tell their children; and when the unseasoned wood of their new homes warps and the wind blows almost as strongly inside as out, they stuff rags in the chinks and stumble off to church through the snow, stopping occasionally to marvel at sunsets laced with mother-of-pearl and vast skies filled with churning clouds.

In February as the grip of winter slackens, three men who have been wintering in Illinois round up their livestock and head west, crossing the Missouri River and staking out a claim on North Middle Creek about ten miles northwest of Osawatomie. Their names are Owen, Salmon, and Frederick Brown. They call their settlement Brown's Station.

Back in North Elba, New York, their father, John, receives letters describing the "curses" of slavery his sons have seen en route to Kansas. They ask him to send them Colt revolvers, rifles, and Bowie knives; and John Brown—who believes he holds a commission directly from God to end slavery—not only agrees, he promises to join them sometime in late summer or early fall to win Kansas for God and abolition by any means necessary.

On the same morning John Brown goes out to buy the hat he will still be wearing four years later when he is hanged for treason, William carries a straight-backed chair into the front yard so Carrie can sit in the sunshine and sketch. The snow has melted, and the long grasses have turned twenty different shades of red and brown. Bent and flattened by winter storms, they form beautiful shapes that she hopes to capture on her sketch pad and send to Professor Gray at Harvard.

Clutching William's arm, Carrie lets him help her to the chair. They walk slowly past the rain barrel, the big iron kettle they use for boiling laundry, the woodshed, and the sod hut that serves as a stable. The baby is two weeks overdue, and Carrie feels large and awkward, like an egg that might crack unexpectedly. Settling her on the chair, William wraps her legs in a buffalo robe and drapes a shawl around her shoulders. Then he goes to the woodshed and gets an empty nail keg. Placing the keg beside her to serve as a table, he brings out her sketching materials and a pot of hot tea wrapped in the muffler she gave him for Christmas. It's a rather strange muffler since knitting is not her strong point: about twice as long as necessary, made of bright red wool and uneven as a buffalo track.

"If you keep spoiling me like this, I may become insufferable," she says.

"Don't worry." William grins wickedly. "Immediately after you give birth, I expect you to rise from bed, go outside, split logs, lug them into the house, stoke up the fire, and cook me dinner. Fried ham and beaten biscuits will be acceptable. A pie would not be out of place. After I've eaten my fill, and you've done the dishes, you'll be free to take a bucket down to the river. The water barrel needs topping off, and the floor needs scrubbing—" She interrupts him with a kiss, and they both laugh.

"Seriously," he says, "are you sure you'll be all right here by yourself? I hate to leave you alone even for an hour."

"Don't worry about me. Go tend to Mr. Crane's lumbago. I'll be fine and I need the fresh air. If I feel so much as a twinge, I'll go inside."

"Second babies can come very fast."

"Good. Then it will hurt less." She gives him another kiss and slaps him on the rump. "Now go."

After he leaves, she pours herself a cup of tea and sits for a while, sipping it and enjoying the sunshine. The sky is a clear, deep blue, and there's not a cloud in sight. After she finishes off the tea, she opens her pad, picks up her chalk, and begins to sketch a patch of grass that has not been bent by snow. The blades are soft pink, speckled with brown. Plumed and ethereal-looking, they resemble the tail feathers of some tropical bird.

For half an hour she thinks about nothing but color, form, and composition. When she finally looks up, she notices the sun is about to disappear behind a cloud. Deciding the best of the day is over, she prepares to put away her sketch pad, but before she can close it, a strong wind rises up and rips it out of her hand.

She watches as the pad is thrown into the air and the individual sheets torn off and tossed in all directions. Within seconds the wind triples in force. With it comes snow—not the first few flakes of impending snowstorms that she remembers from her childhood, but a curtain of the stuff mixed with sleet. For a few minutes, she sits there watching the world turn white around her. The effect is extraordinarily beautiful.

When she finally turns her attention back to herself, she realizes she's shivering. It's time to go back in the house. Picking up the teapot, she stands and begins to walk slowly across the yard, careful not to trip. As she does so, she heads into a wind so cold it takes her breath away. The snow is falling even faster now. The patch of grass she just sketched is already beginning to bend a little under it, and the sheets on the clothesline look as if they are starting to freeze.

She considers taking the sheets down and carrying them inside, but decides to leave them for William. Grabbing onto the railing, she pulls herself up the front steps. As she pushes open the front door, she feels the first cramping pain.

The sudden onslaught of the storm takes everyone by surprise. Sweeping down from the Arctic, a Kansas blizzard can lower the temperature forty degrees in an hour, blot out all traces of roads, and make it impossible to hear human voices at a distance of six feet. In Lawrence everyone makes it safely to shelter, but in other parts of the territory, people freeze to death trying to walk less than a hundred yards, while others suffocate on the snow.

By the time William gets home, there is half a foot on the roof, the wash on the clothesline has frozen, and the water barrel is rimmed with ice.

"Carrie," he calls as he steps onto the front porch. She doesn't answer. Worried, he enters the house and discovers the fire has gone out. Carrie is lying on the bed under a pile of blankets and buffalo robes. The water in the basin beside her is frozen solid.

"Carrie!"

She looks up at him, moans, and grips his hand. "The baby's coming, and it hurts! Damn it, why couldn't God have given women buttons!"

Scooping her up in his arms, William kisses her and reassures her that everything will be fine. He holds her through the next two pains, then lays her back down, tucks her in, relights the fire, and sets a kettle of water on to boil. By the time he goes outside to get more wood and check on his horse, the snow is coming down so hard he has to duck his head to breathe.

Probably no man in Lawrence has as much experience with blizzards as he has. Five years ago, he strapped on snowshoes and walked out of the Sierra Nevada Mountains to get help. An entire wagon train depended on him. True, that blizzard was over by the time he began the trek, but he knows the treachery of snow, the seductiveness of cold so intense that it makes a man want to lie down, close his eyes, and give up. Carrie is safe inside the house, but they are going to need fuel to keep the fire going, and in ten minutes or so he isn't going to be able to find his way to the woodshed.

Staggering to the stable, he checks on the mare, feeds her a carrot, and piles up enough fresh hay to last her a week. Pleased by the unexpected treats, the mare nuzzles him and whinnies. The sod walls are thick and the roof is solid. Even if the entire stable is buried, she should be fine.

When he goes back outside, he can't see the house. He walks in a straight line, heel to toe, until he runs into the clothesline. Cutting it off the posts, he continues until he reaches the house. After that things become easier. He ties the line to the porch rail and then walks in the general direction of the woodshed. The first three times he comes to the end of the line before he locates it, but the fourth time he sees it looming up out of the whiteness. Tying the loose end of the line to the shed, he grabs as much wood as he can carry and follows the line back to the house.

Before he opens the front door, he stops and says a quick prayer. He's never been a religious man, but he doesn't want Carrie to see how frightened he is, and she's always been able to read his face.

Dear God, he prays, *let this baby come into the world easily. Let it be healthy. Let it thrive. Let Carrie's labor be short; let her pain be light. Let her not suffer too much . . .*

The wind shrieks around him and the windows of the house disappear, glowing under the snow like buried lanterns. Out in the front yard, the chair Carrie was sitting on topples over and disappears. William thinks of the women he has seen bleed to death giving birth, women who could not deliver their babies at all, women who labored until they died of exhaustion.

Please don't take her from me.

Is God hearing this? Does He exist? Is that His voice in the roaring of the blizzard? For a few more seconds, he stands on the porch as the storm turns him into a white statue. Then he shakes off the snow, stomps off his boots, and goes inside to help Alice/Edward come into the world.

Sometimes, Carrie thinks, nature is merciful. Later, she remembers the warmth of the hot brick William put at her feet, the fire in the stove casting shadows on the walls, the pain coming in waves, but most of the day she gave birth to Teddy is a blank. She has a dim recollection of cursing, and crying, and screaming; of gripping William's arm so hard she bruises it; of biting her lips and yelling that she will never have another child if she has to give up lovemaking for the rest of her life, but it all seems like a dream someone else dreamed.

The thing she remembers most clearly is Teddy actually being born, the relief of finally pushing him out into the world, the joy of hearing him cry and knowing he's alive. She remembers taking him in her arms for the first time, feeling him wet and squirming against her, and loving him beyond reason from the first moment she holds him.

She even recalls looking up at William, saying, "Thank you," and breaking into tears. William must have comforted her, taken the baby from her, washed him, bundled him up, given him back to her to hold. He must have told her he loved her, but she can't remember any of this.

What comes next is the transition from ice to fire. In the midst of the fever, when she is out of her head and raving incoherently, she believes she is back in the hospital of the Casa de Misericórdia. She speaks to William in Portuguese, and when he hears this, he believes he's going to lose her.

He does not panic, nor does he purge and bleed her as other doctors would have done. Instead, he sponges her down with alcohol, and persuades her to drink tea made from licorice root, thyme, and hyssop. Once, she swims up from the depths of the pit of fire she has been thrown into to find him bending over her.

"Is this childbed fever?" she asks him.

"Yes."

"My mother died of it."

"You won't die, Carrie."

"Are you sure?"

"Yes," he says so firmly she believes him. Then she looks into his eyes and realizes he's lying. "If I do die, will you take care of Teddy as if he were your own son?"

"Yes."

"You won't let Deacon take him?"

"Never."

"I'm burning alive," she says. "Put me out in the snow." He refuses. For a while she is angry; then she forgets snow exists.

What dreams does she have during the time she hovers between life and death? Does Mae Seja come to comfort her? Does she see her mother? She remembers nothing. All she knows is that one morning she wakes to find herself lying in her own bed with Teddy nursing at her breast. Sunlight is streaming in through the windows. Most of the snow has melted, and the sky is so blue it looks like the petals of a giant cornflower.

She puts her hand on Teddy's head. *My son,* she thinks. He is an unusually pretty baby: dark hair as fine as silk, red cheeks, a tiny straight nose, long eyelashes that would be the envy of any girl. Everything about him is small and perfect and compact right down to his tiny fingernails. His eyes are blue, but the color often changes. Will they turn green like Deacon's?

Perhaps they will. She can see traces of Deacon in his face, but her son's eyes will never be catlike and sly. Already they are rounder, softer. Teddy will laugh with his eyes. She and William will love him. He will be a happy child.

When she looks in his face, she sees not only herself. She sees her mother, her father, her grandparents. What a mystery children are. How many births did it take to produce this particular baby? How many centuries was he in the making?

In Mae Seja's *quilombo,* people gave their babies names like *Iyabo,* which means *Mother Is Back*; or *Babatunji, Father Has Woken Up.* They not only believed children were the dead returning; they believed a child who died young would be reborn from the womb of the same mother. Teddy could be Willa come back to her. No wonder every religion has some way to bless children.

She kisses him on the forehead and whispers foolish, loving words in his ear. *I'll bless him with the names of the Brazilian and African gods,* she thinks, *and then I'll take him to church and have him christened.*

But perhaps it's not a good idea to mix gods, because two weeks later, she throws the *buzios,* and they tell her she'll lose him. "Stupid, lying shells!" she cries. "What am I doing practicing witchcraft?" Gathering up the *buzios,* she carries them to the waste bucket and drops them in. They hit the bottom with a deafening rattle. She looks down to see if any have been chipped, but they all appear whole.

Suddenly she feels foolish. A handful of shells cannot predict the future. The messages she reads in them exist only in her imagination. Teddy is in no danger.

She tilts the bucket, fishes the *buzios* out, and stuffs them back into their bag. Going over to Teddy's cradle, she picks him up and clasps him to her so tightly he begins to cry.

"I am never going to let anything hurt you!" she promises. "Do you hear me? I'll never lose you. Never!"

Chapter Twenty-five

Washington, D.C., July 1855

Deacon Presgrove sits at the gaming table in Mrs. Springer's parlor staring into a handsome face and eyes so cold they make his hands shake. The full lips, red cheeks, soft skin, and curly white-blond hair belong to Henry Clark. Deacon isn't given to flights of imagination, but when he looks at Clark he can't help but see bodies piling up in heaps.

Lily comes up behind him smelling of expensive French perfume. Reaching back, Deacon takes her hand in his. Maybe he takes it for courage; maybe he takes it because if Clark pulls a gun, he can heave Lily in front of him. He's too spooked to figure out which.

"What do you want?" he asks.

Clark smiles. It is a charming smile, but Deacon, who has often used such smiles himself to great advantage, is not deceived. He looks at Clark's even, white teeth and thinks *shark*.

"Money," Clark says.

"Why should I give you money?"

"Because you're my friend."

"I am?" Deacon's cravat feels too tight. He starts to loosen it and then realizes Clark will take the gesture as a sign of weakness.

"We drank together. We whored together." Clark's smile broadens. "Remember that little quadroon beauty in Savannah? You kept putting whiskey on her nipples. Then you did something that set her screaming. Remember that? When her pimp came in and saw how you'd damaged his property, he decided to shoot you dead. But I saved your life. Remember?"

"I don't remember anything. I was drunk." A lie. Deacon remembers the whole incident all too well.

"I killed him," Clark says. "Remember?"

"Yes," Deacon admits, "you did."

"In a nasty way."

"Very nasty." Deacon can feel circles of perspiration forming under his arms. "When I woke up the next day the memory of what you did to him was worse than my hangover."

"I enjoyed it. I took out my pocket watch and timed his screaming. He set a new record."

Deacon very much wants this conversation to end. He wishes he had a gun. Shooting Clark would be a public service, but maybe Clark would shoot him first. "How much do you want?"

"Don't you want to know what I want the money for?"

"To keep quiet about the whore, I imagine."

"You imagine wrong. When I heard your father speak in Savannah, he said Yankee abolitionists were taking over Kansas. 'An abomination,' he said. 'Sodom and Gomorrah.' That's when it came to me. That's when I found my calling." Clark leans so close, Deacon can smell the whiskey on his breath. "Think of me as Christ in the wilderness; or if you'd rather, the Beast of Revelation."

"You want money to go to Kansas?"

"Not just me. I want to lead my own band. Like Mangas Coloradas."

In the last fifteen seconds, Clark has compared himself to the Beast of Revelation, an Apache chief, and Jesus Christ. *Clearly he is insane,* Deacon thinks. He clears his throat and tries to look as if such a thought never occurred to him.

"So if I sponsor you and your men, you'll immediately head for the Kansas Territory?" *And put a thousand miles between us?*

"I'll come down on those free-soilers like the wolf on the fold."

When a man with eyes like glass marbles sits across a poker table from you quoting Byron, it's dangerous to bargain, but Deacon has never handed over money without getting something in return, and his mouth works before his brain has time to warn him of the risk he's taking."

"Find my wife."

"Your wife?"

Deacon immediately regrets having spoken. Carrie threatened to shoot him if he came after her, and damned if she wouldn't do it. Could he tell Clark to forget about her? No. If he does, Clark will think he's weak and indecisive. Deacon decides that there is no use imagining what Clark will do to him if he appears vulnerable. Talking to the man is like having a conversation with a panther. You have to look him straight in the eye and act as if he's the one who should be afraid. It's a difficult role, but Deacon has played a lot of difficult roles in his time.

He wills his own eyes to turn to marbles. Perhaps they do; perhaps they don't. He can't tell without a mirror, but when he speaks, he hears the voice he used when he played Caligula.

"I have reason to believe my wife is in Kansas, but those abolitionist bastards are such a closed-mouth bunch they wouldn't tell you the time if you showed them a watch. I've made numerous inquiries, but so far I haven't been able to locate her." He wonders if he should tell Clark about the child and decides against it. The less Clark knows about his personal life, the better. "I'll give you a list of names she may be using, possible whereabouts, and so forth."

"You want me to kill her?"

"For God's sake no! I just want you to tell me where she is, and then I'll go get her myself. You aren't to hurt her or threaten her or even let her know you're there. Just find out if she's living in the Kansas Territory."

"I think you should give me something extra for that." Clark lifts his left hand and brushes his thumb and fingers together. Strong hands that could break a man's neck so fast that—Deacon pushes the thought out of his mind. For a few seconds, Clark holds his hand in front of Deacon's face, then swoops down and begins to paw through the pile of jewelry that lies next to the ashtray holding Deacon's cigar.

"Your stake?"

"Yes."

"Looks like you're pressed for ready cash."

"I'll win everything back tonight and more."

Clark picks up a silver bracelet, slips it on his wrist, and admires it. "What happened to that gold cigar case Nettie gave you?"

"It was stolen."

Clark makes a clicking sound that might possibly be interpreted as sympathy but which is more likely disappointment. "I see two wedding rings here. Have you converted to Mormonism? If you have, I suggest you recant. I've always held that it's easier to cheat on one wife than support two."

"Both rings belonged to my late stepmother. My father gave her the large gold band. The smaller ring, the one studded with sapphires, came from her previous husband. She was a widow when my father married her."

"*Was*, as in no longer with us? *Late*, as in *dead*?"

Deacon nods.

"My sympathies." Clark picks up a gold ring guard and holds it to the light. "Are these real diamonds?"

"Yes."

"Ah, I thought so. Well, if you don't object, I think I'll take all this as a down payment."

"Help yourself."

Clark scoops up the jewelry and stuffs it into his pocket. As he straightens up, his coat flares open revealing a fancy nickel-plated revolver with an ivory grip.

"I could use a drink," he says.

Deacon turns to Lily. "Get us some whiskey," he orders. Whatever Clark wants, he can have. There will be no more bargaining.

PART 5

John Brown

Elizabeth

Excerpt from *A Free Woman of Color in Bleeding Kansas*
By Mrs. Elizabeth Newberry
Vol. II, pp. 76–79. Pub. Thayer and Eldridge, Boston, 1867

In February of '55, the big blizzard killed our milk cow leaving my grandbabies with nothing but salt to put on their porridge. Before the snow melted, bushwhackers began streaming across the border again to vote in the spring election. As soon as they got on Kansas soil, they loaded up their wagons with whiskey, guns, and more ammunition than it took to win the Mexican War. Some flew black flags decorated with skulls and crossbones; others taunted us with hemp hangmen's nooses.

A thousand or more headed straight to Lawrence, but enough came to Osawatomie that those of us who had black skin kept out of sight. We might proudly write F.W.C. and F.M.C. after our names to let the world know we were Free Men and Women of Color (and have the papers to prove it in court), but we knew from bitter experience that the slavers would not hesitate to kidnap us and sell us south.

When the voting was over, those "permanent residents of the territory" piled back in their wagons and left so fast you would have thought they had itching powder in their pants. They said they would hang Governor Reeder if he refused to declare the election valid, never mind that more people had voted than lived in all of Kansas.

Once they got back to Missouri, they traded in their ox teams for horses and the raids began in earnest. There had been raids all along, of course, but now the bushwhackers came at us in packs, burning cabins and shooting down men in cold blood. The worst gang was led by Henry Clark, a pretty, baby-faced boy who enjoyed killing the way a baby enjoys sucking a sugar tit.

In late spring, when my son Prosser drove me up to Lawrence to get some cough medicine for my grandbabies, I found William Saylor and the other men fortifying the town with earthworks. Carrie Vinton took me over to see a new hotel called the Free State, built out of concrete with loopholes on the roof so you could take aim without making yourself into a target.

Carrie was still thin from the fever she'd had after she gave birth to her son, Teddy, but even so, she told me she had been teaching some of the women how to shoot those Sharps rifles they were secretly getting from New England. When I left, she embraced me as if she feared she would never see me again. "Take care of yourself, Elizabeth," she said. "Remember, you can always bring your family up to Lawrence to stay with us."

For reasons I was not then at liberty to tell her, I was unable to leave Osawatomie, but she was right to worry. In July, the fraudulently elected pro-slave legislature met and passed a series of laws aimed at getting me and mine back into chains. Only pro-slavery men could hold office and sit on juries. Anyone who denied that white men had a God-given right to own slaves could to be sent to prison. If you said so much as a word that could be interpreted as supporting slave insurrection, they'd hang you. If a white man wanted to vote, *he had to raise his right hand and swear on a Bible to uphold all these laws. As for black people, we knew what they had in mind for us. We'd seen those nooses they wore in their lapels.*

It was then we began talking about arming ourselves in self-defense. I had always taught my sons that violence was something they should avoid if possible, but if we were going to remain in Kansas, we needed to be able to fight.

"We fled from the South," Toussaint said. "Must we now flee from Osawatomie?"

"We have built our homes here, Mama," Prosser said. "We have crops in the ground."

"We will stay in Osawatomie," I promised my boys, and then I told them about a plan I had conceived the previous November when I was on my way to Lawrence to rescue three fugitives who were about to be lynched. My plan was not for warfare. The bushwhackers outnumbered us a hundred times over and attacking them openly would have been suicide. It was a strategy for self-defense, and a good one if I do say so myself.

We already had the manpower, but what we did not have were the weapons. The day after we decided to stand our ground, I wrote to John Brown. (I had never met him in person, but as an Underground Railroad conductor I knew him by reputation, and his sons, who lived over on North Middle Creek, were our neighbors.)

"Come out to Kansas soon," I told him. "There is a place you need to see." I did not tell him what the place was called or why it would suit his plans. If you have been running slaves to freedom for twenty years as I have, you do not make the mistake of saying something like that in a letter that could be intercepted by your enemies. Still, just in case Mr. Brown did not take my meaning, I wrote the numbers 66-13-10 under my name.

I knew that as soon as he saw those numbers, he would realize I had given him a piece of Bible code. Sixty-six is the sixty-sixth book of the Bible—in other words, the Book of Revelation—thirteen the chapter, ten the verse that reads: "He that killeth with the sword must be killed with the sword."

Imagine my surprise when he actually showed up in Osawatomie with broadswords. By now, everybody knows what John Brown used those swords for, but the first time I saw them, I thought: He damn well have better brought guns, too.

Chapter Twenty-six

Eastern Kansas, mid-April 1856

Prairie violets, Chickasaw plums, wild strawberries, purple anemones, and everywhere the tall grass sprouting new growth under a sky so huge Carrie feels as if she has swum out of winter into an ocean of spring. Usually on such a day she would have brought her sketch pad, but this afternoon she is riding from Lawrence to Osawatomie with her medical kit, a rifle, and Teddy strapped to her back in a Kaw cradleboard. The cradleboard is decorated with fine beadwork and has a deerskin shade that protects his head from the sun. It was a gift from one of her patients. Teddy is getting a little big for it, but he loves it, there's no more secure way to carry a child on a horse, and she wouldn't trade it for the finest perambulator money can buy.

Three armed men are riding with her. All have the same long, straight noses and deeply set eyes, and all share the last name Brown. The Browns are brothers. For about a year now, they have been living on North Middle Creek not far from Osawatomie. Frederick Brown is the handsomest of the three: round-faced and innocent-looking as a baby although he must be at least twenty-five. Red-haired Owen Brown, whose beard reminds Carrie of a spade, has a crippled right arm. Salmon Brown, the youngest, has the air of a preacher who has been dragged out on Sunday for an excursion he doesn't approve of.

Carrie knows almost nothing about the Browns, but she's glad to have them with her. These days she never ventures out unarmed and unaccompanied. Only a few months ago, the bushwhackers surrounded Lawrence again. This time there were fifteen hundred of them, and they came with cannons, guns, and a hatred so intense you could almost smell it. During the second siege she dreamed terrible dreams. Even now when she thinks about them, they make her shudder. The worst is, she can't remember what they were. All she can recall is waking up shaking and sweating. At the last minute, a peace was negotiated, but she isn't taking any chances. Even though things have quieted down considerably, only a fool would ride to Osawatomie alone.

On the other hand, if she believed they were in any real danger of being attacked, she wouldn't have brought Teddy with her. Leaving him at home isn't easy since he's still nursing, but she would have found a way. Mrs. Crane's niece might have agreed to nurse him along with her own newborn, but whenever possible Carrie prefers to take him with her. *I'll never lose you*, she promised him when he was only a few days old, and not losing him means keeping him close.

Up ahead, a cloud of dust appears. That should be Mr. Trout. He agreed to meet them and accompany them to Osawatomie, and he's right on time. But just in case it isn't him—

Carrie pulls out her rifle and the Browns follow suit. She wonders how bushwhackers would react to the sight of an armed woman with a baby on her back. She hopes she never has occasion to find out. So far they haven't killed women and children. In fact, April is proving to be a relatively peaceful month. Over in Lecompton, a

Congressional investigation into charges of election fraud is in process, and while the committee is hearing testimony, neither side wants to rock the boat.

Mr. Trout comes into view riding on a mule. Catching sight of their party, he takes off his hat and waves. Carrie and the Browns lower their guns, and Carrie waves back. When he gets within shouting distance, Trout yells, "Howdy!"

"Howdy!" Carrie replies. The Browns, who are silent men, say nothing.

Trout rides up to them, reins in his mule, nods to the Browns, pulls out a bandanna, and wipes his forehead. "Afternoon, Miz Vinton."

"Good afternoon, Mr. Trout."

"I hear you're headed to Osawatomie because your friend Mrs. Newberry is sick."

"Yes, sir, very." Carrie gestures toward the Browns. "She sent these gentlemen to fetch me."

"What's her complaint? Ain't cholera, is it?"

"No, Mr. Trout. If it had been cholera, Dr. Saylor would have come. Mrs. Newberry stepped on a nail and the wound has become infected."

"You sure about that? You don't want to be bringin' a babe in arms to no house what got cholera or suchlike in it."

"I'm sure."

"Humph. Well, you're the doctor's lady, so I suppose you'd know." He points at Carrie's rifle. "Can you shoot that thing as well as you can shoot a pistol, Miz Vinton?"

"Yes, Mr. Trout."

"Well then if the Browns here don't have any objection, I reckon I'll ride beside you. As you know, I don't fancy turning my back on an armed woman. I believe I told you the story of my gun-toting former fiancée when we first became acquainted, but in case it's done slipped your mind . . ."

For the next five hours, as the Browns ride in silence, Mr. Trout talks incessantly. Just before sunset, they reach the outskirts of Osawatomie. Carrie thanks the Browns for seeing her safely to her destination. After they depart for their homes, she presses a pouch of chewing tobacco into Mr. Trout's hand and gives him a packet of pills for his lung congestion. She'd like to give the Brown brothers something, too, but so far she has seen no sign that they chew tobacco or drink or indulge in any other vices known to mankind. The only thing she could reliably give the Browns are Bibles, and she suspects they already have a sufficient supply.

Dismounting, she walks to Elizabeth's cabin. It's one of three set in a semicircle not far from the place where Pottawatomie Creek flows into the Marais des Cygnes River. The other two cabins are occupied by Prosser and Toussaint and their families. Carrie knocks on Elizabeth's door, and to her surprise, Elizabeth herself answers.

"Thank God you're here!" Elizabeth says. Her voice is steady, but when Carrie looks at her face, she has a sense of staring into unknown territory. Enfolding Carrie in her arms, Elizabeth embraces her, baby, cradleboard, and all. Her hair gives off a strange scent Carrie doesn't recognize. Perhaps it's the odor of infection.

"Which foot did the nail go into?" Carrie asks her.

"Neither." Elizabeth releases her and steps back. "I've brought you here on false pretenses. I have calluses you couldn't drive a nail through with a hammer, but I had to get you to Osawatomie. I'll tell you the details later. Right now, we have to go over to the Adairs' cabin before it's too late."

"What do you mean 'too late'? Is one of the Adairs sick?"

"No, they're both in good health, but last night we found a man draped over a fence rail. I think the bushwhackers left him as a warning, or maybe they just left him to die in the first convenient place that presented itself. In any event, he's horribly burned. What takes tar off skin?"

"Alcohol or kerosene."

"Spartacus!" Elizabeth cries. Carrie notices Elizabeth's youngest son standing in the shadows. He looks terrified. How old is he now: fourteen, fifteen? She can't remember. He's a foot taller than the last time she saw him, skinny but strong-looking. Starting to become a man, but not one yet by a long shot.

"Spartacus, draw a jug of kerosene from the barrel. Then run over to Mrs. Gate's and ask her if we can borrow some of her husband's whiskey for medicinal purposes. Bring the kerosene and whiskey over to Reverend Adair's as fast as your legs will carry you."

"Yes, Mama." Spartacus pauses and his lower lip trembles. "I'm scared."

"When your daddy preached of a Sunday, he used to say, 'If the Lord is the strength of my life, of whom shall I be afraid.' You recognize that, son?"

"Yes, Momma. Psalm Twenty-seven."

"You repeat those verses to yourself as you run over to Mrs. Gate's, and you come back to me brave."

"Yes, ma'am," Spartacus says.

The Adair's cabin is a two-room fortress made out of logs chinked with mud. The chimney is short and squat, the windows small. When Carrie and Elizabeth arrive, they find Reverend Adair and his wife standing in the doorway peering down the road anxiously. Reverend Adair appears to have aged since Carrie last saw him.

When Mrs. Adair catches sight of Carrie, she steps forward. She's a determined-looking woman with deeply set eyes, a slightly pointed nose, and a face that forms such a perfect oval that it looks as if it had been drawn with a compass.

"Miss Vinton," she says, "you are welcome. We have no doctors in Osawatomie. I understand you have apprenticed yourself to Dr. Saylor and have a reputation for healing. I cannot tell you how happy we are to see you. My husband and I have been desperate with worry. We fear the poor man will not survive the night. Please come in."

The cabin is large as frontier cabins go, with whitewashed walls, a rag rug on the floor, and little luxuries like a walnut-framed mirror mounted above the washstand. A small fire is burning in the fireplace, taking off the spring chill. Sitting in front of it in a cane-bottomed rocking chair is an old man dressed in a black suit, white shirt, and black leather tie. His hair is cropped short and combed straight back to reveal a high brow. His nose is long and aquiline, his eyes deep-set like Mrs. Adair's. It's a weathered, weary face set on a head that seems too small for his lanky body.

"Miss Vinton," says Mrs. Adair, "may I present my brother, Mr. Brown." Mrs. Adair does not offer Carrie her brother's first name. Later Carrie will realize this is John, the radical brother-in-law Reverend Adair spoke about over dinner in the Gilliss House, the one who believes he is the right hand of God, but at the moment her mind is on other things.

"Good evening, Miss Vinton," Mr. Brown says. "I am pleased to make your acquaintance."

"Good evening, Mr. Brown. Are you by any chance related to the three Browns who saw me safely from Lawrence to Osawatomie?"

"Indeed I am. They are my sons." As he speaks, he leans forward, the light catches his face, and Carrie sees the most startling eyes she has ever encountered. There is nothing unusual about their color—they are an ordinary shade of gray—but they are fierce, determined, and absolutely steady. For a moment she has the sense of having walked into the presence of a judging god. Then the old man catches sight of Teddy, and his gaze softens.

"A baby," he says.

"My son, Edward. 'Teddy,' we call him."

"How old is he?"

"Fourteen months."

"Such a sweet child." The old man stretches out both arms. "May I hold him?"

Carrie looks at Elizabeth, and Elizabeth nods. Reassured, Carrie hands the old man Teddy. He takes the cradleboard with sure hands, bends over it, and kisses Teddy on the forehead. "Cootchie-cootchie-coo," he croons. Teddy laughs and begins to babble happily. Mr. Brown looks up and smiles at Carrie. "I think Teddy and I are going to get along just fine."

"My brother has always had a way with babies," Mrs. Adair observes.

"How many children do you have?" Carrie asks him.

"Twenty," he says. Later Carrie learns that nine of John Brown's twenty children are dead, and that he mourns them so much he can hardly speak of them without weeping.

Brown brushes a strand of hair off Teddy's forehead and looks at him fondly. "I'll unbind him from the cradleboard and amuse him while you're in the smokehouse."

"The smokehouse?"

"Yes," Reverend Adair says. "That's where one of them is."

"There's more than one injured man?"

"Yes, two. One's only slightly wounded. The other is suffering quite horribly. The wounded man is a fugitive. We've hidden him in the smokehouse. We've put the man who is dying in our own bed."

"I take it the bushwhackers tarred and feathered the one who's dying."

Reverend Adair looks at her grimly, and Mrs. Adair makes a muffled, gasping sound. The old man rocks with his face bent over

Teddy. For a few seconds the only sound in the cabin is the creaking of the rocking chair and the ticking of the clock over the mantel. Then Elizabeth speaks.

"No," she says. "I wish it had been tar and feathers. You can pull off feathers by grabbing the quills. They used hot tar and cotton."

The man who lies in the Adairs' bed is white, but you cannot easily tell this by looking at him. The bushwhackers who attacked him smeared boiling tar on his body before they rolled him in the cotton. He's blind and terribly burned and will no doubt die—perhaps be better off dead. The only mercy is that his burns are so deep, he can no longer feel pain. When he hears Carrie bend over him he gives her a smile so far away it seems to come from another world.

"Lie still," she tells him, "and I'll clean you up." But when she starts to apply the kerosene, she realizes there's no way to remove the tar without taking his skin along with it. Dropping the rag into the basin, she puts the basin back on the washstand and picks up the jug of whiskey. The whiskey gives off a warm scent that partially covers the singed odor that fills the sickroom, the same odor, Carrie realizes, she detected in Elizabeth's hair.

"Here," she says as she puts the jug to the man's lips, "drink all you want."

The man opens his lips, which have mostly escaped the tar, and gulps some of the whiskey. While Carrie waits for it to take effect, she tries to pick the cotton off him, but there's no way to remove thousands of small strands embedded in tar, and even if she gets them off, he will not be any more comfortable or any more likely to live. Usually when men are tarred and feathered, the mob uses cooler tar. This is murder, plain and simple.

"Who did this to you?" The man makes a noise that sounds like "Cork" or perhaps "Clark." Given the condition he's in, it's a miracle he understood her question. Maybe he didn't. She wonders what he did to attract the attention of the bushwhackers. *The Herald of Freedom* recently ran a story about a lawyer up near Fort Leavenworth who was tarred and feathered for publicly observing that the pro-slave legislature had been elected illegally. Maybe this man made the same error. Or maybe one of his neighbors found out he was a free-soiler.

The man coughs and fumbles for the jug. His hand encounters Carrie's arm, and he draws back with a murmur of what sounds like an apology. Carrie puts the jug to his lips again, lets him finish off most of the whiskey, and watches him fall asleep. There is cotton on his cheeks, his forehead, his eyelids. He looks like a rag doll that has come unstuffed.

Elizabeth and the Adairs have not put the second man in the smokehouse proper but in a secret room under the smokehouse floor designed to conceal fugitive slaves. His skin is black, but he wears the buckskin leggings and moccasins of a Kaw warrior. He is in his early twenties, his head is partly shaved, and his right arm is in a hastily cobbled-together sling made from two knotted bandannas.

"Ni," Elizabeth says, "this is Miss Vinton. She's going to tend to your arm."

"How do you do, Ni," Carrie says. "How did you hurt your arm?" The man remains silent, looking at her in a way she can't decipher.

"Best not to ask questions," Elizabeth says. "He's taken a vow."

"A vow not to talk to me, not to talk to white people, or not to talk to women?"

"Not to talk to anyone about where he's been or what's happened to him."

"I realize that when you're running an Underground Railroad station, there are secrets you can't share, but he has to speak to me or I can't help him." Carrie turns back to the injured man.

"It won't do any good for you to remain silent, sir, and it may do a great deal of harm. I'll never breathe a word that might help your owners recapture you. Besides, I can tell a lot about you just by looking at you. For example, I can tell you've been living with the Kaw or at least bought clothing from them. That's Kaw beadwork on your leggings. I have a cradleboard with Kaw beadwork on it. Your moccasins are badly worn, which leads me to believe you've been walking for a long time. Since the Kaw have recently been driven off their land, I imagine you've been trying to get to Canada before the bushwhackers get hold of you and return you to your master or sell you south. Reverend Adair and his wife have already told me you're a fugitive, and there's no other possible explanation for your presence in this room.

"I am not a doctor, but I am as close to one as you're likely to get, and from what little I can see of your arm, I'd say you might lose it unless you let me fix your injury. To treat you, I need to examine you, and to do that, I need you to talk to me. Please trust me."

"Y'all sure you need me to talk?" Ni says. Carrie is surprised. She had not expected him to reply. He speaks with a Southern accent tempered by some other influence.

"Yes. You're the only person who can tell me about yourself."

"That makes sense." Ni pushes his injured arm toward her. "Have at it."

Carrie carefully unties the sling, exposing a bloody shirt sleeve. Selecting a pair of sharp scissors, she cuts away the sleeve to reveal a wound that could only have been made by a bullet.

"Who shot you?"

"Shot myself."

"How?"

"Foolin' around."

Carrie sighs and sits back. "You're right-handed, aren't you."

"Yes."

"Then I find it very hard to believe that you could have shot yourself in your right forearm. But you're going to stick to that story, aren't you?"

"Yes, ma'am."

"You're lucky. The bullet has gone in, missed the bone, and come out the other side. The wound appears to be clean. Do you know what gangrene is?"

"I've seen men die of it."

"Well then, you'll be happy to know you don't show any signs of it. However, even though your wound is only slightly infected, most doctors would consider taking off your arm just to make sure. I'm not going to do that."

"I'm pleased to hear that."

"I'm going to poke around a bit to make sure there are no bone fragments in there. Then I'm going to wash that wound with soap and water until it hurts so much you'll wish I *had* taken your arm off. Then I'm going to sew it up. Then we'll see what happens. If the wound festers, you'll need to have Elizabeth send for me immediately, and when I say *immediately*, I don't mean the next day."

"You remind me of my mama. No bossier woman ever lived. My wife, Jane, is bossy, too, but—no offense intended, ma'am—you and Mama take the cake."

"No offense taken. I am going to consider being compared to your mother a compliment." Carrie opens her satchel and takes out a jar of liquid soap. She pours some into a basin of hot water, dips a cloth into the foaming mixture, and begins to clean Ni's wound. The scrubbing must hurt, but he doesn't flinch. When she has the wound as clean as soap and water can get it, she puts the basin and cloth aside.

"In about two seconds, I'm going to start poking around in your arm with a metal hook. You want something to bite down on?"

"Nah," Ni says. "Not for a little thing like that."

W hen she returns to the Adairs' cabin, Carrie finds Mr. Brown holding Teddy in his arms, rocking him gently and crooning a lullaby. When he sees Carrie, he stops singing. "How are they?" he asks.

"The one they tarred will probably die."

"The man is a martyr. His suffering has been great, but God will welcome him into heaven with trumpets and hosannas. And the wounded man?"

"He'll live to shoot again. Let's just hope that next time he doesn't practice contortionism."

"I do not take your meaning."

"He tells me he shot himself in the right forearm. This is clearly impossible. Obviously someone else shot him. Do you happen to know who that someone might be?"

The old man does not answer. Kissing Teddy on the forehead, he hands him to Carrie. "Teddy is your husband's child," he says, "is he not? And yet, I hear you do not live with your husband, but with another man."

Carrie stiffens. "What business is it of yours whose son Teddy is or whom I live with?"

"You mistake my meaning. You see, you, too, are a martyr, Mrs. Presgrove."

Carrie is so shocked to hear him say *Mrs. Presgrove* that she's rendered speechless. Bending forward, Mr. Brown stares at her intently. She sees gray eyes, wild and deep, love and hatred mixed together, rage and peace—nothing simple or unmixed. "You are Carrie Vinton Presgrove."

She nods.

"Your husband is Deacon Presgrove, son of Kentucky Senator Bennett Presgrove."

Again she nods.

"You wonder how I know all this? I cannot tell you. I hear you left your husband despite the fact that you were with child by him because he believes in slavery and you abhor it. Is this true?"

"Yes," she whispers.

"Marriage is sacred. I never urge wives to leave their husbands even if those husbands are slave owners, but in your case, I approve. Deacon Presgrove and his father are tools of Satan. They smuggle slaves into this country against the laws of God and man. Thus you are like unto the slave who flees an evil master: blameless and righteous.

"No matter how harshly other people judge you, Mrs. Presgrove, my sons and I will stand with you. You have the courage of Jael, who put her hand to the nail and her right hand to the workman's hammer, drove that nail into Sisera's head, and for this deed God gave victory to Israel. There is no sin in your abandonment of a wicked man who is an enemy of human freedom, and there is no sin in protecting an innocent child from an evil father. The sin is slavery, and all those who struggle against it are loved by the Lord."

Carrie finally finds her voice. "Who are you?"

The old man's eyes glitter with something bright she has no name for. "I am merely Mrs. Adair's brother. I have been many things in my time: a farmer, a shepherd, a surveyor. When I was a child, I saw a boy my own age brutally beaten with an iron fire shovel. The boy was a slave; the man who wielded the shovel was his master. That boy's screams still haunt me. On the day I saw him suffer, I became a determined foe of slavery. I have come to Kansas to help defeat Satan and his legions, and I have heard the thundering voice of Jehovah exhorting me to slaughter the border ruffians as He called

Gideon to slay the Midianites." He pauses and sits back. "Am I frightening you?"

"Yes."

"I apologize. Sometimes I speak the truth more forcefully than people are prepared to hear it. Your boy is sleeping peacefully. I am no danger to you or to him. Please go outside and ask Mrs. Newberry to come to me. I have something to tell her."

F ive minutes after Elizabeth enters the Adairs' cabin, she comes out, folds her arms across her chest, and looks at Carrie thoughtfully. "Congratulations," she says. "It appears you passed the test."

"What test? I didn't know I was being tested?"

"Mr. Brown has given me permission to show you something."

"Mr. Brown is in charge around here?"

"Yes. Can you imagine him not being in charge of whatever he puts his hand to?"

Carrie peers into the cabin. Brown is still sitting by the fire. All she can see is the back of his head and his long-fingered hands spread out on the arms of the rocker. She motions to Elizabeth to follow her to a place where they can't be overheard.

They walk out into the night and down toward the river. When they reach the riverbank, Carrie shifts Teddy to her other hip and turns to Elizabeth. "Before you show me whatever Mr. Brown gave you permission to show me, I need to ask you a question: He just said some very kind things to me, but he said them in a way I find unsettling. He knows things I thought no one but William and I knew. I'm not sure I want to share his secrets. I'm impressed by how dedicated he is to ending slavery, but he quotes the Old Testament constantly and speaks so violently that I'm not sure he's entirely sane. Is he, Elizabeth?"

"That's a hard question to answer. You know your Bible as well as I do. Were Isaiah, Jeremiah, and Ezekiel sane? Was John the Revelator?"

"Frankly, I've never been sure."

"I've never been sure either, particularly about John. Don't bother asking me if I mean John the Revelator or John Brown. Both hear what the rest of us don't hear and see what the rest of us don't see, and both preach with the terrifying tongues of angels. One thing I'd say about Mr. Brown, though: You don't ever want to cross him."

"I'll keep that in mind," Carrie says. "So what's the secret?"

Chapter Twenty-seven

The prairie is dappled with dim light, deeply shadowed, trackless, easy to get lost in. The only sound is the soft rustling of the wind, the creak of the saddles, and the clopping of the horses' hooves. Carrie rides next to Elizabeth close enough to hear her whispered directions. No one guards them tonight, not the Browns, not Elizabeth's sons, not even Mr. Trout.

Carrie has left Teddy back in Osawatomie with Prosser's wife, Eulie. "Don't worry about him for a minute," Eulie said when Carrie handed him over. "I'm still nursing my youngest and have milk enough for two." Eulie lowered her voice and bent forward so her mother-in-law couldn't hear. "Besides, Keyhole Draw's no place to take a child."

"Describe it to me," Carrie asked Elizabeth as they set out. "Give me some idea where we're headed."

"It's better if you just see it," Elizabeth said. "Then I'll explain." So the mystery continues. All Carrie knows is that she and Elizabeth are headed somewhere that makes grown women lower their voices and look around to make sure they aren't being overheard when they speak of it. She has kept many secrets in her time, but this one appears to be buried deeper than all the rest put together.

Keyhole Draw. She takes the words apart like a puzzle. Since a *draw* is a ravine and a *keyhole* is small and narrow, they are probably riding to a narrow ravine where fugitive slaves are hidden until they can be passed on to the next Underground Railroad station. But perhaps she's wrong. According to Elizabeth, even the Adairs don't know Keyhole Draw exists. That doesn't make sense. The Adairs are the stationmasters at Osawatomie. They've been working with Elizabeth for two years. They built the secret room under their smokehouse where Carrie tended to Ni's arm. How can Carrie have passed John Brown's test when his own sister and brother-in-law have failed it?

"You're the only white woman in Osawatomie Mr. Brown is letting in on the secret," Elizabeth told her. "The only others who know about the draw are his own wife, Mary Ann, and his sons' wives, and all of them are living up at Brown's Station along North Middle Creek. To tell the truth, I'm not even sure Mrs. Brown and his sons' wives know."

Know what? Carrie wonders. *What kind of secret do you keep from your wife and your sons' wives, and how far away is this place? We've been riding for over an hour, doubling back and coming at the place from different angles. Who does Elizabeth think might follow us at this time of night? Osawatomie is an abolitionist town, and as for bushwhackers—why would they be out in the middle of nowhere at five in the morning? Those Missouri boys like their warm campfires and whiskey. Even if they were out looking for trouble, they'd follow the California Road or go someplace where they could find cabins to burn and stores to loot. There's no glory in tar and feathering gophers.*

She is just wondering if she might be able to persuade Elizabeth to stop taking evasive action and make a beeline for the place, when

Elizabeth reigns in her horse and points to a dim line of low hills. The hills are forested most of the way up and so dark they appear only as silhouettes against the moonlit sky.

"We're almost at the entrance. Before we draw any closer, we need to wait to make sure no one is following us. Also, I want you to see the place by daylight."

By now, Carrie knows better than to ask questions. They ride toward a stand of bushes. The leaves are small this time of year, but the tangle is thick enough to provide cover. While they wait, Carrie picks a leaf and tries to figure out what kind of bush is sheltering them. The leaf has teeth. Hazelnut, perhaps, but it's too dark to be sure. Gradually the darkness thins, and the eastern sky turns milky. Clouds drift in from the west and begin to take on a reddish tinge. Carrie looks down and sees she is holding a hazelnut leaf. Pleased with herself, she tosses it to the ground. "What now?" she asks.

"Wait a little longer."

Birds begin to sing, and slowly the prairie emerges, lapping at the base of the hills and spreading out in three directions for as far as Carrie can see. Elizabeth produces a small pair of binoculars and scans the horizon. Satisfied they're alone, she folds them up with a click and puts them back in her saddlebag.

"Collapsible opera glasses," she says. "Very handy."

Just before the sun tops the horizon, they ride on toward the hills. Carrie can see no sign of a draw or break of any kind. Just a low, forested rise as uniform as a wall.

"You can't see the entrance from here," Elizabeth remarks. As they draw closer, the ground grows marshy, and they come upon a small creek, which runs out of the forest only to disappear into the ground almost immediately. If you didn't know it was there, you'd have a hard time finding it.

When they reach the trees, Elizabeth dismounts and motions for

Carrie to do the same. "Come help me," she says. They walk to a place where a tangle of dead underbrush has piled up over the creek. The brush does not block the flow of the creek, but it's too thick to ride through.

Elizabeth grabs the nearest branch and tells Carrie to do the same. Together they begin to tug, but the brush doesn't budge. "Lift," Elizabeth orders. Carrie lifts her side, and suddenly the entire center section moves forward. Leaves, branches, twigs, and brambles have been woven into a mat. Where there was once an impassible tangle, there is now an opening that leads into a narrow rift between the hills.

"Think of it as a trapdoor," Elizabeth says. "Weaving in the blackberry brambles was the hardest part. Prosser and Toussaint wanted to add poison ivy, but I drew the line."

Remounting their horses, they ride up the creek through a steeply walled, narrow gully lined with willows and cottonwoods. Most of the year, the creek is probably dry, but it is running fairly high this morning, bottomed with slippery mud and stones, so they go slowly.

As they climb, the draw opens up and the cottonwoods give way to oaks, sycamores, and walnuts. They come to another draw that branches off to the left, steeper and even more narrow. No water flows through it. Elizabeth stops. Pursing her lips together, she produces the call of a blue jay. Another jay answers. Elizabeth grins. "You just heard the song of a jayhawk," she says.

They ride up the smaller draw. Again they stop. Again Elizabeth makes the sound of a bird, this time an owl. Unlike jays, owls don't fly about in the daytime, but an owl answers.

"Count to ten," Elizabeth says.

Carrie starts to count. Before she gets to eight, two men slide out of the brush.

"Peet!" Carrie cries. "Ebenezer!"

"Welcome to Keyhole Draw," Peet says and waves them on.

* * *

They ride for another three minutes or so before they come to the top of the ridge. There they halt, and Carrie finds herself looking down on a small cluster of sod huts grouped around a pond. No smoke is coming from the huts, but people are moving around doing various things. One appears to be sharpening a knife on a grinding wheel. Another is hanging wash on a clothesline.

"Who are they?" she asks.

"Fugitive slaves." Elizabeth points at the huts. "You're looking at a small community of them hidden in the best natural fortress in the territory. Sentries posted on the crest can see almost to Osawatomie. Any attackers are forced to approach in single file. Ten men can hold off fifty if they have guns, are properly trained, and know what they're doing."

"It's a *quilombo*! I didn't know they existed in Kansas!"

"*Quilombo*? I've never heard the word. You can explain it to me some other time. The point is, Keyhole Draw has been almost two years in the making. At first it happened by accident. We ran three slaves out of Missouri. They'd fled their masters and were tired of running. They wanted to live together right here in Kansas. Bilander, Cush, and Marcellus. Remember? You saw them at Trout's."

"Yes. I remember. William helped them escape."

"That he did. He and his band of Jayhawkers left them at Trout's Hotel, and Mr. Trout turned them over to me. At first they lived in Osawatomie with Prosser's family, but there was a price on their heads, so we decided they needed a safer place. Without telling the Adairs, Prosser, Toussaint, and I scouted around and found Keyhole Draw.

"For a while that's how new people came to us. They'd run away, decide they wanted to stay in Kansas, and we'd take them here. Then

I showed Mr. Brown the place and before I knew it, he was running fugitive slaves to Keyhole Draw instead of Canada."

"Why?"

"Because he's training up an army. Right now there are fourteen men down there. Some arrived with wives and children or elderly male relatives. We're hiding them with Mrs. Hulett. You remember her? The white woman who pretended to be our mistress so me and mine could get through Missouri without being taken by slavers? She's living at a place called Two Rivers on the bank of the Marais des Cygnes not far from Osawatomie. Grows rope hemp mostly, plus a little corn and tobacco.

"When any of the slavers ask her why she has such an odd collection of field hands, she tells them she divided an inheritance with her brother, and he got all the able-bodied men. She's very convincing, has ladylike airs, and can speak with a Southern accent that makes her sound as if she were born and raised in Tennessee, which is where she claims to be from. Since there are real slave owners living only a few miles from her, no one thinks it odd that she's working slaves so close to an abolitionist town like Osawatomie.

"There are no women in Keyhole Draw. It's strictly a military camp, or at least it would be if the men had enough weapons and horses. The Browns have been trying to turn them into a cavalry unit since last October."

"I'd like to get a closer look." Carrie starts to kick her horse forward, but Elizabeth grabs the bridle.

"You can't go down there. Mr. Brown said you were to be like Moses on the mountain: You get to look at the Promised Land but you don't get to enter it."

"Why not?"

"No one, man or woman, black or white, gets to visit Keyhole Draw. There are too many secrets."

"What sort of secrets?"

"If I told you, they wouldn't be secrets, would they?"

"No, I suppose they wouldn't, but if I can only gaze at this place from afar, what was the point of bringing me here?"

"Mr. Brown's orders. He wanted you to see that he was training up an army of fugitive slaves to liberate other slaves. When they drill, the men sometimes get hurt. There are no doctors closer than Westport and they're all pro-slavers. Mr. Brown wants you and William to move to Osawatomie and set up a clinic.

"And there's something else, something I'm not supposed to tell you, but I don't see how I can ask you to move to Osawatomie if I don't. Mr. Brown and I don't see eye to eye about this. When the bushwhacker legislature started passing pro-slavery laws that carried the death penalty for anyone who defied them, I wanted the blacks in Osawatomie to have guns so we could defend ourselves, but Mr. Brown had a different notion. He's training those men down there to attack."

"You mean raid?"

"No, ride in like a real cavalry, free slaves, and start an insurrection."

"But there are only a few plantations in Kansas and not many slaves to free except the ones along the Missouri border."

"Mr. Brown doesn't intend to use these men in Kansas. His plan is to smuggle them into the South and start a slave revolt. He wants general civil war."

"Into the South! They'll all be massacred!"

"That's what I think. I tried to tell Mr. Brown that, but he said I needed to 'gird my loins and take up the sword.' Carrie, I don't know what to do. Mr. Brown is the greatest man I've ever met. No one has ever treated me and my family with more love and respect, but I also fear he may lead all who follow him to destruction.

"Sometimes I think: So be it. If it takes martyrdom to free my people, let us be martyrs. But then I look at my grandbabies and think how much I would like to see them grow up, and I wake in the middle of the night afraid that if I die and my sons and their families die and all those men down there die, nothing will change, and our lives will have been wasted."

Carrie thinks of fourteen men sent into the heart of the South to start a revolution. No matter how brave they are, no matter how well-armed, no matter how well-trained or how determined . . . Does John Brown understand something she doesn't? Does he really hear the voice of God?

Suppose he's right. Suppose this is the spark that will ignite the great civil war the *buzios* say is coming. Suppose his death and the deaths of these fourteen men will end slavery forever. Suppose only John Brown is capable of seeing this. Suppose he knows exactly what he's doing. Could his plan work? She's almost sure it couldn't, but what if she's the one who's mistaken?

"It all keeps coming back to John the Revelator, doesn't it?" she says.

Elizabeth sighs wearily. "Crazy or sane," she says. "I wish to God I knew which."

Chapter Twenty-eight

Lawrence, Kansas, late April 1856

Mrs. Presgrove?" An old lady's voice, high and shaking. Carrie wheels around. The street is empty except for a man who is standing beside his horse inspecting the cinch on his saddle. As she walks toward him, he straightens up and turns toward her. He has red cheeks, curly white-blond hair, and blue eyes that seem slightly glassy.

"Excuse me, sir," she says, "did you hear someone call out a name?"

"No, ma'am."

"You didn't hear an old woman?"

"No, ma'am."

"Thank you. I'm sorry to have troubled you."

"No trouble at all, ma'am." He tips his hat. "Pleased to have been of service."

Carrie walks on, wondering if she imagined it. Behind her, Henry Clark finishes tightening the cinch on his saddle. "Mrs. Presgrove?" he whispers in a trembling, old-lady voice. He laughs and slaps his horse on the rump. *Found her!* he thinks.

Chapter Twenty-nine

Missouri, May 1856

On a warm day in late spring, a paddlewheel steamer pulls up to the Kansas Landing, double-stacked, three-decked, gold and white, pretty as a wedding cake. The passengers hang over the rails, four hundred men and not a single woman except a lady missionary from Providence, Rhode Island, who got on by accident in St. Louis and has regretted it ever since.

As the boat docks, the men wave their hats, church bells ring, and a brass band strikes up "Cheer Boys Cheer." Six years from now that song will be the anthem of a group of Confederate guerillas, but on this warm spring afternoon, it merely provides a stirring musical background as the gangplank is rolled out and four hundred men from Alabama, Georgia, and South Carolina march onto Missouri soil in military formation carrying banners that read: KANSAS THE OUTPOST! SOUTHERN RIGHTS! and SUPREMECY OF THE WHITE RACE!

The man who organized this massive emigration of pro-slavers is Major Jefferson Buford of Eufaula, Alabama, but the man who paid for much of it is Deacon Presgrove, or to be more precise, Carrie, since Deacon used her money. By right of having made the second largest contribution, Deacon walks just behind Buford, leading the procession.

When Carrie lived with him, Deacon dressed in elegant suits—silk cravat tied just so, gold watch chain draped over his stomach, gray kid gloves on his hands, silk top hat on his head; but all that has changed. Today he wears a broad-brimmed western hat, a red flannel shirt, and homespun trousers tucked into cowhide boots. His belt, tooled with Mexican silver, is almost as wide as the palm of his hand. He bristles with pistols and a knife so long the scabbard impedes his progress, but he bears this inconvenience with a smile.

White teeth, glowing green eyes, flushed face: Deacon is happy, triumphant, ready to make a name for himself. His father has convinced him to stop wasting time in Mrs. Springer's parlor. He has promised Deacon that if he goes to the Kansas Territory with Buford, the deeds he performs there will win him a fame that will carry him to the Senate—not the Senate that presently meets in Washington City, but a new Senate composed of Southern states that will soon meet in Charleston or Richmond, or perhaps even Louisville.

"Go to Kansas, kill some of those abolitionist bastards, and find your wife," Bennett said. "You can't afford to have her running loose if you plan to enter politics. A cuckold is a fool and an object of ridicule. I don't care to open *Leslie's Illustrated* and see a cartoon featuring my son in horns."

Good advice, but easier to give than take. Deacon is just wondering if Henry Clark has had any luck locating Carrie, when he looks into the waiting throng and finds his answer. A pair of cold blue eyes is staring straight at him. Henry Clark smiles. Pursing his lips, he blows Deacon a kiss. For a moment Deacon feels like a small bird that has suddenly encountered an affectionate cobra.

He's found her, Deacon thinks, *or else he wouldn't be here wait-*

ing for me. He looks away and pretends to examine the bluff up ahead. The joy goes out of the day, and he feels as if something heavy has settled on his chest. The truth is, he doesn't want Carrie back. He has her money; the rest is just trouble piled on trouble. Still there is his reputation to consider and the child of course. If his stepmother hadn't started babbling about the little brat on her death-bed, he might have never known Carrie was breeding when she de-camped. Deacon wonders if he is presently the father of a boy or a girl. *Father,* as in owner. He hopes this one hasn't died like the last one. He'll be able to make Carrie do anything he wants once he gets hold of her child.

Marry me, Carrie my dear, he thinks. *And we'll make some little hostages together.* He grins at his own wit. Then he remembers those cold blue eyes. When he looks into the waiting crowd, they are still fixed on him.

If Clark has found Carrie, it's going to cost a bundle to pry her whereabouts out of him. Deacon would rather keep the money; he really would. But there are a dozen men standing around Clark, each more evil-looking than the next: big, unshaven men with dirty kerchiefs around their necks and rifles slung over their backs. Clark's band. Or maybe they're Mangas Coloradas's band, or the Beast of Revelation's, or Jesus Christ's. Deacon can't tell by looking who Clark is this afternoon, but even a fool can see it would be a bad idea to try to cheat him out of what he's been promised. Those ruf-fians in the kerchiefs would probably be happy to kill a man for sport.

Deacon imagines himself stuck to a barn door with Bowie knives. He wonders if they would scalp him first, what parts of him they would cut off. *Damn,* he thinks.

He looks at the muddy path that leads up the bluff to the newly constructed pro-slaver hotel. The sun is ridiculously hot, the crowd has begun to cheer in a way that implies terminal drunkenness, the entire landing smells of manure, and he is bound to ruin his new boots before he gets to the top. He wishes his long underwear did not itch, wishes he were in bed romping with Lily, wishes Henry Clark would stop staring at him with those lunatic eyes.

Chapter Thirty

Just before dawn. A faint paling of the eastern horizon, the rustle of small animals moving through the grass toward their burrows. Carrie and William get up, yawn, stretch, and trade morning kisses. They light a lantern, and while Carrie nurses Teddy, William stokes up the fire in the stove and makes breakfast. Fried ham, eggs, leftover cornbread from last night, a little reheated oatmeal for Teddy, a pot of coffee.

William eats rapidly. When he has drained the last sip of coffee from his cup, he grabs his rifle, slaps on his hat, kisses Teddy and Carrie good-bye, and hurries into town to relieve the men who are guarding the Free State Hotel. A little while later, half a dozen early risers stroll down Massachusetts Street to unlock their stores. When they reach the Free State, they stop to learn the latest news.

A peaceful night, William and the other guards tell them. *No sign of trouble so far.*

Good, they say. *Glad to hear it.*

The bad news is that the pro-slaver legislature over in Lecompton has issued treason indictments against us, and we hear their boy,

Sheriff Jones, plans to show up sometime this morning with a posse.
He intends to disarm us, arrest us, and shoot any man who resists.
We'll fight back.
That we will.
God in His mercy keep us.

The store owners walk on. Over Lawrence, Mount Oread looms
like a great, black-pelted beast. At last the sun rises, hot and orange
and so huge it looks like the mouth of a fiery tunnel. As the light
strikes the slopes of Mount Oread, it reveals a mob of pro-slavers
poised to descend on Lawrence. Armed with cannons, pistols, rifles,
knives, swords, and hangmen's nooses, they still bear the banners that
read KANSAS THE OUTPOST! SOUTHERN RIGHTS! and SUPREMECY OF
THE WHITE RACE!, but there is a new banner on Mount Oread this
morning, one more terrible than all the rest. It is the banner of Henry
Clark's Raiders: an oblong of white cotton cut out of a bed sheet and
dipped in blood.

There is no motto on Clark's flag, only the blood, dried to reddish black. It comes from a pig slaughtered at Beau Rivage, the Missouri plantation of Clark's cousin, Jedediah Clark, but whenever
someone asks, Henry Clark claims it's the blood of an abolitionist.

"Kill 'em all!" Clark yells, slapping Deacon Presgrove on the
back. Deacon flinches and turns pale as around him Clark's men
cheer and discharge their pistols into the air.

D own below, Carrie hears the sound of gunfire. Abandoning the
breakfast dishes, she walks to the window and sees the army
of pro-slavers gathered on Mount Oread. More gunfire. The sound
of men cheering, but no movement yet. Their flags whip in the wind.
Sunlight glints off the barrels of their cannons.

Suddenly, she feels sick with fear. She's never witnessed a battle
and never wants to. She imagines walls coming down, roofs blown

off, the ugly hole in Ni's arm that a single bullet made. The pro-slavers have promised to spare women and children, but she wouldn't put it past them to use her house for target practice.

More gunfire. She starts and puts her hand over her mouth to keep from crying out. *Why can't they leave us alone? Why can't they let us live in peace? We don't want this war!* Turning, she hurries to Teddy, scoops him up in her arms, and holds him close. The second he catches sight of her face, he begins to howl.

"Don't cry, sweetheart," she pleads, but he can feel her fear, and he knows with that blind, perfect instinct of very young children that something is going on worth crying about.

U p on Mount Oread, Clark pulls out a spyglass and peers down at Lawrence. Lowering the glass, he turns to Deacon with a look of disgust. "The craven milksops are still negotiating."

By "craven milksops" Deacon presumes Clark means Sheriff Jones and the Eldridge brothers who own the Free State Hotel. If this is true, it's good news. The attack still might be called off. Deacon doesn't relish the prospect of walking into a wall of abolitionist gunfire or being shot in the back by one of Clark's drunken henchmen.

Clark suddenly lifts his rifle and aims toward Lawrence. He hums cheerfully as he moves the barrel around searching for a target.

"What in God's name are you preparing to do!" Deacon cries.

"I intend to shoot the Eldridge brothers. Quiet, please. It's hard to tell those damn abolitionists apart at this distance. They're all wearing black suits. If the Eldridges would just wear some kind of uniform, this would be infinitely easier. Peaked hats, perhaps. Dunces' caps. Ah-ha!" Clark locks on his target.

It takes Deacon less than a tenth of a second to figure out that if Clark pulls the trigger there will be hell to pay. Lunging forward, he grabs the rifle barrel and shoves it to one side just as Clark shoots.

The rifle goes off with a deafening bang, and he feels the recoil sting his hand. Shaken, he looks up to see Clark smiling at him.

"Thank you," Clark says. "As you realized, rifles are not accurate at this range. I might have hit Sheriff Jones."

"You're welcome." Deacon stutters. He is shaking so hard he can hardly keep his teeth from chattering. Whatever possessed him to foil Clark's shot? Crossing the man is like taunting a mad dog.

Clark slings his rifle over his back and retrieves his spyglass. "She's down there," he says, using the glass as a pointer. "Last house on the right by the river."

"Who?"

"Your wife. Mrs. Deacon Presgrove. Down there, living in sin with your own brother. Mangas Coloradas wouldn't have tolerated it. If you like, we can ride down and pay her a visit while the rest of the army is otherwise occupied."

"No, thank you, Henry. That's a generous offer, but I would rather deal with Carrie by myself."

"Suit yourself." There is a moment of silence, and then Clark speaks again. "She has pretty hair. Blonde and curly. Rather like mine." Clark runs his fingers through his hair and looks up at his flag. He's clearly thinking about something. Whatever it is, Deacon hopes he keeps it to himself.

At noon, the men guarding the Free State are served roast beef sandwiches, slices of pie, and hot coffee. Up on Mount Oread, the only thing being served is whiskey, and even that is running low. Around one o'clock, a carriage rolls up the dirt track that leads to the crest. In it sits David Rice Atchison, the former Senator from Missouri. Due to a bureaucratic technicality, Atchison was once President of the United States for a single day. Ever since, he has been looking for a country to lead, and in Kansas he believes he has found it.

Atchison has previously called on pro-slavery Missourians to kill every abolitionist in the territory. Now, too portly to mount a horse, he stands in his specially re-enforced carriage and gives a speech that makes Deacon shudder.

"Kansas will be ours!" Atchison thunders. "We'll teach those damned abolitionists a lesson they'll remember until the day they die! Remember: if a woman picks up a rifle, she's no longer a woman. Trample her under your feet as you would a snake! Blow her to hell with a chunk of cold lead!"

The pro-slavers cheer until they are hoarse. Fixing their bayonets, they begin to march down the slope toward Lawrence.

Below, Carrie sits in a straight-backed chair with Teddy on her lap and a Sharps rifle across her knees. She hears gunshots, a confusion of voices. Ten minutes pass. Fifteen. Suddenly there is a knock on the door.

"Who's there?" she demands.

"It's Donald Lane, madam. Please let me in. I bring you news of Doctor Saylor." The voice is unfamiliar, clipped vowels, British accent. If Carrie had ever seen a one-act farce entitled *Mr. Buckstone's Ascent of Mount Parnassus*, she might have recognized it as the voice of the hero, Mr. Buckstone.

Getting up, she walks over to the bed, puts Teddy down, and pulls the quilt over him. "Stay there and be quiet," she whispers. Returning to the door, she tries to look through the cracks and is rewarded with the sight of a bit of red that could be part of a flannel shirt.

"I don't know a Mr. Lane."

"Madam, please! The bushwhackers have attacked the town, and Doctor Saylor has been wounded!"

"Wounded!" Drawing back the bar, Carrie opens the door and finds herself face-to-face with Deacon. Uttering a cry of surprise, she tries to slam it shut, but before she can close it, she's thrown off balance by an explosion so violent it rattles the windowpanes.

D own on Massachusetts Street, the Free State Hotel disappears in a geyser of black smoke and fire. Bits of plaster and concrete rain down, coating everything with a layer of fine white dust. As the pieces of the hotel fall on Clark, he throws back his head, opens his mouth, and licks at them as if they were bits of honeycomb.

The bushwhacker who is holding William at gunpoint gives a yip of triumph. Lowering his pistol, he turns and begins to run toward the dry goods store. Before he can reach the other side of Massachusetts Street, a man on horseback rides him down.

The bushwhacker screams and writhes in pain. For a few seconds, William watches him curse and claw at the dust. It's supposed to be enjoyable to see someone who has threatened to kill you suffer, but it isn't. He hurries to the injured man.

"I'm a doctor," he says. "I can help you."

"Damn it, damn it, damn it!" the man yells. "You shot me in the back, you abolitionist bastard!"

"You haven't been shot. You're not making sense. You were ridden down by a horse and may have suffered a concussion." But the injured man won't listen. Standing up, he staggers forward and throws himself on William. His fingers close around William's throat.

"Let go, you crazy fool!" William gasps.

"Crazy?" the man snarls. "Yeah, you abolitionist son of a bitch, I'm crazy!"

William sees red spots, long swirls of black, and flames that dance and flicker in front of his eyes. As he struggles to pry the madman's hands from his throat, he realizes the flames are real. He can feel the heat of them scorching the back of his jacket.

There is another explosion and a crash of breaking glass. More gunfire. The bushwhackers are destroying *The Kansas Free State* and *The Herald of Freedom*, smashing the presses, throwing the type out the windows. Others are looting stores and private homes. They parade the sidewalks of Lawrence wrapped in silk curtains and stolen hats, dump canned goods into their saddle bags, seize hams and sausages, break dishes, bash in the sides of flour barrels for sport. Most search for whiskey, but Henry Clark and his men go looking for guns.

Chapter Thirty-one

Carrie hits the door from one side as Deacon hits it from the other. Seizing a broom, she jams the handle into the nearest bracket and throws her weight against it. The broom handle bends under the force of his assault, but for the moment it holds. It's a poor substitute for the wooden bar that goes all the way across the door, but the bar and rifle are both out of reach. If she tries to get to either one, she'll have to let go, and Deacon is hitting the door like a battering ram, commanding her to open up, yelling that he's come to take her back to Washington.

"You're my wife," he bellows. "I won't have you living in concubinage with my stepbrother. You'll come, you damnable bitch!"

She'd yell back, but it would be a waste of breath, and she needs every bit she has. He hits the door again and begins to pound on it like a madman. He's saying crazy things about how he intends to run for the Senate and how she's getting in his way. She can feel his blows through the planks. The door shudders, and the broom handle smashes against her fingers and creaks as if it's about to snap. How long can she hold him off? Maybe a neighbor will hear the noise and come to her rescue or maybe William will show up.

All at once, the pounding stops. Exhausted, she leans against the door, shaking and terrified. Has he given up? Suddenly, she hears him running across the front porch. She braces herself, but he hits the door with such force that the broom handle splinters and the door springs open, throwing her to the floor. Rolling onto her hands and knees, she scrambles toward her rifle, but before she can get to it, he kicks her arms out from under her and slams his boot down on her back pinning her in place.

She looks up at him and sees those familiar, catlike green eyes staring down at her. And then she sees the revolver. He has the barrel pointed at her head, and at this range, not even he can miss.

"Get the hell up," he commands, removing his boot from her back. Carrie rises to her feet. Her arms don't appear to be broken, but her hands are full of splinters, her hair has come down around her shoulders, and the left sleeve of her dress is ripped.

"You look like hell. Like a slut. Where's my son?"

"Teddy's not yours. He's William's." She fights an urge to look over her shoulder and make sure Teddy is still hidden under the quilt. She can't let Deacon see how afraid she is. He's a coward and a bully, and if he thinks he's succeeded in terrorizing her, things will only get worse.

"Liar. My stepmother told me you were breeding when you ran off." He readjusts the revolver so it points at her chest. Will he shoot her? He's dressed like a bushwhacker. What's he been doing since she left him? What's he capable of?

She sets her jaw stubbornly and stares at him until he lowers his eyes, but he doesn't lower the gun, which continues to waver between her chest and head. Maybe she intimidates him, or maybe he decides it's time to change tactics. Whatever the reason, his voice grows slick, and wheedling. "Be reasonable, Carrie. Tell me where the boy is. What harm can it do for me to see him?"

How "reasonable" does he think she's likely to be at the wrong end of a gun? Could she wrest it out of his hand if she charged straight at him? No, with Teddy hiding nearby, the risk of stray bullets is too great.

Deacon's voice becomes oily enough to gag on. "If the boy—Teddy?—really is William's, then this is your chance to take him to see his grandmother. Matilda asks after him constantly. Poor woman. So ill, and at her age, well one never knows how long—"

"Liar!" She tosses the word back at him and watches with satisfaction as it hits. "Matilda's dead. She's been dead for nearly a year. We get newspapers out here in Kansas. We read obituaries. How did she die? Did you and your *porcaria* of a father poison her? William wanted to go back east and force you to confess, but I persuaded him the satisfaction wasn't worth—"

Deacon lunges at her, and she steps back, sure he's going to hit her. "Shut up!" he yells.

"I won't shut up! I know a lot of things about you that you wouldn't want made public. I even know about that slave-smuggling operation you and Bennett are running out of Brazil. What are you going to say to the custom agents when I tell them what kind of cargo Presgrove Sugar has been off-loading on the Sea Islands of South Carolina? If you take that gun out of my face and get out of here, maybe I won't tell them, maybe—"

Deacon grabs her by the shoulder and shoves her aside. "Teddy!" he yells. "Where are you? Come here! Your daddy has some candy for you!"

Carrie whirls around, but it's too late. Teddy has thrown off the quilt and is sitting up. As Deacon starts toward him, she steps between them, grabs the barrel of the revolver, and leans against it.

"Go ahead. Pull the trigger. You'll have to kill me to get to him!"

"Get out of my way, you crazy bitch!" Ramming the barrel into her chest so hard it knocks the wind out of her lungs, he gives her another shove that sends her stumbling backward. She clutches at the air and falls, hitting her head on the stove on the way down. The blow stuns her, and she lies on her back unable to move as the room turns around her in a sickening circle.

Deacon picks up her rifle and throws it of reach. Grabbing Teddy, he stuffs him under his arm like a parcel, walks over to where Carrie is lying, and stands over her. By now Teddy is terrified and screaming, but Deacon ignores him.

"I'll give you one more chance. Come back to Washington with me. Be my wife. I won't force you into my bed, if that's what you're worried about, but if you don't leave with me right now, you're never going to see the little brat again."

Her head throbs, she's bitten her tongue, and she can taste blood in her mouth. If there's anything more she can do to make him put Teddy down and go away, she's not capable of thinking of it. "I'll—" she gasps.

"You'll what? Come with me?" She nods and stretches out her hand, but he bats it aside. "What kind of fool do you think I am? Get up on your own."

Rising to her knees, she slowly struggles to her feet. As she stands, the wind catches the door and rattles it. Looking toward the sound, she sees William standing in the doorway holding his pistol in one hand and an iron skillet in the other.

Deacon doesn't turn around. He's too busy doing his victory dance. *You miserable* safado, she thinks. She looks at him standing there like a pompous fool, and feels a mixture of relief and anger that makes her glad she didn't try to grab his gun. They're going to get Teddy away from him without a shot being fired.

"Life's like poker," Deacon's saying, "and you just drew losing cards."

Carrie nods weakly as if she's given up and has no more fight left in her. Weaving a little, she grabs at the edge of the stove to steady herself—the perfect picture of a woman about to swoon. If Deacon knew her better—if he had ever really known her at all—he'd realize she wasn't the fainting type, but the only person he's ever studied is himself.

"None of that, now," he says. "I've got no time for female fainting fits. Go get your bonnet. There's—"

Suddenly she plunges toward him hitting his arm, knocking the revolver out of his hand, and grabbing Teddy on the way down. *Whap!* William steps up behind Deacon and poleaxes him with the skillet.

When Deacon opens his eyes a few minutes later, he finds himself staring down the barrel of William's gun. To Carrie's surprise and amusement, his first reaction is to scream like someone is tearing out his fingernails.

"Don't shoot me!" he shrieks.

"This isn't one of your melodramas," William says. "Pull yourself together, man, and get to your feet."

Deacon stands up. His face is as white as a cotton pillowcase, and he's shaking so violently Carrie almost pities him. For a few seconds William stares at him without speaking. Then he says: "If you ever come anywhere near Carrie and Teddy again, I'll blow your damn head off. Do you understand?" Deacon makes a squeaking sound like a rat caught in a trap. He opens his mouth but no words come out.

"Get the hell out of here," William says.

After Deacon leaves, William stays with Carrie and Teddy for the rest of the day. By nightfall the sack of Lawrence is over. The next morning, Atchison marches his men through town one last time and loads them onto a boat that will take them back to Missouri. That day and the next, William and Carrie pitch in to help clean up the mess, and on Friday a band of bushwhackers comes back in the middle of the night and burns down their house.

Who dips those rags in kerosene, sets them on fire, and throws them onto the thatch? Did Deacon send them? William and Carrie never know for sure, but they wake to the smell of smoke and the sound of riders leaving at a gallop.

The men who burn their house also steal William's horse, but even if the bushwhackers had left the mare in the stable, William and Carrie are too busy trying to put out the fire to pursue the arsonists, so their identity remains a mystery.

Scooping up Teddy, they escape unharmed. They save William's medical instruments and books; Carrie's art supplies, drawings, and plant presses; the quilt; two of the buffalo robes, a tin box full of dried plants, and a trunk of clothing; but the rag rug, the hand-carved butter molds, the churn, and the blue calico curtains go up in flames.

The memory that stays with Carrie longest is the sight of the newspapers she pasted to the walls. One by one, they curl and twist, blacken and fall to the ground as ash. After the ashes cool, she picks up a handful and throws them into the air. As they drift away, she silently lists all the places she's lived: houses in Rio, huts along the upper Amazon, Mae Seja's *quilombo*, Grandfather Hampton's place in Bloomington, Grandfather Vinton's in Mitchellville, her cabin on *The Frances Scott*, that mansion in Washington Bennett Presgrove rented. This house was different. This was the first real home she ever had, the first she expected to live in for the rest of her life. Months ago, the *buzios* warned fire would take something from her. She thought she'd be able to bear the loss, but now— Picking up another handful of ashes she stares at them and begins to cry.

William puts his arms around her and draws her close. "We can rebuild."

"I know we can, but it won't ever be the same."

"We'll make it better. I could live in a tent with you and Teddy and think of it as a palace."

He's right. Nothing important has been lost. They still have each other and Teddy. She rests in his arms for a while. Then she steps back and gives him a kiss. Walking over to the remains of their house, she bends down and retrieves a scrap of paper that survived the flames.

January, it says. No year, no date, but a good beginning.

That afternoon, as they are sifting through the ruins looking for their frying pans and Carrie's sewing scissors, Mrs. Crane comes running up with a special edition of *The Beacon of Freedom,* an abolitionist paper that has just arrived from Westport by special courier. She stops in front of Carrie, gasping for breath.

"Have you heard?" she pants. "Oh, my dear Miss Vinton and Doctor Saylor, what a horror!"

Carrie takes the newspaper from her, William reads over her shoulder, and together they learn that two days ago, after making a speech entitled "The Crime Against Kansas," Senator Sumner of Massachusetts was savagely attacked on the floor of the United States Senate. According to the article, his attackers beat him to the ground, hitting him so hard they ripped his desk off its bolts. When Sumner staggered up the main aisle of the Senate Chamber blinded by his own blood, his assailants pursued him and continued to batter him until they broke their canes over his body. Throwing the pieces at him, they walked out, leaving bloody footprints on the marble floor.

Infamy! the article cries. *In the opinion of this publication, the canning of Senator Sumner is the most shameful event ever to take place in the United States Senate. Congressman Brook's and Senator*

Presgrove's cowardly attack on an unarmed United States senator is
an act worthy of a dictatorship, not a democracy, and the fact that it
is going unpunished makes it all the more reprehensible—

There is more, but Carrie has stopped on two words and cannot read on. *Senator Presgrove.*

"They're sending the damnable devils new canes," Mrs. Crane says. Ordinarily Carrie would be shocked to hear the matronly Mrs. Crane use such language, but she is still stuck on those two words.

"The canes are inscribed with the motto 'Hit Him Again.' They're being sent by University of Virginia students, young ladies, respectable matrons, doctors, lawyers, planters. Why canes are coming in so fast, they have to be stacked like cordwood. Brooks and Presgrove have become heroes in the South. It's an evil day, Miss Vinton and Doctor Saylor. An evil day for America."

"Yes," Carrie mutters. "Yes it is." She puts her finger on the word "Presgrove," and as she does so, she sees Bennett as she saw him the first time they met: crooked nose, yellowed eyes, long gray hair, spotted skin; and in his hand a heavy, gold-headed walking stick.

Perhaps what comes next is the only real vision she will ever have, or perhaps it's merely a logical extension of the troubles she's witnessed, but as she stands there holding Bennett Presgrove in her mind's eye, his face fades and is replaced by another face, weathered and weary with fierce gray eyes.

"When John Brown hears about this, he's going to do something terrible," she says.

"Begging your pardon," Mrs. Crane says, "but who is John Brown?"

Chapter Thirty-two

Cicadas humming in a steady drone, trembling poplars, the sheen of moonlight on white gravel and water, a large, dead tree arched like a bridge. John Brown reaches out, puts his hand on the trunk, feels the soft, decaying bark. Using the tree to steady himself, he crosses Pottawatomie Creek. Behind him, he can hear his sons and the volunteers splashing through the water. He turns and puts his fingers to his lips. *Silently*, he says with gestures. *Revenge must begin silently.*

He thinks of Sumner bleeding on the floor of the Senate, of the Free State Hotel burned, of Lawrence looted, of the unspeakable evils of slavery and the cowardice of men who refuse to act on what they believe. Suddenly, he comes to an abrupt halt, overtaken by an anger so great he can taste it.

Up ahead is a clump of maples and beyond them a cabin sitting cold and quiet in the darkness. In that cabin, the pro-slavers are asleep. He and his men must do nothing to alarm or wake them. This is war. An eye for an eye, a tooth for a tooth.

One by one, his sons cross the creek and come to stand beside him. Each carries one of the broadswords he brought to Kansas. *Freshly sharpened,* he thinks, *edges ground so fine a man could shave with them.* He looks at his sons, strong around him, brave warriors all, righteous in their lives, righteous in their dedication to ending slavery. God granted him such sons because of this night and the nights to follow. They are soldiers in the Army of the North, a small army perhaps, but one that will grow until the Lord's work is done.

He lowers his head, in prayer and feels the power of God fill him with certainty. When he has finished praying, they walk on toward the cabin. The only sign of their presence is the moonlight glinting off the edges of their swords.

John Brown lifts his hands over his head, drawing down the Holy Ghost and bringing them all to a stop. Straightening his leather tie as if about to pay a social call, he starts toward the cabin alone. He will be the one to knock on the door and sound the trumpet of judgment. If the pro-slavers do not fight him, perhaps he will even give them time to repent. Not that they deserve anything but hell-fire.

He has almost reached the cabin when two bulldogs come hurtling out of the darkness, barking and snarling. The dogs run on either side of him as if they cannot smell him or see him and hurl themselves on his sons, but before they can do any damage, Frederick beheads one with his sword, and Salmon stabs the other and sends it howling into the forest.

No need for silence now. John Brown approaches the cabin again and knocks. He expects to be greeted with a rifle barrel and has steeled himself to be shot or even to die a martyr, but instead the pro-slaver opens up. As soon as the door swings back, Brown charges in, and his sons follow, guns drawn, swords ready. They knock over a table, and a china pitcher and washbasin hurtle to the floor.

"Mr. Doyle!" Brown cries. "The Army of the North has arrived and demands your surrender!"

A man in a nightshirt faces him, dazed and uncomprehending. A woman stands behind him, her face still creased with sleep. A small girl clings to the woman's nightgown. On the other side of the cabin, three young men rise from their pallets.

"Army?" Doyle says. "Surrender? What the hell are you talking about, Mr. Brown?"

"We have declared war on you and on all who support slavery."

"Hold on. You can't just go and declare war all on your own. Congress has to declare . . ."

"Take the men outside!" Brown orders.

Mrs. Doyle screams and clutches at her husband. "No!" she cries. "No! Please!"

"Madam," John Brown says, "I cannot spare them. They have committed unpardonable crimes against the African people."

"My son, John," Mrs. Doyle begins to sob, "dear God, he's only fourteen! Please, Mr. Brown, leave me my boy!"

John Brown looks at John Doyle. He's slight, thin, short, fresh-faced, and crying. It's the crying that does it. Only a coward or a child would shed tears.

"Leave the boy," he orders. Owen Brown throws John Doyle toward his mother, who catches him. The two fall to their knees dragging the little girl down with them and kneel there weeping, but John Brown has had enough. In time of war, mercy has limits.

"Out!" he orders.

The Browns shove Doyle and his two older sons out into the night. The wind has risen and the trees are thrashing. For a moment, John Brown feels as if he is being touched by the breath of God, but it's only a storm coming in.

They walk down the road that leads from the cabin, pushing the Doyles ahead of them with the barrels of their guns and the tips of their swords, catching them when they stumble. John Brown thinks of the sheep he has herded to slaughter, how the terror in the eyes of these men is like the terror in the eyes of those sheep. He stops in a patch of moonlight.

"Here," he says. "Now!" As his sons raise their swords, he turns away and looks off into the darkness. He hears the sound of screaming and pleading, the sound of metal blades cutting through flesh and bone, the thud of falling bodies.

When he turns back again to the scene of the execution, he sees Doyle and Doyle's oldest son lying dead in the road. A little farther on, the other son lies half-hidden in the grass, his arms severed from his body. Salmon and Owen stand near the bodies, splashed with blood that looks black in the moonlight.

"So let all thine enemies perish, O Lord," John Brown says. He stares at the bodies and waits for some sign that he has done the right thing, but the taste of anger remains in his mouth, so bitter he feels as if he's choking on it.

Pulling his pistol out of his pocket, he walks over to Doyle, bends down, and shoots him in the forehead. When he straightens up, Owen and Salmon are still there, drenched in the blood of the enemies of human freedom. Beside them stand the rest of the soldiers of the Army of the North.

"Come," John Brown says. "We need to move on. We have more of the Lord's work to do tonight."

Chapter Thirty-three

WAR! scream the headlines of the Westport *Border Times* and *The Leavenworth Herald. MURDER ON POTTAWAT-OMIE CREEK! MASSACRE!* All over Missouri, pro-slave newspapers cry for the extermination of every abolitionist in Kansas, while in Massachusetts guns and money pour in for the defense of free-state settlements.

Chaos, looting, burned homesteads, sudden violent death. Lawrence and Topeka blockaded by pro-slavers; forts built around abolitionist towns to cut them off from contact with the outside world: *My brother-in-law has triggered a terrible guerilla war,* Samuel Adair writes. *Brown's Station lies in ruins, burned to the ground, cattle stolen, wives and children fled in terror to parts unknown.*

John Brown goes into hiding no one knows where as Federal troops and the Missouri Militia scour southeastern Kansas looking for him. Troops from a pro-slavery Kansas militia join them. Instead of finding John Brown, they find John Junior crouching in a wooded ravine by the Adairs' cabin. Chaining him to a tent pole, they beat him with their fists and the butts of their rifles until he goes insane.

As they torture him, he cries that he was not at Pottawatomie Creek, that he had nothing to do with the executions, but the pro-slavers do not care. He is a Brown.

An eye for an eye! they yell. *A tooth for a tooth!* Brown's son is too crazed with pain to tell them that this is also one of his father's favorite quotations.

On the second of June, John Brown fights a battle with a pro-slavery militia at a place called Black Jack Springs. To everyone's astonishment, he wins. Two days later, perhaps in retaliation, a band of bushwhackers burns Trout's Hotel.

Trout and his Yankee cook run for it and hide in the creek until the raiders leave, taking every horse, chicken, cow, keg of nails, bag of salt, and bolt of calico with them. When Trout returns to the site of his hotel, all he finds is a pile of smoking boards and a circle of blackened prairie. Throwing down his hat, he kicks it into the ashes.

"Damnation!" he yells. "I'm ruined! Wiped clean out!" Tears stream down his cheeks leaving sooty streaks. He coughs, takes out his bandanna and blows his nose. "Begging your pardon for the cursin' and the cryin', Miz Witherspoon, but I done been pushed to the edge! I came here with the money I inherited from my mama and built my hotel, and now it's all ashes and cinders. It's enough to break a man's heart.

"To hell with Kansas! Who needs her? Bloody battleground, that's what she is. Well, the abolitionists and slavers can let the blood flow without me! I don't wanna be no part of their war! I'm leaving, yes, ma'am, I am. If I can get enough money together to buy a horse, maybe I'll move on further west where there's only rattlesnakes and hostile Indians to worry a man."

Mrs. Witherspoon stands next to him staring at the ashes. After a while, she goes to the root cellar, which the raiders have over-looked in their haste to get away with their loot. Pulling up the hatch, she climbs down the ladder and emerges with a jar of peaches preserved in whiskey.

"I know you don't usually drink, Mr. Trout," she says, offering the jar to him, "but there's a time for everything." Trout accepts the jar, takes a pull on it, sits down on the ground, and takes another pull.

"What was that flag those bushwhackers were carrying?" Mrs. Witherspoon asks as she spreads her skirts and settles down beside him.

"I got no idea, but the consarned thing looked like it had been dipped in blood."

Mrs. Witherspoon shudders.

"Sorry for the cussin', ma'am, but I've just lost my hotel, and I ain't drunk a dram of whiskey since Fifty-four when I had that terrible toothache."

"I understand perfectly," Mrs. Witherspoon says, reaching for the jar.

The day after the burning of Trout's Hotel, Carrie and William buy a mule, load everything they salvaged from their house into a wagon, make Teddy a pallet in the back, and join a group of six armed men on their way to reinforce the defenses at Osawatomie. Passing through the Missouri Militia blockade, they are taunted by the pro-slavers but not attacked.

All day they follow the California Road. That night their party pitches camp and posts sentries. Ever since the news of Pottawatomie Creek came to Lawrence, Carrie has known Kansas is in a state of civil war, but not until she wakes just before dawn and sees three grim-faced men staring off into the darkness with their guns drawn does the reality of it hit home.

Pulling Teddy close, she curls up against William, and lies there listening for the sound of approaching horses, but all she hears is the rustling of the grass and the sentries coughing and talking in low whispers.

Late the next morning, before they reach Osawatomie, William and Carrie say good-bye to their escorts and turn onto the dirt track that leads to Two Rivers. Elizabeth said Mrs. Hulett and the fugitives who lived with her grew rope hemp on the plantation. Carrie has always imagined hemp would look like rope—brown and uninteresting—but instead she finds herself rolling past tall, green plants with delicately feathered leaves. The hemp is planted densely, forming a wall that sways in the wind. Carrie decides it's the closest thing to a jungle she's seen since she left Brazil.

The main house is less impressive than the hemp that surrounds it. Constructed of unpainted boards and sporting a thatched roof, it has nothing in common with the great, white-pillared mansions of the old South. Although much larger than the cabin Carrie and William built in Lawrence it looks similar except that instead of a small porch suitable for knocking the mud off your boots before you enter, the main house at Two Rivers has a wraparound veranda that curves in a protective circle so no matter which door you go out of, you always find yourself with a shaded place to sit.

Behind the house, lined up along the river, are a series of slave cabins. The cabins, which are also constructed of unpainted boards, are in remarkably good repair but still . . .

Carrie wonders if Mrs. Hulett's guests live in them. Surely that would bring back very unpleasant memories if you had once been a slave.

No," Mrs. Hulett tells Carrie and William after they have washed up, put Teddy down for a nap, and are taking tea with her on the veranda. "All of us live here in the big house, except for Ni's wife, Jane, and their two daughters. Jane asked to move her family into one of the cabins. The rest of us have a dormitory arrangement. I'm somewhat abashed to admit that my guests have insisted I have an entire room to myself. I thought we should all share the inconvenience equally, but they laid down the law. They said I was too old and that besides, I snored. 'If you had to take out your teeth every night, you'd snore, too,'" I told them.

She leans forward, picks up the teapot, and refills Carrie's and William's cups. "They won't let me work in the fields either, but I'm not alone in that. The old men don't work in the fields and neither do the children. That's the glory of rope hemp. In April you have a few days hard work planting it, but then you can turn your back on it until August. We're using China seed instead of Old Kentucky, and it's so vigorous, you can lie in your bed at night and hear it growing."

She shrugs. "Actually, if we could get away with it, we'd grow nothing, but we have to keep up appearances. We've had visitors. Pro-slavers, of course, since they think I'm one of them. For a while most people in Osawatomie didn't know the truth, but the day after Pottawatomie Creek Elizabeth told them who 'my slaves' really are. As long as they keep their mouths shut, we should be safe here and so should you and your child."

"That's the main reason we came," Carrie says. "For Teddy's sake. Also, like your guests, we need to disappear for a while."

Mrs. Hulett takes a sip of tea and looks at William with renewed interest. "There is still a price on your head, Doctor Saylor, is there not?"

"Yes. Recently, I was pleased to hear the slavers had raised the reward for my carcass to two hundred dollars. A man doesn't like to be undervalued."

"Someone is also likely to be hunting for me," Carrie says. "He may even be offering a reward. We aren't sure if he is, but I wouldn't put it past him."

"A pro-slaver, I take it?"

"Famously a pro-slaver."

"Can you tell me his name?"

"Deacon Presgrove."

"Deacon Presgrove!" Mrs. Hulett almost drops her tea cup. "Not the son of that wicked man who savagely beat Senator Sumner!"

"The very one, I'm sorry to say."

Mrs. Hulett puts down her cup, and stares at Carrie and William with a mixture of admiration and astonishment. "I'll ask no more questions. You can have a cabin for your clinic, and another for yourselves if you'd like privacy. They're clean and the roofs are watertight, and since it's summer, you'll be warm enough.

"Of course, if any pro-slavers come down the road, I'll introduce you as my cousin and her husband, and you'll have to pretend to be living in the main house, but I don't think that's likely. Right now, my neighbors are occupied with plotting the destruction of Osawatomie, burning free-state homesteads, and hunting for John Brown. As far as they know, I'm just an old lady in bad health with a bunch of nearly-useless slaves.

"In short, you're welcome. The clinic will be a blessing to all of us here at Two Rivers, not to mention the people in Osawatomie and the men who are living at—" She stops abruptly.

William reaches out and takes her hands in his. "My dear Mrs. Hulett, I don't know how we'll ever repay you for taking us in."

"Fiddlesticks, Doctor Saylor! You have a reputation for keeping your patients alive. It's going to be a comfort to have you and Miss Vinton here, and if you find you have too much free time on your hands, you can always help us with the hemp harvest. I don't know what we're going to do with it, but come late August we're going to have to cut it down."

"Maybe you could burn it and blame the fire on free-state gueril-las," Carrie suggests.

Mrs. Hulett smiles and shakes her head. "You don't know much about hemp, do you Miss Vinton?"

One month later to the day, a lone rider comes down the road that leads to Two Rivers. Stopping at the main house, he dis-mounts, knocks on the door, and asks one of the "slaves" if he can have a drink of water. Ni's wife, Jane, brings him the dipper, watches him drink, and takes the dipper back when he is finished.

"Is your mistress at home," the man asks.

"Yes, Massa," she says. It's a carefully rehearsed reply, one they have all discussed and agreed on. Distasteful, but necessary.

"Go get her."

"She's upstairs takin' a nap, Massa. She's real old and sickly."

At that moment, Carrie walks out of the clinic carrying a wash-basin full of water. Throwing the water on the ground, she turns and goes back inside. She does not notice Jane standing on the porch or the stranger standing next to her.

The stranger stares at the clinic. Jane doesn't like the expression on his face. "You want me to go wake the old mistress up, Massa?"

The stranger turns and looks at her with cold, blue eyes. His hair is the color of flax, his lips so red, they almost look painted. "No," he says. "No need. Let her sleep. I already have the answer to the question I was going to ask her."

PART 6

Henry Clark

Carrie

September 1856

*W*illiam, my darling, in token of our love, I offer you this memory of our last night together written in a small sketchbook that I will give you when I rescue you from Henry Clark and his bloody band of murderers. In defiance of Henry Clark, I offer you us together in our bed. I offer you that single, perfect night when we made love and did not see into the future.

Do you remember it? August 29, 1856. We lay together in our cabin at Two Rivers, new curtains at the windows, candle lit, our boy asleep on his pallet. Do you remember Teddy's face in the candlelight, the innocence and sweetness of him? You took such good care of him and loved him so well, and he loved you so much in return. Do you remember how soundly he slept that night? I don't think he will ever sleep as soundly again.

It was hot. We lay on top of the quilt I had made from scraps of old dresses Nettie Wiggins gave me. I ripped those dresses to pieces when I found out she was having an affair with Deacon, but I kept some of the scraps. They were silk and beautiful and hard to part

with. Perhaps I suspected someday I would need to make a quilt for
our bed.

It was a light quilt, soft as a cloud. I was glad I had saved it from
the fire that burned our home in Lawrence, and I can still remember
the caress of it on my flesh mixed with the caress of your hands as you
made love to me. When you touched me, I always came alive in a
special way. Even before I lost the baby fat from giving birth to
Teddy, you always made me feel like a beautiful, sleek wild animal.

That night, as we began, I closed my eyes and imagined the two
of us together lying in a double hammock by the banks of the Rio
Branco under trees laced with purple orchids. I felt the heat of the
tropical sun on my skin and heard the jungle singing. Jungles sing,
you know. They hum day and night, alive with frogs, and insects, and
birds. That's what I heard when we began to make love: that soft
song beating against my ears. When I opened my eyes I realized it
was the beating of your heart.

You always brought the jungle to me even in Kansas, even in the
dead of winter. But on that last summer night before so many terrible
things happened, the jungle was already waiting for me before we lay
down. I often thought of you as a tiger turning me in great soft paws,
rolling me over and over, loving me. But I thought of you as yourself,
too, as a man. I loved the hardness of your arms, the hair on your
chest, the soft brush of your beard against my face.

I loved the way you looked at me as we made love. You were
sweet and passionate, fierce and gentle. You took me with a pleasure that sometimes seemed half-mad, yet at the same time you never
once hurt me or forgot me or left me behind. We were always together, always equals the way we had been ever since we were children. Not many men can carry that off, but you could, and I loved
you for it.

Do you remember our shadows on the walls? How they took on
color in the candlelight? Do you remember putting your hand over

my mouth so I would not wake our boy? Do you remember how I opened myself to you, threw my legs around you, loved you with all my strength and heart? How I bit you on the shoulder in passion and then apologized, and how you laughed and whispered, "Bite me again, my love; bite all you want."

Do you remember how many times I relaxed and rested against you, only to find peace replaced by passion? Do you remember the sounds you made, how you had to bite your own lips to keep from crying out? Were two people ever better matched in desire? Did two people ever love each other more or love each other longer without their love fading or going stale?

Each time with you was like the first. No, each time was better than the first, better than the one before. Our love constantly grew stronger. That was our secret.

We were both blind that night. Blind and blessed. Henry Clark had already found us, but we did not know it. We did not know we would never again be able to look at our sleeping boy without feeling an urge to take him in our arms and defend him.

When we lay back satisfied from our lovemaking, when we curled up in each other's arms, when we whispered our good-nights and kissed our last kiss, we did not suspect what the next day would bring.

I remember dreaming the most ordinary dreams. Butter un-churned. Dishes not washed. Teddy eating oatmeal. Long grass swaying. Sunflowers, cicadas, walls of green hemp.

Chapter Thirty-four

Kansas, August 30, 1856

The prairie is dry, the wheat fields are stubble, and two hundred and fifty Missourians have attacked Osawatomie, burned it to the ground, defeated John Brown, shot his son Frederick through the heart and left him dead beside the Marais des Cygnes. Now Henry Clark and his men are bringing the news to Two Rivers.

With them rides Deacon Presgrove. Deacon looks like one of Clark's Raiders now. The costume he put on to come to Kansas has taken on a reality that terrifies him. He still has his pistols, his rifle, and his oversized knife, but his broad-brimmed hat is battered almost out of recognition, the kerchief around his neck reeks of sweat, and his trousers are so stiff with dirt they could stand up without him. Worst of all are his boots. Deacon can hardly bear to look at them. They are splattered with blood, great dark stains of it.

Will all great Neptune's ocean wash this blood . . . Macbeth, *Act Two, Scene Two . . . I am going insane*, Deacon thinks. *I am riding with a madman bent on committing murder.* He looks up and sees Clark's flag snapping above him, rolling and unrolling in the wind like a message from hell. The blood on it is bright red, fresh, not pig's blood any longer.

Carrie isn't worth this. Nothing is. Deacon would run if he could, take off into the brush and hide like John Brown, but if he does, Clark will shoot him. Clark has made that clear.

I'm not going to bring your wife and son to you, Clark said on the day he told Deacon he had found Carrie for the second time. *You're going to come with me. When a man's wife runs away, he should go after her. Shoot her lover. Make things right. Honor needs to be satisfied.*

Then he had stepped up to Deacon, put a finger on the bottom button of Deacon's flannel shirt, and crawled up finger by finger, button by button to the top. It was a crazy gesture, threatening, terrifying.

You aren't afraid, are you? Clark asked as he touched the first button. *Not a coward?* as he touched the second. *Because then,* he touched the third; *then,* he touched the fourth; *well, then, Deacon* . . .

Clark's finger had rested on the fifth button, then the sixth. He had not completed the sentence.

Chapter Thirty-five

The sky above Two Rivers is the color of fire. For the rest of her life Carrie remembers the intensity of that sunset, how it tinted the hemp, turned the unpainted boards of the main house and the cabins rose-colored, and spread crimson ripples along the banks of the Marais des Cygnes.

She is in the clinic with Jane, removing a thorn from Jane's knuckle. William, who is rolling pills, has his back to them. Carrie and Jane have become close in the time Carrie has lived on the plantation. Their children play together, and they both like to read the books Mrs. Hulett has arranged on the mantel in the parlor. It's a small library, but well-chosen. So far Jane and Carrie have discussed *David Copperfield, Paradise Lost,* and *The Stones of Venice.* This week they are taking turns reading Mrs. Gaskell's latest novel out loud to each other.

Jane is a tall, quiet woman with blue-black skin and long, graceful fingers calloused by years of sewing. She's not one to complain, so as Carrie probes around with the needle trying to get under the tip of the thorn, she knows it must hurt when Jane winces.

"Sorry," Carrie says.

"Y'all going to soap this up afterwards?"

"We soap up everything," William says without looking up.

"Indeed we do," Carrie agrees.

"Remind me not to get a speck in my eye then. I don't fancy having my eyes washed out with Mrs. Hulett's soap. She always puts in enough lye to take the skin off a mule."

In front of the main house, Jane's daughters and Teddy are playing together. On the veranda, the old men are sitting in their rocking chairs watching the sun set. Mrs. Hulett is sitting beside them in a straight-backed chair, plucking a chicken. The rest of the women are in the shed milking the cows, in the garden picking beans and digging up potatoes, or in the springhouse skimming cream so they can churn butter. One woman is in the woodshed splitting kindling. Another is down at the river getting water.

"There," Carrie says, as she extracts the thorn from Jane's knuckle. She is about to say more when she is interrupted by a high-pitched scream. Jumping to their feet, she and Jane hurry to the window. William comes up behind them. They look, but can't see anything out of the ordinary. The children are still playing in the front yard; the old men are still sitting in their rocking chairs.

Suddenly they hear the sound of approaching horses.

"Teddy!" Carrie cries.

"Lara! Franny!" Jane yells. "Run! run!"

Chapter Thirty-six

Clark's Raiders gallop out of the hemp fields howling like demons, ride up to the main house, and throw lighted torches onto the roof. When Mrs. Hulett tries to escape the flames, they shoot her and leave her dead on the veranda. They capture the old men—not worth much, but worth taking alive. They ride down Jane's daughters, throw them to the ground, and tie their hands behind their backs.

As Teddy stands in the middle of the yard screaming in terror, they break into two groups and ride around him. He's too little to go anywhere, and they have their orders. *You're not to harm a hair on the little brat's head,* Clark has told them. *He comes up with one scratch, and—*Clark rarely needs to finish his sentences these days.

Clark rides past the main house, stops, pulls back on the reins, and forces his horse to rear up on its hind legs. The red light of the sunset turns his hair to bronze and for an instant he looks like a monument to the violence that is tearing Kansas apart. "There's the clinic," he tells Deacon, pointing to the last unpainted cabin in the row. "There's where you'll find your wife."

Deacon opens his mouth, but nothing comes out.

"Are you deaf? I just said that's the clinic." Clark grabs a lighted torch from one of his men and thrusts it into Deacon's hand. "Burn it down. Smoke them out." Deacon takes the torch, holds it for a few seconds, then drops it.

"You're a pitiable excuse for a man." Clark grabs another torch. With a high, yipping yell, he gallops up to the clinic and tosses it onto the thatched roof. "Come out, you abolitionist bastards!" he yells. He rides back to Deacon. "Take aim, man. This is going to be like shooting fish in a barrel."

Reassured, Deacon recovers his senses, pulls out his pistols, and points them at the door of the clinic. Smoke is billowing from the windows and flames are consuming the thatch. Deacon inhales burning grass and wood and coughs on the ashes.

Come out, you stubborn bitch! he thinks. *Don't burn to death in there!*

But it is Jane, not Carrie, who runs out of the door screaming for her children. William runs after her, throws himself on her, and tries to shield her body with his. Jane trips and falls to the ground, and William falls with her.

Perfect targets, Deacon thinks, and discharges one of the pistols. He has never been an especially good shot, but this time luck is with him. He hears William yell, and sees him grab at his leg. Only lamed. Not dead. Too bad. But Deacon has shot him. He looks around for Clark, wants him to see this moment and approve it, but Clark has gone off somewhere.

A few seconds ago, Deacon would have been terrified to discover he was alone, but his stepbrother is wounded and unarmed, and what can a wounded, unarmed man do against a man with loaded pistols and a knife?

The female slave William has been shielding gets up and begins to run toward the main house. Deacon lets her go. Clark's men will catch her. Kicking his horse into a slow walk, he rides toward William to finish him off.

He is just taking aim when Carrie charges out of the burning clinic holding a double-barreled shotgun. Deacon sees her point the gun at him.

"Don't!" he yells, but his plea is drowned out by the sound of the shotgun going off. The next thing he knows he is flying through the air, knocked off his horse with his chest on fire. The pain is terrible and the fall to the ground seems to take an extraordinarily long time. When he finally hits the dirt, he screams and thrashes like a beached fish.

Looking up, he sees Carrie bending over him. She puts the shotgun to his head.

"Don't kill me," he begs.

"Why not?" she says.

Chapter Thirty-seven

Would she have killed Deacon as he lay there helpless, and if she had, would it have been murder or an act of war? John Brown could have told her, but he is twenty miles away riding for his life after his defeat at Osawatomie.

Carrie is so full of rage that all she can think is that Deacon has brought death to Two Rivers and she wants him to pay for it. Still, she pauses. Perhaps that means she would not have pulled the trigger after all. In any event, she never has a chance to find out, because before she can decide whether to let Deacon live or send him to hell, a shadow falls over both of them, and she hears a voice say: "Drop the gun."

When she looks up, she sees a young man mounted on a brown stallion. She sees his hair—curly and blond—his cold blue eyes, his nickel-plated revolver, the red bandanna around his neck. He is not pointing his revolver at her. He doesn't need to because in his right hand he holds something more powerful than any weapon, holds it upside down by the ankles like a dead rabbit.

Clark gives Teddy a shake and lifts him higher so Carrie can get the full benefit of the sight of her little boy screaming for his mama to come rescue him. "Drop the gun now."

"Teddy!" William yells. Clark ignores him. Deacon's wife's lover can only crawl now and not very fast at that. So let him yell, threaten, curse, command. It's all just noise. He grabs Teddy's head with his free hand.

"Drop the gun. I'm going to start counting. If it isn't on the ground by the time I reach three, I'll snap his spine. One . . ."

"For God's sake!" Carrie begs. "Please, don't hurt my boy!"

"Two . . ."

Carrie throws down the shotgun, steps back, and lifts her hands over her head. "Don't hurt Teddy! I'll do whatever you want. Just don't hurt him!"

Clark ignores her. "Rab!" he yells.

The raider who goes by the name of Rabbit trots over. He's a big, bucktoothed man, the kind who kills for sport. The only human being Rabbit has ever feared is Henry Clark. Reining in his horse, Rab touches the brim of his hat respectfully.

"Yes, sir, Capt'n?"

"Hold this," Clark says, handing him Teddy. Rab takes Teddy by one arm, and Teddy begins to scream with redoubled fury.

"Don't dislocate the little brat's shoulder, you idiot! Hold him like you were his mama, but if this one," Clark points to Carrie, "or that one," he points to William, "give me any trouble, dash his brains out on that chopping block over there."

"Yes, sir, Capt'n."

"My God!" Carrie says. "Teddy's just a baby—"

"Shut up."

Carrie closes her mouth and bites her lips to keep from screaming at him.

The evil-looking raider with the buckteeth has ridden off a few paces. He's holding Teddy under the arms now, shaking him to make him shut up. Everything in Carrie urges her to run to Teddy and pull him out of the bushwhacker's grip, but she's afraid if she does, Clark will carry out his threat.

Clark dismounts and inspects Deacon. "Looks like you're fixing to die," he says.

Deacon has clasped his hands over his chest. His fingers are stained with blood, and those green eyes Carrie saw for the first time in her parlor in Brazil are growing cloudy.

"I'll make it," Deacon gasps. He grits his teeth, spits in Carrie's direction. "Bitch shot me."

"You've always had a talent for the obvious," Clark says. He steps over Deacon and walks to where William lies. "Good evening, Doctor Saylor. I'm Henry Clark."

"I don't care who you are, you evil bastard."

"I don't fancy being cursed at," Clark says. "If you were a whole man, I'd have to call you out, but since you're crippled, I'll just warn you: Keep quiet, or you're going to see that child's brains scattered all over creation." Clark turns his back on William and cups his hands to his mouth.

"Zeb!" he yells. Another raider gallops up to join the group in front of the clinic. This one is burly and short with a barrel chest and powerful arms.

"Drag the doctor over to Mr. Presgrove," Clark orders. "The doctor can't walk, and I don't want to soil my hands on him."

Zeb grabs William under the arms and lugs him to where Deacon lies. It must hurt, but although William turns pale, he doesn't make a sound. Carrie also remains silent, afraid of what will happen if she speaks. She wants to go to William, tend to his leg, stop the bleeding, and wash out the wound before it festers. Tears fill her eyes, but she chokes them back. She won't give Clark the satisfaction of seeing how terrified she is. If he hurts Teddy or hurts William any more than William is already hurt, he had better kill her, because she will never rest until she has hunted him down.

"Turn Mr. Presgrove on his side so he can see the doctor."

Zeb shambles over to Deacon, grabs his left shoulder, and starts to turn him on his side. As he does so, Deacon shrieks.

"Hurt?" Clark says. "I'm afraid that's something you must endure. Turn him, Zeb."

Zeb turns Deacon so Deacon is facing William. A small pool of blood begins to form on the ground between the two, most of it Deacon's. Clark puts his hands on his hips, looks down at Deacon, and shakes his head. He looks disappointed. Not horrified, not upset, not even angry. Just disappointed.

"You didn't kill your wife's lover, Deacon. You botched things as usual, and honor hasn't been satisfied. So what do you want me to do with him? Shoot him dead where he lies? Torture him for a while? Hang him? I'm offering—"

"No!" Carrie cries. Clark turns and looks at her. Clapping her hands over her mouth, she falls silent.

He turns back to Deacon. "I'm offering you a choice of revenge. How would you like this man who has sullied your name to die? It's a free lunch. Pick your dish."

Deacon spits out a mouthful of blood. "Hang the abolitionist son of a bitch," he gasps.

"Excellent choice. I'm always happy to oblige a friend. How are you doing? Still in pain?"

Deacon nods and groans.

"Bad, is it?"

Again Deacon nods.

"Well, I wouldn't let a dog suffer like you're suffering. I think it's time to put you out of your misery." Clark draws his pistols and approaches Deacon.

"No!" Deacon screams.

"Hush now," Clark says, and putting one of the pistols to Deacon's temple, he fires.

Chapter Thirty-eight

Ice pick, knife blade, sewing scissors, twine: Carrie is sitting on a rock making a weapon no one in Kansas has ever seen, although anyone living on the upper Amazon would recognize it immediately. The weapon consists of a straight tube four feet long and about two inches in diameter. If she were in Brazil, she would construct the tube from bamboo, but she has been forced to make do with a stick, and finding a piece that fits her needs has been difficult.

She holds the stick at arm's length and sights down it to make sure it's perfectly straight. Satisfied that it is, she slices it in half lengthwise and begins to dig out the center. She works mostly with the knife blade, but for the final hollowing she uses the tip of the ice pick. She was lucky to find the pick in the ruins of the main house at Two Rivers and even more lucky that Mrs. Hulett brought it with her from New England. They never had ice in their drinks at the plantation, never even saw it—although presumably the Marais des Cygnes froze in winter. Perhaps Mrs. Hulett kept the pick around to remind herself that someday, when Kansas came into the Union as a free state, there would be icehouses in every town and cold lemonade in August.

Poor Mrs. Hulett. Every time Carrie thinks of her, she begins to cry. Shot down in cold blood: a gentle, intelligent woman who had dedicated her life to abolishing slavery. Despite the way she died, hers was a life to be proud of; but still, what a sad, terrible waste.

Carrie wipes away her tears and goes back to hollowing out the stick. She cries a lot now that there is no one to see her do it: cries when she remembers finding Mrs. Hulett lying in the ashes; cries when she thinks of the men, women, and children Henry Clark kidnapped, all of whom he will undoubtedly sell into slavery if she can't rescue them.

She does not cry about William and Teddy—at least not in the daytime. At night when she lies in the tall grass shivering and not daring to light a fire, she sobs herself to sleep. But in the daytime when she thinks of William and Teddy, she only feels anger. She never knew she could be so full of rage. She will never forgive Henry Clark. She wants him dead for what he has done, and if she goes to hell for killing him and those bastards who ride with him, it will be worth the price.

Clark should have shot her when he had the chance. Instead he left her alive to suffer. He thought that was all she would do. After all, she was only a woman. He has no idea how straight she can shoot, how ingenious she is, what a deadly adversary she can be.

"I'm leaving you Deacon's horse," Clark said as he and his gang rode off. "Go to what's left of Osawatomie and tell your New England friends what happens to abolitionists. Tell them to get out of Kansas or we'll shoot them down like dogs, hang them, chop them into mincemeat." He smiled when he said this as if he were merely informing her that tomorrow was likely to be exceptionally warm. Carrie will never forgive Clark for that smile.

His men had brought chains with them to shackle the black residents of Two Rivers. As they left, they drove their captives down the road moaning and crying. Carrie will never forget the sight of Jane's little girls stumbling and being whipped for falling.

The bucktoothed raider had held Teddy in front of him, trussed up to the neck in a pillow case like a kitten about to be drowned. Clark bound and gagged William, tied him to his horse, slipped a noose around his neck, stood back, and mocked him.

"Hemp," Clark said pointing to the rope. "Highest quality." He turned to Carrie. "You can ride out and cut your paramour down when we're finished, but not until we're finished. If you follow us—" Clark had a habit of not finishing his sentences.

He and his men had ridden off leaving Carrie behind. As William rode past, he gave her a look that could have meant *Don't come after me. Be careful. Save yourself. Go for help.* It could have even meant *Good-bye. I love you.* In fact, that's what Carrie is afraid it meant.

She spent almost no time grieving. If she didn't follow them at once, she might lose the trail, so as soon as Clark and his men were out of sight, she ran to where the main house had stood and started digging in the ashes. They were still hot, but she didn't have time to wait for them to cool. She needed a weapon because Clark's men had taken all the guns. *Knives don't burn,* she thought; and sure enough, where the kitchen had been, she found a knife blade. A few moments later, she also found the ice pick. A gift, perhaps even a good sign.

As soon as she located the knife and the pick, she ran to her cabin. The raiders had looted it but had not bothered to burn it. Inside, she found her sewing basket, a feather pillow, a bottle of glue, the *buzios,* some dried meat, and the tin box that contained the plants she'd brought from Brazil. She took a moment to stuff a dozen packets of dried herbs into a saddlebag that had once contained Deacon's socks and cigars, but what she was really after was a small gourd that contained a sticky, black substance used by the Indians of the Upper Amazon to tip their hunting arrows. There were all sorts of things in that black mixture, including the secretions of poisonous frogs, but the main ingredient was the sap of a pretty, white-flowered plant called *Strychnos toxifera,* commonly known as *curare.*

Now that gourd sits at her feet next to the ball of twine. As soon as she has hollowed out the stick properly, she will bind the halves back together with the twine. Then she will take her sewing needles and glue feathers to them. The needles will become tiny darts which she will dip in the curare. Curare kills slowly but effectively. In fact, if she pricks herself with one of her own needles she will die within ten or fifteen minutes. It won't be a pretty death. Her lungs will stop working, and she will suffocate. But she doesn't intend to die.

For three days, she has been tracking Clark and his men, and every hour of those three days she has feared she will find William's body dangling from the rope Clark threw around his neck.

A knife, an ice pick, a pack of needles, a handful of chicken feathers, sap from a tropical plant, and an ordinary bottle of glue. They are no use against men with guns—unless, of course, you know what to do with them.

Chapter Thirty-nine

That night Clark's men begin to die. The first walks away from the campfire to relieve himself. In the morning, the others find him facedown in a patch of poison ivy. Clark strolls up to the body and kicks it over with the toe of his boot.

"Dick must have died of natural causes," he says. "There's not a mark on him." He nudges the body again. "Blue lips. That's odd." He stands there for a few seconds trying to figure out what might turn a man's lips blue. Poisonous mushrooms? Apoplexy? In the end it doesn't much matter. A dead man is useless. "Strip him," he commands.

Clark's men strip the dead raider of his guns, knives, tobacco, money, and ammunition and leave his body for the vultures. By seven, they are on their way again, driving their captives in front of them, and by seven-twenty Carrie is riding after them wearing Dick's hat and boots, all too big for her but better than no hat and no boots, which was what she had before.

Clark's band originally consisted of Clark and thirteen men.

Clark killed Deacon; now she has killed Dick. That leaves a total of twelve armed men between her and the prisoners. Given enough time, she can probably eliminate all twelve, but does she have time? She has to take them out one by one, and they are obviously headed somewhere specific.

Yesterday they crossed into Missouri. When they reach their destination, more pro-slavers may join them. Twelve men could easily turn into twenty, thirty, even a hundred. The best she can hope for between now and then is to spread terror. If Clark's men panic, they may desert before he gets reinforcements.

She lists her advantages. The blowgun is silent and the darts small and hard to notice. It's unlikely that Clark or any of his men are acquainted with the effects of curare. Since the slaves are not only on foot but chained together in a coffle, the raiders are forced to travel slowly. Unaware that they are being followed, they are making no attempt to hide their tracks. Still, she needs to be extremely cautious. Although she aches to catch a glimpse of William or Teddy, she must keep her distance.

Actually, the hardest part may prove to be not catching up with Clark's men by accident. The chains are heavy and the captives often stumble, bringing the entire coffle to a halt. Sometimes no amount of whipping can make them go on—at least no amount that won't permanently hurt Clark's chances of getting a good price for them. So from time to time, the raiders are obliged to halt and let their human cargo rest.

Once Carrie nearly rides straight into them. She's only saved by the sound of metal hitting rock. Dismounting, she crawls up, peers through the grass, and sees that the sound is being made by the prisoners' chains. They are leaning their heads on one another's shoulders, perhaps for comfort, perhaps because they are so tired they can no longer sit upright. They don't speak. Maybe Clark has forbidden them to. A skinny raider with a sunken chest passes down the line distributing water from a folding leather bucket. Jane refuses it. She once told Carrie she would rather die than be a slave.

Drink the water, Carrie thinks. *Don't despair. Hang on. I'm going to rescue you and the girls.* But Jane can't hear her. Reaching out, Jane tries to touch six-year-old Franny, but the chain is too short. For a little while, Jane's fingers grope at the empty space that separates her from her daughter. Then she lets her arm drop.

Carrie feels her eyes filling with tears again. *Oh, Jane!* she thinks. She puts her hand over her mouth to keep from making a sound that will give her away. The tears choke her, and she comes within a second of sneezing. She is far too close to the raider with the bucket. She should not have been tempted to draw so near.

Silently, she inches her way back to a safer distance. She had hoped to at least catch a glimpse of William and Teddy, but she doesn't dare linger, so for another day she goes without seeing them.

That evening just after dusk, she puts a dart into the neck of Zeb, the burly raider who dragged William over to Deacon. Zeb swears and slaps at the needle as if it were a mosquito bite. He must knock it loose, because fifteen minutes later when he drops dead, the raiders can find no indication of what killed him.

Now they begin to panic. Carrie has decided that she can no longer risk getting close enough to watch, but what she hears tells her the tide is beginning to turn.

"Come quick! Zeb ain't breathin'!"

"By God, his lips is blue just like Dick's!"

"You reckon it's the cholera?"

"You damn fool, a man don't die that quick of cholera."

"Well then what the hell killed him?"

"Snakebite."

"I ain't seein' no signs of no snakebite."

"First Dick, now Zeb!"

"Maybe it's the smallpox."

"Them slaves musta brought it with 'em."

"We should kill 'em all before we all die of it."

"They ain't sick."

Suddenly she hears Clark's voice, scared, screaming: "Shut up! Shut up all of you!"

More yelling, more cursing, Clark bellowing threats, the sound of Teddy crying. Again Carrie wants to run to Teddy and get him out of there, but she can't; so she bites her lips, grabs at the ground, digs in, and waits. William must still be gagged because she doesn't hear his voice. Instead, she hears Clark's men fighting, and then the sound of a pistol going off.

Suddenly the raiders are rounding up their horses, throwing dirt over their fires, and breaking camp. One of them rides past her, so close she could reach out and touch him. He is followed by a second man, then a third. The others take off in the opposite direction, driving their prisoners in front of them with oaths and curses. They've never traveled at night before, so they must be running scared.

Carrie forces herself to wait until Clark and his remaining men are out of earshot. When she rides into the abandoned camp, she finds two bodies. One belongs to Zeb. The second is that of a large, black-bearded raider whose name she never learns. Cause of death: gunshot wound to the chest.

Seven left, she thinks. Henry Clark is almost as efficient a killer as curare.

She gets one more raider before they panic completely. His name is either Mike or Mark—she only hears it once and not clearly even then. Unfortunately this time the needle stays in his neck, the

raiders find it, and Henry Clark, who may be many things but who
is no fool, figures out what is going on.

Grabbing William, he pulls him into the firelight and puts a knife
to his throat. "If you kill another of my men, Carrie Vinton, I'll cut
off his balls and nose, flay him alive, and roast him over a slow fire.
If I see another of your needles, he's a dead man, and when I've finished with him, I'll do the same to that little bastard of yours. Do
you hear me, bitch?"

Carrie hears. She puts away the blowgun and waits until the raiders break camp. She continues to wait all night and all the next day.
When night falls, she starts following them again. By now their trail
is cold, but she has no trouble finding it.

The broken grasses, bent twigs, overturned rocks, and hoofprints
lead her to the south bank of the Missouri River to a cotton plantation named Beau Rivage. The cotton is starting to mature and the
fields look as if they have been sprinkled with snow.

Tethering her horse in a stand of willows, Carrie walks to the
crest of a bluff that overlooks the plantation and climbs a tree. From
it, she can see slaves crouching between the rows of cotton, chopping out weeds with short-handled hoes. She can't make out their
features, but at least one looks like a woman. A white man—probably
an overseer—stands near them. He appears to be unarmed, but at
this distance it's hard to tell.

The prisoners from Two Rivers have been unchained and herded
into a slave pen next to a horse corral. Two men are guarding them.
Clark's men? Again, she can't tell. A least half a dozen other men
appear to be living in the barn. She tries, without success, to figure
out if they are part of Clark's original gang or reinforcements.
What she wouldn't give right now for those folding opera glasses of
Elizabeth's.

William and Teddy are nowhere in sight. Maybe Clark has imprisoned William in the stable or in the windowless shed next to the barn. Of course, he could have done something else with him. If you killed a man and threw his body into the Missouri River—

She forces herself to stop borrowing trouble. William is down there somewhere and so is Teddy. The main house is built of yellow-gray limestone. It looks solid and cool. She hopes they are both inside out of the heat.

For the rest of the day she continues to spy on Beau Rivage, but nothing of importance happens. Clark does not put in an appearance. Perhaps he's asleep or perhaps he's ridden to a nearby town to make arrangements to sell his captives. Twice she sees a white woman emerge from the main house. The woman throws feed to the chickens and picks some roses. Around three in the afternoon, a heavyset, dark-skinned woman opens the back door, walks across the backyard to the woodshed, and returns with an armful of kindling. House slave? Cook?

Near sunset, two men approach the slave pens and dump mush into a wooden trough. As Carrie watches Jane's little girls dip their hands into it, she feels sick with despair. She has wasted a whole day spying on the plantation. She needs to do something soon, but what? She's desperate to know what fate Clark has in store for his captives, but Clark knows she's still following him—or at least he must suspect she is. If she goes down there, she's likely to get everyone killed including herself. She's one woman against who knows how many armed men. Her only weapons are a knife blade, an ice pick, and a glorified pea shooter that has to be aimed ten times more slowly and carefully than a gun.

She sits in the tree until night falls and mist rises up off the river. The lights in the main house go out one by one. Overhead, a full moon rides through the sky, veiled and ominous.

Shutting her eyes against the moonlight, she leans her forehead against the trunk of the tree and looks into the dark places inside herself. She is afraid she has come to the end of her ability to do anything useful. She can't attack the plantation single-handed. Clark's men will kill her long before she gets to the slave pens, and her death won't save William and Teddy and the people from Two Rivers.

Mae Seja, she whispers, *come to me. Tell me what to do.* But Mae Seja doesn't come. *Jesus,* she prays, *come to me, help me.* But the mist settles in, the tree grows slippery, and Jesus doesn't come either.

Around midnight, she climbs down from her perch, walks back to the thicket where she tethered her horse, and makes him lie down. Curling up against him for warmth, she buries her face in his mane. Around her, the forest has come alive. She hears the sound of frogs croaking, the hum of cicadas, the hoot of an owl. Restless, she turns over and the horse stirs, perhaps wondering why she's so agitated.

She turns again and feels the *buzios* in her pocket. The pointed end of one of the shells presses into her side. *Hellfire and damnation,* she thinks. *It's hard enough to sleep without being stabbed by a cowry shell.* Sitting up, she pulls the bag out of her pocket and prepares to toss it aside.

What causes her to hesitate? Why does she dump the *buzios* out into the palm of her hand, lean forward, and throw them into a patch of moonlight? Does she make the cast because she hopes magic will work where prayer has failed? Or does she do it because she has run out of hope so completely that only habit remains?

Later she is never able to understand what prompts her to impulsively cast the *buzios* that night instead of tossing them aside and going back to sleep, but in any event, she does and they come to rest on the ground: sixteen shiny, pearl-white half-moons, five upright, eleven upside down.

Do the shells speak to her? No, she doesn't think they do. But somehow they allow her to speak to herself, not to her frightened self, but to the self that saw her through the death of Willa, her marriage to Deacon, the long trip to Kansas, the blizzard, the birth of Teddy, the sacking of Lawrence, and the pillaging of Two Rivers. It is her old self, her real self, the one that has been with her as long as she can remember.

What shall I do? she asks it. And to her surprise, it tells her.

Chapter Forty

Henry Clark sits on a bale of hay smoking a cigarette and carefully tapping the ashes into the palm of his hand. He enjoys setting fires, but burning down his cousin's stable is not on his agenda this morning. Besides killing Jed's horses, it might get out of control and kill Saylor before they can hang him.

"So, Doctor," Clark says, blowing a smoke ring and admiring its climb toward the rafters, "as I was saying: I get these headaches every so often." He pauses and blows another smoke ring. "When I get them, I see odd things: flashes of light, colors. Sometimes I see a wall built out of one-inch-square blocks. The blocks pile up around me when I close my eyes, and then as soon as I try to look at them, they go away."

He stares at William as if expecting an answer, but William does not supply one. Leaning forward, Clark jerks the bandanna out of his mouth. "Care to hazard a diagnosis?"

"You bastard! What have you done with my son?"

"Wrong answer." Clark stuffs the bandanna back into William's mouth. "In the first place, he's not your son. And in the second place—"

Clark sighs and sits back. This is becoming tedious. It's convenient to have a doctor around, particularly when you have a tendency to suspect there are all sorts of things wrong with you. So far he has managed to get William to reassure him that he doesn't have consumption, a diseased liver, or the French pox; but there are other symptoms he would like to discuss, and time is running out.

Once again it all comes down to the fact that people aren't grateful when you do them favors. He could have strung William up five minutes after they rode out of Two Rivers, but he has kept him alive for more than a week now and even let him supervise the cleaning of the bullet wound in his leg. Ever since they arrived, Jed's slaves have been running back and forth between the main house and the stable with hot water and clean bandages. Result: There's no sign of gangrene in William's wound and thus no need for amputation. He could probably hobble around if his ankles weren't tied together. *Saylor should be thanking me,* Clark thinks. *But instead he's becoming increasingly stubborn.*

He takes a deep breath and reminds himself to be patient. A few hours from now, he isn't going to have a doctor to consult, and while William is still able to talk, they might as well make the most of it.

"Let me put it to you this way: I'm curious to know what's causing my headaches. If you tell me, I might consider getting one of my cousin's slaves to bring you something to eat. How long has it been since you had a real meal? Three days now? Four? I've lost track, but I imagine you're hungry. There's going to be a big party later this afternoon. The cook's making fried chicken and apple pies. Tell me what's causing my headaches, and I'll see that you get a piece of white meat and a wedge of pie before the guests arrive."

Clark wonders if William suspects the party Jed and Emma are throwing is a necktie party. The hanging is scheduled to take place right after the slave sale, so if William talks, this will be his last meal.

Most men would hang him without feeding him fried chicken. Again, William's luckier than he knows.

Clark blows a chain of interlinked smoke rings toward William, and a choking sound comes from beneath the gag. He considers pinching William's nose shut and decides against it. He wants an accurate diagnosis, and when you push a man too hard, he's liable to say anything.

"Let's try again. What in your professional opinion is causing my headaches? Are these what are known as 'migraines' or are they something else? Do you think, for example, that I might have a brain tumor? I'd worry that your mistress shot me with one of her deadly little darts, but I've had these headaches for as long as I can remember, so for once she's in the clear." He leans forward and takes the gag out of William's mouth again. "Speak."

"Go to hell!"

Clark frowns and crams the gag back into William's mouth. This is taking much longer than he anticipated. The problem is, the man is stubborn and doesn't scare easily. Would telling him that he's going to die this afternoon speed things up? Probably not. Once William knows he has nothing left to lose, he's likely to clam up entirely. What else might shock him into cooperating? If he knew his stepfather was dead, would that do it? Senator Bennett Presgrove, felled by apoplexy on the floor of the U.S. Senate while making an impassioned speech in favor of extending slavery into every state in the Union: The news is two days old, but as far as Clark knows, no one has mentioned it to William.

He opens his mouth, then reconsiders and closes it. No, bad idea. William never liked his stepfather. Plus as soon as he hears Bennett Presgrove is dead, he will realize Teddy is the heir to his grandfather's estate as well as Deacon's. It will only take him a few seconds to realize that it doesn't matter if he cooperates and diagnoses Clark's headaches. To get at Teddy's money, Clark is going to have to remove any suspicion that Teddy is William's child, which means Clark is going to have to kill him.

Putting the cigarette back between his lips, Clark inhales deeply. *What would Mangas Coloradas do?* he wonders. He wishes he had Deacon here to tell him. Pity he had to shoot Deacon, but Deacon was dying anyway. Tilting his head toward the ceiling, he blows three perfect smoke rings. The circles rise and expand like the rims of wagon wheels. *It's hard to lose a friend,* he thinks.

He closes his eyes and the little square blocks start fencing him in. *Click,* he thinks as they drop into place. *Click, click, click. If I poked my finger in my eye, could I put it through that wall they're making?*

An hour after Clark gives up on William, a boat pulls up to the Beau Rivage landing, and three men disembark. Two are local planters who are in the market for new field hands. The third is Sheridan Thompson, a middleman who buys slaves and ships them South to his associates who in turn sell them to large landowners. The slaves who labor in the Southern cane and cotton fields die every year at a steady rate, so the demand for replacements is always brisk.

Jed Clark greets his guests with a friendly handshake and conducts them to the slave pen. Jed is a portly, jolly-looking man. Perhaps he was once as handsome as his cousin Henry, but if so, age has melted him down like a candle, piling his cheeks on his chin and his nose on his upper lip. There is something clownlike about his face that always makes strangers smile when they first meet him, but this morning the potential buyers stop smiling as soon as they see the merchandise he's offering. None of them have ever seen a sorrier lot of slaves.

"What is this?" Thompson asks. "An asylum for the infirm?"

"I admit they're no great shakes," Jed says, "but they come cheap, gentlemen. The women recently worked on a hemp plantation. Worked right hard, too, with no fussing or complaining. Why they didn't even have to be driven out into the fields. They went on their own, nice as you please, no overseer needed. You don't get obedience like that every day.

"As for that one," he points to Jane, "she can cook and clean and sew like nobody's business."

"She has a sullen look," one of the local planters observes. "I reckon she's trouble."

"No matter to me," Thompson says. "Where I'll send her she won't be raising a fuss if she wants to keep skin on her back. A slave that can cook fetches a higher price."

"She can read, too," Jed says.

Thompson frowns. "I don't find that an attractive quality in a slave and neither will those who bid for her. Teaching a slave to read is illegal all over the South. Fines are imposed, sir, hefty ones. Teach a slave her letters and the next thing you know, she's reading abolitionist tracts and plotting to poison you in your sleep."

He rests his hands on the top rail and stares at Jane, who glares back at him defiantly. "If I take this one, you're going to have to knock down the price you're asking considerably, plus throw in the old men for free."

"I wouldn't take her at any price," says one of the planters, "but those two pretty little girls of hers—"

The men all laugh.

"You'll have to outbid me for those two beauties," Thompson says. "Fatten them up, wash them, pick the nits out of their hair, and ship them off to New Orleans, and—well I shouldn't say this because I reckon Mr. Clark here will raise his price on me—but the owners of every pleasure palace in the city will be lining up to buy them." He turns to Jed. "That's assuming they're virgins. They are, yes?"

"Since they look to be about five and six years old, I reckon they are."

"I'm going to need to inspect their teeth and tongues before I bid on them, make sure they're in good health and free of blemishes. Get one of your men in there to make the mother let go of them, Mr. Clark, and we'll get started."

A tall bluff with muddy sides, and below it, a brown, coiled river and bottomlands white with cotton. Beau Rivage: beautiful to look at from a distance, but horrifying when examined more closely.

For four days, four nights, and the better part of a fifth day, Carrie has ridden until she was too tired to sit up in the saddle; ridden until her horse died under her; then she stole another horse and set out riding again. In that time, she has been to Osawatomie and, with Elizabeth's help, armed the men of Keyhole Draw with the guns John Brown took from the pro-slavery militia at the Battle of Black Jack and mounted them on the horses Brown took at the same battle. With Brown's blessing, she has led his secretly trained cavalry back to Missouri to this bend in the river where Henry Clark and his men have set up camp; and every second she has been afraid she will arrive too late, that the slaves will already have been sold, Teddy disposed of, William hanged.

She stares at the slave pen through Elizabeth's collapsible opera glasses. The lenses make the air between what she looks at and what she sees as visible as water. Waves of moisture rise from the fields twisting like serpents. Near the main house, four men in dark suits walk toward the pen. Their faces are pinkish blanks rimmed with hair and beards, and their bodies waver like badly drawn watercolors. They lean on the fence, stare at the slaves, and gesture. Carrie sees Jane's daughters torn out of her embrace and led off toward the main house. She sees Jane throw herself against the fence of the slave pen and beat on it with her fists. Jane's mouth opens in an O of rage and lamentation.

Carrie can't bear to continue watching Jane suffer. Folding up the opera glasses, she stuffs them in her pocket. Behind her are fifteen men ready to die to set Jane and the other captives free, fifteen men eager to take on Henry Clark and his band of murderers. Carrie has led them to Beau Rivage. Now it's their turn to take over. They've agreed that Ni and Ebenezer will lead the attack: Ni because he saw something of warfare when he lived with the Kaw; and Ebenezer because he served his master during the Mexican War.

Carrie closes her eyes and thinks of Elizabeth. *I'd come with you,* Elizabeth had said, *but I'm too old to ride that fast and that far. God bless you. God keep you.*

After Elizabeth blessed Carrie, she went to each man, and blessed him by name: Abel, Andrew, Bilander, Caesar, Cush, Charles, Ebenezer, Ishmael, Jack, Jordan, Marcellus, Ni, Peet, and Samuel. When she got to Spartacus, she drew him to her and kissed him on the forehead. *Be as brave as your brothers and stay alive if you can. You're my last living child, my last chick out of the nest.*

Carrie decides that if Spartacus is to return to his mother in one piece, they will need more information than she can get through a pair of collapsible opera glasses. Someone has to go down to Beau Rivage and find out where William and Teddy are and how many men Clark has. There are signs that more raiders have arrived in her absence. The number of horses in the corral has doubled and there are tents pitched in the pasture.

We'll take them by surprise, Ni said.

We'll trap them between the bluff and the river, Ebenezer promised her.

Is this possible? Will it work? They're clearly outnumbered now, but how badly? There's only one way to find out.

Chapter Forty-one

Used properly, powdered fustic wood produces an evil, yellowish brown that suggests age and illness. No woman in her right mind dyes her hair with fustic if she wants men to look at her with interest; but if she does not want men to look at her at all . . . *Well then*, Carrie thinks, *it's perfect, particularly when you combine it with a ragged head scarf, a bundle filled with herbs, a dirty face, and a limp.*

Thanks to this disguise, she has passed unnoticed through the gates of Beau Rivage, counted Clark's men, and determined that there are now at least thirty, plus Clark himself who fortunately is nowhere in sight. She has also spotted the four men in dark suits sitting on straight-backed chairs under a tree drinking something out of glass tumblers. Three appear to be carrying sidearms. The fourth has tipped his chair back against the tree trunk and flung his coat open. If he is carrying anything more deadly than a penknife, Carrie can't see it.

She intended to find out where William and Teddy were being kept, but there were so many of Clark's men walking around she didn't dare linger any longer than it took her to walk from the front of the house to the back. Now she is in the kitchen standing beside the cook who is in the process of examining a pack of needles, a partly used bottle of glue, and half a dozen packets of herbs that Carrie has spread out on the table in front of her.

The cook is the same tall, heavyset, dark-skinned woman Carrie saw fetching firewood. She wears a coarse smock under her apron and a pair of old boots out at the toes. If they were in Kansas, she might be free, but here in Missouri she is undoubtedly a slave. Since it costs a great deal to take a woman out of the fields and put her in the kitchen, the owners of Beau Rivage must be prospering.

"What's this here?" the cook asks, poking at one of the packets.

"That's for worms."

The cook frowns and nudges at the packet again. "How fast it work?"

"Fast."

"Can y'all use it to worm hogs?"

"Nothing better."

The cook picks up the packet, opens it, and cautiously sniffs the contents. As she does so, Carrie hears a sound that makes her stiffen. Somewhere in the house, Teddy is crying. *My boy, my baby!* she thinks. *Where are you!* She grits her teeth. For Teddy's sake, she can't afford to betray what she's feeling.

"Does your mistress have a child?" she asks. She can hear her voice trembling, but the cook must not for she says:

"It ain't hers. She just takin' care of it for a spell. Then it going South."

"South?"

"With the new slaves. They sellin' 'em all South. Not keepin' a single one. I was hopin' they give me a girl for the kitchen. I need help in here, but they sellin' 'em all at auction this afternoon. The buyers done already arrived. How much you want for this worm medicine?"

"Seven cents." Carrie nearly chokes on the words.

"You think we made of money here? I go ask Miss Emily for seven cents for wormin' hogs, and she think I crazy."

"How about five?"

The cook nods her head. "That be more like it. You stay here. I be right back." Carrie knows she needs to avoid exciting suspicion, but she can't stop herself.

"Are they selling the child, too?"

"Now you the crazy one. That's a white child. You think they gonna sell a white child? No, they gonna give him to some folk who own a big place down in Lus'ana or Georgia or sumwheres."

"Doesn't the child have a mother or father?"

"Oh yeah, he got a father, but there a price on his head. Massa Clark gonna hang him for helpin' slaves escape. That's the law here in Missouri."

"When are they going to hang him?"

The cook looks at her warily. "Late afternoon or thereabouts, I reckon. Massa Clark say he want to do it before the guests et their dinner, but Miss Emily say hangin' put folks off their feed. What you care anyways?"

"Just curious." Clark plans to hang William in two or three hours! Carrie's mind begins to move in all directions, making plans, discarding them, making more plans. If she had returned from Osawatomie a day later—even a few hours later—William would be dead; Teddy and the others gone . . .

She can't think about any of this now. She has to concentrate on playing the role she has created for herself. She forces herself to smile at the cook. "I always enjoy a good hanging."

The cook frowns and shrugs. "Most white folks do, but I'm the one who got to cook the vittles for the big party my masters throwing. You bake pies and fry chicken in here this time of year and it get so hot you near to smother." She slips the packet of worm medicine into her apron pocket.

"Now you stay put, and I'll go see if I can talk Miss Emily into givin' you five cents for this stuff. Of course if you was to lower the price—"

"Three cents," Carrie says.

Five minutes later, the cook returns to the kitchen with three pennies only to find that the peddler lady has disappeared. Deciding this is her lucky day, she slips the pennies into her apron pocket and sets about rolling out the crusts for the pies.

Chapter Forty-two

During the course of their married life, Miss Emily has won every argument she has had with her husband except the one that brought her to Missouri. She wanted to stay in Tennessee so she could be near her mama and papa, but Jed dragged her to Beau Rivage, and she has been making him pay for it ever since. As a result of her refusal to yield an inch in the direction of compromise, everyone is eating dinner before the hanging this afternoon, not after.

The slaves have all been put up on the block and auctioned off. Mr. Thompson bought most of them, including the sullen-looking one and her two little daughters; the planters bought the rest, grumbling at the quality of the merchandise but pleased by the price. Did Jed make a profit from these sales? Miss Emily neither knows nor cares. At present the slaves are back in the slave pen, out of sight awaiting transport, which means, as far as she is concerned, they have vanished as completely as morning dew.

While the auction was going on, the slaves of Beau Rivage placed sawhorses in the front yard, covered them with planks, and brought out every bench, stool, and chair in the house, including a cane-bottomed rocker that really should be reglued before anyone sits in it. On the table intended for Miss Emily, her husband, and his cousin, the planters, and Mr. Thompson, the cook spread a white linen cloth. The other tables, where Mr. MacNally the overseer and Henry Clark's men were to sit, had to make do with ordinary cotton.

Miss Emily entrusted her good china and silver plate to all the tables, despite the fact that some of the men who ride with her husband's cousin look like ruffians who wouldn't know a fish knife from a marrow spoon. She fears breakage and depredation, but she cannot resist bringing out her best. Of course there are not enough Wedgwood dinner plates to go around, but on the whole she is pleased. She loves to put on parties, particularly ones where she is the only woman present and thus can flirt outrageously without fear of censure.

Unfortunately only the two planters and Mr. Thompson are worth flirting with. Henry Clark also would be a possibility, except there is something about him that bothers her. She can't quite put her finger on it. He's handsome enough, but whenever she looks into his eyes, she feels as if she's staring at a blind man. He doesn't appear to see her, and this annoys her no end.

"May I offer you another serving of chicken?" she asks, hoping to force him into a civil conversation.

"Yes, thank you, Cousin Emily." Clark flashes her a smile that reveals teeth so perfect they look as if they've been dipped in whitewash.

"Messlina," Miss Emily commands, "provide Mr. Clark with some chicken." The cook hurries forward and offers Clark the platter. Picking up his fork, Clark spears a drumstick.

"Where's the boy?" he asks as he deposits it on his plate and sets about eating.

"Upstairs taking a nap. He's just the cutest little thing. I love him to bits."

"I'd be obliged if you'd wake him and bring him out to the table."

Miss Emily represses an impulse to ask why her husband's cousin wants the little brat at an adult gathering when all he will do is drool, scream, and break things.

"Why certainly," she says, giving him her most charming smile. Again she turns to the cook. "Messlina, hand that platter to Lucy and go upstairs and fetch . . ." For an instant, she cannot recall the child's name. ". . . Teddy. Before you bring him down, make sure his face and hands are clean."

Without waiting for Messlina to reply, Miss Emily turns back to Clark. "It's uncommon to allow such a young child to witness a hanging. May I ask why you want him present?"

Clark puts down the chicken leg and wipes his lips with one of Miss Emily's linen napkins. "I doubt the boy will remember the execution of Doctor Saylor," he says, "but Doctor Saylor will see him and—"

"And what?" Miss Emily prompts.

Clark lifts his eyebrows as if imparting a secret. He lowers his voice and leans close to Miss Emily—unpleasantly close, actually. "Well, let's simply say that the doctor could have avoided the sight by being more cooperative. And then—" Clark puts down his napkin and stares at the remains of the drumstick. Miss Emily follows his eyes and sees some scraps of skin and a well-picked bone.

"And then?" she prompts again.

He does not reply. Despairing of further engaging him in conversation, she turns and begins to talk to Mr. Thompson.

Up on the bluff concealed from view, Carrie lies between Ni and Ebenezer. Ebenezer is peering down at Beau Rivage through Elizabeth's opera glasses.

"What are they doing now?" she asks.

"Still eating."

"Is Clark's flag still flying in the front yard?"

"Yes."

"And Jane and the girls?"

"Still in the slave pen with the others."

"How many of Clark's men are guarding them?"

"One. The other two appear to have joined the dinner party."

"Any sign of William?"

"Not yet."

"We can't attack until we know where he is."

"I don't think we need to worry about finding him. I think they're going to bring him out soon. One of Clark's men just put a chair under the big tree. It's right under a limb and no one's sitting in it."

After the chair has been placed under the hanging tree, Henry Clark stands up and taps on his water goblet with his fork, calling both tables to silence.

"Cousin Emily, Cousin Jed, gentlemen, boys, Mr. MacNally, we now come to what the French call the 'resistance piece.' In a little while, after you have enjoyed Miss Emily's pies and finished your coffee, we are going to hang an infamous abolitionist."

The guests break into applause, and some of Clark's men give hoots of approval. Clark glares at the men who made rude noises. Clearing his throat, he looks down the length of the tables. It's a sight of devastation: plates piled with bones and scraps, platters smeared with the remains of mashed potatoes, green beans swimming in pot liquor, crumbled cornbread, broken biscuits, tablecloths so spotted with congealed cream gravy that a man could probably eat off them for a week.

"Saylor didn't get a trial because he didn't deserve one. He's been wanted for slave stealing since fifty-four, and we caught him red-handed harboring fugitives. But this presents us with a problem. In the ordinary course of things, a man who's been condemned to death sits in jail for a few weeks thinking about how that rope is going to feel as it tightens around his neck. There's no use hanging a man so fast he doesn't know what's happening to him, so I propose we give our Kansas Jayhawker time to understand that the feet he's got planted on the seat of that kitchen chair over there are going to dance him straight to hell."

"Bring the son of a bitch out here now!" Jed yells. Cousin Emily flinches as if someone has dropped a hot coal on her head. Henry Clark suppresses a grin. Jed is going to spend years paying for that one. It will be a miracle if he gets laid before the Second Coming.

Upstairs, Messlina is washing Teddy's face and hands. She speaks to him pleasantly and doesn't pull his hair when she runs the comb through it. Teddy likes her a lot better than the other lady, who frightens him.

"Where?" he asks.

"Are you asking me where you goin', baby?"

Teddy nods.

"Well, I reckon you goin' to see your daddy."

For the first time in days, Teddy smiles.

Ten minutes later, when Messlina brings him out of the house, all the pies have been eaten, and the guests are drinking sweet coffee laced with chicory.

"Put the boy on the table," Clark orders.

Messlina lifts Teddy up and sets him down on the main table. He stands there, bewildered. Where is his daddy? The lady told him he was going to see his daddy.

Ignoring him, Clark points at the barn. "Dan," he says, "go get Saylor and take the rope with you."

All during dinner, the raider named Dan has had a rope slung over the back of his chair. Now he stands up, grabs it, and displays the noose. "We're gonna hang us a Jayhawker!" he yells.

Clark's men begin cheering and pounding the handles of their knifes on the table. After a few seconds, everyone except Miss Emily joins in. Miss Emily knows she should retreat inside and not watch what's coming next. This is no place for a lady, but she has never seen a hanging, and when the raiders bring the condemned man out of the stable she cannot tear herself away from the sight of him being led across the yard like a dog on a leash.

She watches as Clark's men force William to step up on the chair, watches as they throw the rope over the tree limb and secure it. She hasn't expected the doctor to be so handsome nor to look so much like a gentleman. It seems a waste to hang a man with his looks.

As William turns toward the tables, Teddy stretches out his arms and gives a squeal of delight. "Daddy!" he cries.

Scooping up the boy, Clark lifts him over his head and settles him on his shoulders. As he strolls toward the hanging tree, he is rewarded with the sight of William's face. Is it the fear of dying or the sight of Teddy riding on the shoulders of his worst enemy that makes him look so distressed? Hard to tell. Any man balanced unsteadily on a chair with a noose around his neck is likely to look anxious, even a brave one. Is William brave? Clark intends to find out.

"My boys tell me you almost got your hands loose," he says. "I'm impressed. You're more dangerous than I thought. So, how shall we hang you? Slow or fast? I've been thinking it over: When I kick that chair out from under you, your feet are going to be about eighteen inches above the ground. It would take a lot longer fall to break your neck, so you'll strangle. You won't die for a few minutes, but you'll lose consciousness within seconds. I imagine being a doctor, you can figure the exact time it will take better than I can, but the point is, that's much too fast.

"So I'm going to do what you were trying to do before my boys interrupted you: I'm going to cut your hands loose. That way, when I kick the chair out from under you, you can decide how fast you want to die. Do nothing, and you'll leave this world of toil and woe behind you in no time. But if you reach up and grab the rope with both hands, you can prolong your life. The question is: How long can you hold on?

"My boys have already started laying bets. Most think you won't last ten minutes, but some have more faith in you. Some think you'll hang on for as long as twenty.

"Just to make things even more interesting, I'm going to let the boy here hang you. Of course, he won't know what he's doing, but when he's older, I'll make sure his new parents tell him how he executed the wicked man who murdered his father."

Drawing closer to William, Clark lowers his voice. "I really wish you had been willing to tell me what causes my headaches. I didn't enjoy the dinner party nearly as much as I might have, and it's not often I get served hot apple pie. I'm very displeased. I don't care to hear any last words from you, so if you pull that gag out of your mouth when I free your hands, I'll just shoot you and be done with it."

Clark steps back and motions for one of his men to grab the back of the chair so it won't fall over prematurely. Drawing his knife, he saws through the ropes that bind William's wrists. "Let go of the chair," he orders. The raider lets go of the chair and it wobbles: right, left, center; left, right, left; center, stop. Satisfied, Clark nods, turns away from William and walks back to the tables. When he reaches Miss Emily, he takes Teddy off his shoulders and puts him down on the ground. "Teddy, run to your daddy and give him a big hug."

With a cry of delight, Teddy runs toward William and throws his arms around William's legs. As the chair topples over, William grabs the rope with both hands, Teddy screams, Miss Emily's dinner guests cheer, and Henry Clark takes out his pocket watch.

"One, two, three, four, five!" he cries. "How many seconds will the abolitionist hang on ladies and gentlemen? Place your bets now before it's too late."

William kicks at air and the world turns around him like a steam-powered carousel, trees blending into grass, grass into the white of the big house, white of the big house into the brown smear of the river. He feels his fingers slipping on the rope and growing numb, feels the hemp biting into his neck.

Black spots swirl before his eyes, alternating with the blue dome of the sky and the burning disk of the sun. Round and round he goes, hanging on. The noose suddenly tightens and his breath jams in his throat like a clump of dry sticks.

Faces: white, black, Clark's, the raiders'. The face of a tall woman dressed all in white. Four men in dark suits, their beards black smears. The rope swings him around again. Now he faces the stable, sees details so fine he could never have imagined it possible: the grain of the wood in the boards pulsing like a heartbeat; shadows of ivy fluttering like wings; a chicken pecking in the dust; great sweeps of knife-edged, silver clouds frozen over the roof as if time itself has come to a stop.

Again the rope turns, and Carrie's face suddenly appears in front of him, floating and turning with him. She opens her mouth, and moves her lips. *I love you*, she says. Her voice rings in his ears like a thousand silver bells. Oxygen deprivation. Asphyxia. Hallucination. Part of his mind knows this. Part denies it. Part keeps him hanging onto the rope. He can no longer feel his hands and a sharp pain has begun to crawl across his chest.

William, dearest William, Carrie says. Her blonde hair springs away from her face, and the amber flecks in her eyes flash and spin like pinwheels. She is beautiful beyond description, and he has never loved her more than he loves her at this moment.

I'm dying, he thinks. Words that make no sense fill his mind. He sees something silver falling from the sky, jagged like scraps of torn paper. Carrie's face blossoms in front of him like a great, white gardenia, and he smells the scent of the flowers in her father's garden, sees the sea shining out in the bay beyond Rio, feels the touch of her hand on his forehead light as a kiss.

William, hang on!

These words, which she cannot possibly have spoken, shock him back to reality. He clutches the rope more tightly and with great effort, lifts himself up, loosening the noose a little. He inhales and feels air fill his lungs. Somehow he manages to spit out the gag. Again he turns. Now he faces Clark. Clark has a grip on Teddy's collar. Teddy is crying and struggling to get away.

"Let go of my boy, you son of a bitch!" William gasps.

"Four and a half minutes," Clark says.

Suddenly another sound fills the air. It's a dull pounding like hail on a wood-shingled roof. Behind Clark, William can see the dinner guests springing to their feet. Again he hears Carrie yell, "William, hang on!" Only this time he could swear it's really her.

Chapter Forty-three

The raiders' own horses come stampeding toward them, driven by riders who bear down on the dinner party from all directions. Ebenezer leads one group, stripped to the waist and bearing the scars of his burns like medals. Next to him rides Spartacus; next to Spartacus, Carrie; behind Carrie, Sam and Peet. Coming toward the tables, closing the trap, Ni leads Jordan and Marcellus, Andrew and Charles, little Cush with the fierce eyes, Bilander, who can split a rail with a single blow, Caesar whose master once whipped him half to death, Abel who was sold away from his mother at the age of five.

The men come yelling the battle cries that John Brown and his sons taught them, come yelling the war cries of Africa, come screaming Bible verses or singing hymns or cursing, or just yelling, giving voice to their wives and children and friends and ancestors who have been enslaved for over two hundred years.

As they charge out of the willows that border the river, gallop out of the fields, and ride up the main road driving the stampeding horses before them, Miss Emily leaps to her feet.

"Soldiers!" she shrieks. And then she turns to Mr. Thompson and says in a voice full of amazement. "Why, they're black!" Paralyzed by the impossibility of this, the men stare at the approaching riders. One of Clark's Raiders starts to draw his gun, then hesitates.

"What the hell are you waiting for!" Clark yells. "Shoot the bastards, damn it, and turn those horses around!"

Shocked into action, the men draw their pistols and kick over the tables to form a barricade, forgetting that the tables are merely planks set on sawhorses. The barricades dissolve into a heap of lumber, broken china, shattered crystal, and soiled linen. As the stampeding horses plunge into the wreckage, Miss Emily turns in circles screaming for help. Around her, men are being knocked down and trampled. Some of the raiders try to hold their ground. Others break and run, only to find themselves ridden down and taken prisoner.

Clark takes refuge behind the hanging tree as the panicked horses thunder by. Drawing his pistol, he shoots at the nearest soldier and scores a hit. As the man falls to the ground, Clark runs out and tries to grab the reins of his horse, but they slip through his fingers.

Dan has made it to the stable and mounted Jed's brown mare. Now he comes bursting out the door, heading straight for Clark as if he's going to trample him.

"Coward!" Clark screams. "Deserter!" Lifting his pistol, he aims it at Dan and shoots. In the instant between the moment the gun fires and the moment Dan falls, Clark recognizes him. Seizing the reins, he steps over Dan's body and starts to swing himself into the saddle. Then he realizes he has forgotten something.

"Teddy," he commands, "come here!" But the boy isn't where he left him. He's over on the far side of the yard, running toward the river like a spooked rabbit.

Chapter Forty-four

Carrie gallops up to the hanging tree and cuts William down. How long has he been dangling? Three minutes? Four? Dismounting, she kneels beside him, loosens the noose, and shakes him. "Breathe!" she yells. "Breathe!"

William struggles to obey, but his throat has gone into a spasm, or maybe it's his lungs that don't work. When he was hanging, he saw colors. Now all he sees is blackness creeping in from all sides like spilled ink. He fights to shove it away, but it keeps spreading, stuffing him into a black bag with no bottom.

Putting her lips to his, Carrie breathes into his mouth until the knot in his throat opens and her breath enters his lungs. He coughs and gulps in a mouthful of air. Breathing hurts so much he's tempted to stop. "Clark . . ." he gasps. "Teddy . . ."

He points, and Carrie looks up just in time to see Henry Clark swoop down on Teddy, grab him by the shirttails, and jerk him off his feet.

* * *

Let go!" Teddy screams.

"Shut up!" Clark yells. Throwing Teddy behind the fork of his saddle, he wheels around and kicks his horse into a fast gallop only to discover he's headed straight at Carrie, who's riding toward him with a pistol leveled at his chest. For a second, he feels a fear so intense his heart nearly explodes, but then he realizes she can't fire, because if she does she may hit her son.

Wheeling around, he gallops back toward the river. He can hear her coming after him, but he's got a good head start, and the trail that runs along the riverbank passes through a stand of willows before it comes out near the landing. If she loses her senses and takes a shot at him, the chances of her hitting him from a moving horse are small. Once they get into the willows where no one can see them, he'll turn around, stop, and surprise her by offering to let her buy back her son.

All Deacon's money, he'll say. *All Bennett's. All yours, if you still have any left.* While she's trying to decide if he's serious, he'll blow her off her horse. Simple as that. His enemies always underestimate him, but he can outthink them.

Teddy will inherit the money, and there will be ways to get at it. Forged documents. A will from Deacon, perhaps, that appoints his dear friend Henry Clark as the boy's guardian. Then whores and whiskey, the green felt of New Orleans gaming tables. Perhaps he'll buy a gold-headed walking stick, or perhaps he'll just help himself to one of those canes the slavers sent Bennett after he thrashed Sumner.

A willow twig slaps him in the face. That's the problem with galloping through brush. He's been riding for at least a minute now, maybe two, and he can hear Carrie gaining on him. Pulling back on the reins, he halts and turns his horse around. He is in a natural alley with a row of willows on one side and the river on the other. Perfect. He's only going to get one shot at her but in a place like this, a blind man couldn't miss.

Grabbing Teddy by the hair, he jerks the boy upright so his face will be the first thing his mother sees. Then he draws his pistol and holds it by his side, concealing it under the edge of his jacket.

"Carrie Vinton!" he yells as she comes crashing out of the brush. "Stop! I have an offer for you!"

Carrie takes one look at her boy, jerks up short, and lowers her pistol. Clark realizes there's no need to actually go through the charade of making her an offer. She's holding still and couldn't be a better target if she had a bull's-eye painted on her forehead. He lifts his revolver and points it at her.

"Say good-bye to your mama," he tells Teddy. And that's when it happens: Just as he pulls the trigger the little brat, who up until now has done nothing but scream, suddenly turns on him like a snake and bites through his thumb.

With a yell of fury, Clark drops the pistol and flings Teddy into the river. Before he can mourn the loss of thousands of dollars' worth of boy flesh, Carrie raises her gun and pulls the trigger. For an instant, Clark is sure he's been shot; then he realizes she's clicked on an empty chamber.

Throwing back his head, he howls like a coyote.

"You're crazy!" Carrie screams.

Clark can see blood staining the left leg of her trousers. He may not have killed her, but he's hit her. He starts to ride toward her figuring he can finish her off with his knife, but then he sees she's drawn another gun. Two to his one. Hardly fair, but this hasn't been his lucky day. Wheeling around again, he runs for it.

* * *

As soon as he's out of sight, Carrie dismounts and plunges into the river. The wound on her leg stings as she staggers through the muck and reeds that line the bank. Just beyond the shallows, Teddy is thrashing around, going down and coming up. As she dives into the current and swims toward him, she can still hear Clark in the distance, yipping like a madman.

She grabs Teddy by the collar, and they both go under. When they come up, choking and coated with silt, Teddy clutches at her shirt and hangs on. He doesn't fight her, so she's able to keep his head above water as she swims toward shore.

When she can touch bottom again, she stands up, takes Teddy in her arms, and stumbles through the reeds. A few moments later, they are both sitting on the riverbank. She's shaking, Teddy is crying, and both of them are plastered with mud from head to foot.

"Good boy," she says as she rocks him and picks the waterweeds out of his hair. She's so busy comforting him that she doesn't bother to look at her leg. The wound Clark gave her hardly hurts, and she figures she can tend to it later.

Chapter Forty-five

When Henry Clark comes riding out of the willows, he looks toward the main house and sees the planters and a dozen of his own men standing by the ruins of the dinner party with their hands raised over their heads. Jed is standing with them waving a white napkin, and the black soldiers are holding them all at gunpoint. Where are the rest of Clark's Raiders, the fiercest band of bushwhackers in Missouri and Kansas combined? Nowhere, that's where. Not a one in sight unless you count three dead men, one of whom he himself killed.

Clark feels a wave of disgust. His men never deserved him. They're disloyal, cowardly, traitorous scum. If he ever meets up with the ones who ran, he may have to shoot them.

Up ahead, he can see the boat that brought the planters to Beau Rivage rocking lazily beside the dock as if all the trouble going on is nothing to get excited about. Now that he doesn't have to lead a bunch of cowards, he can ride onto the boat, cut it loose from its moorings, drift downriver, and disembark at his leisure. Money won't be a problem. He still has one of the gold rings he took from

Deacon. He can pawn it and treat himself to a hot bath, a shave, and a whore.

His only real regret, besides losing the boy, is that he'll never be able to tell anyone what happened today. If he did, bushwhackers would be lining up for a chance to hunt down the men who attacked Beau Rivage. He would only have to say the magic words "black men with guns," and he could just sit back and watch. They'd string up free blacks and fugitives both from here to Topeka without even asking if they'd been part of the raiding party and maybe lynch a dozen Jayhawkers for good measure. While he's at it, he could probably get them to do away with Carrie Vinton and that doctor lover of hers in some satisfyingly unpleasant way, get the boy back if the little brat hasn't drowned, and start spending Deacon's money. But to do all that he'd have to admit he's been outshot and outsmarted by a band of black soldiers, a woman, and a toddler with teeth like a serpent. He'd never live it down.

Clark kicks his horse into a fast walk. The only thing that stands between him and the boat now is the slave pen, but he never notices slaves unless he's selling them, buying them, or entertaining himself with them, which is why, when a tall black woman walks out of the gate and stands in front of him blocking the road, he is so taken by surprise that he doesn't notice she's holding a rifle.

"Henry Clark!" she yells. "My name is Jane and you hurt my babies!" And lifting the rifle, she pulls the trigger and becomes the death Henry Clark never thought he would meet.

As he lies in the dust bleeding and in pain, she draws close and bends over him. Clark looks up at her with eyes filled with resentment. "You had no right to shoot me," he gasps. "I should only be shot by a white man."

"Sometimes you got to take what you can get," Jane says.

"Is that so?"

"It is."

Clark blinks and his blue eyes grow opaque. He licks his lips and groans. "It—" he says. He lifts up his hands as if to ward off something big. "It—" he repeats.

"'It' what?" Jane asks, but Henry Clark, who has made a habit of not finishing his sentences, does not reply. Waving his hands in an agitated way, he stares at a place just over her left shoulder with a look of such terror that Jane is glad she cannot see whatever he is seeing.

Carrie

*S*waying, bone-jarring jolts, the smell of mules—I opened my eyes to find myself lying on a straw pallet in a wagon that was bumping along much too fast for comfort. Someone had strung a piece of canvas over my head, and rain was rattling against it like corn on a drumhead. I was wrapped in a fancy white quilt like the sort people give to a bride on her wedding day. There was a goose down pillow under my head and a warm brick at my feet, but I had never felt so cold. My fingers were almost numb, and I was so weak and sick to my stomach that I wasn't sure I could lift my head. Where was I and what was wrong with me? The last thing I remembered was pulling Teddy out of the river.

"You're awake," a familiar voice said. I heard the scratch of a match. Lantern light flared suddenly, and I saw vinelike lines moving above me like snakes. They reminded me of the time Mae Seja gave me the black drink, but I couldn't possibly be in Brazil.

"Are you warm enough?"

With great effort, I managed to turn my head. William was sitting beside me, looking at me with concern. There was an ugly purple bruise around his neck, his shirt was torn, his hair was matted with dust, and he needed a shave. But it was his voice that startled me most. It was wheezing and hoarse, as if he still had the hanging rope around his neck. I wondered if he'd ever talk normally again. He must have seen this question in my eyes for he said: "Don't worry. I'll sound like myself again in a week or two. How about you? How do you feel?"

"Horrible. What happened?"

"Clark shot you in the leg, and you nearly bled to death."

Alarmed, I tried to sit up, only to fall back and collapse in helpless tears. I felt dizzy and breathless and confused. I wanted to be home in Lawrence in my own bed.

Pulling out his pocket handkerchief, William gently applied it to my eyes. "Hush, sweetheart. Hush. You're very weak, but you'll be fine. We found you in time. Hush. Rest and let me take care of you."

"Teddy—" I sobbed.

"Teddy's safe. Jed Clark's cook is taking care of him in the other wagon."

"Ni and Ebenezer, Sam and Spartacus, Peet and—"

"All of them are fine. They were outnumbered at two to one, but they had surprise on their side. I hear Ni and Ebenezer planned the attack. Generals in a regular army couldn't have done better. That stampede was a stroke of genius. Most of Clark's men broke and ran like rabbits. The ones we took prisoner are keeping Jed Clark and his wife company in the slave pen. You should have heard Jed's wife shriek when her own slaves put chains on her. As for Henry Clark, he's dead. Jane shot him."

I lay there trying to take all this in. The news seemed too good to be true. As a matter of fact, it was. Five of our men had been wounded, two gravely, but at the time William didn't think I was up to hearing about it, and he was probably right.

He stroked my cheek tenderly. "There. That's better. There's no need to cry, and I have a surprise for you." Reaching into his pocket, he pulled out a ring, took my left hand in his, and slipped it on my third finger. I looked down and saw a gold band set with blue sapphires. "My father gave this to my mother on the day they were married."

"How—?"

"How did I come by it? I'll tell you the details later, but for now let's just say it was brought to Beau Rivage by the last man we'd have expected to bring it." He leaned over and softly brushed his lips against mine. "Carrie, sweetheart, will you marry me?"

I had already said "yes" twice before, but no matter how often he asked me that question, my answer was always going to be the same. I nodded, and he smiled.

For a long time William sat beside me holding my hand. Gradually, I felt peace stealing over me. After a while the wagon came to a halt, the rain stopped, the lantern went out, and in that almost perfect silence between dark and birdsong, I slept.

Author's Note

The history of the Kansas Territory is not a simple subject. Between 1854 and 1861, the territory had ten governors, seven capitals, and four constitutions. At times a pro-slavery legislature and a free-state legislature were meeting simultaneously, both claiming to be the only legal legislature. In the interests of not driving the reader mad with details, I have intentionally omitted descriptions of various events, some of them major, including several murders that would lend themselves nicely to a noir mystery novel should any future author care to undertake one.

Although some of the language has been modified for modern ears, for the most part I have chosen to record things as they actually happened. For example, on May 21, 1856, an army of pro-slavers attacked Lawrence, smashing printing presses, burning the Free State Hotel, and looting homes and stores. Three days later, John Brown and his sons rode to Pottawatomie Creek and—unlikely as it may seem—killed five pro-slavers with broadswords.

On various occasions, I have exercised the novelist's prerogative to create fictional events. Although Brown and the Adairs once hid eleven fugitive slaves for over a month in a cabin four miles west of the present town of Lane, Kansas, there is no indication Brown trained an African-American cavalry unit like the one that defeats Clark's Raiders. However, there is a reasonable possibility that such a unit could have existed. At one point, Brown told fellow abolitionists about a plan to arm former slaves and send them into the Allegheny Mountains to fight a guerilla war against slave owners. It is unlikely that he began to implement this plan while living in Kansas, but John Brown was a man who kept many secrets.

Although Henry Clark is loosely modeled on William Quantrill, the Confederate raider who attacked Lawrence in 1863, he is a fictional character. There was never a senator from Kentucky named Bennett Presgrove, nor did the fictional Senator Presgrove attack real Massachusetts Senator Charles Sumner on the floor of the U.S. Senate. Senator Sumner was brutally beaten by South Carolina Representative Preston Brooks. I was the one who placed the cane in Bennett's hand and let him share Brooks's infamy.

I have previously written about the Civil War in my novel *The Notorious Mrs. Winston*. One question I am frequently asked is: "Was the Civil War fought over slavery?" In Kansas, slavery was the only real issue. Although it sometimes masqueraded under the banner of States' Rights or Southern Rights, the question of whether or not Kansas was going to enter the Union free or slave was the explosive problem that polarized America, pitted North against South, and helped get Abraham Lincoln elected president. It is telling that Kansas was only admitted to the Union as a free state in January of 1861, after South Carolina, Mississippi, Florida, Alabama, Georgia, and Louisiana had already seceded.

I like to imagine that if the men of Keyhole Draw had existed, Elizabeth and the Adairs would have made sure they were swiftly conducted to Canada and freedom after the Battle of Beau Rivage. When the Civil War officially began, perhaps some would have returned to Kansas to fight with the First Kansas Colored Infantry Regiment, which had the distinction of being the first unit composed of men of African descent to engage in battle with Confederate troops.

Acknowledgments

I am indebted to many people who helped me during the process of writing *The Widow's War*. First, I would like to thank novelist Sheldon Greene who read every draft multiple times. As always, his feedback and suggestions were invaluable. Thanks also to Donald Worster; Beverley Worster; Wes Jackson; Paul Kamen; the members of the WELL Experts Topic; Roy L. Hudson of the National Railway Historical Society; Jackie Cantor, my wonderful editor at Berkley Books; and my husband, Angus Wright, who, besides giving me support and encouragement, accompanied me on a research trip through Kansas and Missouri in the summer of 2006. A historian and native-born Kansan, Angus led me to the place that served as the model for Keyhole Draw and provided me with information and insights not to be found elsewhere.